征服、重构与回归
蒂姆·温顿小说的生态解读

CONQUEST, REESTABLISHMENT AND RETREAT
AN ECOCRITICAL READING OF TIM WINTON'S FICTION

徐显静　著

世界图书出版公司

上海·西安·北京·广州

图书在版编目(CIP)数据

征服、重构与回归:蒂姆·温顿小说的生态解读:英文/徐显静著.—上海:上海世界图书出版公司,2016.9

ISBN 978-7-5192-1639-9

Ⅰ.①征… Ⅱ.①徐… Ⅲ.①蒂姆·温顿-小说研究-英文 Ⅳ.①I611.074

中国版本图书馆 CIP 数据核字(2016)第 189986 号

责任编辑:吴柯茜
责任校对:石佳达
装帧设计:车皓楠

征服、重构与回归:蒂姆·温顿小说的生态解读

徐显静 著

上海世界图书出版公司 出版发行
上海市广中路 88 号 9—10 楼
邮政编码 200083
上海景条印刷有限公司印刷
如发现印装质量问题,请与印刷厂联系
(质检科电话:021-59815625)
各地新华书店经销

开本:890×1240 1/32 印张:8.25 字数:300 000
2016 年 9 月第 1 版 2016 年 9 月第 1 次印刷
ISBN 978-7-5192-1639-9/I·57
定价:38.00 元
http://www.wpcsh.com

摘　要

当代著名澳大利亚作家蒂姆·温顿(Tim Winton)(1960—)是澳大利亚文学史上首位四次“迈尔斯·弗兰克林奖”获得者。因故乡西澳大利亚自然景观在其文本中的重要地位,他被冠以“景观作家”的称号。作家亦作为环保运动的积极参与者和赞助人为人熟知。遗憾的是,尽管作品中的地方主义特色、归属感、非典型男性气质、厌女倾向等重要论题得到了评论界的足够重视,批评者们也关注到了自然景观在其创作中的突出地位,但对其生态意义的解读还不够系统深刻。温顿作品始终关注人与自然环境的关系问题,具有布伊尔所谓的“环境取向的作品”的所有特质,因此利用生态文学批评理论解读该作家可以建立起其作为景观作家和环保主义者身份之间的内在逻辑,具有特殊意义。

生态主题是温顿创作的重要元素之一,体现了以作家本人为代表的后定居者——当代澳大利亚白人对这片土地、海洋及栖息于此万物的全方位的爱恋和生态关怀。细读作家所有作品后,笔者认为尽管作者的生态理念呈现散漫式分布,但仍可勾勒出一个清晰的发展脉络。在相关前期成果不十分丰富的情况下,本书选取温顿生态主题较为突出的几部作品,如《浅滩》《土乐》《洛基·伦纳德,浮渣清除者》《蓝背鱼》《露天泳者》《呼吸》以及短篇小说《荒野》等,对其生态主题进行纵向分析。

笔者经深入分析发现,作家的生态思想遵循着征服、重构和回归的思想轨迹。所谓征服指作品中温顿不遗余力地揭示出在西方文化中人与自然二元对立价值观指导下,白人在两个多世纪里对澳洲土地和海洋资源的恣意掠夺。瓦尔·普拉姆伍德(Val Plumwood)

对二元论的深入分析将为解读这种人与自然的征服与被征服关系提供理论支持。文本中暗示白人罔顾澳洲大陆的自然条件恣意建立田园牧歌似的阿卡迪亚,结果却是过度农业垦殖遗留下土地退化;采矿业造成生态破坏,并进一步造成人自身的异化。温顿对人类征服海洋的揭示则主要集中于捕鲸业造成的人类精神生态失衡,以及少年读物《洛基·伦纳德,浮渣清除者》中作者用夸张笔墨展现的海岸污染严重威胁人之生存。作者构建新型的人与自然,更准确地说是澳洲白人与这片土地的脐带关系的灵感部分来源于20世纪以来西方生态批评的重要成果,如阿尔贝特·施韦泽(Albert Schweitzer)的"敬畏生命"、奥尔多·利奥波德(Aldo Leopold)的"大地伦理",同时也来源于澳大利亚土著文化中的"关爱大地"的世界观。三者在本质上并行不悖,共同为解读温顿作品中重构生态和谐的努力提供理论依据。在作者处女作《露天泳者》中,人物在对待陆生的袋鼠、海洋中的鱼时,充分体现出了一种对生命应有的敬畏,《土乐》中暗示出农业文化中理应秉持的环境伦理。其次,温顿积极塑造典型的自然之子/女形象,并使他们成为构建人与自然亲情关系的主要践行者。其中《浅滩》中的昆尼代表了20世纪70年代末生态意识觉醒的先行者,她不顾丈夫反对投入到一场拯救海洋生物鲸鱼的环保行动中。温顿的生态乌托邦小说《蓝背鱼》则展示了主人公属于海洋、与其和谐共生、终生守望的动人画卷,表达了作者对生态文明美好未来的企盼。回归荒野在温顿的生态思想体系中举足轻重,具有重要的生态和社会意义。回归荒野有利于高度城市化的当代澳洲白人通过与自然亲密互动,产生亲情和归属感,摆脱疏离的"无根"状态实现本土化,从而构建与大地休戚相关的新型民族身份,并且加强人类与自然的纽带关系,培养人类对自然的生态关怀。此外,回归自然也是对社会上普遍存在的发展与消费主义神话的不满与反抗。温顿作品一再证明了浪漫主义之父让·雅克·卢梭的观点，即被人类社会所累的主人公在荒野中才能恢复纯良本性。如《露天泳者》中杰拉在荒野中经历了水与火的洗礼，净化了心灵，摆脱了负罪感，克服了友情危机、乱伦情欲而得以成长；《土乐》中鲁德·福克斯同样经受住了荒野生存的各种挑战，历经从求死到求生的蜕变，最终实现了自我和解。温顿还暗示，这种和解不仅在于主人公与个人的过往，而且在于种族间和物种间，并最终实现人类与自然间的和解。

总之，蒂姆·温顿的个人生态哲学突出地关注构建澳洲白人与土地的亲情关系，他本人热切希望像其作品中的人物那样，澳大利亚白人可以从荒野自然中获得净化、顿悟、救赎和活力，并感受到他们的个人及民族身份与澳洲大陆血肉相连，从而实现人与自然和谐共生的生态理想。

关键词：蒂姆·温顿；生态批评；征服；重构；回归

Abstract

The contemporary Australian author Tim Winton (1960—) is the only four-time winner of the most prestigious literary prize in Australia—Miles Franklin Award. He is known as a landscape writer on account of his preoccupation with describing the landscapes in Western Australia in his oeuvre. Meanwhile, he is also an avid environmentalist who participates, leads and patronizes many an organization and campaign to keep the primal beauty of wilderness in Australia. Pitifully, although adequate criticism zooms in on such major topics as regionalism, sense of belonging, the non-typical masculinities, the propensity of misogyny and so on, rarely have literary critics noted the link between his being a landscape author and an environmentalist, which prompts me to study his works from the perspective of ecocriticism.

Virtually, the motif of environmentalism has always been an indispensable theme in Tim Winton's works, representing his passionate love for and ecological care towards the land. A close reading of his fiction reveals that his ecological thoughts are scattered yet prevalent in all his works and this research focuses mainly upon such works as *Shallows*, *Dirt Music*, *Scumbuster*, *Blueback*, *An Open Swimmer*, *Breath*, and short story "Wilderness".

This book concludes that Tim Winton's ecosophy mainly includes three components, namely, conquest, reestablishment and retreat. Conquest denotes the depiction of white Australians' wanton plunder of natural resources in the past two centuries on account of the dichotomy of man and nature in western culture. Val Plumwood's argumentation on the five features of dualism offers the fundamental theoretical support for the exploration into the estranged relationship of conquest. It is implied that the European settlers' dream of building idyllic Arcadia disregarding the wrong natural conditions in Australia inevitably results in land degradation, ecological disruption and the mining industry causes human alienation. The conquest of the sea is vividly embodied in the brutal whaling industry as well as in coastal contamination. *Shallows* discloses that the whaling industry eventually leads to the disequilibrium of people's spiritual ecology prominently embodied in collapsed faith, as well as in minor forms of bully, barbarity, sodomy, aloofness, abandonment, betrayal, and even cannibalism. And *Scumbuster* points out that coastal pollution is the unavoidable consequence of illegal industrial discharge superficially and of the mentality of colonizing nature essentially.

Both western ecocritical theories and Aboriginal eco-wisdom become accessible inspiration for the author to reestablish the umbilical bond between white Australians and the adopted land, the second aspect of Tim Winton's ecosophy. Borrowing ideas from Albert Schweitzer and Aldo Leopold, the author advocates reverence for life in dealing with non-human animals in nature and basic environmental ethics in agricultural development. Succinctly, Winton's ecological care towards animals goes from "reverence for life" (in *An Open Swimmer*) to protection of wildlife (in *Shallows*) and then to a harmonious coexistence with animals (in *Blueback*). Secondly, Tim Winton portrays a new kind of protagonists as nature's children who are ennatured rather than alienated and are voluntarily converted to firm land caretakers in time. Queenie Coupar in *Shallows* involves herself in the environmental campaigns launched by a foreign green organization to prevent whales from extinction, which helps to awaken people's eco-responsibility. The ecotopia *Blueback* depicts the harmonious symbiosis between humanity and nature in a utopian world where the protagonists claim to belong to the sea, make moderate use of its resources, and in the meantime take pains to protect it in return, the way the Aborigines take care of their country. In a way, *Blueback* implies the author's eco-ideal in its highest form.

Retreating to the wilderness is the third element in Winton's ecosophy. Retreat is of great ecological and communal significance because it brings the highly urbanized modern Australians into intimate contact with nature, cultivating a sense of kinship and belonging and thus indigenizing them in a land that they still feel alien. Retreat to wilderness not only strengthens the bond between man and nature but cultivates ecological care towards nature and furthermore helps to shape a new type of national identity. Jean-Jacque rousseau advocates going back to nature to regain the natural state of human goodness that has been corrupted by human civilization. Hence, withdrawal to wilderness is also an antidote to and a reaction against the myth of development and consumerism prevalent in modern society. It is proved that nature possesses the magical power to tranquilize one and appease one's trauma. Hence, after removing the guilt and uncertainty and experiencing catharsis in the fire and water in the coastal bush, Jerra in *An Open Swimmer* overcomes the crises in growth. Likewise, Luther Fox undergoes an alchemical shift from seeking death to seeking life and becomes a better and more unified man in the wilderness of the unmanned small island.

In brief, Tim Winton's ecosophy concerns with constructing the umbilical bond between his white compatriots and the adopted land of Australia. The author enthusiastically wishes that like his fictional characters they can also acquire catharsis, epiphany, redemption and vitality from the wilderness and feel that one's identity is tied to immediate nature. Hopefully, reconciliation can be achieved between white Australians and Aboriginal Australians, culture and nature, human and non-human species, and eventually between man and nature.

Key Words: Tim Winton; Ecocriticism; Conquest; Reestablishment; Retreat

Contents

Introduction

In Australia, Tim Winton is known under several titles: literary prodigy, landscape writer, and environmentalist. He began to write and publish at 22 and decided to be a writer at 10. Therefore, he won the name of a writing "prodigy". His writing career is brilliant because he is the only four-time winner of the most prestigious literary prize in Australia — Miles Franklin Award. He is full of affection for the land that bred him and he wants the world to know that there is such a wonderful region on the western verge of the largest island continent — Australia. He is also known as a landscape writer. In addition, as a Western Australian who lives along the coastal area facing the Indian Ocean and backed by the vast arid or semi-arid area of the continent, Winton is an avid surfer, diver, fisher and even a beachcomber, which naturally leads to another important title for him — the enthusiastic patron of the marine environmental protection.

Winton was born to a working-class family in Karrinyup, Western Australia in 1960. His father was a policeman and his mother a switchboard operator. When he was 12 years old, his family moved to Albany, a major southern port, where he spent three years. Winton grew up largely at Scarborough, a suburb of Perth. The family Christmas holidays that were often spent "in a shack at the mouth of the Greenough River", four-hour drive north of Perth, had an enormous impact on the author's future career (Winton, *Land's Edge* 12). In his memory, there are two distinct childhoods, "the one contained and clothed, between fences" in the suburban area and "the other rambling, windblown, half-naked" in the coastal area. Winton admits that he "lived the coastal life harder, with more passion", for the outdoor life on the beach activates every cell in the boy (*Land's Edge* 9). And Winton attributes his becoming an author partly to the summer time spent in the house library "with four walls of books" at Greenough. Besides, his summer holidays are full of "the briny smell of the sea", which accounts for the author's obsessive interest in the littoral life (*Land's Edge* 14). House library and coastal life initiate him into a writing career as a landscape writer.

Later, Tim Winton had his name enrolled in a course of creative writing under the tutelage of Elizabeth Jolley, the famous Australian novelist, at the WAIT (the West Australia Institute of Technology, now Curtin University), albeit he spent most of his energy writing his virgin work *An Open Swimmer* which won him The Australian Vogel Literary Award.

After marriage, Winton lived for several years in Lancelin, "a hamlet for fishermen, north of Perth, a life away from the city" (Ben-Messahe, *Mind the Country* 4). This "redneck crayfishing town of six hundred people and seven hundred dogs" (Hefner 23), according to Ben-Messahe, is the "haven for the landscape writer" with its "long stretches of white sand beside the Indian Ocean", which "have certainly provided Winton with a wealth of material" (*Mind the Country* 5). A grant from the Literature Board of the Australia Council permitted him to sojourn in such European countries as France, Greece, Italy and Ireland from 1987 to 1989, during which he embarked upon the writing of *Cloudstreet* (1991). The experiences themselves become the major materials for *The Riders* (1994). Winton is now living at Fremantle, a small town at the mouth of the Swan River with a population of 25,000.

Up to now, Tim Winton has published nine novels, namely *An Open Swimmer* (1982), *Shallows* (1984), *That Eye, that Sky* (1986), *In the Winter Dark* (1988), *Cloudstreet* (1991), *The Riders* (1994), *Dirt Music* (2001), *Breath* (2008) and *Eyrie* (2013), among which *Shallows* and *Cloudstreet* have been translated into Chinese. Winton's writing career has been accompanied by honors and applauses ever since the publication of his virgin work and almost all his novels have won prizes. Here, I hope to mention the most significant honors since a full list of awards and nominations is found in the appendix attached to this book. Tim Winton sets an unparalleled record as the first and only four-time winner of the most important literary prize in Australia — the Miles Franklin Award, respectively for *Breath* in 2009, *Dirt Music* in 2002, *Cloudstreet* in 1992 and for *Shallows* in 1984. Additionally, Winton was twice short-listed for the Booker prize with *The Riders* in 1995 and *Dirt Music* in 2002. Besides, *Cloudstreet* and *Dirt Music* rated first and fourth respectively among the top 40 Australian books in the poll conducted by the Australian Society of Authors in 2003. In December 2012, *Cloudstreet* topped the list of Top 50 Aussie Books voted by Australian ABC Viewers with *The Riders* coming in the nineteenth. On account of the brilliance achieved by the author, Winton was declared "an Australian National Living Treasure" in 1997 (O'Reilly, "Mind the Country" 359) and listed amongst Western Australia's 100 most influential people in 2006 (qtd. in Kuhlenbeck 57).

Winton is also an excellent short story writer and has three short story collections to his name, i.e. *Scission* (1985), *Minimum of Two* (1987) and *The Turning* (2005), among which *Scission* "won the 1985 Western Australian Council Week Literary Award" (Wilde 822). Two of his short stories "Neighbours" (from *Scission*) and "On her Knees" (from *The Turning*) have been rendered into Chinese. As a professional author since 1981, he also composes seven books for younger readers including *Jesse* (1990), the trilogy *Lockie Leonard* (1990—1997), *The Bugalugs Bum Thief* (1991), *Blueback* (1997) and *The Deep* (2004) and three plays *Rising Water* (2011), *Signs of life* (2012) and *Shrine* (2013).

Given the wide popularity, Winton's works have been successfully adapted for stage, screen and radio. Some of his books, like *That Eye*,

The Sky and *In the Winter Dark* were turned to movies respectively in 1994 and 1998 while *Lockie Leonard* series and *Cloudstreet* were adapted to TV series in 2007 and 2011. It's interesting to note that the author sometimes gets personally involved in the adaptations of his own works. His prize winners *Cloudstreet*, *Dirt Music* and *The Riders* are all now being converted into movies. On the publication of his novel *Dirt Music*, he collaborated with broadcaster, Lucky Oceans, to produce a compilation CD, *Dirt Music — Music for a Novel*. His plays have achieved equal success on stage. In the non-fiction sector, he has solely or cooperatively published four books including *Smalltown* (2009), *Down to Earth* (1999), *Local Colour*: *Travels in the Other Australia* (1994), and *Land's Edge* (1993). *Land's Edge* is often taken as his "autobiographical meditations about his obsession with the coast"① and "his relationship with place" (Wilde 822).

Tim Winton admits that the early literary influences come from American writers such as Mark Twain who teaches him that one can write with the language that one speaks; William Faulkner whose regional writing gives him the very inspiration for depicting Western Australia the way one deals with a character. The author also feels indebted to Nathaniel Hawthorne, Earnest Hemingway, F. Scott Fitzgerald and a group of American Southern novelists, with Flannery O'Connor on the top of the list, whose works depend heavily on the regional settings. Among Australian writers who have influence on him, Winton singles out Randolph Stow, Christopher Koch, Helen Garner and Les Murray (Kuhlenbeck 57). The author said that "it was unusual when he was a boy to read about Western Australian places and people in fiction"② (刘，《外国文学》151). Many Western Australian writers such as

① From the back blurb of the book.

② This and other quotes of the same interview all derive from the English version of the interview offered by the interviewer Yunqiu Liu.

Dorothy Hewett, Elizabeth Jolley, and Randolph Stow, especially the latter, set him good examples by presenting the special place in Western Australia and by employing the vernacular there. Winton adopts his home state as his literary province and further develops the regional writing to a higher degree by describing the indigenous flora and fauna there to impress his readers with the unique natural landscape of the coastal area of Western Australia.

Winton feels akin to Stow also because of their resemblance in the attitude towards nature. Again, as Winton puts it in a recent interview, "I'm more interested in Stow, perhaps because he has a kind of humility towards the landscapes". Then he further illustrates that "Stow seemed to be putting himself in more ways at the mercy of the natural world, in a kind of humility" (刘,《外国文学》151). To remain humble towards nature is something that recent western culture dearly lacks. Winton intends to cultivate such an attitude towards nature in his fiction to reconstruct a close link between man and nature. He portrays quite a few characters that live in the bush along the coast, far away from city life and in awe of the power of nature. As Bruce Bennett comments:

> In his revisiting of this coastline, Winton meets fishermen and beachcombers who are held up as examples for urban sophisticates of stoical, humorous, bloody-minded independents who are, in some respects, the legatees of Henry Lawson's bush men and women. Winton is keen to show that such characters still exist at land's edge, though now at the edges of Australian consciousness. (283)

Notwithstanding the trends of urbanization, industrialization, commercialization as well as globalization, Winton stresses that at land's edge where his hometown lies, there are such natural individuals who are able to survive in wilderness. Such people are "stoical, humorous, and bloody-minded." They take things from nature just to meet the vital needs and never take more than necessary so that they live as an organic part of nature and are on harmonious terms with other species and the natural environment. In brief, they are the genuine members in nature.

Winton stresses that he is more influenced by the presence of natural forms, landscapes and space. Landscape is the primary source of inspiration for Winton who comes from a large island continent where there is more landscape than there are people (刘,《外国文学》149~150). In a way, all these memories and experiences of a littoral life have become part of the author and thus have inexplicably marked his body and shaped his identity. Obviously, he feels deeply attached to the land where he grew up so that its contours, its sounds and its smells are all stored in his brain and then depicted in his works.

Likewise, the author who claims himself "not the standard issue green ideologue" but "redneck greenie" is a spontaneous environmental activist (Rolley 28). Tim Winton is an avid environmentalist who participates, leads and patronizes many an organization and campaign to keep the primal state of wilderness in the vast areas of Western Australia as well as their coastal zones.

As an active marine conservationist, he is a patron of the Australian Marine Conservation Society (AMCS) and has actively campaigned for marine species such as turtles, dugongs, dolphins and whales (Skatssoon 42). He has also fought against shark finning with AMCS. Winton delivered a speech in 2010 to raise awareness of the plight of sharks and called on Australians to stop being accomplices in driving sharks out of existence.

Like Judith Wright who campaigned relentlessly for the Great Barrier Reef in the eastern coast of Australia, Winton donated his $25,000 prize in the New South Wales Premier's Literary Awards for *Dirt Music* in the year 2002 to halt development of the coral Ningaloo Reef, a fringing reef off Western Australia's mid north coast. In the following year, he was awarded the inaugural Australian Society of Authors (ASA) Medal in recognition for his work in the campaign to save the Ningaloo Reef①. Again in 2002, he joined an increasingly damaging boycott of one of Australia's richest literary prizes and withdrew his novel *Dirt Music* from the $40,000 Tasmania Pacific Fiction Prize in protest over logging of the island's old-growth forests (Andrew Darby 9).

In 2010, Winton contributed to the whaling debate with an article "No Humane Way to Kill a Whale" on the Last Whale website, and he is a prominent advocate of the Save Moreton Bay organization, the Environment Defender's Office, Australian Wildlife Conservancy. He also patronizes the Stop the Toad Foundation②.

As a writer who cherishes the uniqueness of the landscapes and seascapes in his homeland and as a patriot who devotes himself to the reconstruction of the link between white Australians and their landscapes and to the construction of a new national identity, Tim Winton is a responsible caretaker and eulogist of the land of Australia.

Tim Winton is undoubtedly one of the most successful contemporary full-time writers and "arguably the most popular Australian writer" (O'Reilly, "Mind the Country" 359). The fact that his works are often launched simultaneously in Australia as well as in the U.S. or U.K. and that his books have been translated into eighteen languages brings him wide international readership. Oddly enough, Tim Winton has been seriously underresearched in the academic milieu.

Robert Dixon③, the former president of the Association for the Study of Australian Literature (ASAL) (1995—1997), and the current Chair of Australian Literature at the University of Sydney, notes this unusual phenomenon and attempts to explain it by placing Winton's

①② http://en.wikipedia.org/wiki/Tim_Winton.

③ Robert Dixon is also the past-judge of the Miles Franklin Literary Award (2004 — 2009). More information about Robert Dixon is found at webpage <http://www.austlit.edu.au/austlit/page/A24056>.

success in the context of the development of Australian literature from the early 1980s on. He puts "the whole system involved in the production and reception of Australian literature" and Winton's fiction under close scrutiny to seek the link between the two (245). He quotes David Carter's view that "the field of Australian literature has achieved a certain maturity or 'density'" in the last two decades of the 20th century to conclude that Tim Winton is "an artifact" (247) of the time and of the system of Australian literature, which means Winton's brilliant career as a novelist exactly corresponds with the maturation of Australian literature (248). In contrast, his tutor at WAIT Elizabeth Jolley had to wait till she was in her fifties to have her works published. Coincidentally, their fame both began to soar in the 1980s, "a key moment in the growth and maturity of the field of Australian literature" (249). In fact, it is believed that Winton's success lies more in the effective commercial promotion which creates a wide readership than in academic literary criticism, which attests to Nathanael O'Reilly's opinion that "surprisingly little criticism has been published on Winton's work, especially when compared to Peter Carey and David Malouf, both of whom published their first novels not long before Winton (in 1981 and 1975 respectively)" ("Mind the Country" 359). Numerous interviews, book reviews, comments from reader groups rather than from university literature professors are published on newspapers, magazines and web pages. Besides, Winton's works are frequently adapted to stages, movies or TV series. All these elements in the system lend a hand to boost the reception and consumption of Tim Winton domestically and internationally. That Winton's fiction has long been listed in secondary school curriculum in Australia further certifies "his popularity with the general rather than the academic reader" (Dixon 251). All these factors ensure the author's stable success in the market but give rise to the awkward situation of Tim Winton studies.

Tim Winton is lucky to be born in the right time and chooses the right career in which he makes a dent. Meanwhile, Tim Winton is also unlucky to be involved in the controversy over whether he is a writer worthy of serious academic consideration or he is just the time pet who manages to earn enough to have a shelter over his head with spare money to donate to some green activities. When Robert Dixon's article "Tim Winton, *Cloudstreet* and the Field of Australian Literature" was published in 2005, the status quo then was that the "readings of Winton's works have been less theoretical and text-based, preferring instead author-centered, thematic and regional approaches" (249). However, the staggering number of national and international literary awards and the hit created by the launch of each and every of his work eventually prove that he certainly deserves serious academic scrutiny. In a way, the fourth Miles Franklin Prize further confirms the author's special contribution to the national literature and demonstrates his steadfast determination to write something that is read by people and influences them rather than something put on the book shelf for decoration. An undeniable fact is that his latest work in 2013 *Eyrie* was again shortlisted for the 2014 Miles Franklin Literary Award. Therefore, the second decade of the new century has witnessed a wave of Tim Winton studies and a rapid proliferation in the number of academic essays on top literary journals as well as theses and dissertations by graduates. In March 2013 CMII (Centre for Memory, Imagination and Invention) of Deakin University declared that it would embark upon a comprehensive academic research into Tim Winton's works and his readership from such perspectives as gender, race, religion and nationality①. It is alleged that the project is to explore the special contributions made by Winton's fiction to Australian national culture and the roles played by literature in understanding places and identity construction. The project is said to be the first attempt of its kind and

① http://www.deakin.edu.au/research/grants/stories/2013/03/21/the-legacy-of-tim-winton.

will be a milestone in Tim Winton studies, which indicates a steady rise of the significance of his fiction in the international academic circle. The heads of the panel are Professor Lyn McCredden from Deakin University in Australia and Dr Nathanael O'Reilly from Texas Southern University in the United States and the symposium *Tim Winton: Critical Essays* (2014) has been recently published by UWAP (University of Western Australia Press), covering articles contributed by researchers from Australia, the U.S., France, Spain, Germany as well as China. Professor McCredden also plans to publish a monograph in the coming year.

Up till now, five books have been published on Tim Winton studies: *Mind the Country: Tim Winton's Fiction* (2006), a monograph by Dr. Salhia Ben-Messahel, a French critic who had published several essays and interviews before publishing the book ; *Reading Tim Winton* (1993) co-edited by Richard Rossiter and Lyn Jacobs and *Tim Winton: Critical Essays* (2014) co-edited by Lyn McCredden and Nathanael O'Reilly, two collections of academic articles; *Tim Winton: the Writer and His Work* (1999), a learner's guide written by Michael McGirr; and *Tim Winton: a Celebration* (1999) edited by Hilary McPhee. Criticism on Winton's fiction is frequently indispensable chapters in books and dissertations. Journals and newspapers are also common media for the researches on Tim Winton's works. The following is a detailed survey of the chief perspectives of Tim Winton studies.

1. Author-centered researches constitute a major part of Tim Winton studies. The three books on Tim Winton published in the 1990s all belong to this category. *Reading Tim Winton* (1993) is a collection of six essays by excellent critics whose topics cover the major elements in his early works, such as his attachment to place, the spiritual aspect, the problems of gender and class, childhood and history. These essays attempt to establish some link between the major themes in fiction and the author's personal experiences and make engaging and instructive

reading till today. *Tim Winton: the Writer and His Work* (1999) follows the similar train of thought and is of limited academic significance in that it's written mainly to help the students appreciate seven of Winton's early novels. *Tim Winton: a Celebration* (1999) edited by Hilary McPhee is a volume concerning the novelist's life and work written by his friend Helen Garner, his former publisher Hilary McGirr and so on. Robert Dixon points out succinctly that "the issues and approaches that dominate the three books about Winton are author-centered. and thematic, focusing especially on the biographical and regional issues" (251). Additionally, researches "in the form of interviews, feature articles in newspapers and magazines, and on radio and television" should be included in this group (Dixon 249). Self-admittedly, interviews made immediately after the launch of a new book contribute much to the promotion and interpretation of the work. But it's equally undeniable that interviews conducted by renowned literary critics such as Andrew Taylor (in 1996), Richard Rossiter (in 2004), Britta Kuhlenbeck (in 2006), Salhia Ben-Messahel (in 2010, 2012), and Yunqiu Liu (in 2013), to name a few, are insightful, inspiring and instructional for serious studies. Author-centered researches help me understand the umbilical bond between Tim Winton and his hometown, which greatly facilitates my study into his eco-care towards it through fiction as well as action.

2. Another significant perspective for Tim Winton studies is regionalist writing. These essays are concerned with the striking local features of Winton's works. Many a critic notices that Winton places most of his protagonists in Western Australia, especially the coastal area of the state. Vanessa Richard's "Land and the Self" (2009) focuses on Winton's persistent concern with the relation of the land to the individual identity. Salhia Ben-Messaha discusses regionalism in her monograph *Mind the Country*, which will be introduced in more details later. In *A Companion to Australian literature since 1900* (2007), co-edited by Nicholas Birns and Rebecca McNeer, a chapter by Lyn Jacob devotes to

the exploration of the relationship between Tim Winton and Western Australian Writing. During an interview, Winton comments that unlike the U.S. or Europe, there are no real dialect or accent differences in Australia, so "you can't push the regional idea too far" (qtd. in Ben-Messaha, *Mind the Country* 231). Obviously, Tim Winton does not think highly of the label of regionalism. Despite this, many critics choose to explore this feature of his writing and they even dig out the origin of his regional style. In Watzke's interview, Winton said: "I like the way the region was always a character in the novel" ("Where Pigs Speak" 96 ~ 97). The writer also admitted he was intrigued by American regionalist writers of the South. What's more, when Winton received the Premier's Book Award for *Dirt Music* in 2001, the judges' comment goes: "Winton has given us the quintessential West Australian novel ..." (qtd. in Kuhlenbeck 55). Undoubtedly, regionalism is an appropriate hallmark attached to his works.

In the monograph *Rewriting Spatiality — The Production of Space in the Pilbara Region in Western Australia* (2009) by the German critic Britta Kuhlenbeck, the critic explores the production of the Thirdspace in *Dirt Music*. The male protagonist Luther Fox is portrayed in the image of a poacher, which, as Kuhlenbeck sees it, implies transgression, a notion proposed by Tim Cresswell. On the surface, Fox is poaching lobster. But on the deeper level, his behavior of poaching is transgressing territory, or is a critique of boundaries. When Fox and Georgie meet, the spatial transgression develops to a deconstruction of power relations in the community. Then the discussion zooms in on Luther Fox's walking through the wilderness, which is an all-round proprioceptive involvement with nature and thus yields empathy, meaning and understanding. Kuhlenbeck points out that the intimacy developed between human and space/nature is beneficial for a process of reconciliation with the land and its Indigenous ethnic groups in Australia in particular, and for a re-evaluation of space in ecological terms. This opinion gives me much inspiration and instruction for my interpretation of Luther Fox's self-rehabilitation in the wilderness of the deserted island in Chapter Ⅲ.

Kuhlenbeck also discerns that many elements of environmentalist writing prescribed by the renowned ecocritic Lawrence Buell can be identified in *Dirt Music*'s Thirdspace representation and explores the ecological factors in *Dirt Music*. However, it is a pity that she does not bother to dig out more details in the text to explore the author's serious concern with the environment, though she does mention that Winton's environmental concern lies in his criticism of the idea that the environment's value can be measured by its "utility"; in his "critique of spoiling the beauty of the environment through human presence and endeavour" etc. (128); though she also notices that Winton's engagement with the environment results from his attachment to the land.

What's worthy of mention is Appendix 1 attached to Kuhlenbeck's monograph, a full script of the interview with Tim Winton by the critic in 2006, in which questions are about space, place, environment, land, landscapes, sense of belonging, the relationship to the land, relationship between self and landscape, between protagonists and nature, the role of an author and his writing with respect to conservation of the environment etc. Kuhlenbeck's study and interview are the few achievements of research that touch upon the ecocritical significance of the Winton's oeuvre and thus are of special meaning to this research.

3. The portrayals of unconventional, manipulative or matriarchal female protagonists render the boom of criticism from the feminist perspective. The novelist is even blamed by some critics for misogyny, although the author himself thought it ridiculous and denied the censure in the talk with Salhia Ben-Messahel in 2010. Hannah Schürholz is a major critic in this aspect and the female characters in Tim Winton's fiction become the constant objects for her studies. In her PhD thesis, she makes a deconstructive interpretation of them by employing such theoretical tools as feminism, memory and self-harm ("Gendered

Space" 79). In her essay "Shadow of the Dead", she analyzes the female characters in Winton's early fiction such as *An Open Swimmer*, *Shallows*, and *In the Winter Dark* to explore the link between death and woman in Winton's works. According to Schürholz, death is traditionally held as "a gendered metaphor in literature and visual arts" in western culture and it shares with the female the attribute of being the other (164). She discovers that "death here becomes an allegory that exposes feminity as simultaneously a threatening and regulating force within dominant social-cultural discourse and a pre-condition for the healing and maturation of the male protagonists" (166). Hence, Winton's intention to fracture traditional gendered roles in family and in patriarchal community is often offset by his "appropriation of the female body as a nexus of male experience and enlightenment" (178 ~ 179). Like in most other male narratives, the female protagonists remain to be the *locus* of "trauma, transience and otherness" (179). So Winton's novels consequently tend to intensify stereotypes of genders that he has intended to deconstruct. In another essay on the domesticity in Winton's later works *Dirt Music*, *The Riders* and *Breath*, she confirms that "only male protagonists are granted the rite of passage to recovery" ("Gendered Space" 75) while female protagonists are always displaced, marginalized and fragmented as "traumatized and traumatizing Other" ("Gendered Space" 74). Schürholz contributes another article to *Tim Winton: Critical Essays* — the latest collection in 2014, in which she continues her feminist questioning of Winton's gender politics by asking why the female characters in Winton's oeuvre always "show a strong tendency towards self-threatening behaviour, transience and ferocity" (96).

Colleen McGloin points out that the only female protagonist Eva in *Breath* is obviously portrayed in a misogynistic way. Hence, critical readings of the character are accordingly negative since "*Breath*'s narrative positions readers to comply with a very specific view of her" prescribed by the author (111). Elizabeth Guy notes that under "Winton's overtly masculine gaze, women are seen as 'other' and the feminine is erotic, desired and feared and the maternal is placed as both whore and Madonna" (31). She proceeds to explore a variety of ruptured factors in Winton's works, such as the ruptured desire, ruptured patriarchal structure, and ruptured control of sexuality's feral power, and eventually ruptured stereotypes of genders, which are held by Tim Winton as a convenient approach to explore the unconventional, sensitive and vulnerable male and to uncover "what lies outside the rational male" gaze (35). Ma Pilar Baines Alarcos publishes an essay entitled "She Lures, She Guides and She Quits", in which she zooms in on three female characters in *The Riders* to conclude that "Winton's fictional women are normally portrayed according to female archetypes in Australian social and cultural contexts and thus they are presented as ambivalent beings who are therefore unreliable and even dangerous" (7). The Chinese critic Chunjuan Zhan also believes that in Winton's fiction feminity is subject to the invisible and disguised power of masculinity despite Winton's seeming subversion in ideals of masculinity and feminity in a pro-feminist way. So women images in his novels are negative and dangerous (117).

Feminist interpretations make me discreet in dealing with female characters in the fiction. They deepen my comprehension of the female character Jewel in Winton's virgin fiction, *An Open Swimmer*. Seen from ecocritical perspective, women protagonists such as Queenie Coupar, Dora Jackson are eco-warriors rather than the erotic or the feared other.

4. Since Winton's fictional clans are predominantly male, issues of masculinity become the next perspective of analysis. In "Changing Masculinities: Disruption and Anxiety in Contemporary Australian Writing", Linzi Murrie comments that in Winton's fiction there is an obvious "feminine" side to the male protagonists who have some non-rational traits in their personalities and who are mainly involved in domestic sphere in their searching for meaning and identity. This

"disrupts dominant construction of the public sphere as the site of male proving and of the 'home' as emasculating" (Murrie 174). But he also notes that the empowerment of the male characters, like in *Cloudstreet*, is corresponded with the disempowerment of women, for example, the marginalization of the maternal in the two characters of Oriel and Dolly, which echoes the suspect of gender prejudice held by Elizabeth Guy etc. Barbara Arizti Martin analyzes the crisis of masculinity in Tim Winton's *The Riders* and concludes that the depictions of both masculinity and femininity are contradictory and the end of novel stands for reconciliation between the two. Roie Thomas investigates *Breath* within "a framework of theistic existentialism alongside a critique of masculinities in the Australian context" in the essay "Inspire, Expire: Masculinity, Mortality and Meaning in Tim Winton's *Breath*" (54). In their articles in *Tim Winton: Critical Essays*, Bridge Grogan focuses on the melancholic masculinity in *The Turning* by dwelling on the dialectic relationship between "love and loss" (199~220) and Nathanael O'Reilly explores the non-traditional fatherhood and father-son relationships that allow intimacy, shedding light on the untypical masculinity in *Scission* (161~182).

In fact, the discussion of masculinity is inseparable from that of femininity. They are the double sides of the same coin. Gender studies will continue to be a major research perspective due to Winton's depiction of unconventional "weak" males and "strong" females, which the author himself partly attributes to the influence from his family tradition.

5. Frequent employment of Christian instructions and direct Bible quotations in Winton's fiction make criticism from the theological perspective unavoidable. The topics may center on sin, grace, and redemption and so on. "Sea, Spirit, and Salvation: a Theological Reflection on the Writings of Tim Winton" by Chris Beal, an Anglican priest, is a case in point. Beal claims that we cannot fully appreciate his

work without taking into the author's religious conviction into account and he deems that Winton's fiction is "both prophetic and mystical in the classic Christian sense; is written from a deep well of personal faith and spirituality" (48). Lisa Jacobson's "Surprised by Grace: Mourning and Redemption in Tim Winton's *Dirt Music*" is another probe into the element of Christianity in Winton's composition. These essays draw my attention to the factor of religion in the interpretation of Winton's fiction. As I will argue later, religion can be conveniently employed to unfold spiritual disequilibrium and convey eco-warning.

6. The motifs like trauma, identity, family, the sense of belonging constitute another major study perspective. Solitary souls in Winton's fiction strive for a way to come to terms with personal traumas and to re-define concepts of home and to earn, refresh and renew the sense of belonging and to reconstruct individual and national identity (qtd. in Kuhlenbeck 120). Martin Flanagan explores Winton's sense of place and belonging in *Tim Winton: a Celebration*. Michael McGirr writes about his major themes of love and family in "Go Home Said Fish" and Salhia Ben-Messahe focuses upon family love in her essay "Family Stories, Brawling Love and Loving Hate". She also notes the metaphorical significance implied in the *Cloudstreet*'s protagonists who suggestively symbolize the post-settler white Australians that have to cope with the difficult historical trauma inflicted by their ancestors upon the indigenous. To construct the new national identity, reconciliation must be achieved between races as implied in his fiction. Chinese researcher Zaizhong Xu's essay "A Thematic Reading of Reconciliation in Tim Winton's *Cloudstreet*" "explores the theme of reconciliation from four aspects: the reconciliation within the family, the reconciliation between neighbors, the reconciliation between people of different races and the reconciliation between man and environment" (139).

Other topics for research includes Winton's obsession with the themes of coming-of-age or childhood; solidarity; his non-elitism and identification with working-class; his strong sense of time and history; his nostalgia and anti-suburbanism and so on. Psychoanalysis is applicable to a broad spectrum of text readings. Tim Winton study is no exception. "Land and Self" is an insightful psychoanalysis of Winton's three novels, i. e. *Dirt Music*, *The Riders*, and *That Eye, the Sky*. Zaizhong Xu's recent article on *Contemporary Foreign literature*, a highly regarded quarterly publication featuring essays, interviews, translations of fiction and poetry, analyzes *Breath* against the backdrop of Counterculture Movement in 1970s in Australia. Fei Hou explores elements of the hippie subculture in *That Eye, the Sky* in her article published in *Journal of Yan'an University* in Aug. 2014.

I think it necessary to dwell a while on *Mind the Country: Tim Winton's Fiction* (2006), the only monograph on Tim Winton studies. Nathanael O'Reilly wrote an eponymous essay claiming that the book fills "a huge gap in Australian literary criticism" and his comments are candid and objective:

> Although the nationality of the author and the presence in the bibliography of names such as Lacan, Barthes, Bachelard, Poulet and Sartre may lead readers to expect a highly theoretical approach and opaque prose, Ben-Messahel's writing is usually clear and direct, and she favours close reading over engagement with theory. (359)

Hence, the book is more text-centered than theoretically-driven. The book mainly focuses on Winton's major fiction like *Cloudstreet*, *Shallows*, *Dirt Music* and *The Riders* far more than others. Ben-Messahel incorporates a map of Western Australia with the fictional places in Winton's oeuvre marked out in the book, which shows visually the author's obsession with the littoral landscapes in Western Australia. Self-admittedly, the book is never short of original ideas and pertinent comments on these works. The weaknesses of the monograph are apparent. One is that it does not pay due attention to the major essays by influential literary critics such as Stuart Murray, Jennifer Rutherford, Anthony Hassall, Andrew Taylor, Robert Dixon and Bill Ashcroft, as O'Reilly points out ("Mind the Country" 359). The other is, as I see it, Ben-Messahel frequently jumps from one novel to another in her discussion so that it is difficult to read and the research on a specific work is unsystematic and discursive. Despite all these flaws, *Mind the Country* gives an insightful analysis of the major themes of Winton's fiction, emphasizes the importance of landscapes in his fictional world, and explores the regionalism in Winton's writing[①].

The latest research result is an anthology *Tim Winton: Critical Essays* that came out in July 2014. Targeting at the academic circle, the collection is a thematic study by an international panel whose articles cover all the works from *Shallows to Eyrie*. Generally speaking, the book shows deeper insight into traditional research motifs such as spiritualities, masculinity, childhood, love, death, nostalgia and special significance attached to water by the author in his oeuvre etc. Some critics take the author's place and reception in domestic and international market into critical consideration.

Besides, quite a few theses and dissertations put Winton's works under academic scrutiny. Hervé Cantero's doctoral thesis "Representations of Innocence and Experience" (2010) is a comparative research into how notions of innocence and experience are demonstrated in the novels of Robert Drewe and Tim Winton and the fourth chapter of the paper is on how the characters fall from innocence to experience in Tim Winton's fiction. Nathanael David O'Reilly from Michigan University explores such themes as anti-suburbanism, indigenous Australians and the struggle for belonging in Winton's *Cloudstreet* in the fourth chapter of his PhD

① Comments from the back blurb of *Mind the Country: Winton's Fiction.*

dissertation "Between the City and the Bush: Suburbia in the Contemporary Australian Novel" (2008). Gillian Mary Tyas from Deakin University analyzes the element of landscape in *Shallows* in the dissertation "Transformations: Landscape in Recent Australian Fiction" (1995). In recent years many Chinese graduates choose to study fiction by Tim Winton in their theses and it can be foreseen that more papers can be expected in the near future.

Tim Winton begins to draw attention from Chinese critics since 2010 when Zaizhong Xu published an essay introducing *Breath* and more than ten articles have been found on the academic journals to date. Besides, two interviews by Yunqiu Liu are worthy of mention since she is the first Chinese critic who has talked with the author face to face. Her interview covers thematic questions such as environmentalism, loneliness and alienation, religion, and philosophy; formal questions such as narrative perspectives and language. Self-admittedly, landscapes and seascapes, regionalism and ecology are key questions that cannot be avoided in any interview with Winton. Xianjing Xu and Yunyi Zhu both cast their critical sight on the author's ecological thoughts in *Shallows*.

Understandably, I cannot possibly exhaust all the academic achievements made by critics around the globe due to the constant development in Tim Winton studies. To sum up, all these researches should help to deepen comprehension of his works and more importantly, arouse interest in further research. I will now turn to elucidate causes for this study and the contribution it may make.

As noticed by the critics mentioned above, succeeding other well-known Western Australians of letters ranging from Peter Cowan, Randolph Stow, Elizabeth Jolley, Mudrooroo and to Robert Drewe, Tim Winton demonstrates a profound preoccupation with depicting his home state in some form of fictional reconstruction. That land and landscape are foregrounded in all of Winton's works, as to me, reveals his passion for place and more significantly, his ecological aspiration for reestablishing a harmonious relationship between mankind and nature through depicting nurturing, redemptive land with spirit. "Winton's strength is not only the subtlety of his characterisation but also his passion for place; not just scenery, although there are wonderfully scenic descriptions, but the spirit of the land" (Walker 42). As aforementioned, Britta Kuhlenbeck does note the ecological element in *Dirt Music* but fails to give adequate analysis of it. Among other critics who do research from ecocritical perspective are John P Turner and Kylie Crane. Turner discusses the link between the novel *Shallows* and the end of whaling in Australia. Kylie Crane shows strong curiosity about the role played by wilderness in the post-settler narrative *Dirt Music* in her journal articles as well as her monograph *Myths of Wilderness in Contemporary Narratives: Environmental Postcolonialism in Australia and Canada* (2012) based on her dissertation at the University of Erlangen-Nuremberg, Germany. Yet, it's obvious that the ecological implications prevalent in Winton's oeuvre haven't been paid due attention to though relevant questions are frequently asked in interviews and newspapers often report on Winton's participation in a variety of green campaigns for the protection of indigenous species or primal landscapes etc.

Given the inadequacy of the researches and his being a landscape writer as well as an environmentalist, I consider ecocriticism a promising perspective from which to read his fiction. Hopefully, my work will contribute to making readers aware of Winton's ecological care toward his motherland and the indigenous wildlife on it, which well corresponds to Winton's active involvement in environmental campaigns.

The difficulties of this research are also self-evident. Firstly, as a study from a comparatively new perspective, it naturally involves a lot of pioneering work which calls for both insight and courage. I'll try to make use of the research results that can shed light on my illustration to avoid being subjective. Secondly, the theory of ecocriticism itself is multi-vocal with the loudest voices from the U.S. and European countries. Therefore, it requires discriminating ability to locate the right theoretical support from a wide scope of views and arguments. Thirdly, applying American and European eco-theories to Australian works sometimes meet special problems of acclimatization, which must be handled carefully. Fourthly, the most challenging task before me is the abstraction of the discursive yet prevalent ecological information in all his works in a logical and systematic way to form a continuation of change and development of Winton's ecological thoughts, or ecosophy, a term coined by the Norwegian father of deep ecology Arne Naess, which means one's own personal code of values applied to questions involving ourselves and nature (Naess, *Ecology, Community and Lifestyle* 36). Ecosophy is synonymous with ecological wisdom. In accordance with Naess' explanation, ecosophy is "a philosophy of ecological harmony or equilibrium."① Unlike ecophilosophy which is a descriptive study of problems common to ecology and philosophy appropriate to a university milieu, ecosophy concerns itself more with practical situations and offers guidance for one's own decisions in handling the relationship with nature (Naess, *Ecology, Community and Lifestyle* 36 ~ 37). Each person may develop one's own ecosophy.

The research process naturally involves arduous close reading and in-depth analysis with ambition and conviction. Finally, like other Chinese researchers into foreign literature, I also face the challenge of obtaining necessary foreign references and getting the latest research results.

Despite all these obstacles, the significance of the research will certainly reward the efforts. Firstly, a comparatively new research perspective of ecocriticism is added to the international Tim Winton studies. Western ecocriticism and the rich ecological wisdom from

① http://en.wikipedia.org/wiki/Ecosophy.

Australian Aboriginal culture constitute the major sources of theoretical framework, which will greatly facilitate the evaluation and exploration of the author's ecosophy. The analysis will set a good example of equal dialogue between Western culture and Aboriginal culture, which will not only enrich the developing theory of green studies but encourage the communication between races as desired by the novelist. Secondly, it will contribute to domestic researches into Tim Winton, which is something new. At the 14th International Conference of Australian Studies in China held in July 2014, I noticed two keywords: Tim Winton and ecocriticism. A couple of conference articles are on Tim Winton's works, among which one is an analysis of *Shallows* from ecocritical perspective. Thirdly, my research will lend a hand to the argument that Winton is both a literary and a popular author, further confirming the academic significance of Winton's works. Fourthly, ecocritical reading of literature is of much contemporary relevance in an era of continuous deterioration of the environment and ecosystem. Through the interpretation, subconscious intuition will be uplifted to the consciousness to promote the improvement of man/nature relationship in general.

It is clear enough that this research will mainly be conducted within the framework of western ecocriticism. So a brief introduction of the theoretical background is necessary. In his essay in 1978, William Rueckert first coined the term "ecocriticism", "a literature-based approach within a still loosely federated but emerging field" (Hochman 187). Lawrence Buell stresses that ecocriticism is "conducted in a spirit of commitment to environmental praxis" (*Environmental Imagination* 430). Apparently, no other school of literary theory relates itself so tightly to contemporary social and historical reality than ecocriticism. The age of environmental crisis determines ecocriticism a major perspective for aesthetic researches into literature. A popular definition goes that "ecocriticism is the study of the relationship between literature and the physical environment" (Glotfelty, Introduction xviii). In circulations are other synonymous terms like "*ecopoetics*, *environmental literary criticism*, and *green cultural studies*" (qtd. in Glotfelty, Introduction XX). The advent of ecocriticsm reflects the common desire to restore the harmony or slow down the deterioration of man-nature relationship held by literary scholars. In effect, literature has long been used as a vehicle by eco-authors to convey eco-awareness and give warnings. Although European and American ecocriticism initiated from the 1970s and didn't mature until the 1990s, it has proved to be a significant job to reinterpret literary canons by authors with ecological bent such as D.H. Lawrence, Thomas Hardy, Herman Melville and Earnest Hemingway etc. from ecocritical perspective. So to speak, ecocrisis is prompting all disciplines of humanities such as philosophy, psychology, anthropology as well as theology to incorporate ecological and environmental dimensions in their respective field of study. Thus, ecocriticism has grown into a polyphonic open system with voices from different fields. The interdisciplinarity of ecocriticism also gives rise to a variety of subfields in recent years, such as environmental ethics, deep ecology, ecofeminism, postcolonial ecocriticism, ecotheology and so on. The openness of ecocriticism is also embodied in its embracing ancient, Eastern, Native or Aboriginal, and pantheistic and other non western, non main-stream belief systems that are assumed to "contain more wisdom about nature and spirituality" (Glotfelty, Introduction XXII).

Several theories and concepts will be employed for the text interpretations in this research. The five features of dualism will be viewed as the key to interpreting the tradition of taming nature and plundering natural resources in western culture. Val Plumwood's argumentations will be the major source of theoretical glimpse. Karl Marx's concept of estranged labor will be borrowed in the analysis of conquerors' spiritual disequilibrium and Rachel Carson's theories on marine ecology will also be frequently referred to. The second major source of theory derives from land care thoughts in Aboriginal ecophilosophy, which exerts subliminal impact upon the author. Other theories like Albert Schweitzer's "reverence for life" and Aldo Leopold's land ethic will be employed to interpret the author's efforts to reestablish harmonious relationship with the land. The third theoretical support comes from the theory of wilderness, a key setting in Winton's oeuvre and a core concept in ecocriticism. After tracing down the historical changes in the connotation of the concept, I further compare different notions concerning "wilderness" held by westerners and Australian Aboriginals to conclude that Winton's concept of wilderness is mainly a western one but peppered by the later.

As far as the organization of this book is concerned, it is made up of five parts. Introduction gives a detailed description of the profile of Tim Winton, including his life and oeuvre. After combing international studies on him, I put forward my research proposal and succinctly mention the contribution to be made by this study. Thereafter the major theoretical framework and the composition of this research are presented. Conclusion summarizes the main arguments as well as the originality of the study.

Chapter Ⅰ centers on digging out the details from the texts that unfold the white settlers' wanton conquest of nature in Western Australia. The conquest of land is analyzed through the landscapes of wheatbelt and mining towns. The depictions of wheatbelt in *Cloudstreet* and *Dirt Music* reveal the ecological disasters of massive land degradation and salinization on account of over-exploitation, which results in the collapse of both farm and ecosystem. It is also argued that Western Australia's fame as a great deposit of mineral resources seems to be a boon but turns out a curse. *Dirt Music* sheds light on both the ecological catastrophes caused by mining on the land as well as human alienation in the form of painful physical diseases caused by excessive exploitation of mineral resources and *Eyrie* reveals the complications of environmental problems in modern society. Settlers' conquest of the sea is approached from two perspectives, whale fishery, which leads to the near extinction of the biggest marine life and spiritual disequilibrium of whalemen; and marine pollution caused by industry, which is presented in impressive way in the fiction *Leonard Torpedo, Scumbuster*.

Chapter Ⅱ focuses on the author's endeavors to reestablish the umbilical bond between white Australians, i. e. post-settlers, and the land, in the way the Aboriginals link to their country. Firstly, borrowing Albert Schweitzer's famous "reverence for life", though Aboriginal thoughts remain a major source of reference, the paper anatomizes the characters' attitudes to animals in nature. Jerra and the nameless old recluse in *An Open Swimmer* (hence *Swimmer*) will be cited as the examples to highlight the eco-ethics observed by his characters. Secondly, the paper zooms in on a group of characters that are depicted to be children of nature to reveal Winton's deep affiliation to the land. Bruce Pike in *Breath* and Queenie Coupar in *Shallows* will be the examples for detailed analysis. Intimate contact with nature removes the alienation and estrangement between humanity and nature and creates in them deep affection for the land of Australia as well as for nature. Thirdly, delving again deeply into Winton's eco-fiction offers the opportunity to see his efforts in awakening people's environmental consciousness through the depiction of Queenie Coupar, the pioneer local eco-warrior at Angelus in *Shallows*. Fourthly, Winton's ecological ideal is best represented in *Blueback*. In this ecotopia of Tim Winton, the harmony between man and nature is reestablished.

Chapter Ⅲ analyzes the author's obvious tendency to return his protagonists to wilderness as a solution to their personal issues, attesting to the novelist's ecological awareness in relinking his protagonists to nature to rid them of the alienation between man/nature relationships. Firstly, wilderness is the place where the outcast character Jerra in *Swimmer* retreats to overcome the growing crises caused by incestuous love and the loss of childhood friendship. Secondly, Winton's short story

"Wilderness" seems to lay bare an awkward fact about modern people who pretend to return but cannot manage to, a dilemma trapping all the three characters. Thirdly, an in-depth analysis of *Dirt Music* shows that reconciliation can be hopefully achieved in wilderness, not only reconciliation between an individual and his past, but that between many other pairs of binary opposition, like white Australians and Aboriginal Australians, culture and nature, human and non-human species, and eventually man and nature.

Chapter Ⅰ Conquest of Nature

1.1 Conquest of Nature in Western Culture

The conquest of nature can be said to be an unavoidable result of western philosophy which features dualism, because the dualistic mindset almost always leads to the conquest of the inferior parts of the numerous pairs of binary oppositions, like human/nature, mind/body and male/female. In this section, I will introduce the philosophic background of human's taming of nature in western culture by tracing it back to dualism — the deep root in modern western philosophy. Theories developed in *Feminism and the Mastery of Nature* (1993) by Val Plumwood, an Australian ecofeminist intellectual and activist, will be the major source of theoretical support.

According to Val Plumwood, dualism possesses five basic features, i. e. backgrounding (denial), radical exclusion (hyperseparation), incorporation (relational definition), instrumentalism (objectification) and homogenization or stereotyping (*Feminism* 48 ~ 53). What concerns ecocritics is what happens if these structural features are applied to the specific human/nature dichotomy. They serve as a convenient short-cut to the comprehension of people's colonization of nature.

Backgrounding derives from denied dependence, in this case the denial of humanity's dependence on nature for survival, which is a simple fact but has been purposefully ignored in modern western culture ever since the advent of rationalism advocated by René Descartes in the 17th century. It is not until the later half of the 20th century when the western culture began to undergo a kind of self-criticism with environmental orientation that nature finally became visible to people again. Since the European Renaissance, humanism has risen up so high that in literature it is routine to describe natural settings as the coil to human feelings and emotions. Although Romanticism rejuvenates poets' enthusiasm for nature, their works cannot throw off the shackles of anthropocentrism, that is, the landscapes are just the stage on which human drama is played.

Radical exclusion "corresponds to the conception of self as self-contained and of other as alien which denies relationship and continuity" (Plumwood, *Feminism* 155). Put it another way, this feature separates human race away from nature on the ground that it is assumed that humanity is self-contained and nature is alien. There is a chasm between them so man and nature are not only separated but hyperseparated.

Incorporation is "that the underside of a dualistically conceived pair is defined in relation to the upperside as a lack, a negativity", "defining the other only in relation to the self, or the self's needs" (Plumwood, *Feminism* 52). That is to say, nature is recognized only to the extent that it is incorporated into human and his systems of desires, namely, only as the object to be exploited and colonized by the human race. Nature is reduced to "a mere servant of human purpose" (Oelschlaeger 182 ~ 183).

The feature of instrumentalism (objectification) is most conspicuous to human/nature dichotomy. Nature is "objectified, without ends of its own which demand consideration on their own account". And nature is also constructed instrumentally as resources. Human, as the dualizing master self, "does not empathically recognize others as moral kin, and does not recognise them as a centre of desires or needs on their own account. Hence on both accounts, he is free to impose his own ends" (Plumwood, *Feminism* 53).

Homogenisation or stereotyping means differences among the inferiorized group are disregarded (Hartsock 160 ~ 161). A typical example of this feature is the word by Ronald Reagan, the then governor of California, "If you've seen one redwood you've seen them all", a catchword cited by many an ecocritic to indicate people's general "insensitivity to the incredible diversity and richness of nature". The word "nature" itself is also quite representative because it sweeps entities as diverse as plants, animals, microorganism and so on under the general term, "treating beings in nature as all alike in their defectiveness, their lack of human qualities" (Plumwood, *Feminism* 70).

The features discussed above are the major clues to understanding the split of the relationship between the human race and the earth and they will greatly facilitate the interpretation and exploration of the anti-ecological behaviors of the white settlers and their descendents in the past two centuries in Australia as depicted in Tim Winton's fiction. In the discussion of man's conquest of land and sea, I will frequently refer to them to argue that the estranged relationship between man and nature developed over long history in the west is the genuine root of the environmental and ecological crisis in contemporary Australia. Moreover, the mentality of nature colonization, one of the numerous varieties of binary oppositions, further exacerbates the discordant relationship.

1.2 Land Degradation due to Over-exploitation

In Tim Winton's fiction, the farmland or the wheatbelt is an important scene for exploring the split of the relation between white settlers and nature. Firstly, the wheatbelt satisfies the settlers' desire of land conquest and is the most outspoken achievement of colonizing nature. Secondly, it is the most common artificial landscape until now in Western Australia, the author's homeland. Thirdly, the wheatbelt is now experiencing the most obvious crisis of degeneration. Fourthly, the wheatbelt is widely blamed for a broad spectrum of environmental problems, such as the salinization of the farming soils, the decline of biodiversity, even the general trend of ecological disequilibrium caused by long-term clearing the land of its native flora and fauna practiced by farmers for agricultural cultivation. Therefore, I choose to begin the discussion with the scene of wheatbelt in Winton's two novels — *Cloudstreet* (1991) and *Dirt Music* (2001) to analyze Winton's ecological concern about the over-exploitation of land and the concomitant environmental problems.

A glimpse at the history of wheat planting in Western Australia seems to be necessary and beneficial for the interpretation of the stories and the exploration of its ecological significance. Although Australia Aborigines① have been living on this isolated continent for at least 50,000 and possibly 60,000 or more years, most of them were hunter-gatherers. "Only in the most fertile and populous areas have they lived in semi-permanent settlement".② After conducting in-depth research into the culture and history of the Aboriginals, Deborah Bird Rose concludes:

> Aboriginal people's land management practices, especially their skilled use of fire, were responsible for the long-term productivity and biodiversity of its continent. In addition to fire, other practices include selective harvesting, extensive organization of sanctuaries, and the promotion of regeneration of plants and animals. (*Nourishing Terrains* 10)

That is to say, advanced methods of land management had been developed and practiced by them over tens of millennia before European settlement, though farming has never been confirmed to be the common means of production among the Aborigines③. However, this remains largely unrecognized by settler ideology and the landscapes are likewise

① The Latin term *Ab Origins* means those who were here from the beginning (Macintyre 5).

②③ https://en.wikipedia.org/wiki/Prehistory_of_Australia? oldid=46569316.

not taken as "the product of Aboriginal knowledge and labour" (Rose, *Nourishing Terrains* 75). The history of Australia since 1788 when the colony was officially established can be summarized by Julius Caesar's famous slogan *Veni*, *Vedi*, *Vici*, namely, I came, I saw, I conquered.

During the early period of colony, there was little to encourage anyone to believe that the foundations of a great nation could be laid, for the land gave no welcome to the newcomers. Some even believed that this country must be the "outcast of God's works" (Palmer and MacLeod 25). Tim Flannery, an Australian environmentalist and global warming activist, makes it clear that the soils in Australia are "by far the poorest and most fragile of any continent, its rainfall the most variable, and its rivers the most ephemeral" (37).

Despite the bareness of the soils, the tenacious early settlers had never let go of their dream of building a pastoral Arcadia. In Western culture, the pastoral landscape was celebrated at least as early as in Roman literature, and has been working itself out over millennia, further strengthened by the biblical tradition of pastoralism (Spirn 57). Understandably, wherever the westerners go and despite the great variety of climates and terrains, their dream of constructing idyllic home never wavers because it becomes deep-enduring and persistent over time and place (ibid.). Therefore, during the pioneering time the settlers broke their back trying to transform an inhospitable land to a productive one. "The pressures to clear land, both for food and for timber, were enormous and it's clear that the native vegetation was seen to have little intrinsic value other than that for sustaining the colony" (Bradshaw 14). So they cleared the bush, which in Australian mythologies masks an immense diversity of landscapes, and cut down gum trees that had been guarding the land for thousands of years, to grow crops and graze cattle. Winton puts it in an interview, "We tore down a whole incredibly diverse woodland, to make our wheat belt, which feeds everybody" (Brown and Bisley). Agriculture soon spreads to the most favorable locations in the region (qtd. in Bell 180). Western Australia's wheat country, the last of the wheatbelts in Australia, didn't take shape until the 1890s in response to the gold rush.

"Emboldened by good seasons and high prices, grain farmers pushed right out into the drylands". By the end of World War Two Australia could produce enough food not only for the domestic need but for exports. "At the time it must have seemed that nature itself was surrendering to human ingenuity and the vigour of a new settler culture" (Winton, "Silent Country" 30). Optimism was the prevailing mood in the mid-20th century although some people began to adopt cautious attitude to the land. For example, Sir David Rivett, a distinguished scientist, warned in a memorial lecture in 1944:

> The tragedies of over-exploitation in the past must cease. The sins of cattle-men who devoured the vegetation capital of the back country instead of being content to live on its income must not be repeated. We must take a firm grip of those two-thirds of Australia which we and the rabbits are murdering by various methods, not the least being surface erosion. (qtd. in Palmer and MacLeod, *After the First* 176~177)

However, most people were overwhelmed by the rapid progress in agriculture and so his warning was disregarded.

Notwithstanding the temporary success on the farm in early settlement, there has been always a lack of love and care for the alien land felt by the toilers who were mostly transplanted involuntarily from other continents. The estrangement felt by the settlers is succinctly expounded by Tim Flannery:

> For a start it left many colonial Australians unable to see the subtle beauty and biological richness of the land, and what they could not understand they strove to destroy as alien and useless. For most of the last two centuries we have believed that we could remake the continent in the

> image of Europe-turn the rivers inland and force the truculent soils to yield. (37)

This description partly explains why the natural environment deteriorated rapidly within the past two centuries on the land with the arrival of the Europeans, though it is undeniable that the "development of agriculture, particularly wheat production, in this region was vital to the stability and growth of European settlement in Western Australia" (qtd. in Bell 179). Today, the wheatbelt area still covers the entire south-west agricultural region, including the coastal zone.

The wheat land is where Quick hunts the kangaroos to earn a living in Winton's *Cloudstreet* (1991). Quick somehow feels that he should be partially responsible for the accident that has almost drowned his younger brother Fish who was once a smart and cheerful boy but becomes retarded hereafter. Unable to come to terms with himself, Quick runs away from his home at the Cloud Street one night. After experiencing some difficulties, he wins the reputation as an excellent hunter of kangaroos and begins to earn a handsome pay on the farm.

Western culture has one of the most common dichotomies between the cultivated and the uncultivated land:

> Primal nature (chaos) is conceived as initially fallen and disordered; *logos* undertakes to do for this disorderly other that he finds in nature the same task that he undertakes for slaves, free-living animals, female forces and other 'disorderly' elements; *logos* orders and rules the world of nature, conceived as chaotic and disorderly, in a relation of domination conceived as the imposition of a rational order. (Plumwood, *Feminism* 84)

In the matrix of western culture, transforming primal landscape to cultivated landscape, which was similar to the order in Eden created by God who has assigned man the dominion over other species on the earth

(Callicott 14), is taken as "an effort to return everything to the divinely sanctioned order" (Hornborg 207). Hence, the uncultivated land is wild, chaotic and dangerous whereas the cultivated land is tamed, controlled and desirable. Winton depicts the landscape of the wheat land on the eve of the harvest thus: "the wheat is its own map, neat and dogmatic in its boundaries" (*Cloudstreet* 195).

In Western Australia every inch of arable land has been developed so that "from the ground level, the wheat belt is the whole world" (ibid.). The white settlers have decisively changed the original landscape. Unfortunately, the wheat land soon becomes "anthropogenic 'wild'" in that the fields turn out to be "deadly places for insects, birds, animals and anything beyond the desired monoculture" (Harvey 284). Turning the land into crop field serves the sole interest of human beings but removes the natural habitat for a great variety of endemic inhabitants in the bio-community and thus reduces the diversity of species in the region. Rachel Carson insightfully points out the poignant fact that "nature has introduced great variety into the landscape, but man has displayed a passion for simplifying it". "Single-crop farming" should take responsibility for it (*Silent Spring* 9). It's reported that "seventy-one percent of the original vegetation was cleared to establish agriculture and settlements" (qtd. in Bell 179). As a result, "beneath the clouds of crows it's hard to find a feature" and the scene of wheatbelt looks forlorn. Here the landscape of the wheatbelt turns out to be "a strap of land surrounded by the rest of the world", the way an isolated island surrounded by the immense sea (*Cloudstreet* 195). Man's toiling seems trivial and funny in the context of the whole natural world. However, the whole world is now endangered by human activity, which seems to be an oxymoron. The irony is that if the ecosystem breaks down its disastrous consequences will be universal.

Given the poor natural conditions in Australia, human beings resort to agricultural technology for help, which disturbs Winton. His sarcasm is found in the description that you can "see the sun in it (the wheat), the prodigal rain, the magic tons of superphosphate" (ibid.). It is self-evident that sunshine and water are necessary for growing wheat. But the third element deserves special attention. As has been mentioned above, the surface soil in large area of Australia is far from fertile. So, "the development of agriculture on low fertility soils was largely dependent on innovations in agricultural science and technology, including superphosphate and trace element fertilizers, and nitrogen fixing crops and pastures" (qtd. in Bell 179). But the tragedy is, as Winton writes in a later essay "Silent Country", that the "fragile soil exposed by all this tree grubbing was quickly depleted; then it was laced with billions of tonnes of the miracle additive superphosphate, which lured two generations of farmers into the delusion that their operations were sustainable" (30). The adjective "magic" appears both in this essay and the description in *Cloudstreet*. Here we would like to ask whether technology is really "magic" as proclaimed. I am afraid the result will surely be most undesirable in the ecological sense, especially when "tons" of those things are widely used in the wheat field. Rachel Carson wrote *Silent Spring* (1962) to denounce the crime of excessive use of pesticides and herbicides in American agriculture. Agricultural technology, like technology in other fields, can never be expected to solve all the problems and conversely it may be the cause of the problems.

If superphosphate is not desirable, why not use phosphate, the ideal natural fertilizer? This question leads to another interesting plot in *Cloudstreet*. Sam, who is to become Quick's father-in-law later, works on an island "fifty miles out to the sea" (9) to "mine guano for phosphate" (12). In this episode, the author implies that Australia is lucky to have rich storage of accessible natural sources of phosphate on the nearby islands. But the commercial development of such resources may pose hidden danger to the micro-ecology, since these islands are the habitats to numerous birds. Dr. Glen Phillips, the emeritus professor of literature and wheatbelt poet in Western Australia confirms this speculation. He explains the history of mining guano thus:

> Many islands in the Indian and Pacific Oceans had been nesting sites for thousands of years for sea-birds so their accumulated excrement (manure) built up hugely and turned into a kind of soft rock. When it was realised this could be mined for use as an effective fertiliser for growing wheat and other grains, many companies were set up to transport and process it to use to grow crops. This was the 19th Century. Most of it is now used up and chemical fertilisers (artificially made) can be substituted. However, once upon a time the guano industry in Western Australia was very large. But without the superphosphate to put on the wheat fields each year, WA could never have succeeded to grow wheat on a large scale.①

The booming "shit" mining industry depicted in *Cloudstreet* impresses upon readers the massive scale of its exploitation: "Dozers scooped it, trucked it and dumped it on barges" (12). Undeniably, with the commercial development comes another ecological disaster — the disruption of the fragile island ecosystems, for "the ships destroyed the pristine coastal regions at the port areas, birds trying to nest were disturbed and killed and much of the jungle etc. would have been destroyed."② Modern grains only survive their unnatural environments by continuous injection of manufactured nutrients and human efforts to eradicate competition (Harvey 269). Hence, this mode of production can hardly sustain.

Guide our attention to the farmland itself once more. Generations of farmers in Australia work hard to eliminate any flora or fauna that stands in the way of a good harvest, as indicated in an Australian motto: if it moves, shoot it; if it doesn't, chop it. They treat all plants other than

①② From Glen Philipps' Email to me on Jan. 3, 2014.

the crops as weeds. Therefore, "what had provided a home for myriad creatures was reduced to smoke and ash, a diverse biotic community transformed into a biological monoculture that soon depleted the soil" (Oelschlaeger 183). The process of clearing the land was in essence the history of "ecological annihilation" (Hughes-d'Aeth 56). "Wild Radishes", a popular poem by a famous contemporary Western Australian ecological poet John Kinsella, depicts the scene of a farmer's family "scouring the crop" for wild radishes. To the farmers, "wild radishes missed will destroy the yield". The poet depicts "the absence of crow and parrot talk" on the farm, which sounds quite odd as they are the most common endemic birds in the region (63). By unfolding the fact that in the wheatbelt wild radishes and birds are all to be removed by farmers, the poem attests to Rachel Carson's alarming prediction of a silent world. As a Western Australian author, Winton demonstrates similar care and concern about the wild local species. In Winton's depiction of the farmland, the readers feel the deep sympathy and a sort of agricultural environmental ethic held by the author towards the kangaroos that are killed in the wheat land.

In *Cloudstreet*, the kangaroos become "poachers", the way the Aborigines become displaced others on their own land, because they try to seek food on the farmland. So the kangaroos have to be eliminated, especially on the eve of the harvest season. According to the widely accepted values in western culture, "property is formed from the rational labours of white European Heroes upon a passive, captive virgin earth called 'nature'" (Plumwood, *Environmental Culture* 21). Since the settlers have tilled the wheat field, they have the right to reap the harvest and to protect their property. "Poacher" is an ironic title here used to address such wild animals as kangaroos. What they want is satisfying the basic need for food and water to survive. Yet when this need is in conflict with man's benefits, they have to be eliminated. This is the anthropocentric logic that has always been taken for granted but now begins to be questioned by philosophers, ecologists, authors as well as anyone who cares about the destiny of mankind or the future of the planet.

As the native herbivores, kangaroos are now living in an ever shrinking area of habitat and their natural food sources are becoming increasingly inadequate on account of man's expanding agricultural territory and the general deterioration of the environment. So sometimes they have to turn to wheat for food. However, the destiny awaiting them is clear enough. Winton exposes man's callousness in the killing and protests against his hegemony endowed by modern weapon in the relationship between man and wildlife. In his depiction of Quick's kangaroo hunting, a series of single syllable verbs such as "shoot, load, aim, shoot", remindful of Hemingway's style, are used to demonstrate the hunter's swiftness and ingenuity in the job. But in fact, what the author intends to unfold is the animals' miserable destiny under man's guns. Seen through the lens of the hunter, these kangaroos are dumb and slow in reaction so that Quick is able to shoot them "from left to right without haste". The kangaroos' dumbness and the hunter's adeptness constitute a sharp contrast. Winton also draws the readers' attention to the comparison of the sizes of the two sides: the hunter is then only a teenager but what he kills is a group of kangaroos, including "a couple of big bucks among them" (197). The power comparison indicates a margin in the kangaroos' favor, which makes the outcome more melodramatic and tragic. With the aid of the gun, the product of modern technology, even a teenager can be immediately turned to a callous killer and accomplish the job of killing a group of strong adult kangaroos. The censure against weapons can hardly be ignored.

Winton admits being influenced by the American writer Ernest Hemingway, who is known to be good at telling stories of hunting. Hemingway's attitudes toward preys are ambiguous in that he believes they must be conquered but in the meantime they are to be respected. In contrast, Winton holds the firm belief that the wildlife is entitled to live and to be revered. This view reminds of Aboriginal philosophy that "life requires no justification". Put it another way, "there is no justification required in asserting that other ... things also want to live, and have the right to live their own lives" (Rose, *Nourishing Terrains* 10).

Let's return to the hunting scene to see the reactions of the kangaroos that are to be killed. The kangaroos "went rigid and opened their eyes to him". They may have felt the approaching danger, but they are "unable to tear themselves away" (197). Winton narrates what happens to them later in a reserved coolness, again in Hemingwayesque style: Some get killed while others escape to be hunted another day. Since "the central goal of agriculture is understood in terms of production", the kangaroos have to be killed (Thomson 45). In other words, anthropocentrism sometimes does not allow the space for other species' survival. In contrast, the Aboriginal culture holds the holistic concept that "other species, as well as humans, have the right to the conditions which enable their lives to continue through time: minimally to the waters and foods on which they depend, and to the sanctuaries in which they cannot be hunted or gathered or mutilated in any way" (Rose, *Nourishing Terrains* 10). In Australia, the most arid inhabited continent on earth, water has always been the most precious resource that makes the difference between life and death. Therefore, this depiction is a censure on the immorality of mankind's depriving the kangaroos of their rightful access to water.

Careful readers find that bad luck often visits those characters that are not on good terms with nature in Winton's fictional world. In *Cloudstreet*, men who do the job of guano mining are obviously not blessed. Sam lost his four fingers of "the working hand" (15) when "the cable caught his glove" (13). Similar accident also happens to Nowles, a pioneer whaler in *Shallows* (1984). Likewise, Quick is doomed to be seriously injured by the kangaroo that dies soon after counterattacking him. Killing soon incurs revenge. To the individual, it is a lesson but to the human race it is a warning that nature will fight back and punish those who have gone too far breaking the balance of nature. Interpreting Tim Winton's writings through the lens of Christianity, Chris Beal, an Anglican priest, claims that "Tim's writing is both prophetic and mystical in the classic Christian sense" (48). In my eyes, Christian concepts like sin and salvation can be handily employed not only for evangelizing, but for transmitting a warning against human's anti-ecological behaviors. That is to say, as to Winton, over-exploitation or abuse of nature is sinful and will incur revenge and punishment in one way or another and salvation derives from being friendly with nature and being respectful to nature.

In addition to hiring cullers, the farmers themselves take actions to keep the kangaroos away because as the harvest time is drawing near, herds of them are pouring into the farming area and "eating their way overland". Tim Winton caricatures the scene of expelling kangaroos by farmers: "mobs of blokes hurtle around the paddocks at night with shotguns and crates of Swan Lager". He ironically points out that they virtually do "more damage to the crop than the plague itself". Sarcastically, the guns blow "each other's ears off in a regular fashion" rather than killing the kangaroos as intended (204). Isn't it a story of black humor employed by Winton to revenge on anthropocentric farmers? The whole matter sounds more like a farce, which is a mockery of man's intention to monopolize all the resources bequeathed by nature. The teasing tone in the text implies the author's resentment towards man's selfishness and foolishness in their attempts to eliminate kangaroos which enjoy the same entitlement as other common and ancient indigenous feral fauna in Australia to continue to be there and thus coexist with human race.

After recovery from the injury, Quick resumes his job as a shooter. But on a subsequent culling expedition, Quick begins to be pestered by a vision under which he sees himself "right in the sights, right under the first pressure of trigger" (205). As a matter of fact, Quick has experienced similar hallucination before the injury. In that case, he sees his brother Fish, who is "rowing a (fruit) box across the top of the wheat" (200). All these make Quick even suspect whether he is insane. As a result, the hunting business has to be called a halt.

There is much discussion concerning this plot among critics. Beth Watzke takes it as surrealism. Tim Winton expresses his dislike of traditional realism due to its exclusion of anything numinous, which denies the author "a wedge of material" in composition. In addition, he shows his disapproval of surrealism in that it fakes in order to "escape restraint". Thus, neither realism nor surrealism meets the demand of the author who wants to include both realms, for in his eyes the supernatural and the natural can be accepted as one thing, as inclusive, which is Winton's special version of "true realism" (Watzke, "Where Pigs Speak" 97). Interestingly, Winton's version of realism coincides with the alchemical and situated realism put forward by Patrick D. Murphy in his monograph *Farther Afield* (2000). According to *The American Heritage College Dictionary* (3rd Edition), the second definition of "alchemy" goes "a seemingly magical power or process of transmuting" (qtd. in P. D. Murphy, *Farther Afield* 31). "A situated realism is one that relies on the consensual reality of a given people in a given locale, but that is not represented as a universal truth" (Murphy, *Farther Afield* 30 ~ 31). Murphy further expounds that this type of realism is quite common in many indigenous cultures. "Alchemical realist novels do not treat their supernatural depictions as fabulous contrarealistic devices but as part of a referential orientation toward a different conception of reality than the culturally dominant one". Besides, it's different from magic realism in that "as part of the postmodernist literary movement, magic realism foregrounds the unreality, the absurdity of their magical devices in order to emphasize their figurative and allusive signification" (P.D.

Murphy, *Farther Afield* 35). In the same interview conducted by Beth Watzke, Winton frankly admits "the term magical realism really upsets me. It assumes trickery. The weird things that happen in my books aren't devices. [...] this is the kind of world where pigs speak in tongues and angels come and go. And I'm not speaking metaphor here. The world is a weird place" (Watzke, "Where Pigs Speak" 97). So Winton's realism sounds akin to alchemical and situated realism rather than magic realism. Like religion factor discussed above, this "true realism" of Winton, as I see it, is also sometimes employed to transmit ecological information. Here, Quick is forced out of the business of killing kangaroos by the messages sent in a special way. Although the status quo does not change much with one culler's quitting, yet it at least partially embodies the author's romantic inclination to dismantle the westerners' stereotyped anthropocentric mode of thinking and acting.

Ecological care and worries about the endemic plants, animals and the land itself are prevalent in the depiction of the wheat land in *Cloudstreet* and warnings are issued through various means such as religious and mysterious devices to make people aware of the impending ecological dangers. However, the warnings are not heeded. After an interval of ten years, when *Dirt Music* was published in 2001, some nightmares came true. As a scrupulous observer and loyal guardian of his homeland, Winton describes in *Dirt Music* the changes of landscapes due to the settlers' long-term cultivation in spite of the "wrong" soils and climates.

Along with the male protagonist's trip north through Western Australia, every trivial change in colors and forms in the land is perceived in the vision and relayed honestly through his lens. The descriptions show the author's sensitivity to the shifts of the landscapes in physical surroundings on the route. Tim Winton stresses that the most obvious changes in the landscapes are that only "remnant stand of gums, cockatoos" are seen on the paddock (218). The adjective "remnant" hints at a history of clearing the land of its native vegetation for cultivation. Gum trees and mangroves are cut down. Consequently, the cockatoos lose their natural habitat. Some cockatoos move to the farming areas to seek wheat as food, and thus become pests to the local farmers and are killed. So in the local farmers' eyes, the endemic plants are "weeds" whereas the birds are vermin and thus both have to be eliminated. The word "remnant" unfolds the author's increasing anxiety about the status quo in Western Australia. And it's not hard to imagine how he desires to awaken the local farmers of their eco-consciousness, which is the first thing to do to protect the environment.

Winton portrays the decline of farm along the route. At the beginning of the trip, Luther Fox sees the harvesters working on the field, which "raise clouds of chaff and dust across the rolling hills" in the midlands wheatbelt (218). As the protagonist moves on, the country becomes drier and the soil grows thinner, and wheat farm is replaced first by "sheep paddocks" and then by "squat mulga scrub" and finally "just olive dabs of vegetation spread over stony yellow dirt" (219). A more severe attack on the ecosystem is the quick development of the seemingly lucrative husbandry. D. B. Rose comments that when the land is used for grazing, the destruction of the vulnerable ecosystem is accelerated due to the fact that the introduced cattle and sheep not only eat up the vegetation but vastly change the soil (*Nourishing Terrains* 76). Thus, when he gets off at Mount Magnet, the gold mining town, Lu discovers that "farm fences are gone and soil has long been replaced by dust or grit" (221). It sounds to be the continuation of the plot in *Cloudstreet*. The reality is that the adopted land today becomes even more desolate after two centuries' over-cultivation by the white settlers. With the degradation of the natural environment, many farmers give up their struggle against the poor soil, leaving behind a bleak and miserable scene of eco-disequilibrium, as Winton describes in his article "Silent Country":

> In the great sickle-shaped hinterland of the Western Australian wheat belt, trees have been exterminated. Like embroidered motifs at the hem of a bleached and threadbare rug, a few lonely specimens mark the corners of paddocks. Now and then you'll encounter a remnant stand of wandoos spared because of hulking domes of granite underfoot, but most of what you see is a land scraped utterly naked. (30)

All the worst predictions have come true then. The original vegetation has almost completely gone with the lean topsoil. With the depletion of the indigenous wild plants comes the desertification and with agricultural irrigation comes salinization of the farm land. Tim Flannery frankly points out that "salination will destroy the majority of Western Australia's wheat belt in our lifetime if nothing is done" (37). It's worthwhile to point out that the collapse of wheat farming does not come singly, for it is accompanied by the deterioration of pasture and the destruction of the whole ecosystem as well. In the same essay, Winton points out that "less than a century ago this bit of country was a series of eucalypt woodlands of remarkable biodiversity, but it was bulldozed and burned at the urging of successive governments to make way for cultivation" ("Silent Country" 30). The depictions of the battered ecosystem in Western Australia imply the author's deep suspicion whether it can regain their first fertility since it has been so irrevocably damaged. In effect, homo sapiens is pushing himself to the edge of the abyss by destroying the physical environment. The failure of farming in Western Australia is just one of numerous such examples.

"Relations between landscape and text have been fundamental to understandings of the inscription of meaning on newly discovered lands during the course of European colonial expansion, [...] as work on Australia and South Africa has revealed" (qtd. in Cosgrove 33). Developing vast area of farm land was the usual way of engraving prints on the new territory as can be testified by such examples as the United

States and Australia. But it seems that the settlers in Australia are not as lucky as their counterparts in the US who grabbed vast fertile arable lands and pastures from the Indians. What the European Australians seized seems to be "the most nutrient-poor soils to be found on the face of this earth" (Bradshaw 14). Despite all these disadvantages, wheatbelt has left an indelible imprint on the land. Moreover, farmland degradation in forms of salinization and desertification from over-use turn up with the development of agriculture. "As Geoffrey Bolton makes so clear in his book, agriculture has always been a disaster in WA — despite many claims to the contrary" (Bradshaw 13). Therefore, "agrarian ideals of noble farmers or stoic outback battlers are coexistent in Australian mythologies with images of environmental destruction and exploitation, communities in crisis and global corporate domination" (Bell 177). Rereading Winton's depiction of the wheatbelt in *Cloudstreet* and *Dirt Music* from an ecocritical perspective, we get to understand the author's doubt and worry about the current state of agribusiness as "the wheatbelt is increasingly associated with discourses of crisis and is less associated with romantic myths of the rural battler" (qtd. in Bell 184). The farmers are more concerned about their crops than the wholesomeness of the ecosphere. Farming activities do not bring them spiritually closer to the soil and larger organic process but render nature of use value only, for their motivation is mercantile. They regard the soil as "property, or means of living", namely, nature is recognized only to the extent that it is incorporated into his system of desires as objects to be exploited, "thus the landscape is deformed, and the farmer leads the meanest of lives. He knows Nature but as a robber" (Thoreau, *Walden* qtd. in Oelschlaeger 160). Moreover, Winton's protest against man's killing aboriginal fauna is perceptible and his care and concern about animals will be further explored in other chapters of the book, which proves that Winton is consciously aware of the ethics that should be observed when dealing with them.

1.3 Human Alienation due to Resources Abuse

If wheat farming is one of the major forms of land exploitation and appropriation on the surface, mining is definitely an important underground means of land exploration. Or in Rod Giblett's words, "where soil erosion 'rapes' the surface of the earth, mining 'rapes' its depths" (175). Having explored one of the major representative forms of land exploration in Western Australia — the wheatbelt, in this section, I will focus on the ecological significance of the depiction of the mines and mining towns in Winton's fiction.

It's widely agreed that Australia has the most infertile topsoil in the world. However, it's equally discernable that Australia has the most enviable deposits of a variety of mines. Marcia Langton claims that "Australia is a rich first-world nation, largely because of this mineral wealth" (49). The local Chamber of Mines described Western Australia as having been "endowed with rich mineral resources (Griffiths 109)." In his latest novel *Eyrie* (2013), Winton defines his home state as the "booming state" that is "thin-skinned" but "rich beyond dreaming". Western Australia is also "the nation's quarry" and "China's staggering enabler" with its "greatest ore deposit in the world" (5).

"Western Australia's dependence on mining incomes is a particular feature of the national economy" (Langton 54). Gold mines were discovered in Western Australia in the 1890s and the first decade of the twentieth century, which caused an influx of migrants from the eastern states as well as new immigrants from Europe. Other mines, such as iron, asbestos, lead, bauxite, nickel, oil and gas are successively discovered and explored. Mining brings huge amount of fortune but in the meantime it also causes environmental destruction. It's reasonable to attribute this mode of mine exploration to the settlers' attitude to the land. In recent western culture the earth is constructed as a passive and compliant object to be exploited and the emphasis has always been on "resource-exploitation, or greed and gluttony" (Giblett 168). Namely, nature is objectified and constructed instrumentally as resources that have no intrinsic value but gain meaning via meeting certain needs of humanity. What's worse, the greed of the settlers leads them to exhaust any resource that they can lay their hands on at whatever expense. In the history of Western Australia, the development of mine resources is usually accompanied by the rising of mining towns. Some of them develop into permanent settlements especially when the infrastructure is established well enough for long-term inhabitance while others decline with the exhaustion of the resources and the worsening of the environment.

Dirt Music, the Miles Franklin winner in 2002, was acclaimed as "the poetry of the landscape" by *HQ* and "a drama that needs to be played out against and over terrain as rigorous and baleful as Winton's West" by *Australian Book Review. Sunday Telegraph* commented that "Winton evokes the Australian landscape superbly"①. The above discussion has focused on the ecological significance implied in the text's depiction of the changes of land forms and vegetation along the character's journey. In *Dirt Music*, Winton not only depicts the prosperous appearance of the mining industry, but concerns himself with the influence of mining industry on people's physical and mental health and on the land's health. This critic wants to stress that Winton is an ecological writer who is good at revealing the scar and trauma left by the environmental-unfriendly activities of mining. Thus, rereading scenes of mining and deserted mining towns in *Dirt Music* contributes to awakening people's consciousness of environmental protection.

Britta Kuhlenbeck discovers that "although Tim Winton's novel evidently is a work of fiction, the itinerary of Luther Fox's journey to the

---

① From "Praise for Dirt Music" listed before the title page of the novel.

northern coast of Western Australia is nevertheless related to representations of real places on the Australian map" (63). I would add that not only names of real places are adopted, but histories of mining at those spots are honestly borrowed, which make the story somewhat facts-filled. That is to say, the landscapes represented in the novel correspond with the peculiar local geographical and historical features in reality. *Dirt Music* offers a perfect opportunity for the author to lay bare the ecological catastrophes caused by mining on these spots and in the meantime it's a window through which readers can observe the landscape which "absorbs the events played out on its surface" and "inters the marks of past practices as much as it also bears its traces" (DeLue and Elkins 100).

Three mining towns are mentioned, among which the first one is "the old minetown of Cue". Cue is a small town in the Mid West region of Western Australia, located 620 km north-east of Perth. In fact, not much is said about this iron town in the novel. We are only told that it seems that the whole town is dusty and rusty, which is one of the reasons for the failure of the nearby farms that Lu has passed by. Funny enough, Winton gives the name Rusty to the driver who offers Lu a lift to echo the scene before the eyes. Winton tersely presents Cue as a place "where diggings and slagheaps become landscape" (225). This is the most common scene in the mine areas. "Diggings and slagheaps" are ugly scars left on the land, which is vividly reminiscent of the argument made by Rod Giblett in his book *Living with the Earth* (2004): "they construct the earth as a passive and compliant object to be exploited, and then expect the earth to absorb or hide their wastes in return" (168). The sad fact is that the miners together with the company behind them have been playing the role of plunders for several decades.

Mining almost always pollutes the physical environment, as depicted in *Dirt Music*: "long-term mining at Cue stains the tar streets and the vehicles and buildings along them" (226). What's more, it alienates man from nature so that after more than two centuries' settlement, white Australians are still stricken by a sense of rootlessness and struggling for a sense of belonging. The state of rupture endures really too long so the gap cannot be filled overnight. In addition, "the earth is red", which indicates the rich iron deposits in the region (225). Then how to strike the balance between resource exploitation and environment protection? It's a tough issue posed at the whole world and it's more complicated in Australia because the nation is born out of a former settler colony, which means there is a congenital lack of natural link between the people and the land. So Australians, especially the European post-settlers have to learn to love and take care of the land. Maybe they should slow down to listen to the voice of the original owner of the land. The local Aborigines hold disparate ideas about mining, as an Aboriginal poet Errol West writes in his poem: "you rip out her heart, her spleen and liver — mining, digging, drilling, a cancer attacking the essence of my life" (qtd. in Giblett 173). So mining is cancer to the Aborigines because they feel deep sympathy with the mother land. If the settlers can develop similar attachment to the land, if they try acting as the caretakers rather than the plunders, they may figure out appropriate means in handling the tough issue.

Newman is the second iron mining town that Lu passes by. It locates within the "stupendous iron ranges" in Pilbara, a thinly populated region in the north of Western Australia (227). Unlike Cue, Newman looks complacent with "lush lawns", flowers, "neat bungalows and company shops". Winton points out succinctly that three things matter here: water, iron ore and money (228). Newman is a typical town booming with the rise of the iron mining. Since it's a dry area, "mists of pumped water" not only softens its profile but creates an appearance that looks dreamy, luxurious and unnatural. But the temporary, artificial beauty of the mining town serves only as a foil to the dazzlingly intoxicating natural beauty of the Opthalmia Ranges, approximately 20 km north of Newman, with all its pristine features of landscape. The natural scenery there is depicted in its splendor. More than ten colors create impressive visual impact on the viewer; the primal land forms, the aboriginal vegetation and endemic birds are all described in poetic language. Winton is never stingy at eulogizing and highlighting the beauty of its original landscape without the interference of the settlers' mining activities:

> ... the Opthalmia Ranges whose bluffs and peaks and mesas rise crimson, black, burgundy, terracotta, orange against the cloudless sky. Gully shadows are purple up there and the rugged layers of iron lie dotted with a greenish furze of spinifex. You sense hidden rivers. Your ears pop with altitude. Closer to the road, on scree slopes the colour of dry blood, the smooth white trunks of snappy gums suspend crowns of leaves so green it's shocking. Mobs of white cockatoos explode from their boughs. (228)

Ophthalmia Range is a range in the Pilbara region which not only has rich deposits of mines but is "one of the 34 most biodiverse regions in the world". "Hidden rivers" are precious sources of life and imply the abundance of life forms. According to Tim Nicol, a Liaison Officer with the Conservation Council of Western Australia, "the diverse ancient landscape has created a high level of endemism (native speciation), where individual hills or salt lakes may be host to species found nowhere else on earth" (12). Under the colorful appearance, biologists and ecologists may discover many endemic species unique only to the local ecosystem.

Newman and the Ophthalmia Range are both places with sources of fresh water. Since Australia is the most arid continent, water is naturally highly valued and cherished. Places with sources of fresh water are desirable nesting and breeding sites. The Aborigines hold these places as Dreaming sites or sanctuary where hunting is prohibited, which effectively creates a refuge for all the species free from human predation

(Rose 49). But when the miners come, they monopolize the dear water resource and use it in a wasteful way only for the sole welfare of human race. The act itself may pose enough threat to the ecosystem, let alone the mining activities.

Tim Winton depicts the beauty of the Ophthalmia Range to remind readers that this is the most valuable treasure, more valuable than iron ores. When one mine is depleted, man can always transfer to other spots. But if the primitive habitats of some species are destroyed, the unique species will disappear forever. Mining boom in most cases leads to environmental disasters. The soils may be poisoned and the sources of water polluted. Decades of mining practices in Western Australia have destroyed many beautiful landscapes like this and killed numerous species before we even have opportunity to know them. Besides, man can never estimate the significance those species held for the equilibrium of the local ecosystem. Therefore, the potential risks to biodiversity and landscapes presented by mining can never afford to be ignored. People need to pay due attention to the "profound impact of mining on the plants and animals that grow and live on these hills, with many providing homes to unique species before exploration". Since mining inevitably produces an impact on the environment, we can never be too cautious. In other words, "mining needs to be approved with consideration of long-term effects to the environment but not short-term passing benefits" (Nicol 13).

Then Lu reaches the third mining town called Wittenoom, a hellish place that has "orphaned him" (221). At Wittenoom, the tragic consequence of mining turns out to be the downfall of the asbestos mines going hand in hand with the collapse of the town itself and the miners' physical health.

The name Wittenoom, to many Western Australians, has become the synonym for asbestos because crocidolite (blue asbestos) was mined at Wittenoom by the Australian Blue Asbestos Company from 1943 to

1966 (qtd. in Musk 312). When Lu's father was "a sandy-haired young fella", he worked here, leaving his family behind because if he earned adequate money he could achieve the ambition of owning a pasture down south. Lu recalls that his father used to speak of the north with pride and fear in his voice (221). Abundant natural resources ensure steady and handsome pay, which is the most irresistible temptation to young fellows like Lu's father. The tragedy is that the miners are not aware of the danger of the blue asbestos "billowing in drifts all around them" (235). To make matters worse, the mining proprietors just keep it a secret. Ben Hills, the Walkley Award① winning Australian freelance journalist and author, published a book entitled the *Blue Murder* in 1989, narrating the Wittenoom asbestos mine disaster and the victims' battle for compensation. Through Ben Hill's stubborn efforts, many facts are exposed. In 2001 he wrote an essay "Every Breath You Take; INSIGHT" published on *Sydney Morning Herald*, in which the history of asbestos mining in Australia was combed. According to this essay, James Hardie Asbestos pioneered asbestos manufacturing in Australia in 1916 and ran the business until 1979, during which deposits were mined in Tasmania, in Western Australia's Pilbara, and at Baryulgil in northern NSW (Hill 11). It was not until 1966 that James Hardie partner CSR Ltd closed its asbestos mine at Wittenoom after more than 100 cases of lung disease among workers and their families were confirmed. It's reported that during 1973—1974 Wittenoom toll reaches 175, with 27 known dead (ibid.). Worse still, right up until 1986, long after the dangers of asbestos were well documented, and multimillion-dollar compensation awards had been made to victims in United States courts, the company continued to manufacture asbestos, and to deny its products could kill (ibid.). The historical fact is that the operation of mining blue asbestos

① More information about the prize is found at the webpage: http://www.walkleys.com/walkley-awards.

at Wittenoom created "the most lethal industrial disaster in Australian history" (Knox 69).

The dark history causes the family tragedy of Luther Fox, who summarizes the whole story about Lu's father and the asbestos mine thus: "the mesothelioma and the monumental bastardry of the cover-up". Nonetheless, the agony of the occupational disease is given a detailed description in the text. "The yellow slaughteryard eyes, the horrible swelling trunk. The falling down and liquid shitting and desperate respiration". The horrible scene in hospital when his father was in the final stage of the disease deeply engraves on his soul: "Lying there like a man being held down in a tub of water. Neck straining at the end of him as though he might get his head out and take a clean breath if only he pushed hard enough" (229). This episode is a silent accusation of the inhuman crime of covering the truth committed by the mining company. Moreover, it is by means of presenting the extreme agony Fox's father experienced that Winton reveals man's alienation in the process of grabbing resources in the land. In this alien form of labor, man is not only estranged from nature but from himself, which echoes Karl Marx's concept of estranged labor that concerns "the relation of labour to the *act of production* within the *labour* process" (Marx 73, emphases original). Marx further illustrates that in that case "labour is external to the worker, [...] in his work, therefore, he does not affirm himself but denies himself, does not feel content but unhappy, does not develop freely his physical and mental energy but mortifies his body and ruins his mind" (Marx 72). The work of mining brings Lu's father and his fellow miners the plague of mesothelioma and inflicts upon them a painful death.

The hellish scenes at the deserted mining town of Wittenoom are presented through Lu's lens: Every step puffs up asbestos, which is an insult to your health (237). "Remnant gardens", "low neighbourly fence, exotic trees, trellises with bougainvillea and jasmine wound through" betray yesterday's glory. Only "house stumps" and "a forlorn school sign" indicate that it was once a town with miners and their families as the residents and that it was once a place for the young Aussie battlers to fight for their dreams. But today "almost everything has been pulled down and carted off to stop people living here" (234). Still, a few people persist despite the health warnings here and there. They are here witnessing the downfall of the mining town and the agonizing death of their mates and themselves, as predicted by Lu's father — "Let the dead bury their dead" (237). The town is not only inhospitable but unapproachable. It is a living warning for the mining industry and human race as a whole. If we continue this mode of production and resource exploitation, we shall virtually ruin ourselves. If the land itself has been poisoned to death, then humanity is on the brink of apocalypse.

Is the land really dead as it appears? The answer is both Yes and No depending on whose perspective one adopts. In a westerner's eyes, it is yes on account of the poisoning of the land. It's necessary to take the Indigenous viewpoint into account. Winton gives enough cues in the fiction hinting at the other system of world view. When sleeping in the open on the ground, Lu feels stored in the earth the energy and power that is linked to its former caretaker: "The earth thrums beneath him, stirs with a thousand grinding clanks and groans like the deck of a ship in heavy weather. He feels it twist and flex and murmur and, deep down, between rivety stones, there's an endlessly repetitive vibration like a priston-chant foghorn drone. Whorrr, whorrrr, whorrrrr" (232). Verbs like thrumming, stirring, twisting, flexing and murmuring animate the earth and conjure up a corroboree[①], an event or ceremony which usually involves dancing and singing, through which Australian Aborigines interact

① In the Pilbara, corroborees are called *yanda or jalarra*.

with the Dreamtime[①]. In Australian Aboriginal culture, corroborees are held on different occasions and for diverse purposes. When a corroboree is led by the tribal elders, it can be very solemn and formal. Through corroborees the elders are able to communicate with the tribe ancestors, who are "variously known as spirits, dead bodies, the old people, or the ancestors". On these occasions, special costumes are worn, songs sung and dances performed. In Aboriginal culture, "the people who belonged to country in life continue to belong to it in death" and "people say that when they sing the dead listen" and songs, "especially the sacred songs constitute a language which the dead can hear". Old people or rather the spirits of their ancestors are "part of the life of the country; their involvement keeps the country productive, and also assists living people (their descendents) in their own use of the country" (Rose 71). Here, Winton fancies that the Aborigines are having a corroboree to recover the land's vitality and fertility.

In history, many Aborigines died of either fights or diseases like typhoid in the course of being colonized. The remnants either became fringe dwellers around white settlement or were displaced from their own country to the Reserves disregarding their connection with particular land that they call their country. As to Aboriginals, "identity is based on the links between the community, the land and ancestral beings" (qtd. in Plumwood, *Feminism* 102). The foundation of this unity is the particularity of tribal land, which contains both the remains of past generations of kin and the other living beings it fosters and will foster. The particularity of these ties to land yields a framework for human identity which underlies responsibility for and connection to both the land and the generations of the past and the future. Moreover, in Aboriginal culture, concepts such

---

① In the animist framework of Australian Aboriginal mythology, Dreamtime is a sacred era in which ancestral totemic spirit beings created the world. <http://en.wikipedia.org/wiki/Dreamtime>.

as death, extinction and so on have disparate implications from those held by the westerners. Aboriginal philosophy interprets death as a return to the land. For instance, "for the Gagadju people, death is treated as a means of realizing human continuity with the earth" (qtd. in Plumwood, *Feminism* 102). They believe their spirits do not disappear although their physical forms perish. Death, to them, means entering a new stage of life; or taking a different form of life. They may become a gum tree, a cockatoo, a stone, or a small stream. Therefore, everything in nature is interlinked through the kinship. What's more, the spirits of their ancestors are guarding their people and country all the time. That is to say, although the tribe may be removed, or the land may be destroyed, their ancient caretakers are still keeping an eye on everything on the land. And the country itself is not dead resources for exploitation. As Deborah Bird Rose describes in her book *Nourishing Terrain* (1996):

> People say that country is aware, it knows what's going on, it knows who is there, and it knows if they have a right to be there. Other animals also watch, laugh at our mistakes, and take notice of our better actions. So too do all the people who have passed away who are still there in their own country, taking care of it. (70)

When the Aborigines are in desperate situations, they may plea the spirits of their ancestors to rescue them and punish the intruders by manipulating four elemental forces from water, fire, wind and earth. This is what happens in the aboriginal author Alexis Wright's novel *Carpentaria* (2006), the 2007 Miles Franklin Award winner. The Gulf of Carpentaria was a place with rich resources in fishery and mining. The white men established Gurfurritt International there, claimed to be the biggest mining company of its type in the world. As can be expected, the country was soon contaminated by "mining, shipping, barges spilling ore and waste" (Wright 401). Birds "flocked to the chemical-ridden tailings dams", drank water that was "highly concentrated with lead" and were mutated (Wright 395). Eventually the great spiritual ancestors belonging to other worlds roared out of the dusty, polluted sea (Wright 401). Taking the forms of cyclone and fire, they helped their descendents burn down the mine and its entire buried pipeline leading all the way to the port. By using the forces from the cyclones and floods, they even tore down the mining town Desperance and created a small island in the sea out of the frames of houses and rubbish discarded by the white, which is a parody of the Ark of Noah.

Traces of Aboriginal culture's animism can be obviously felt in Winton's narration, which implies the possible existence of Aboriginal spirits on the land that the settlers fail to properly exploit and cannot really understand. Driving through an animistic world, Luther Fox feels "these ranges look to him like some dormant creature whose stillness is only momentary, as though the sunblasted, dusty hide of the place might shudder and shake itself off, rise to its bowed and saurian feet and stalk away at any moment" (236). Luther Fox feels the throbbing of the ancient imperishable spirits and shudders at the immense power stored in the land. "Whereas traditional societies, such as the aboriginal tribes in Australia, revere the earth as Great Mother and so as a living person, modern societies abuse the earth as dead matter" (Giblett 168). Winton is trying to highlight that the land is not dead matter as is assumed in western culture. The post-settlers should show due respect to the land and learn from the Aborigines about the ways to take care of it rather than deal with it by "ceaseless digging and blasting" (221).

Mining is the only significant industry in the remote region of the Pilbara which has made its name in iron ore (Langton 53). "Previously, few questions had been asked about the way the industry operated; governments had encouraged unfettered exploration and new operations because of their contribution to economic growth" (Langton 58). Gradually, people come to realize that "in the process of mining, the land, rivers, underground water and vegetation are irreparably and irreversibly altered" (Langton 61). Hence, like any other mineral resource pool, the area is also faced with issues of "resource curse" or "paradox of plenty", terms coined by Richard Auty, emeritus professor of geography at the University of Lancaster, denoting "the social and economic phenomenon in which many natural-resource-rich countries experience poor economic growth, conflict and declining standards of democracy" (Langton 52). Obviously, Auty uses these terms mainly for economic and political purposes. As to me, they are equally applicable to the ecological situations. That is to say, the natural-resource-rich regions can hardly escape the curse of environmental destruction and ecological disequilibrium though they benefit tremendously in economic way. The curses in the context of the mining towns are embodied in the poisoned streams, "ghost towns, dust diseases, the dispossession of indigenous owners" and so on (Knox 70). As can be seen from *Dirt Music*, the miners are highly alienated on account that they mutilate both the land and themselves in the course of working.

Then the situation has to be improved as it is not sustainable. And both the government and mining companies must take some measures to avoid the undesirable consequence. It's true that "the mining industry and the Environment Protection Authority (EPA) in Western Australia have worked on better practices and assessments". Yet Philip Jennings, President of the Conservation Council of Western Australia, "warned that significant impacts still happen" (Nicol 12). Tim Winton concerns himself persistently with the nation's mining industry. In his latest book *Eyrie* published in 2013, some conspiracy involving the government and the mining companies is implied:

> Because they'd always be a whisper, a Cabinet leak, a buried press release about another government cave-in, fresh permission to drill, strip, fill or blast. The industrial momentum was feverish. Oil, gas, iron, gold,

lead, bauxite and nickel — it was the boom of all booms, and in a decade it had taken hostage every institution from government to education. The media was bedazzled. There was pentecostal ecstasy in the air, and to resist it is heresy. (Winton 6)

Despite the deterioration of the environment, the protest of the Indigenous groups and NGO (Non-governmental Organizations), the government keeps conceding to the mining industry. Australians' traditional distrust of the government is also embodied in the issue of exploiting minerals because many cases confirm that sometimes the governmental institutions are accomplices in the crime of reaping lucrative economic interests at the expense of environment. Even the mass media and universities may be bought over. A plot in *Eyrie* conveys the author's serious concern with this corruption. One day Keely, the former leader and eloquent spokesperson for a green NGO, bumps into Damien, a young environmental science graduate who has participated in the wetland campaign led by him. In their brief encounter, Keely realizes that:

> If the iron giants hadn't bought him (Damien) it could only be oil and gas. These days they were co-opting them as undergrads, paying their tuition. Miners employed more ecologists, marine scientists and geology graduates than six governments. In order to smooth the way, before they literally scraped the place bare. All that harmless data owned and warehoused. It was brilliant. (Winton, *Eyrie* 191)

In the strife between environmental protection organizations and the mining companies, the latter seem to be increasingly tricky and gaining an upper hand. In *Eyrie*, the sharp contrast between the two parties is embodied in the portrayal of the two protagonists: Damien is a young scientist hired by some lucrative mine with handsome pay, "his flash mountain bike laden with wholesome/organic produce"; Keely, his former boss, is standing "ravaged and unsteady outside the roughest liquor store in town", with "brown bags cradled in his arm" (Winton, *Eyrie* 191). Unemployed, divorced and obsolete, Keely is down and out physically as well as spiritually. The comparison betrays an obvious mood of pessimism in the author about the complications of the issue of environmental protection.

That the mining companies always work to improve their public image is a long-term practice in Australia. Traditionally, they have been pleasing the government and the people by constructing the infrastructure in the mining towns. No wonder some claim "the industry of mining made the country — made its roads, its railways, its ports, its towns and its cities" (Knox 69). In contemporary era of environmentalism, however, the means they take become more imperceptible and misleading. By paying the tuition for students of ecology, geology, or any other relevant disciplines, they are cultivating the mouthpiece for their sabotage of nature and in the meantime eroding the most eloquent forces for the eco-campaigns. Kill two birds with one stone. Mining industry now gains steady support from their former foes, which paves the way for further abuse of the natural resources disregarding potential negative impacts on the land. Keely seems to be foreseeing a future when the land will be scraped bare and the mine companies seem to be the ones who laugh last and best. To be indignant or to be frustrated, everything leads to one direction: it's always the same story of "the triumph of capital" (Winton, *Eyrie* 7).

By contrast, the voice from the environmentalists sounds rather weak and their appeal to "people's higher nature" is sheepish, hesitant and lack of confidence. Their endeavors to get "Nature itself a fair hearing" waver at the overwhelming propaganda by the miners with assistance from "ecologists" they hire. As Keely puts it, preserving the resources and protecting nature are, "in this state, at such a moment in history, like catching fart in a butterfly net". Fed up with disappointment and poignancy, Keely determines to quit and pretends that he is no longer relevant: "Don't touch that dial. Not the radio, nor the telly. Least of all the laptop. ... Didn't even read the papers any more. Tried not to, at least. Had no need of more stories about 'clean coal'. ... Didn't matter which rag you read, it would be another installment about the triumph of capital" (Winton, *Eyrie* 7).

Like most other characters in Winton's fictional clan, Keely is almost a spontaneous guard of his land. The forced relinquishment (for he was dismissed by the NGO) leaves him no peace. Very much like protagonists in Ernest Hemingway's fictional world who can be destroyed but not defeated, Keely is dismissed but not resigned, for man's eco-unfriendly behaviors keep pricking at his conscience, which never allows him to become indifferent to them. To gain a peaceful mind, people like Keely have no other choice but stand to fight albeit they themselves are not in good shape. But what matters is that the struggle is on. New problems have to be coped with, though old ones are far from being solved and new challenges have to be confronted with.

1.4 Spiritual Disequilibrium due to Whale-exploitation

"It's as if Winton has impatiently bypassed the adolescent revolt stage, and gone straight for the big question", Helen Garner wrote when she reviews Winton's virgin work *An Open Swimmer* (qtd. in McPhee 19~20). As a passionate writer who consciously feels the responsibility for preserving the unique beauty of his motherland, Winton demonstrates deep concern about the land when he firstly embarks upon the writing career. His second novel *Shallows* is an important eco-fiction that was published in 1984 when the author was 24 years old and won him the first Miles Franklin Award. Like many of his other fiction, *Shallows* is "an intense rendering of the Western Australian coast around Albany" (qtd. in Tyas 218). The fiction records the rise and decline of the traditional whale fishery at Angelus, a fictitious small whaling port created from the archetype of Albany. Whale exploitation as a central line goes through the whole story and Winton embeds the whaling story of the 1830s in the form of journal by Queenie's ancestor Nathaniel Coupar in the main framework, which punctuates the narrative with a fictional history (Tyas 219). "Switching back and forth from the Angelus of 1831 to the Angelus of the present, Winton presents a world in which the townsmen are shallow, petty, venal, and cruel" (Willbank 221). In *Shallows*, Winton dexterously tangles the stories about whales and whale hunting with the saga of the Coupar family which spans five generations despite the brevity in the narration of some not so pertinent details of two generations. The Coupar clan is always entangled with the whales. Nathaniel Coupar, the first generation of the lineage, was once a young whaler but was deserted "for lost" at the Bay of Whales — a provisional land-based whaling spot (Winton, *Shallows* 171). Unexpectedly, Queenie Coupar, his great-granddaughter, grows to become the brave local participant in the eco-campaign launched by foreign environmentalists and an outspoken caretaker of the whales. The family saga well mirrors the 150-year history of the small coastal town and its pillar industry of whaling.

Whale exploitation is one of the traditional means of sea conquest. Although mankind's territory is on the land, yet the development of science and technology, especially of shipbuilding, enables them to tap the potential resources in vast oceans. The boom of whale hunting business coincided with the industrial revolution and massive expansion of major capitalist countries in recent centuries. As the American author Herman Melville puts it in his masterpiece *Moby Dick, or the Whale* (1851):

> Dutch in DeWitt's time had admirals of their whaling fleet; Louis XVI of France, at his own expense, fit out whaling ships from Dunkirk; Britain

> between the years 1750 and 1788 paid to her whalemen in bounties and lastly whalemen of America now (in the nineteenth century) outnumber all the rest of the banded whalemen in the world. (124)

Namely, such historical maritime superpowers as Dutch, France and Britain all invariably had jumped on the bandwagon of whale hunting in their heydays. The whale fishery is of special significance to the construction of the new settlement in Australia. "Herman Melville, through his protagonist Ishmael, the narrator in *Moby Dick*, describes the achievements of the American whalemen, crediting them as the greatest explorers in the world and including in their honours the opening of the Pacific and Australia" (Gibbs, "Conflict and Commerce" 3):

> That great America on the other side of the sphere, Australia, was given to the enlightened world by the whalemen. After its first blunder-born discovery by Dutchmen, all other ships long shunned those shores as pestiferously barbarous; but the whaleship touched there. The whaleship is the true mother of that now mighty colony. Moreover, in the infancy of the first Australian settlement, the emigrants were several times saved from starvation by the benevolent biscuit of the whaleship luckily dropping an anchor in their waters. (Melville 125)

Whale hunting did play an important role in the founding period as confirmed by the great historian of whaling, Edouard A Stackpole: "whale ships with their wide-beamed holds were well suited for the transportation of convicts in the early days of the new settlements" (176). And "the temptation was very great to turn a handsome profit with a whale hunt on the return voyage and have the venture underwritten at government expense" (Turner 79). Some writers recognized that the American whalers' contributions were "crucial to the early development of the isolated outposts of Western Australia" (Gibbs, "Conflict and Commerce" 3).

Whaling has always been a major motif for depiction in literature. Again in *Moby Dick*, Melville endows whaling with aesthetically noble associations by claiming that "mighty Job wrote the first account of our Leviathan; Alfred the Great composed the first narrative of a whaling-voyage by taking down the words from the Norwegian whale-hunter; and Edmund Burke pronounced the glowing eulogy in the parliament" (Melville 126). It is unanimously agreed that *Moby Dick* should be listed among the top whaling narratives. When *Shallows* was published 130 years later, memories about *Moby Dick* were evoked and the comparison between the two seems unavoidable by the common readers, book reviewers as well as literary critics. The *Los Angeles Times'* comment is: "The prose and learning stand up to Melville himself ... the elegance of language, the grandeur of nature being described — all this is dazzling. It makes the heart pound."① Carolyn See makes the remarks that *Shallows* is "a dark masterpiece about whaling that ranks with (or above?) *Moby-Dick*" (5). John P. Turner compares the two novels in his essay "Tim Winton's *Shallows* and the End of Whaling in Australia". Despite many similarities, Turner believes the major difference lies in the fact that American author Herman Melville's *Moby Dick* was composed during the heyday of the whaling industry when the whalers were revered as great heroes for they were able to conquer the marine monster "through a hostile environment with pitifully small and inadequate weapons" whereas *Shallows* was written "at the end of its centuries-long history" when a new era of global ecological crisis and species extinction is ushered in (80). Different times produce dissimilar responses. Before reading Winton's whale story, I want to take a brief look at *Moby Dick* from ecocritical perspective.

Moby Dick, the once great epic of whaling, is mainly taken as an

---

① From back blurb of the UK Piccador Edition of *Shallows*.

anti-ecological fiction. In Melville's version of whale story, Ahab as a representative of humanity seeks revenge on a white sperm whale that has mutilated him in the former encounter, which is the most ridiculous and irrational decision made by the seemingly rational captain. Today we tend to agree with Starbuck when he says "Moby Dick seeks thee not. It is thou, thou, that madly seekest him!" (Melville 582). Seen from the ecological perspective, the sperm whale looks innocent while Ahab is the real vengeful demon. If Moby Dick represents the wildlife or even elemental power of nature, then Ahab embodies human's desire to tame the former. In the 19th century, Ahab's activity was eulogized as a form of romantic heroism in that he fought not for any practical objective or economic gains but for the glory of *homo sapiens* as a species. But the eco-critics would argue that Ahab's decision derives from a kind of extreme anthropocentrism which makes him believe that man cannot be defeated and man's reputation is something that must be guarded at any cost. The deep-seated reason consists in the alienated man-nature relationship. "Nature as the non-human world, as the animal world" is taken as an object to be conquered and dominated (Plumwood, *Feminism* 83). However, human beings have to pay a price for the conquest of nature. The whalemen are frequently injured or killed. In *Moby Dick*, Captain Boomer shares similar experience with Ahab in losing his arm in strife with the white whale. But he is quite tolerant and able to come to terms with the defeat and loss. His ship doctor's words justify this resignation:

> Do you know, gentlemen, that the digestive organs of the whale are so inscrutably constructed by Divine Providence, that it is quite impossible for him to completely digest even a man's arm? And he knows it too. So that what you take for the White Whale's malice is only his awkwardness. For he never means to swallow a single limb; he only thinks to terrify by feints. (Melville 458)

Faking attack or not, whales can never escape the destiny of being hunted by human race on account of the economic values they possess. Lawrence Buell believes that in *Moby Dick* whales "are not cast as sinister predators. On the contrary, more often they are typed as prey to the whalers, who themselves get slyly caricatured as the sharkish, cannibalistic ones" (*Endangered World* 210). So we have to admit that in spite of its anti-ecological motif, Melville does harbor some ecological vision on the sea life, which is obviously ahead of his time.

Like Captain Boomer, if man had taken the physical mutilation as a warning from nature, and had moderated the exploitation, undoubtedly severe ecological catastrophes may have been avoided. But the Ahabs' desire can hardly be satisfied. More hostile actions against nature only result in deteriorating relationship and more extreme forms of man-nature binary opposition. Accordingly, the individuals who are involved will receive more severe punishment from nature. Some are physically hurt while others are to experience serious spiritual disequilibrium. This is what happens to Nathaniel Coupar, the whaler who kept the journal of "near-starvation, cannibalism and bitter suffering on sea and land as he battled a recalcitrant landscape for his fortune" (Edelson 65). Being "morally aghast at the conduct of his fellow whalers and at the carnage wrought on the whales in 1831" (Willbanks 221), he was left "a wasted hulk of a man" that was "barely alive, barely a man" (Winton, *Shallows* Ⅻ).

This section is an exploration into how the whalers in the 1830s conquered the sea by whale exploitation at the Bay of Whales, the fictional temporary shore-based whale station, via analyzing the embedded text of Nathaniel's journal in *shallows*. Karl Marx's concept of estranged labor is the handy theoretical tool for the analysis. Firstly, the interpretation intends to uncover the ferocity of the whaling work. This critic would claim that the whaling work goes against man's nature of free, conscious, creative labor and thus alienates man's nature as a species and breaks the natural link between man and nature (here represented by whales). Secondly, the product and process of labor jointly alienates laborers (whalers) and the relationship among them. Thirdly, it is to argue that man's spiritual crisis in religious conviction and psychological disequilibrium would be the sure consequence of the estranged labor of whaling.

Since Karl Marx's concept of estranged labor will be frequently referred to in the discussion, an introduction of the theoretical background serves as a good point of departure. Proceeding from the premises of political economy, Karl Marx developed the key concept of estranged labor in *Economic and Philosophic Manuscripts of* 1844. According to his theory in the 1844 version, the alienation of labor is embodied in four aspects, namely, the alienation of the relation of the worker to the product of labor, the alienation of the relation of labor to the act of production within the labor process, the alienation of man's species nature and the estrangement of man from man. Since the theory itself was later repeatedly revised by Marx himself and many later philosophers, it's not wise to follow the theory point by point. So this critic chooses to conduct the discussion from three perspectives: the alienation of the work itself under desperate conditions; the alienation of interpersonal relationship, and the concomitant spiritual disequilibrium.

Nathaniel Coupar recorded the miserable natural settings that trapped the whalemen in the dreary wet winter of Western Australia in thick descriptions. Struggles against elements of nature and whales pushed the whalers to collapse both physically and spiritually. The scarce cases of successful hunting could hardly cheer the whalers up. Instead, the ferocity of killing, flensing and dissecting whales degraded them to brutes, numbed their humane sympathy towards fellow workers and estranged man's relationship with marine wildlife and nature. In a word, whaling is "a devilish existence that bestialized the worker" (Buell, *Endangered World* 211). In this sense, whale exploitation is the forced, estranged labor that causes all the problems.

The estranged labor is firstly embodied in "the relation of the worker to the *product of labour* as an alien object exercising power over him. This relation is at the same time the relation to the sensual external world, to the objects of nature as an alien world antagonistically opposed to him" (Marx 73, emphasis original). Nathaniel Coupar was stricken with a guilty conscience owing to the inhuman operations performed on a pregnant cow whale: "Cut the calf from the womb of its mother this evening. Wading about in entrails sometimes strikes me as profane". Young Nathaniel was so startled by the work that he associated it with "the feeling of being buried alive" (Winton, *Shallows* 108). In Lawrence Buell's word, "whaling forces many of those involved in it into more bestial lives than they would lead shoreside" (*Endangered World* 212). In a sense, the whale that is dissected, as the object of labor, is exerting power over the whaler by exposing the brutality of humanity and creating doubts as to the legitimacy of man's massacre of whales.

The process of labor is alienating in that the tie between mankind and natural world is severed. Therefore, sometimes it seems that the external natural world is "antagonistically opposed to" the whalemen. Many occurrences confirmed this suspicion. One day they spent the whole day stalking a mother whale and her calf around the bay. Eventually, the cow was caught. But when they were painstakingly towing "her in towards the shore and the fires on the beach" (161), something melodramatic occurred: the great carcass slid away and sank slowly in eight fathoms, almost taking the whalers with it (ibid.). Everyone was shocked and couldn't help taking it as an omen of misfortune. And the disquieting fact behind this was that what they killed was a mother whale who had thrown "herself on top of her young to shield it" and thus "exposed" herself and got killed by the whalemen (ibid.). Nathaniel, the sensitive young whaler, could not be apathetic about the greatness of the cow. Winton makes his readers aware that virtues such as maternal love and self-sacrifice are not exclusively possessed by human race; here, they are best embodied by the cow. It insinuates that "whales emerge as less bestial than one might expect" (Buell, *Endangered World* 212). The self-sacrifice found in the cow has been fascinating scientists all the time. The documents kept by the French environmentalist Fleurier in the fiction have the record that "cows with calf were easy prey for bay whalers because the cow was slowed by her offspring and often ensnared by her own maternal instincts. If a calf was harpooned and towed in, the mother would follow and be slaughtered" (212). Moreover, Winton contrasts the greatness of a mother whale to the barbarity of human race to disturb the reader's clear conscience so that a contemplation of the relation between the two will be triggered off. In this case, the whaler's labor itself becomes an alien one. As Marx puts it,

> This relation is the relation of the worker to his own activity as an alien activity not belonging to himself; it is activity as suffering, strength as weakness, begetting as emasculating, the worker's own physical and mental energy, his personal life or what is life other than activity — as an activity which is turned against him, neither depends on nor belongs to him. (73)

This is what we call "*self-estrangement*" "in the relation of labour to the *act of production* within the *labour* process" (Marx 73~74, emphases original). Young Nathaniel worked as a whaler to pay his debt, but he hated the work that astounded him and left deep psychological trauma on him. He was loath to commit the cruel barbarity of the hunting. In fact, he was anxiously awaiting the arrival of the whaling ship to pick them up and he had decided to quit if he could leave. To him, the sojourn at the whaling spot wore on like years. Nathaniel Coupar, the contemplative participant of the ferocious work, had managed to remain largely aloof from other whalers and their contemptible behaviors. To certain degree, he is also an eyewitness "outsider" who is able to "fashion a mental space in which these matters can be held up for contemplation: how whaling reduces people, how whale-beholding sometimes ennobles whales and impels one to imagine people and whales as semi-interchangeable" (Buell, *Endangered World* 212).

However, the real unbearable aspect of the job lies in the alienation of human relationship. In Marx's words, "an immediate consequence of the fact that man is estranged from the product of his labour, from his life-activity, from his species being is the *estrangement of man* from *man*". Alienated human relationship is the core of Nathaniel's journal. "If a man is confronted by himself, he is confronted by the *other* man. What applies to a man's relation to his work, to the product of his labour and to himself, also holds of a man's relation to the other man, and to the other man's labour and object of labour" (Marx 77, emphases original).

Nathaniel Coupar arrived at the Bay of Whales with the American whaling ship the *Family of Man* in 1831. Ironically, crew members did not treat each other like brothers in a family as indicated by the ship's name. Instead, they frequently fought with each other. As a result, "Leek has knocked out the front teeth of Mountford" (161). Cain has "had his left earlobe torn off in a past fight". Eerily, he was said to have kept "the shrivelled lobe in his sea-chest" (18). In harsh living conditions, human relationship is unfriendly and highly distorted.

Winton's novel "is structured by fragments of historical voices and Biblical allusions" (Tyas 218). Plots in *Shallows* correspond roughly to historical facts. According to Martin Gibbs, the outpost, known as Fredrickstown and later Albany, was declared open for free colonists in 1829 (4). But not much progress was achieved during the first few years in either agriculture or establishment of a new settlement. As far as the whaling is concerned, "it was not until the winter of 1836 that an Albany merchant by the name of Thomas Sherratt was finally able to form a small whaling party on the shores of Doubtful Island Bay, located approximately 150km north-east of Albany". American whale ships also played a role in the founding of whaling station and the settlement in Western Australia in history. In the nineteenth century, the American whalers voyaged around the globe plundering the rich resources in virgin open sea. Their hunting activities along the western coast of Australia and sojourn on the land actually promoted the Australian settlers to embark on the whaling industry. Records proved that the commerce between the American whalers and the early British colony settlers helped to pull them through the most challenging pioneering period. Gibbs also points out that "the fortunes of the Western Australian whaling parties fluctuated through the late 1830s, although small seasonal shore stations were established progressively in various bays" ("Nebinyan's Songs" 3). So when Nathaniel Coupar and his workmates arrived in 1831, they came for short-term visit instead of long-term settlement. The early shore-based whaling spot was provisional in essence and therefore the arduousness of the working and living conditions was beyond imagination. Sustenance could hardly meet the basic need for survival. Supplies of wood and water could be obtained on the land, but if the irreplaceable living materials ran out, they could do nothing but wait for the visitation of their ship for replenishment. That's why the daily supplies must be put under scrupulous control and be allocated by rations. Overconsumption might endanger the survival of their peers and thus was immoral and despicable. Among all kinds of living materials, rum was something dearly precious to the whalers because it helped to pull them through the bleak, wet season of winter. But Nathaniel's diary showed that some stronger crews were shameful bullies because they surreptitiously drank other whalers' share (161). On another occasion:

> A ration of rum (was) issued, though none sent up to Churling in the

> lookout atop the hill. When I mentioned this oversight some man muttered that he, Churling, would need no spirituous warming when he returned. This puzzles me. My senses are dulled by weariness and a sort of revulsion for my comrades. (61)

Innocent young Nathaniel felt confused and indignant at the negation of fundamental morals and values in the desperate circumstance of whale hunting at the outpost.

Miserable working conditions aggravate the alienated relationship among the whalers. Trying to hunt whales with simple and gravely ineffective weapons such as harpoons virtually jeopardizes the whalemen themselves. In *Moby Dick*, we've witnessed mutilations inflicted by whale hunting. Injuries and deaths seem to be the common occurrences. Likewise, in *Shallows* tragedy fell on Nowles who had "stumbled over the clumsy-cleat after striking a black cow and wedged his fingers between rope and gunwhale" (30). Barbarity was implied when Nathaniel hinted at the possibility that Mr. Jamieson had ordered the severance of the fingers but not the rope to prevent capsizing (ibid.). Nathaniel refused to believe this because he still held some illusion about human nature. Although the injury itself was not fatal, the situation deteriorated rapidly for want of medical care. Both Ahab and Captain Boomer received medical care, sympathy and support from their crew members and were held as heroes in *Moby Dick*, but in *Shallows*, when a man was sick or injured he had to endure it lonely and painfully. "A man from Finn's crew is sick. He screams like an animal in the night and throws furniture about" (138). Similarly, Nowles had to toss and pitch his way in the dark helplessly and agonizingly all by himself (31). No one made any effort to alleviate the pains suffered by their workmate. Neither did they care at all although similar calamity might fall upon anyone, anytime. So Nowles had to wait for the approach of death in extreme agony and solitude. Winton puts it: "How lonely is the sound of a man in pain! There is nothing more solitary; it cannot be shared and a man is isolated in his own sea, the swirling rip-current that is pain" (30~31).

The shift in attitudes towards the injured in whaling, with the former being given care and honor and the later being discarded, proves the deepening of the alienation in human relationship in the process of estranged labor. This aloofness towards other's agony, as a matter of fact, degrades men to beasts and throws the journal keeper Nathaniel, the sensitive, delicate, and timid young whaler, into life-long spiritual crisis which deprives him of a peaceful mind and a normal life all together. Witnessing the sufferings of Nowles, he was not sympathetic though deeply disturbed. "Do I wish to share his pain to ease his burden? No, I am ashamed, but I can only hate him for his pain and his noise and I want him away or dead to leave me some peace and some sleep for what is left of the night" (31). His belief in religion made him fully aware of the sin of being mean, callous, and unsympathetic. Self-admittedly, he was incapable of offering any effective help even if he had attempted to. But conscious indifference and incapability to help are different in essence. The former is obviously against the Christian doctrines and constitutes the sin.

However, Nowles' tragedy was not the only sin that obsessed him. His conscience was also stricken with the death of Churling, another weak young whaler like himself. Many traces implied that Nathaniel had some idea about the crime of sodomy against Churling committed by Cain and Leek: he heard "a child weeping" in his sleep; he saw "hanging from a bough near our hut, a pair of trousers" with "drops of dried blood on the legs" (108). These details were later echoed in Cleve's accusation of Nathaniel, "You knew whose they (the pair of trousers) were all the time, [...] you knew, you bugger. They were raping him, and you knew. And never did a thing" (165). Nathaniel also observed that, almost compulsively, Churling had become "haggard and pale", "forsaken", "pathetic", soulless, and "hopeless". Yet, he still felt that "it is not my business to offer help until he asks it of me" and chose to turn a blind eye or fakes ignorance, though he discerned "a feeble expression of disappointment" in Churling's look (109).

Nathaniel didn't respond to the call for help for the third time when he "made no move to go to the aid of the fingers" that "curled from outside the boat, nails denting the wood" (170). Obviously, one of the crew was in danger. Timely help makes the difference between life and death. Unlike Nowles and Churling, the third victim was unnamed and reduced to "the fingers". The synecdoche reveals the growing numbness in Nathaniel. When the fingers disappeared from the boat, another life was lost to the sea and Nathaniel was also driven to the edge of spiritual collapse.

It's not exaggerating to say that the whalemen at the Bay were trapped and isolated from the outside world. For want of support, either materially or spiritually, human relationships were distorted. The alienated relationships among the whalemen were not only demonstrated in forms of barbarity, bully, sodomy and aloofness, but also in abandonment, betrayal, and cannibalism.

Some were driven crazy and then abandoned. "At dust today Finn's crew took the lunatic Bale into the bush, returning without him an hour later. They have left him to his own insane nature" (139). Later, "the petrified form of Bale, the lunatic" happened to be discovered by Nathaniel and he felt there's "a look of bliss" on his face (172). That is, the dead is more blissful and blessed, which echoes Churling's opinion that "it is better to die than to live" (124). More than forty years later, when Nathaniel looked back at his whole life, he still believed it's hard to feel gratitude for his survival. As he put it, "since the days I came here as a young man, since my marooning, I have ceased to live, continued merely to exist" (167). In the final whale hunting voyage, Nathaniel was the only survivor after the nightmare storm on the sea. But when he "stumbled upon the beach of the encampment", he discovered everything was gone. Obviously, the long-awaited ship *Family of Man* had returned, "taken all survivors off the beach and given our crew up for lost", which is another case of ruthless forsaking (171).

With time rolling by, supplies were increasingly inadequate but the work showed slim hope of improvement. Then one day, Cain, Leek and four other men deserted, stealing almost all the food and materials for living and hunting. Moreover, Cain and Leek were the "only remaining harpooneers" they had (162). So to speak, the betrayal threw all others in desperation. Then what lay in store for the traitors? When the forsaken Nathaniel was wondering about after being deserted for lost, he found the "remains of the four deserting crewmen who had accompanied Leek and Cain". He noticed that "much of the men's flesh had been taken, not savaged as if by wild dogs, but butchered with some grim deftness", which clearly indicates cannibalism (172). It won't cause any objection if I take cannibalism as the extreme form of alienated human relationship.

What's more, it is necessary to note the relationship between the white whalers and the aborigines. Firstly, the abuse of aboriginal women draws our immediate attention. Nathaniel noticed one morning "in the poor light a staggering lubra, naked, besmirched and inebriated," who "struck her fists against the door of the hut opposite without response" (108). On another occasion, he saw "two naked women tossed from the headmen's hut. It had been raining and they lay stupefied in the mud as I passed" (109). Aboriginal women are commonly called the "black velvet" by historians in that a large number of them were sexually abused by the white men in the early days. That the abused aboriginal woman was "staggering" and "inebriated" implies another major problem with the aborigines till now-grog-addiction, the second aspect of the alienated relationship between the white Australians and the natives. Grog is virtually a dose of poison that ruins the aboriginal race. Many young aborigines find it hard to stay sober even in today's Australian society. Thirdly, the way they deal with Nowles' blanket represents a dishonorable history of Australia. When Nowles was dead, the "stench in his bedding has rendered it useless", but "Jamieson has suggested we trade his blankets to the blacks" (108 ~ 109). Winton is insinuating an important way of persecuting the aboriginals during the early settlement. The Reverend William Pell in *Shallows* ironically muses, "a hundred years ago, these blankets I'm carrying would have been laced with typhoid" (5). In history, many aborigines died from the diseases transmitted by the blankets they got from the "benevolent" white almsgivers, because thousands of years' isolation renders the aborigines vulnerable to the imported viruses. Blankets laced with various viruses had been consciously used as tools of genocide by the early settlers. Fourthly, it is ironic that the charity blankets are routinely distributed through the clergyman and the church, which represent another force of colonization and appropriation. They aim to replace the traditional aboriginal cultures with Christian culture. The blankets they handed out impair both the physical and the spiritual health of the aborigines. So to speak, Winton's concise narration covers all the major aspects of the alienated relationship between the two races and reveals the root of the racial conflicts.

The barbarism in whale exploitation leads to serious spiritual crisis. The cook Hale finally turned to alcohol to numb his feelings and to turn a blind eye to the occurrences around him. Churling's diary revealed that the crew had lost flesh, blood, and soul. Young whalers such as Churling, Nowles, and Nathaniel were once innocent as the "sand on this bech [beach] was once wite [white]" (sic). However, the alienated work stained their soul and conscience so that they felt themselves non-human. Churling wrote in his diary, "For I am ther animal" (sic) (124). Nathaniel shared this feeling: "We have become animals" although he soon denied associating himself with the others

(162). In fact, Nathaniel always took great pains to disconnect himself from the corrupted. Hence, "Hale, the cook, has twice called me 'High an' Holy' as though in jest" (139). To varying degrees, they are all crucified by the "filth, and hopeless barbarity" of the job of whaling (162).

In Chris Beal's opinion, Tim Winton's "work cannot be fully understood or appreciated without a strong awareness of his Christian faith and spirituality" (48). Nathaniel's journal is essentially a record of someone that spends his whole life negotiating such significant religious propositions as life and death, innocence and sin, abandonment and hope. Nathaniel experienced, observed, mediated, recorded and survived physically but died spiritually. As discussed above, on more than one occasion did he detect the call for help but failed to react, which disgraced his reputation as a religious fellow. Although he held it firmly that he was clean, his conscience never let him go for one second. It's true that "what others do is their own sin, their own salvation, their damnation" (283). However, his "sins of inaction" weighed upon his heart and prevented him from gaining salvation (98).

Realizing all others had been saved but himself, Nathaniel "cursed them all, cursed the sky and the wind and the fish of the sea, berated and spat upon their Creator" (171). Nathaniel was so psychologically impaired by what he had experienced that his conviction collapsed as he explained in his journal "I have looked Evil in the eye and have been confounded since" (174).

We can also interpret it as a sort of trauma left by unutterable experiences. According to Freud, only if one can look at the problem boldly then it begins to heal. In fact, Nathaniel dared not face squarely his own sins of inaction and his claim of innocence was thus weak. "You do not sleep at night, Nathaniel Coupar. Sometimes you are at the brink of all knowledge, others you creep along the crumbling bank of all ignorance. I have no guilt" (174). Deprived of sleep at night, Nathaniel

Coupar, in his senior age, was tormented by the nightmare of his cannibalistic fellow workers Leek and Cain. He believed his sufferings came from "resisting barbarity" (174~175). Nathaniel himself could not tell whether the spiritual disequilibrium derived from "fear or shame" till death (174). Maybe both are contributing factors in alienating man's spirit. Non-participation and "ignorance" are all invalid excuses so they cannot help Nathaniel to shake off the spiritual shackle. Maybe suicide is the only way out. Unable to find salvation, Nathaniel Coupar shot himself in the cave that used to be his sanctuary and was doomed to be his burial ground, after a lifelong painful search. Moreover, "his nineteenth-century travails are brought to bear on the present, on the vain, God-crazed Coupar men who followed him" (Willbanks 221).

1.5 Coastal Pollution due to Industrial Discharge

The historical settlement of Australia has been significantly influenced by its geography. Coastal areas are of special significance to Australians on account of some historical and economic facts. Early settlements were located along the coast owing to its proximity to sources of fresh water and access to shipping for security as well as for trading purposes (qtd. in Brunton 37). And the trend is inherited and continues till today. According to the Coastal Zone Inquiry Final Report released by the Resource Assessment Commission in 1993, eighty-six per cent of Australia's population lives within 50 kilometers of the coast, which means the overwhelming majority of Australians live along the narrow coastal strip. Coastal towns and settlements thus congregate around river mouths, bays and natural harbors all around the nation.

In Ray Willbanks' interview with him in 1991, Tim Winton talked about the importance of coast in his writing:

> The coast just seemed to be where I spent most of my time, and

> where, I suppose in terms of my literary world inside of my head, that's where I go when I'm writing. I don't know if there's anything deeply meaningful in the setting itself, but yes, it's an area I know about; there are people in that area that I know about. I'm a coastal person. (189)

In another interview, Winton owes his love of the coast to the three years spent at Albany in his early teen years. This experience gives him an inexhaustible source of inspiration and the coast remains an omnipresent element in his works ever since his virgin work *An Open Swimmer* (1982) to *Lockie Leonard* (1990—1997) and to *Breath* (2008). The littoral setting has almost become an indispensable character in his fiction.

Yet, Tim Winton stresses that "we are not sea people by way of being great mariners, but more a coastal people, content on the edge of things" (21). "Coast" and "edge" are the keywords commonly employed by Winton as well as the famous American ecologist and pioneer eco-warrior Rachel Carson. Echoing her book *The Edge of the Sea* (1955), Tim Winton wrote his semi-biographical memoir *Land's Edge* (1993) to express his deep fondness for the littoral life. It's easy to discern the link between the two works. However, they have different focus of attention — Carson's care stays with the sea and marine species while Winton's goes to the land. So to speak, Tim Winton and Rachel Carson are concerned with the same thing but from distinct angles of view. Hence, Carson tends to assume "the marginal world" to be the edge of the sea whereas Winton wants to highlight the coastal strip as the land's edge.

Of course, Winton is not the only author who notes the importance of the coast in Australian life. "Robert Drewe has long argued that almost every Australian rite of passage occurs on or near the beach" (Winton, *Edge* 21). However, the depictions of the southern west coast of Western Australia have undoubtedly become a recognizable hallmark of Tim Winton's fiction. Salhia Ben-Messahe discerns that "his stories are rooted in the agrarian and coastal zones operating on the periphery of Perth" (*Mind the Country* 230).

Therefore, the ecological sustainability of the coastal marine environment is vital to Australians. Unfortunately, the coastal areas fall easy victim to human activities. When she was composing *The Sea around Us* in 1950, Rachel Carson once assumed that ocean is the "ultimate sanctuary". However, later she revised the view and pointed out that the "most alarming of all man's assaults upon the environment is the contamination of air, earth, rivers, and sea with dangerous and even lethal materials" (*Silent Spring* 4). By focusing on such marginal places as the coast, *Lockie Leonard, Scumbuster*, the second book of the highly regarded trilogy of Tim Winton centers on how the teenage eco-warriors attempt to lay bare and put an end to the local mills' crime of discharging effluent into the harbor. Winton, an avid surfrat and conservationist, would draw people's attention to the problem of marine pollution. In this section, the topic of sea conquest will be continued by probing into an eco-campaign launched by two teenagers to protect the harbor. Through the analysis, this critic would argue that the fiction shatters the illusion that "the future usually looks after itself" (*Scumbuster* 39) and uncovers the simple fact that environment protection is a career for the common good, which calls for everyone's contribution.

It's interesting to note that the setting for Lockie Leonard trilogy is again in Angelus, the fictional small town where Nathaniel Coupar, the protagonist in *Shallows*, was stranded. In fact, about nine novels and short story collections are placed in this small town created out of Albany as calculated by Salhia Ben-Messahel, an expert in Tim Winton studies. Like his tutor Elizabeth Jolley at college, Winton would like to have his characters travel from one fiction to another. So we are going to meet the Cooksons (Cleve Cookson and Queenie Coupar) who happen to come back for a summer holiday, bringing along their 11-year-old daughter

Dot who like her mother, is adept at surfing, which casts a spell on Lockie on their first encounter on the beach. Lockie develops a crush on her at the first sight, for Dot can surf better than him. Moreover, we are to witness another face-to-face confrontation between the eco-pioneer Queenie and the obstinate environment-victimizer Des Pustling. *Lockie Leonard, Scumbuster*, the 1993 Wilderness Society Environment Award winner, was published nine years after *Shallows*, during which great changes have taken place either in environmental situations or in people's attitudes. It's true "eleven years later, there's whales out there and no whalers", as Lockie puts it. Yet the environmental circumstances are not improving but deteriorating and new problems keep mounting on the ground that economic development opposes man against nature. Businessmen such as Des Pustling would pursue maximum profits at any expense. The good news is that people are increasingly aware of the urgency and necessity of taking actions to stop sabotage against nature committed by industrialists, businessmen and the like. More people are aware of the duty to protect the sole home to all living organisms, as Queenie puts it "Aha. So it's finally happened. Someone's woken up" (72).

Lockie Leonard, Scumbuster (hence *Scumbuster*) was published in the early nineties in the twentieth century. The series include three novels, namely *Lockie Leonard, Human Torpedo* (1990), *Lockie Leonard, Scumbuster* (1993) and *Lockie Leonard, Legend* (1997), which are the anecdotes of a thirteen-year-old boy who is on the cusp of puberty and dooms to experience the pains and confusions caused by transition, displacement, and hormone. Having been dumped by his first girl friend, Lockie is to meet a worthy friend Egg in this episode. After accidently discovering the ugly secret of stealthy discharge of effluent, they decide to launch a campaign to stop it. The theme of this novel is clearly indicated in its title, *Scumbuster*. "Scum" refers to a layer of a dirty or unpleasant substance that forms on the surface of a liquid and

"-buster" is a suffix "used with some nouns to make nouns describing someone or something that attacks or removes something bad," ① like in "crime-buster", "stress-buster". The scumbuster Lockie in this episode would launch a protest to force the mills out of illegal and irresponsible direct discharge of industrial waste water into the bay. Bradford et al. hold that *Scumbuster* is a "realist fiction" in which "the young eco-warriors battle evil polluters". They also observe that such novels are versions of "distinctly anthropocentric environmental literature". Namely, "problems are caused by human greed and disregard for the natural world, and are solved by human intervention" (90). As the novel targets young readers, it is understandable that the narrative does not trace down to its deep cultural root of anthropocentrism behind the phenomenon of industrial pollution. Bradford and his research fellows also argue that

> Children's texts remain constrained by the intrinsic commitment to maturation narratives — narrative structures posited on stories of individual development of subjective agency, or of bildungsroman. This tends to ensure that any environmental literature remains anthropocentric in emphasis, rather than engaging with the biocentrism of 'deep ecology'. (91)

Therefore, by Arne Naess' precepts of deep ecology, *Scumbuster* should be characterized as belonging to the category of "shallow environmentalism". Namely, they launch environmental campaign for human welfare rather than for an essential reorientation of the western civilization. Still, it has "significant implications for any would-be ecocritic of children's literature" (Bradford et al. 91).

Australia is bestowed with nice white sand, beautiful bay, gorgeous

① Interpretation from *Macmillan English-Chinese Dictionary for Advanced Learners* 272, 1869.

stretch of beach by nature, which entitles Australians the opportunity to make a living from the sea or to seek fun along the beach via surfing, diving, swimming, and fishing. In most cases, they take the advantage for granted and never learn to treasure it until it is endangered. One day the harbor in the middle of the small town begins to stink as if bad luck strikes all of a sudden, though in fact the pollution has always been there just that the protagonists are too young to notice it. Ironically, it turns out that the harbor is being spoilt by the local residents themselves. The pattern of life and production sets human race apart from and against other species and the natural world. Industrial development is pursued at the expense of the environment and so it is the town folk who pull themselves in the mire of pollution. Rachel Carson pointed out as early as in the 1960s that "this is an era dominated by industry, in which the right to make a dollar at whatever cost is seldom challenged" (*Silent Spring* 12). Against the backdrop of Angelus at the end of the 1980s in *Scumbuster*, Winton portrays the increasing awareness of the impending threat from industrial pollution among people in spite of the general numbness and improvidence.

Rachel Carson is famous for her deep passion for marine life and the sea. She describes the sea shore as an "ancient" and "difficult" world where "life displays its enormous toughness and vitality by occupying almost every conceivable niche". As a marine biologist, she emphasizes that "the area between the tide lines" is full of vigor and "crowded with plants and animals" (*The Edge of the Sea* 11). Following Carson, Winton demonstrates similar, if not more, enthusiasm for the littoral area. In the epigraph to his documentary *Land's Edge* (1993), Winton admits the supremacy of untamed power of nature at the marginal place of coast by citing W. J. Dakin's word: "We speak of course of that narrow strip of land over which the ocean waves and moon-powered tides are masters — that margin of territory that remains wild despite the proximity of cities of land surfaces modified by industry" (5). From it we have good reason to speculate that Winton agrees with Dakin that the land of cities is dominated by industry while the seashore remains to be the territory of elemental forces of nature. But as far as the industrial pollution is concerned, the demarcation between the territories disappears immediately. Despite its immensity, the ocean has long felt the impact of human activities. In the above section, whale hunting has been explored as one traditional way of marine resource exploitation, which seriously endangers the survival of the species. As a matter of fact, seawater pollution is virtually even more pressing and cannot be ignored as an environmental threat to marine ecosystems.

The pollution of ocean results from a great variety of reasons, petrol spills, fertilizer runoff, garbage dumping, sewage disposal, and toxic chemicals from pesticide and other chemicals used on farms, to name a few. Productive activities of industrial and urban development such as mining, oil and gas exploration and production, city expansion, and tourism all pose threat to this environment because they affect "water and sediment quality, habitat and marine bio-diversity" (Rudiyanto 6~7). It is unanimously agreed that land based sources of marine pollution (LBMP) constitutes the major cause for marine pollution, some sources put it at eighty per cent whereas others indicate a percentage of seventy with ship-based sources and ocean dumping comprising ten per cent each (qtd. in Brunton 37). The emerging scientific evidence has also identified LBMP as the most serious threat to the long term health of marine ecology (ibid.).

> Similarly, in April 1991, the House of Representatives Standing Committee on Environment, Recreation and the Arts tabled a report on the protection of the coastal environment which concluded that the disposal of sewage by offshore outfalls into the ocean is one of the principal human impacts on the coast and is the major source of pollution of coastal waters. (Brunton 37)

Left unsolved, marine pollution will soon change the way the world runs in a dynamic state of balance. Therefore, both communities and individuals should take the ecological responsibility and contribute to the common welfare, which is something Winton wants to inform his young readers in *Scumbuster*.

When paddling the tin kayak across the shallow waters along the coast, Lockie and Egg bump into a patch of reeds: "Lockie felt the kayak brushing into a bank of reeds where the water was really foul" (*Scumbuster* 32). As they push on, they hear that "a pouring sound, a kind of gurgling came from somewhere back in the reeds". What's more, "it got louder all the time, and water got smellier. Lockie eyes began to water" (34). A hellish scene of water pollution is gradually unfolded before the readers' eyes and it turns out that the effluent is discharged secretly by the local mills. It's meaningful that the secret is discovered accidentally by two teenagers who are shocked as well as alarmed. Of course, we won't expect children to understand that "such dumping of effluent has been a practice of industry since the Industrial Revolution" (Bradford et al. 91). But the undeniable fact is where there is industry, there is pollution. Despite young ages, 13 and 14 respectively, Lockie and Egg don't waver in the face of powerful industrious polluters. They only know this: people couldn't swim and fish "in industrial sludge" (39).

Winton endeavors to uncover the ugly crime of pollution in the harbor. We are impressed by the thickness of the layer of algae on the surface of the water: "In the sunlight the water was dark green and thick as soup" (124) and "you could almost walk on it". Hence, when Lockie and Egg are paddling, they have to "snag" it (34). "Snag" indicates that the booming algae are like a blanket covering the surface of the water, which insulates oxygen and sunshine and suffocates other sea life living below. Thus it's widely known that the multiplication of algae can be lethal. Pollution caused by algae is something worthy of further elaboration. In the text we'll read further discussions about the causes and harms of algae over propagation between the protagonists. Then what enables algae microorganism to multiply? To answer the question, Winton gives some scientific facts: it is the "nitrogen and phosphates, mostly from fertilizer" that "makes algae grow" (50). Then how come is there a surplus of nitrogen and phosphates? Pushed further, the question leads back to the development of the modern agribusiness in Australia. We have observed in Chapter I that agriculture depends heavily on modern technology owing to the bareness of its soil in Australia. On low fertility soils, there is a lack of basic elements such as phosphates and nitrogen. Then fertilizer can replenish the want. But these artificial nutrients may seep into underground water in the long run. Furthermore, when it rains, some find their way into the nearby rivers together with particles from the surface soil, which, in most cases, eventually ends in the harbor. The phenomenon had been noted by Rachel Carson when she did the research into the effects of DDT: "Chemicals that have been applied to farmlands have been leached out of the ground by rains to become part of the universal seaward movement of water" (*Silent Spring* 37). A quote from Wikipedia well explains the problem:

> The pollution often comes from nonpoint sources such as agricultural runoff, wind-blown debris and dust. Nutrient pollution, a form of water pollution, refers to contamination by excessive inputs of nutrients. It is a primary cause of eutrophication of surface waters, in which excess nutrients, usually nitrogen or phosphorus, stimulate algal growth. ①

Since it's a story for young readers, Winton chooses to explain the whole matter in lucid language rather than by using difficult jargons like

① http://en.wikipedia.org/wiki/Marine_pollution.

runoff, cutrophication etc. The youngsters are informed that "ninety per cent of the seagrass meadows that fish and stuff live and breed in are gone" because algae prevent light from getting through. And with the death of seagrass comes the death of the harbor (50).

However, one more thing makes the matters even worse: the local fertilizer mill is discharging industrial effluent into the harbor through the pipelines hidden "somewhere back in the reeds". And they "could get away with it" (34) although "two years ago the EPA demanded a clean-up" (59 ~ 60). People can't help wondering why "NOTHING HAS BEEN DONE" (60 emphases original). These details not only indicate a conspiracy against the public and the natural environment but provoke strong indignation amidst people when they come to realize the truth. As is always the case elsewhere, despite the supposed security ensured by legislation, the public are usually exposed to serious dangers for years before "slowly moving legal processes can bring the situation under control" (Carson, *Silent Spring* 214). Here we can feel the typical Australian suspicion of the government. In many cases, they prefer to take immediate actions rather than wait for the authorities to adopt some measures. The matter well corresponds with Rachel Carson's line that it is "an era dominated by industry" (*Silent Spring* 12). But the difference lies in that decades later in a coastal town of Angelus more people won't "endure" it.

Eutrophication is not the only problem with the marine world. A dialogue between Lockie and Egg uncovers another major source of pollution — heavy metals. Egg, one year Lockie's senior, explains that the heavy metals are "mostly from the two factories that pump *gunk* straight into the harbour" (50, emphasis added) — "the fertilizer factory and the wool-mill" (51). Having talked a lot about the fertilizer factory, we'll now transfer the attention to the wool-mill. We wonder why bother to single out the wool-mill for blame among all kinds of industries. According to John P. Turner, wool replaced whales to become the major product in Australia economy in the 1830s (79). Sadly, sheep-grazing poses serious threat to the fragile ecosystem. The delicate topsoil is soon destroyed and many endemic plants are driven into extinction. However, these are not the only destruction and here we'll learn that wool-mill also discharges heavy metals and other pollutants into the waterway and contaminates the water. Winton shows the paradox that the nation renown as one riding on the sheep's back is virtually mutilated by sheep.

Maybe it's a coincidence that Rachel Carson once described the despair implied in the word "gunk": "In rivers really incredible variety of pollutants combine to produce deposits the sanitary engineers can only despairingly refer to as 'gunk'" (*Silent Spring* 36). Winton's description of the lousy scene on the spot attests to Carson's description. It's true that the pollutants come from multiple sources. People's casual disposal of residential waste is one of them. Scattered on the surface of the shallow area of the harbor near Angelus is an inextricable mixture of domestic and other wastes, such as "a few tyres", "a submerged pram", "schools of plastic bags", and "half-sunk dinghies and riverboats with mountains of bird poop growing on them" (*Scumbuster* 30). The appalling deluge of household waste is dumped in the harbor without any interference from either the residents or the local authorities. The pollution caused by life garbage is no less than the pollutants disposed by mills. Yet the difference between them is self-evident: one is done out of heedlessness and ignorance whereas the other is done consciously for some economic gains. Namely, the local mills are clear about the harm and illegality of their practice since they have been required to clear up the act by the government two years before. But the mills haven't done anything about the discharge and neither have they received any punishment. The government's acquiescence and nonfeasance seem odd and dubious.

When the town people are protesting in front of the phosphate factory, instead of coping with the pollution problem with effective measures, the mayor Des Pustling attempts to incite people's outrage against the protesters — "These people want to close down a good business and put a lot of decent hardworking people out of job. And I won't stand for that!" (116~117). He assumes the pose of an individual with high morality and justice in public. However, in private, "it turns out Mr. Pustling — the mayor — owns part of the phosphate factory and some of the wool-mill. He owns the dredges in the harbour ..." (129). The link between the mayor and the mills imply "corruption, greed and stupidity" as Egg's mother curses (90). Strangely, his conspiracy works well enough to stir up "the unions" to come out "against the 'environmentalists'" and to condemn that "the protest threatened jobs" (138). So to speak, the public are insidiously misguided to the "job or harbor" dilemma by the government, or Des Pustling, the mayor. Rachel Carson once raised the doubt: "How could intelligent beings seek to control a few unwanted species by a method that contaminated the entire environment and brought the threat of disease and death even to their own kind?" (*Silent Spring* 7). As to those town people who lived in Angelus in late 1980s, we may wonder how intelligent beings could seek to secure job opportunities in a way that contaminated the entire environment and brought the threat of disease and death even to themselves. Sadly, this is precisely what they choose to do, for people are told that to have jobs, they have to put up with the pollution as necessary by-product or side-effect as if pollution were inevitable and there were no alternative to it. Obviously, in *Scumbuster*, Winton's distrust of politicians and businessmen persists. Either in *Shallows* or here, Des Pustling has always been portrayed as "a liar, a thug", a hypocrite and a representative capitalist (117). "With the rise of capitalism, [...] the economic subject comes increasingly to the fore, and the new form of mastery comes to define rationality as egoism, and sociality as an instrumental association driven by self-interest" (Plumwood, *Feminism* 141). Des Pustling would like to seize every opportunity to maximize his economic benefits. He doesn't care about the welfare of his fellow citizens, let alone ecosystem and environment. The deeply entrenched instrumental mode of thinking may well account for De Pustling's indifference and neglect of duty. The state of radical exclusion in the human/nature relationship in the western outlook is exactly the cultural and philosophic root of the issue. Therefore, the conflicts between Pustling and the eco-warriors are elemental and unavoidable and the struggles will not end until nature gets revered and human race learns to get along harmoniously with the world that he dwells in.

The miserable situation that human beings have flung themselves in is that everything they get out of the harbor and put in dish on the dining table is "poisonous" (50). As a matter of fact, "dead crabs and fish" are seen on "the algae-choked bank" (34). It is also known that all materials that are involved in the ecosystem travel along the food chains. Carson has commented on the circulation of water:

> Water must also be thought of in terms of the chains of life it supports in an endless cyclic transfer of materials from life to life. We know that the necessary minerals in the water are so passed from link to link of the food chains. Can we suppose that poisons we introduce into water will not also enter into these cycles of nature? (*Silent Spring* 42)

This is a worthy question. If the fish and crabs are poisonous, dare we eat them and turn a blind eye to the whole affair? Carson points out that "one of the most sinister features of DDT and related chemicals is the way they are passed on from one organism to another through all the links of the food chains" (*Silent Spring* 20). Likewise, the poisonous sea food will surely arrive in hunter's belly and the heavy metals, many of which are carcinogens, will end up in humans' stomach and eventually cause cancers of all types. Moreover, as a coastal town, the pollution in the harbor will certainly jeopardize both fishing and entertainment industry in the form of surfing or coastal sightseeing. Among all these impacts, the most imminent and impending threat depicted in the novel is the fact that the stink from the harbor is rendering the town inhospitable.

The diction vividly describes the terrible mess at Angelus. The adjectives in "slimy wads of algae", "queasy", "steaming gunk", "Harbour lay rancid and still" (34~35), create strong impact on man's sense organs like eyes, ears and nose. Verbs like "snag", "spew" and "choke" can equally get on your nerve. Let alone some comparisons: "Angelus Harbour smelt like the boys' toilets in any school across the world" (30); "It looked like a football team of giants had blown their noses into this corner of the harbor"; and "What a nostril thrasher. This is sputagenous olfactorizing" (34). What's more, a chapter entitles "Stench" devotes to describing the foulness of the smell from the harbor and people's response on Christmas Day when Australia is in mid-summer. Disgust and nausea are the most appropriate words to express the feelings. All in all, Winton's depiction of the contamination is so impressive and vivid that the readers can even smell the putridity and picture the messy scene in their brain's eyes. No wonder Carson queries whether an individual can escape a pollution that is now so thoroughly distributed throughout our world since man is part of nature, however much he may like to pretend the contrary (*Silent Spring* 180).

In this novel for young readers, it is implied that the harbor pollution derives from conspiracy between the government and the industrialists. Winton encourages people to challenge what is happening and demand change, for the reason that "every problem was everyone's problem" (*Scumbuster* 122). Winton lashes out at the attitude held by the workers' union. "Now the union sees what comes out that pipe as someone else's problem ... and what goes on inside the plant and the mill is their problem" (139). Self-evidently, it won't do to just mind one's own business. If so, workers in the mills become accomplices as well. In Rachel Carson's word, "to assume that we must resign ourselves to turning our waterways into rivers of death is to follow the counsel of despair and defeatism" (*Silent Spring* 130). Therefore, it's definitely urgent to educate and awaken the public to their ecological responsibility and slam on the brake of blind development disregarding nature's welfare. In the story, people's attitudes go through obvious changes as the stink from the harbor becomes increasingly unbearable. The protest begins with the two youngsters but ends with the involvement of many local dwellers and a face-to-face confrontation with the victimizers. Winton's brave woman eco-fighter Queenie adds to the inflammation by lending her aid. Winton makes it clear that we have to cherish and protect the environment even as if for our own sake and he wants to make the public see that shameful acts of pollution and environmental destruction in whatever name must be stopped.

The famous Australian eco-feminist Val Plumwood points out that nature is conventionally backgrounded in almost all areas of human activities: it is "backgrounded in standard economics where, notoriously, no value is given to anything natural or to resources as they stand before they acquire use-value or before human labor is applied, where no account is taken of natural limits and ecological factors are treated as 'externalities'" (*Feminism* 70). Hence, when economic benefits are sought, usually no consideration is given to the effects upon the natural environment. In *Scumbuster*, the mills assume that nature has limitless potential of receiving wastes produced by human race. They turn a blind to the deterioration of the local ecosystem and a deaf ear to the call from the public. Winton spares no efforts in portraying the pong of the harbor to remind people of the intimate relationship with the natural surroundings. Obviously, it's hard to deny man's dependency upon the assumed subordinated other — nature. Since "dualism is a relation of separation and domination inscribed and naturalised in culture and characterised by radical exclusion, distancing and opposition", human beings in western culture, where dualism dominates, unavoidably have long separated themselves from and colonized nature (Plumwood, *Feminism* 47). However, the pollution of the harbor dismantles man's domination, for all things point to the fact that when nature is polluted, man's own survival is endangered.

In summary, this chapter helps the readers gain some insight into the author's depictions of the estranged relationship between white Australians and the territory. He mocks at the ridiculousness of the dream of constructing an Australian version of Arcadia and then proceeds to describe the ecological disasters caused thus. Winton notes mining as another major form of land conquest, which not only destroys the ecosystem but alienates the miners from the labor they do and the product they produce, a vivid case of estranged labor, borrowing Karl Marx's term. The conquest of the sea is also approached from two aspects. Whaling activities, another case of estranged labor, endanger the species, jeopardize the spiritual wholesomeness and leave serious psychological trauma to Nathaniel Coupar, as the analysis of his journal in *Shallows* shows. Once held as the last sanctuary, the ocean is unable to avoid contamination from human activities. In my way of thinking, exploration into fictional details that highlight the conquest of nature on land as well as in the sea not only consolidates Tim Winton as an author with strong ecological consciousness but also provides a foothold for further research into his endeavors in reestablishing a harmonious link between the post-settlers and their inherited land.

Chapter Ⅱ Reestablishment of "Umbilical" Bond

As a settler society, Australia's cultural heritage is mainly European although "white Australians saw themselves as isolated, displaced and on the very margin of the European world" (Quin 3). Dualism is the key to the comprehension and interpretation of western culture and thus of the hyperseparation of man/nature relationship. The discussion above shows that in modern western culture the relationship between man and nature is mainly embodied in conquest and domination, which results in all kinds of undesirable consequences, such as land degradation, human alienation, spiritual disequilibrium and marine pollution. However, to expose the hostile relationship between them is not the objective of eco-authors. Reconstructing a harmonious relationship seems to be a more practical and worthy goal for an author with ecological pursuit, which is the focus of discussion in this chapter. Important theoretical support comes both from western ecocritical doctrines such as Albert Schweitzer's "reverence for life", Aldo Leopold's land ethic and so on, and from Australian aboriginal ecophilosophy. Given its uniqueness and peculiarity, I would give the latter some illustration now.

2.1 Land Care in Aboriginal Tradition

Ecological crisis is believed to be crisis of western culture which mistakes humanity for the conqueror, nature for the object to be conquered. As a matter of fact, western culture has been undergoing changes ever since the appearance of environmental problems. The mainstream culture is constantly enriched and revised by minor cultures, such as Indian culture in North America, Aboriginal culture in Australia. All these cultures contain wisdom and knowledge in handling the man/nature relationship, which offers precious impetus and inspiration for the white people who have long turned a blind eye to their existence. I tend to use the plural form "cultures" on account of the diversity of Aboriginal cultures which vary from one to another despite some common core values. As Deborah Bird Rose, an Australian anthropologist who has worked with the Aboriginals, puts it,

> There is so much to be learned from Aboriginal people — about land management with fire, about the species of the continent, about relationships among living things, and between living things and the seasonal forces, about how to understand human society as a part of living systems, taking humanity seriously without making of it the centre of creation. (*Nourishing Terrains* 4)

Now I'll introduce the philosophy of land care in Aboriginal cultures to show that the animistic cultures of the Aborigines offer a possible way out of the predicament that the white people are trapped. And the following discussion in this chapter will demonstrate how the Australian indigenous cultures as well as other environmental theories from western culture have exerted a subtle influence upon Tim Winton in his exploration of building an "umbilical" bond between the white Australians and the land.

Aboriginal cultures in Australia are in essence animistic in that they "see the natural world as inspirited, not just people, but also animals, plants, and even 'inert' entities such as stones and rivers are perceived as being articulate and at times intelligible subjects, able to communicate and interact with humans for good or ill" (Manes 15). The animism in Aboriginal cultures can be certified by their concept of "country". According to OED (Oxford English Dictionary), "country" firstly refers to the "land occupied by a nation" (265). It is the most usual word to use when you are talking about the major political nations that the world is divided into. It secondly means the "land of a person's birth or citizenship" (ibid.). People are passionate for the country where they are brought up. Hence, "mother country" is a usual metaphor. However, in Aboriginal cultures, "country" is a concept that describes one's home country, the ancestral land where their forefathers have been living over many generations (Jackson 10). Aboriginals are usually highly identified with their country so that if you are talking about me you are talking about my country. Namely, I am my country. Hence, country can also be employed to refer to the individual (ibid.). In short, this word "conveys the holistic, multi-dimensional notion where people, animals, plants, dreaming, underground, the earth, minerals, waters are all encompassed" (ibid.). The concept of country can be taken as the key to comprehending the whole Aboriginal cultures. Deborah Bird Rose's interpretation of country unfolds a totally different cultural perspective:

> Country in Aboriginal English is not only a common noun but also a proper noun. People talk about country in the same way that they would talk about a person: they speak to country, sing to country, visit country, worry about country, and feel sorry for country, and long for country. People say that country knows, hears, smells, takes notice, takes care, and is sorry or happy. Country is not a generalized or undifferentiated type of place, [...] rather; country is a living entity with a yesterday, today and tomorrow, with a consciousness, and a will toward life. Because of this richness, country is home, and peace; nourishment for body, mind, and spirit; heart's ease. (*Nourishing Terrains* 7)

Hence, country is generally assumed to be "alive and articulate" and plays a great diversity of functions in Aboriginals' daily life (Manes

15). Besides, country is a multi-dimensional and all-embracing concept whose scope even covers the sea and sky, for Aboriginal people may use such expressions as land country, sea country and even sky country (Rose, *Nourishing Terrains* 8). Like the way they relate to the land country, the sea country is also "known, named, sung, danced, [...], loved, harvested and cared for". So far as ownership is concerned, "Aboriginal people own both the land and the surrounding waters" (ibid.), though their concept of ownership differs vastly from that in western culture.

As one grows up in such cultural environments, one picks up signs and symbols through which country expresses its moods and gets the knowledge of one's own country. It must be emphasized that knowledge about country can only be acquired by living in it, for knowledge is with distinctive local features. And this local and detailed knowledge that has been tested and built up over time is the basis for being in country (Rose, *Nourishing Terrains* 13). Eric Michaels developed this understanding from his work with Warlpiri people in Yuendumu:

> Aboriginal society de-emphasises material wealth, and values information. Lacking writing, most information is personal property, stored mentally. Dances, designs, stories, and songs are all formats for storing information and for displaying it in ceremonial and educational settings. (qtd. in Rose, *Nourishing Terrains* 32)

Such information is the knowledge that is held dearly by the Aboriginesto which the outsiders usually have no easy access. But one thing is certain: all the information aims to construct a harmonious symbiosis between humanity and the natural world. Predominant in animistic Aboriginal cultures are notions "that all the phenomenal world is alive in the sense of being inspirited — including humans, cultural artifacts, and natural entities, both biological and 'inert'" and "that not only is the nonhuman world alive, but it is filled with articulate subjects, able to communicate with humans" (Lowie 99, 135). Thus, theirs is "a world of autonomous speakers whose intents one ignores at one's peril" (Manes 15).

Since country is treated as a person, the communications between people and country are "two-way" and depend on an individual's capacity to discern and interpret the occurrences and places (Rose, *Nourishing Terrains* 13). As mentioned above, the ability lies in the mastery of the highly localized knowledge that has been passed from mouth to mouth.

In western culture, such ideas tend to be dismissed easily in that they can be relegated to "the realm of superstition and irrationality" (Manes 17). But in Aboriginal cultures, the communications with other species in nature are quite normal. They communicate with the birds, rivers by calling out, singing songs, and they believe the birds can understand them. As a matter of fact, in their cultures, there are many stories that help to trace a sort of kinship between people and some animal species. Aboriginal concept of kinship sharply differs from that held by the Westerners on the ground that it is not decided by blood only. Neither is it limited to the scope of the same species. Bill Neidjie of the Gagudju calls "eagle our brother, /like dingo our brother" (sic) (46). Virtually, it's not difficult to find Aboriginal songs and poems in which trees, animals and even rocks are called our brothers or sisters because in the Aboriginal worldview, "all the trees and the birds are your relations" (Rose, *Nourishing Terrains* 14).

"These multi-faceted relationships are holistic. The purpose and meaning of life are located in the relationships between people, their home countries, their Dreaming, the plants and animals, geological formations and waters, and each other" (Rose, *Nourishing Terrains* 40). In sum, animism is the key to Aboriginal cultures.

Country, the all-inclusive complex, is the "nourishing terrain" to all the creatures including human beings. Conversely, the country is taken care of by the Aborigines. Deborah B. Rose's study indicates that "management of the life of the country constituted one of Aboriginal people's strongest and deepest purposes in life, as well as making up much of their daily lives in so far as it is still possible for people to take care of their country" (Rose, *Nourishing Terrains* 10).

It must be pointed out that Aboriginal people are caretakers of their country for the sake of common welfare rather than for their own sake. In their cultures, all entities in the matrix are interdependent and self-interest cannot exist without common interest and thus is meaningless. If one endangers the interest of the country, one is in essence putting oneself in danger, which constitutes the hard but essential law of interdependence in their life (ibid.). Human beings are only one member in the community of country, neither higher nor lower than other species. Thus, they are not privileged to "take supreme control, or to define the ultimate value of the country" (ibid.). But the Aboriginals generally understand it part of their responsibility to look after their country. The notion that "if you don't look after country, country won't look after you" is prevalent among the tribe members who unanimously agree that the relationship between the tribes and their country is reciprocal (qtd. in Rose, *Nourishing Terrains* 49). Therefore, theirs are typical de-anthropocentric cultures in which humans are linked to ecosystems and reversely entrusted with the responsibility of looking after instead of dominating over nature. Hence, there exists "a fundamental philosophical gap between European cultures of conquest and Aboriginal cultures of balance" (Rose, *Nourishing Terrains* 11). This discrepancy is also discerned by Silas Roberts, the first Chairman of the Northern Land Council①, who recognizes the intimate link between everything that

① See more information about North Land Council at <http://en.wikipedia.org/wiki/Northern_Land_Council>.

is natural and Aboriginals that see themselves as part of nature and cherish the special connection with nature. He proceeds to point out that the westerners tend to adopt the opposite opinion, namely, all things natural on Earth are part of us, or belong to us (qtd. in Rose, *Nourishing Terrains* 26), a mindset unavoidably leading to anthropocentrism.

The aboriginal concept of country highlights people's emotional attachments or spiritual relationship to the land (Jackson 10). Aboriginal people say, "healthy country means healthy people", reflecting a sort of symbiotic concern with the physical environment (ibid.). Dr Sue Jackson, a senior researcher, further illustrates, "the environment — people nexus — implicit in sustainability — brings ways of seeing people's material economic needs and their social values in line with the limits or requirements of the environment", which makes the indigenous an ethic group who are born environment caretakers (10). Moreover, animism, special concepts of kinship and holism well justify the assumption that the Aborigines are spontaneous environmentalists. But Deborah B. Rose cautions that "Aboriginal people were not conservationists in this contemporary sense of the term" because "the terms 'conservation' and 'conservationist' are contemporary terms brought into being by the urgency of the ecological issues which surround us". Yet, to get rid of the ecological crisis, westerners can benefit a lot by referring to how the Aborigines handle the relationship between human and the land. However, in the collaborations between the two, "it is essential to acknowledge that many Aboriginal people take quite different views about conservation from those developed by scientists and other concerned citizens" (Rose, *Nourishing Terrains* 4).

Aborigines' intimate link to their country makes it natural for them to take a holistic attitude. All things in nature are sentient subjects but not lifeless materials or instruments. So humans shouldn't spoil the land and they must be very careful in the use of it. If it is well cared, all will benefit and prosper. In this kinship, "people and country take care of each other" and therefore constitute "a system of reciprocity and respect" (Rose, *Nourishing Terrains* 49, 44).

Moreover, it's meaningful to note that the self in Aboriginal cultures is not estranged or hyperseparated self but relational self and ecological self, for one "includes the goal of the flourishing of earth others and the earth community among its own primary ends, and hence respects or cares for these others for their own sake" (Plumwood, *Feminism* 155). Relational or ecological self is a concept put forward by the Australian eco-philosopher Val Plumwood in 1993 to help remove the deep-rooted binary mode of thinking and reconstruct a friendly relationship with nature. Many similarities are found between her suggestion and the core values honored in Aboriginal cultures except that there is no concept of self/other in the later. Aboriginals implement a kind of democracy among different members of the ecological community in which humans must shoulder the obligations of nurturance. Therefore, Christopher Manes passionately advises that we "leap away from the rhetoric of humanism" and "draw on the ontological humility and egalitarianism of native American or other primal cultures, with their attentiveness to place and local processes" (25). Judith Watson, an artist in residence at Western Australian Academy of Performing Arts, admits "the strong connections that aboriginal people have of the land by their family culture" and believes that "it can be a very valuable learning for anybody from non-aboriginal background" (Dinham and Phillips, *Landscape and You*). Through the learning, she hopes, the white Australians will learn how to respect aboriginal cultures and land (ibid.). In the forword for *Kakadu Man Bill Neidjie*, Clyde Holding, Minister for Aboriginal affairs in 1984, expresses similar opinion:

> I am hopeful that in time, the values of a dominant white community will be sufficiently flexible to encompass within it some of the valuable insights that Aboriginal people learnt in their 50,000 years occupation of

> its land. If that is possible, then Australia will not only be a more compassionate and caring society, it will be a society in harmony with itself and its environment. (9)

He further points out that Aboriginal cultures and values can "provide us with an insight, and possibly an understanding, of a tradition and a culture far older than anything that has thus far prevailed in Europe, and hopefully give all a new insight and perception of our own land, and our need to care for it and preserve it" (Holding 9).

In fact, many Australian artists have been doing the exact thing of exploiting indigenous cultures. Tim Winton, who taps the rich pool of Aboriginal ecological wisdom, is just one case. The coming discussions will uncover traces of Aboriginal philosophy scattered in his works, which indicates a positive cross-cultural stance held by the author. As the historian Stuart Macintyre puts it, "by embracing the Aboriginal past, non-Aboriginal Australians attached themselves to their country" (4).

2.2 Reverence for Life

It can't be denied that western culture never lacks thoughts and values showing care and concern about the natural world. In his famous essay "The Historical Roots of Our Ecological Crisis", Lynn White Jr. advises people to learn from Saint Francis of Assisi (1181? —1226), the greatest radical and spiritual Christian revolutionary, for "his belief in the virtue of humility — not merely for the individual but for man as a species". St. Francis' greatness lies in his efforts to "depose man from his monarchy over creation and set up a democracy of all God's creatures" (13). Max Oelschlaeger also praises Saint Francis of Assisi for his belief in that "God's spirit animates all creation and that humankind is merely one life-form among many" in his monograph *The*

Idea of Wilderness (1991) (72 ~ 73). Pitifully, as an alternative Christian view of nature and of man that rested on a unique sort of pan-psychism, Franciscanism was suppressed and failed (White 12~13). So did a great variety of thoughts and philosophies that had attempted to construct a harmonious relationship between human race and the natural world in the west. But one figure is more or less an exception that is lucky enough not to be buried into history. His name is Albert Schweitzer (1875—1965), the famous German theologian, musician, philosopher and physician. His theory continues to be of increasing theoretical and practical significance and becomes a vital inspiration for many later ecologists in wider ecological ethics so that when the pioneer American ecologist Rachel Carson published her masterpiece *Silent Spring* she dedicates it to Albert Schweitzer, who was lauded as one of the intellectual and moral giants of his age for his great achievements.

It is Albert Schweitzer who expanded the scope of moral care to include all life forms and put forward the conception of "reverence for life". "He repeatedly drew attention to the inadequacy of human-centric thought as a rational critique of the world and sought to widen the scope of ethics to incorporate concern for all manifestations of life" (Barsam X). He was a pioneer of challenging human-centered ethics and establishing life-centered ethics and foresaw contemporary environmental and animal concerns. Not only did Schweitzer help put the issue on the agenda, he also offered philosophical and theological foundations for its solution. And his theory is best represented in the concept of "reverence for life" which implies a sense of spiritual unity with nature. It's not exaggerating to say that "reverence for life" offers us a guideline as regards how to handle animals. In a way, Albert Schweitzer was "an iconic figure in the now burgeoning life-centered ethics movement" (Barsam 120). As to me, the ethic of reverence for life is vividly embodied in *Swimmer*, Winton's virgin fiction.

Swimmer was published in 1982 when the author was 22 years old and garnered him the Vogel Award for the best "first book" by a young writer. Winton demonstrates deep concern with the relationship between mankind and nature from the very beginning of his writing career. In *Swimmer*, the focus is on the relationship between man and fish. As discussed in Chapter I, when his second fiction *Shallows* was published two years later, his attention is fully occupied by the concern about the destiny of the largest marine mammal — whales. Winton soon becomes an outspoken eco-author and environmentalist.

Tim Winton admits the influence from the American author Ernest Hemingway on more than one occasion and careful readers may discern obvious intextuality between *Swimmer* and *The Old Man and the Sea* (hence *Man and Sea*). The prologue of *Swimmer* presents a fight between an eight-year-old boy Jerra and a big fish. Little Jerra fights with the big fish bare-handedly, with his father looking on. Given the sizes and powers of the two sides, it seems to be a fair one. Winton depicts the fish as a real rival for the young boy and endows it with the spirit of perseverance. Virtually, both the boy and the fish demonstrate courage and tenacity which allocates them equal place as a worthy fighter. This plot easily reminds readers of the strife between Santiago and the marlin. Santiago feels the strength and resolution in the fish and thus grows love and respect for his rival in their fight. So is Jerra. In the process of desperate struggle, the fish's strong "will-to-live", in Albert Schweitzer's term, is confronted by the boy. Schweitzer describes the live world thus: "I am life which wills to live, and I exist in the midst of life which wills to live" (*Anthology* 248). Using empathy, Schweitzer admits life of all forms the will and right to live, which directly refutes the western philosophy that emphasizes the privilege of mankind in the world. The fish's firm resolution to fight and strong will to live are given a full display via verbs such as "grunting, threshing, clenching and unclenching, bashing and finally mumbling" (1). To sum up, Winton depicts the fish as a true fighter that can be killed but not possessed.

Likewise, the eight-year-old also acts as a genuine warrior despite the bleeding of his palms and the desire to cry. He is scared but not conquered. They are both Hemingwayesque code heroes that can be destroyed but not defeated.

The intextuality between *Swimmer* and *Man and Sea* also resides in other aspects. Both authors show due respect to wild life and treat them as equals. Their depictions of fish are both humane and compassionate. In *Swimmer*, the fish's mate is cruising in the water during the struggle and doesn't disappear until it dies. Winton's work reveals his belief that animals have love and devotion too. Schweitzer comments that "whenever love and devotion are glimpsed, reverence for life is not far off, since one grows from the other"①. A rereading of *Man and Sea* shows that Hemingway not only depicts a porpoise couple who "plays and makes jokes and loves one another" but also claims that they and the flying fish are all our brothers, an opinion that Tim Winton would concur with (48). Furthermore, Santiago's recollection of hooking one of a pair of marlin further proves the echoing between the texts. When the female fish is hooked and making a desperate fight, the male stays on with her beside the boat all the time as Santiago gaffs and clubs her to death. In Hemingway's text, the male marlin even jumps high into the air to see his lover before departure to the deep ocean (49~50). On seeing this, the old man and his apprentice feel sorry about it and would beg her pardon (Hemingway 50). Similar emotions beset the boy Jerra who wishes that "it would be alive again" and refuses to open it up for the pearl, which is the main purpose of the killing (2). In the meantime, he is also obsessed with sadness and remorse for killing him in the face of his mate, who must be stricken with deep sorrow at losing him at the moment. In other words, the sensitive boy is emotionally tortured by the

① "The Ethics of Reverence for Life" <http://www.chapman.edu/schweitzer/sch.reading4.html>.

dilemma whether to mutilate or to return the fish to its mate. After the incident, a sense of guilt continues to haunt him till his young adulthood. This explains why he denies having seen a big fish die later during the talk with the old hermit. He even tells a lie: "I always clubbed 'em before they suffered. Didn't like to see 'em die" (21).

The deep ecologist Arne Naess once explained in an interview: "When they see a death struggle [...], when they see animals suffering, they may identify with a life form they usually don't identify with. Such situations offer us an opportunity to develop a more mature point of view. [...] these deep feelings are religious" (Bodian 30). While experiencing the desperate struggle of the fish, witnessing the loyalty of its mate, Jerra is deeply touched. The reverence for them is intertwined with a sense of bewilderment and guilt because as a young boy he can neither afford to give up the fight to become a laughing stock before his father nor forgive himself for the killing. In view of his young age, Jerra's feelings are rather complicated.

Winton concerns himself with the relationship between humanity and other-than-human animals all the time. Thus, the topic whether man can really control the fate of fish becomes one worthy of contemplation and negotiation between Jerra, who is now in his early twenties, and Judy, a girl he meets at the bar. Like most common people, Judy believes that once you catch the fish, you can decide its fate (88). So it is a problem of power that mankind exerts over other species. Little Jerra has caught the fish and attempted to control it. However, the turrum negates his power first by demonstrating a firm will in the struggle for the right to stay alive and then by choosing to die rather than to be controlled. Hence, Jerra can't see eye to eye with Judy:

> 'The fish. You said you had power over it; but it's not really true. Put him in the bag. Fine, he's dead; you scale him, gut him, and eat him. But if you throw it back there's no guarantee he's going to live.'

> [...]
>
> 'The fish might survive the hook and the exposure and take off. Or he might be weakened and be easy prey for a bigger fish, or he might die in a couple of minutes, just from shock.'
>
> (Judy:) 'So, the fish decides its own fate?'
>
> 'Sort of. Maybe the fish's strength, or something else; but whether he lives or dies won't be decided by throwing him back.' (92~93)

The discussions sound trivial but they insinuate the negation of power over other species assumed to be held by human beings. That the weak stands as the prey to the strong is the law of nature. Man can kill and eat fish if he is strong enough. But if he chooses to let it go, the fish and other natural factors jointly decide its fate, which has nothing to do with man's will at all and thus depose human racc its self-appointed power to control.

Moreover, the fish, an ordinary aquatic life, actually is a mysterious species out of man's reach: "There was nothing to him like that grunt of surrender, the gentle collapse from deep within, [...] Nothing. Like knowing or believing in subtle defeat" (93). As Schweitzer puts it, "the mystery of life is always too profound for us, and that its value is beyond our capacity to estimate" (*Anthology* 270). Since man cannot understand fish, how can they claim to have power over it?

Some animals have to be killed for others to survive and hunting has been the antique means of adding protein to people's diet. Then, the question is not whether we should kill, but how to kill properly or decently. To an ethical individual, killing without causing too much pain is morally more acceptable than inflicting slow and agonizing death on any live being. And if you eradicate life to satisfy basic needs of survival, you are more well-grounded. These ethics and principles are highly valued by Schweitzer and are observed by Winton's characters when killing becomes necessary in our story.

There is a meaningful dialogue between Jerra and the nameless old hermit about the hunting of a kangaroo by snare:

> (Jerra): 'Take long for a roo to die when you snare it?'
>
> [...]
>
> (Hermit): 'Not if you do a good job. There's ways.'. (sic)
>
> (Jerra): 'What do you do for a snare?'
>
> (Hermit): 'Pinner wire.'
>
> (Jerra): 'Must be painful as hell.'
>
> (Hermit): 'If you make a mess. Bad to mess up an animal. Killin's bad enough without mutilatin'. This one went down with his legs caught, see?' He showed Jerra the raw patches in the fur. 'Lucky I heard 'im go down, or I wouldn't've found him till later in the day. Just slit 'is throat while he was stunned. Didn't take long.'
>
> (Jerra): 'Still, a pretty awful way to go, especially if you don't hear. Could lie there for hours.'
>
> (Hermit): 'You can only try to be around.' (*Swimmer*, 140~141)

Obviously, they both show great care about the sentiency and agony of the trapped. Jerra believes snaring an animal can be "painful as hell" because it usually takes a long time for it to die. The old hermit agrees with Jerra that to let a life die in that way is to "mess up an animal". So after setting a snare, he tries to be around so that when anything is caught he can come to end its life quickly to avoid the slow and painful process of losing its vitality gradually for hours. Both characters treat animals as equals, and they naturally care about his fear and agony as they do with a human being and they can't bear it if the animals are killed in an inhumane way. Schweitzer defines ethics as "nothing else than reverence for all life" (*Anthology* 259). In traditional western culture ethics is only concerned with mankind or rather, the white and then gradually applies to colored races after persistent struggles by the oppressed races. Schweitzer further broadens its scope to cover animal creations of God. Schweitzer believes that reverence for life is "the highest rationality" and should be the fundamental principle of morality (*Anthology* 260).

This episode indicates that Winton takes seriously the value of all living things and shows ethical care towards them. Schweitzer declares if an ethical system is only concerned with the attitude to mankind it is not complete, for it lacks the relationship with the universe (*Anthology* 281 ~ 282). The two characters of Winton are laudable for being sensitive to the pains and sufferings of other living beings and demonstrating ethical care to them.

Schweitzer also puts forward "the law of necessity" for dealing with animals, which allows killing for meeting vital needs. To the nameless beachcomber in *Swimmer*, who has been living a secluded life along the coast for two decades, fishing and hunting are the major modes of sustenance. Obviously, he is well-justified for the killing. While trying to show ethic care towards wildlife, we have to admit that humans are forced to "to live at the cost of other life and to incur again and again the guilt of destroying and injuring life" (qtd. in Barsam 134). Winton's novel underscores that man should make full use of the food he obtains so that the animals are not wasted. Namely, life should not be abused when killed. Similarly, the Aboriginals "look after the animals, birds and land" but also "eat them not to waste it" (qtd. in Rose, *Nourishing Terrains* 67). Traditional station philosophy says that nothing should go to waste. And it is immoral and irresponsible and therefore despicable to waste the wildlife after killing. Gary Snyder points out that "primary peoples are our teachers" "in their practice of killing and eating with gentleness and thanks" (*Practice of the Wild* 20 ~ 21) and he argues that "they (other beings) hate to see themselves wasted" (20). It's interesting to cite another instance from Winton's later work — *Breath*, in which the male character Sando accidentally bumps into a kangaroo while driving. He brings it back home to peel and eat, which is quite odd and rare in the 1970s as can be felt from Bruce Pikelet's repulsion while grudgingly accepting a piece of meat as a gift. Sando's act can also be interpreted by his being a hippie and a member of the Countercultural Movement whose major values include such positive appeals as world peace, gender equality, harmony and environmentalism. Once a hippie, Tim Winton wears an obvious symbol of it — the ponytail till today[①](徐 91).

Besides, as the mutilated character Sam Flack in *That Eye, the Sky* puts it, "everyone who eats vegetables should grow their own at least once, and everyone who eats meat should kill it at least once" so that they see that animals and plants are meaningful and elementary for human survival and human race is accordingly responsible for them (Winton, 85). As a result, humanity, plants and animals form an organic whole.

In the third part of the novel, another battle flares up between young lad Jerra and a huge fish under the sea, for he wants to get the pearl assumed to be in its head. Jerra eventually manages to kill the big fish, which is almost bigger than him in size, a feat of which he is proud. This plot clearly echoes the opening scene of the fight between little boy Jerra and the big fish and hence forms a loop. Sadly, what Jerra finds is only the grey little brain and the pearl in a kinghie's head turns out "an old fisherman's myth" (146). When the seaside recluse learns about this, he fervently yells at Jerra: "What are you? Gotta mutilate fish to find out what you want? Why don't you hack yourself open?" The unnamed beachcomber feels indignant about the whole thing and thinks it is unfair for the big fish, which is "a beautiful blue thing" and is equal to man as a form of life. Winton reveals his viewpoint about

① Translation mine.

killing wildlife through the old man: "Bad enough you hack the poor bastard up; but you just left it there for the bloody bastard seagulls!" (147)

Schweitzer puts it in his *Memoirs of Childhood and Youth*:

> There slowly grew up in me an unshakeable conviction that we have no right to inflict suffering and death on another living creature unless there is some unavoidable necessity for it, and that we ought, all of us, to feel what a horrible thing it is to cause suffering and death out of mere thoughtlessness. (*Anthology* 275)

So it is unethical and unacceptable to kill without justification. As Schweitzer's often quoted statement goes, "good consists in maintaining, assisting and enhancing life, and that to destroy, to harm or to hinder life is evil" (*Anthology* 259 ~ 260). Experienced critics may have noticed many a similarity between theories of environmental ethics by modern western critics and Aboriginal ecophilosophy. The indigenous philosophy holds life to be inherently significant and, rather than mutilating life, celebrating and promoting life have always been the motif of human activity (Rose, *Nourishing Terrain* 11). Bruce Rose notes that "values and judgments which support playing favourites with some species over others do not easily fit into the Aboriginal world view" (qtd. in D. B. Rose, *Nourishing Terrain* 11). Equality is an obvious feature in Aboriginals' attitude to their brother emu or lizard.

The old hermit further points out that it is unbearable for Jerra to have left the fish with "*no guts*" and "*no head*" with those sea birds hovering above (147 emphases original). As a hermit, the old man doesn't care much about material wealth that the ordinary people would mind. However, he lives carefully in awe of elements of nature and hence it's natural for him to be concerned with man's proper behaviors in nature. As he sees it, the killing committed by Jerra is totally nonsensical and unfair to the turrum. He is so enthusiastic to preach ecological justice to Jerra that he forgets that he himself has committed murder by burning his wife when she got pregnant probably with another man and decided to desert him. Is it contradictory and ironic for a murderer to do this? We have to admit that it is. Thus a kind of tension is created between the old man as a natural being who sounds fair and righteous and a social individual who deprives another person's right to live, which alludes to the alienation of mankind in modern society. Then, isn't nature a better guide that cultivates in us a sense of reverence, justice and responsibility?

Then how does Jerra feel about the killing? Is he really proud of his achievement? "I was a crook. Had water in me guts! Jerra couldn't get close enough to the fire. He was freezing and his head pumped" (147). Jerra is experiencing a difficult time and he feels equally bad because of both the unnecessary killing and the disillusion. By sacrificing a turrum, Winton awakens the young man from his nightmare and gets him out of the abyss of incestuous affiliation to the neighbor aunt. In a way, Jerra's soul has experienced a sort of catharsis due to the death of a fish and the disequilibrium of Jerra's spiritual ecology is somewhat resumed.

Reference for life is also embodied in the agricultural environmental ethics. According to Pascalev Assya, agricultural ethics refers to "the values and moral issues involved in food production and farming practices" (23). Agricultural environmental ethics is an important area of ethical inquiry into the interactions between agricultural production and environmental protection aiming to strike a balance between them.

A description of the kangaroo corpse in the landscape of wheat field in *Cloudstreet* engraves deeply on the readers' mind. When the kangaroos die, "the fallen animals lay like a new stone formation, the color of granite" (198). It sounds rather odd to associate animate kangaroos with lifeless stones. These images, combined with the analysis in the preceding paragraphs, easily conjure up discussions about whether animals possess sentience. Albert Schweitzer puts forward the notion of "reverence for life" and theologians Charles Birch and John B. Cobb, Jr. develop it by systematically differentiating the intrinsic value of various life forms:

> First, they find rocks', cells', and plants' experience to be "dim" and holding only "instrumental" value. Entities of this type can "appropriately be treated primarily as means". Second, in animal life, conscious feeling arises. With this "increased complexity of the central nervous system and the development of the brain," they "find every reason to suppose there is increased capacity for richness of experience". In contradistinction to other nonhuman life forms, animals "cannot rightly be treated as mere means"; animals "make a claim upon us," and we have "duties" to them in a way different to other nonhuman beings. Third, human beings, because of their "explosion of intellectual activity" and highest degree of consciousness, are at the summit. (qtd. in Barsam 135)

This division is controversial for its anthropocentricism but at least they believe that animals deserve more care and respect than lifeless stones. In Liu's interview with Winton, the author affirms the influences from such ecological thinkers as John Cobb, Bill McKibben, Charles Birch and A.N. Whitehead (《当代外语研究》64). The readers may easily discern the linkage between the text and the theory by Birch and Cobb quoted above.

Winton's comparison of kangaroos to granite prompts the readers to consider what if animals are treated as stones. *Homo sapiens* would demonstrate maximum indifference and ignorance about other animals' ability to perceive pain and terror. Then they would show no sympathy, no compassion, to say nothing of reverence for them. Here, the bodies of the kangaroos are in effect silent condemnation and people will have a pang of ecological conscience. Furthermore, the fact is laid bare that farmers have always been adopting "short-term profit maximizing practices that are inimical to the long-term ecological stability of the regions in which they farm" (Thomson, *The Spirit of the Soil* 14). Wheat farm virtually becomes a bloody battlefield between *Homo sapiens* and the wildlife. As I see it, here Winton manages to draw people's attention to the customary agricultural practice by generations of farmers to foreground the fact that mankind survives at the expense of other species and they will be extinct if we continue to turn a blind eye to it. The scene of killing kangaroos on the farm is thus meaningful and reveals the author's ecological care and environmental ethics towards endemic wildlife in the wheatbelt.

After finishing his work, Quick could still hear other kangaroos out in the wheat again, "trampling, eating, swishing through". Then he exclaims, "Lord, they were eating up the country!" (198). The ironic fact is that it is human beings, other than the kangaroos, that have been encroaching the natural habitats of a variety of species by clearing the land and cutting down the trees to make room for farmland and that should be responsible for the drastic decline of the diversity of species. Agricultural expansion means less territory for feral fauna and flora. Aboriginal cultures dictate that the "celebration of life is a celebration of the interconnection of life in a particular place, which also includes the humans who celebrate" (Rose, *Nourishing Terrain* 11). Winton's depiction of kangaroo hunting tells us that humanity should make relentless endeavors to protect the system of life while pursuing agricultural development, allowing adequate space for other organisms to thrive and prosper together with human race, which is also showing due reverence for life.

2.3 Birth of Nature's Children

To reestablish the bond between white Australians and the land, Tim Winton depicts a group of protagonists that can be called children of nature, by which I mean characters that grow up more in natural environment than in social surroundings and therefore are at ease in nature but are somewhat misfits in community. In this section, I would explore Tim Winton's "commitment to nurture the birth of a new kind of human being, one who is ennatured rather than alienated" (P. D. Murphy, *Farther Afield* 32). Through the analysis, I am trying to see whether to Winton a harmonious relationship with nature would derive from an intimate direct contact with it. And I'd also check the possible inference that the closer one stays with nature, the more likely that nature is to be loved, revered and protected, and the more likely that a harmonious tie is to be built between them. In this section, several such protagonists will be analyzed to shed light on Winton's attempts to reconstruct a close bond between the white settlers and their adopted land. We may still remember Winton's role as a landscape writer. His identification with his homeland, both as an individual and as literary personae, is best embodied in his fiction in which children of nature protagonists are to be found. Many critics as well as the author himself admit that you can never emphasize too much the significance of the place in his fiction, for it is where they grow up, cope with their pains, come to realize that they are natural beings before cultural beings.

Winton's surfing fiction *Breath*, another Miles Franklin Literary Prize Winner, was published several years after the success of marine environmental protection campaign against the commercial development of the Ningaloo Reef area, which typically represents the unique and pristine landscape of Western Australia. In this campaign the author declares and later reiterates repeatedly in his works as well as in a variety of interviews that Australians share an umbilical bond with the land (Ben-Messahel, "Blokes, Water" 13). In Eleanor Wachtel's interview with the author, Winton is full of pride when talking about "the big blue sky, red dirt, then suddenly white beach" in his homeland and he admits that the landscape in the littoral area of Western

Australia is so much part of him that it becomes his only subject (64). "The coastal environment, a central feature in *Breath*, is not only a backdrop to the story but becomes, like the water, a character and a signifier for the protagonists and for the plot" (Ben-Messahel, "Blokes, Water" 13).

Long coastline and sandy beach inAustralia render it the surfing paradise and breed an ardent love for sea sports among Australians. "Like a number of Australian authors, Winton uses landscape to construct the idea that the land spawns Australian culture, that place is a signifier for culture" (Ben-Messahel, "Blokes, Water" 16). Growing up in close contact with the fabric of the coast, Tim Winton is an avid surfer himself. Partly owing to the author's idiosyncratic addiction to the sea, many of Winton's narratives have a surfing theme or focus (McGloin 110) and quite a few protagonists in Winton's fiction, male or female, children or adults, are superb surfers and divers. The teenage protagonist in his trilogy *Lockie Leonard* is obsessed with surfing. In the first episode, *Human Torpedo*, he organizes a surfing club — the Angelus Boardriders Association. In the second book, his crush on Dot also happens because he is intoxicated by her amazing agility at surfing. *Breath*, "a retrospective narrative of 1970s surfing culture", is another case in point (McGloin 109). It's one of the masterpieces in Australian surfing narratives.

"Winton writes about surfing with an insider's knowledge and an unparalleled lyrical beauty" (O'Reilly, "Testing" 170): "Winton's virtuosity is to move seamlessly from the character's honest speech into an elevated but absolutely direct account of what it is like to fling yourself at great waves" (Hensher 36). As a matter of fact, many surfers themselves find it hard to convey the thrill of the sport, for it brings you momentary ecstasy and it's even harder to take it as the motif in a novel. Thus, the American literary commentator Nathanael O'Reilly believes "*Breath* breaks new literary ground [...] and *Breath* might be the first great surfing novel" ("Testing" 170). Fewer people would link surfing on the roaring sea to stories of teenagers, as what Winton does in *Breath*. Generally, "in this story of surfing, he does what a great writer can do to make us see, while sitting in our armchairs, exactly what it would be like to stand on a bit of hardboard while a 30-foot wave defeats our attempts to float on it" (Hensher 36).

Ever since the Second World War, the Australian government had adopted a large-scale immigration policy for reasons of both development and defence. The program was mainly to draw British immigrants and high levels of immigration continued to the 1970s (Carter 254). The story is set in the 1970s, the period "when Australia was going through radical changes, when complete independence from Britain was surfacing in political discourse, when voices were raised to support the dismantling of colonial remains" (Ben-Messahel, "Blokes, Water" 13). Still, the first generation of immigrants, mainly from Great Britain and other European countries, was then experiencing a difficult process of emotional and cognitive identification with the new land. Winton objectively records the shift in attitudes towards the land of Australia from one generation to another. Before unfolding the motif of the fiction, Winton depicts the life style of the older generation and highlights their aloofness and detachment from the alien land. The typical attitude to the sea was a mixture of indifference and dread. They fished down "the broad shallows of the inlet" and rarely "ventured out" to the sea. Pikelet's father is a good representative who "would never leave the shelter of the estuary and no one, man or boy, could shame him into going further". To the land, "they were equally anxious or ambivalent". As Pikelet puts it, "they always seemed rather municipal" and "in Sawyer you kept to the mill, the town, the river" (12). The attitudes towards the sea and land betray a strong sense of estrangement felt by the inhabitants and insinuate a sad cloud of displacement and their sentimental attachment to their home country in Europe.

In contrast, Pike Bruce (Pikelet) and Loon Ivan (Loonie), the native-born Australians, never hide their love for the land or their obsession with the sea. The younger generation's affiliation with the land is something that the author hopes to highlight: unlike our transplanted ancestors, we are brought up as natives to this land and we belong here. Their attachment to the sea and fascination for surfing can be taken as the convenient signs of purposeful indigenization. So to speak, "his novel is not simply about the waves and the riding of a surfboard, it is also about the individual in context, the individual as a component of place, defined by place as Bruce Pikelet suggests: 'We were little more than animated flotsam' (*Breath* 25)" (Ben-Messahel, "Blokes, Water" 16). Focus of discussion in this section will be on the role played by surfing in the formation story of the two pre-adolescents in *Breath*. My research proposal is that maturation in the course of surfing makes it possible for the sea to shape the individual and communal identity and forges a natural bond between man and sea.

Surfing as a form of extreme sports taps the wildness in an individual and helps to build up the masculinity in a boy. Fed up with the "myth of a national male type based on the literary image of white bushmen" (Moore 44), Winton wants to show that men are capable of something graceful, as expressed in *Breath*: "How strange it was to see men do something beautiful. Something pointless and elegant, as though nobody saw or cared" (28). Seen from historical perspective, surfing as a popular form of sport in Australia has replaced war to become an efficient way of cultivating masculinity due to the fact that such inherent masculine traits as courage, strength, fitness, competiveness and adventure are all put into full play in surfing. *Breath* is an appropriate footnote to "surfing's iconic status in Australia as a national trope" (McGloin 110). Tim Winton happens to have "that hunger for wildness that he gives the boys" (Steger, "The Sea Side" 26).

I agree with the Chinese critic Zaizhong Xu who reads the novel against the cultural backdrop of Countercultural Movement in the 1970s when the hippies like Sando in *Breath* retreated from big cities in the eastern coast such as Sydney and Melbourne to the remoter and smaller places in the western coast to pursue an unconventional life. Xu points out extreme sports are popular with counter-cultural youths due to such features as freedom, simplicity, peril and thrill. In the meantime, they cater well to such ideals as pursuit of freedom, escape from city and connection with nature, and challenge of the physical limit (91). Other reasons also account for this addiction to surfing by the protagonists who are on the cusp of adolescence. For Pikelet and Loonie, to grow up is to be conscious of one's ordinariness and to remove it. Seeing surfing for the first time, Pikelet is deeply intoxicated by its beauty. Captivated by the grace and distinction that go with surfing, they surf to get rid of the drabness of life in the mill-town, the monotony of regular breath and to avoid the ordinariness in themselves. In the 1970s, common people went hunting and fishing only for survival. But they surf for the unique charm and beauty of the sport itself and for demonstration of their personal feat. In a way, what Pikelet and Loonie attempt to do is something unthinkable to the ordinary townsfolk.

From the narration, it's easy to see that Australian coast is the haven for surfers with abundant sites to be exploited. "The characters' initiation to surfing unravels as [...] the discovery of a new world, a world encompassing the real nature of Australia as when the first explorers and settlers reached the shores" (Ben-Messahel, "Blokes, Water" 13). Sando, the former surfing champion and the guru for the two green hands, turns out to be an irresponsible controller who pushes young children too much. Yet, the "escalation of the surfer's ambition is beautifully done, as the two boys and their heroic mentor move away into shark-infested deeps, the open ocean and 30-foot waves" (Hensher 36). The sites for surfing become increasingly remote and perilous as their skill and courage multiply. Barney's is the shark's home. One spring morning witnesses the close contact between the shark that "surfaced like a sub in the channel, rolled over beside Loonie and fixed him with one terrible, black eye before sliding away again" and Loonie who thus won the reputation among surfers. Therefore, Barney's makes them stronger and more mature and is held as the landmark (91). Nautilus, a navigation hazard with multiple warnings on map, is also a "sharkpit" and "a seal colony", but more treacherous (140). The hint that Sando hopes them to attempt at Nautilus sickens Pikelet and drives him to his limit, for in the circle of surfers one's status is decided by the sizes of the ocean swells that one drives.

Virtually, Pikelet and Loonie represent two distinctive ways of coming of age despite the obvious similarities. Loonie embodies the wildest image of an arrogant individual who allows his cocky self to expand limitlessly. But the real fear resides in fearlessness. Loonie's recklessness and Sando's menace both make Pikelet uncomfortable. In contrast, Pikelet feels the charm and glamour in surfing and he admires and reveres the power and beauty in the sea as well. It is also hinted that one has to learn to cooperate with elements of nature to best demonstrate the superb beauty of the art of surfing, which is no less elegant than ballet only that it is performed on the stage of the sea. Looking back at his restless youth days in his middle age, Pike Bruce realizes that they've embarked upon an unusual road of growing up with no return by devoting themselves wholeheartedly to surfing. He now clearly sees the heavy toll it takes on his whole life. Conquering nature is virtually as ridiculous as conquering one's own limits and removing one's ordinariness. Overwhelmed by the desire to conquer and control, one is unable to live in harmony with the outside nature or to live in peace with the inner soul of oneself, the precious thing that can never be regained once lost. In the process of challenging one's physical limits, they taste the "excitement and strangeness" from being "an outrider, a trailblazer" and in the meantime they also open the Pandora's Box without knowing the way to shut it

(143). The oxymoron resides in that surfing is a sport through which man realizes that he can never conquer nature but can achieve marvelous and amazing beauty through perfect cooperation with nature. Surfers are the bold dancers in the seascape and the sea is the spiritual home of mankind's wildest dream of beauty and conquest. As Ben-Messahel puts it, "*Breath* invariably suggests that the individual is a component of place" and place shapes an individual's identity. The strength of the waves and the experience of surfing initiate the innocent boys to manhood. "The ocean is an unearthing element; it operates as a centripetal force compelling nature and culture to mingle in a flowing stream — suggesting that events are part of an ecological system" ("Blokes, Water" 14). Unlike their parents, Pikelet and Loonie grow into quintessential Western Australians who demonstrate natural and strong propensity to identify with its landscapes and seascapes. They manage to root themselves in a land that their parents' generation feels alien to.

Many readers and critics have noticed that Winton's protagonists are overwhelmingly male. Ma Pilar Baines Alarcos finds that Winton's male characters often defy tradition but not female ones. Chinese critic Chunjuan Zhan also deems that Winton's attitude towards women is at most ambivalent though his female protagonists are superficially subversive and somewhat "matriarchal" (117). These censures are not unjustifiable, which at least proves that, Winton, as a male author, does not demonstrate equal ingenuity in depicting female characters to please his feminist readers. However, we cannot deny that Winton's endeavor to portrait images of natural individuals is found in the female protagonists as well. As to me, the characterizations of Queenie in *Shallows* and Dora Jackson in *Blueback* not only defy conventions of female characters but create enduring images of daughters of the sea. Here, the analysis will focus on Queenie, leaving Dora to be discussed in the last section of this chapter.

Young Queenie was a keen listener of the marine world. At the beginning of the novel Winton unfolds that "the lovemaking of the whales out in the bay" was "the sound of her childhood" (3) and "mimicking the sounds of the windmill and the songs of the whales" was her childhood pastime (73). A relation of intimacy is immediately forged between Queenie and the whales. As a young innocent girl who was deserted by parents and brought up by grandparents, fish and other marine lives were her childhood playmates. But in the townfolk's opinion, young Queenie was rather odd, for she often told "stories about conversations with dolphins and hearing God in seashells" (8). This again proves that nature's child is often the misfit in human community. The dissociation from other humans draws her even closer to nature. In her grandfather's eyes, the little girl is more like an amphibian animal than a human being.

Daily contact with the sea not only cultivates a close link between Queenie and marine species, but builds the strong physique of adult Queenie. She is an excellent swimmer with fantastic lung capacity. As she swims, her long legs scissor the water (4). The verb "scissor" impressively depicts the strength and swiftness of her manner of swimming. There is no exaggeration to say that she swims like a fish and the descriptions further consolidate her image of a sea animal rather than a terraneous being. Qualities of shark are borrowed to shed light on the protagonist's ease and nimbleness in water. "She *torpedoed* out of the haze to take him by the legs, shaking him *as a shark shakes its prey*" (4~5 emphases added) to play a trick on her husband. The zoosemic association of Queenie with a shark is interesting and original so that not only her husband but readers can't help wondering that she "ought not to have been born a land mammal" (4). In a way, the portrayal of Queenie blurs the boundary between terrestrial animal and marine life. In reverse, the fish is frequently endowed with such human traits as being bold, curious and attractive (5). Figures of speech like zoosemy and personification stress the similarity between human beings and marine creatures and question the rigidity of the human/animal dualism.

Queenie's belonging in the blue sea is emphasized in "Laps" — a short story that can be taken as *Shallows*' continuation from Winton's celebrated collection *Minimum of Two* (1987). Queenie tells her 6-year-old daughter: "When I did everything else lousy, I knew I could always get in the water and swim like a fish" ("Laps" 83). Interestingly, like her mother, Dot swam before she could talk ("Laps" 76). In a later fiction *Blueback* (1997), Winton's perseverance in portraying images of children of the sea is felt again. The protagonists Abel, his parents and daughter are all able to swim like fish in the sea. The most impressive detail is that Abel's daughter little Dora dives with her parents on her third birthday. The motifs that "We come from water" and that "We belong to it" are reiterated by various personae in different works (*Blueback* 145). In short, their deep affiliation to the ocean cannot be overstressed.

On more than one occasion has Winton pointed out the uniqueness of the coastal landscapes in southwest of Western Australia — a place where the desert meets the sea; an odd kind of situation where the margins blur. Winton once said that the physical surroundings in Western Australia is "odd", "strange", "not picturesque", and "un-European" and therefore "it's taken those of us who are new comers a couple of hundred years to get the hang of it, to feel at home there" (Wachtel 64). But Winton stressed the necessity and significance of "emotional commitment" to the land to make it their genuine home "in the mature way" (Wachtel 74). Despite that European Australians have outnumbered and replaced the indigenous for more than two centuries, they are constantly stricken with a strong sense of homelessness. And the process of constructing a deeply rooted relationship to the land is slow and agonizing in that the estranged account of human identity in western culture would essentially set him "apart from or 'outside of' nature, having no true home in it or allegiance to it". Namely, humans "stand apart from it as masters or external controllers of nature" (Plumwood, *Feminism* 71). In a way, Winton's portrait of children of nature contributes to reversing the horrible trend of the split between mankind and nature and also to reconstructing "umbilical" bond with the land as felt by the author himself. The link between the characters and their environment is more spiritual and emotional than physical and rational. Winton said, "I'd be faking it if I didn't feel it myself. It's a big part of my life. But it's not always easy to explain and fiction is a way of explaining things without being rational" (Steger, "A Big Night" 1). Winton would like to see his characters as a genuine member in the community of nature, the way that fish is a member in the aquatic ecosystem. Winton's efforts to endear the land to white Australians are of special meaning to white Australians.

However, some critics doubt whether these efforts in constructing the bond overshadow or dim the natural link held by aborigines to their country. Ken Gelder and Paul Salzman's opinions are representative. They believe Winton gives the land full depiction in his works to "write the genealogies of the settlers into the landscape itself, which helps link the white Australians to country and in the meantime underwrite their occupation of the land to enable them to belong" (34). McGloin notes that "Winton's characterizations, while ensconced firmly in Australian landscapes, give only 'the briefest of nods to Aboriginal presence'" (110). This is a worthy issue open for further exploration. As to me, the sense of belonging and profound affection frequently underscored by Winton, to some degree, is a conscious appropriation of aboriginals' affiliation to their country. This affinity is firstly embodied in the sense of belonging, which echoes the tenet of aboriginal philosophy that you belong to the land rather than that the land belongs to you. The discrepancy in worldviews between aboriginal and western philosophy is salient so that one has to admit that imperceptibly or subconsciously, aboriginal culture has been exerting a subtle influence on the author and other white settlers, for it caters well to the need for cultivating a sense of belonging. The similarity is also obviously felt in "Laps", in which Queenie attempts to resume a kind of "umbilical bond" with her hometown by taking her daughter back after seven-year absence from it.

Through the analysis, we can see that the creation of characters that are intimately related to nature embodies the author's initial intention to construct the link between white Australians and the land and paves way for further development. All these personae, like the author himself, identify themselves strongly with Australia as the sole, beloved, irreplaceable home. In a way, the particular coastal areas in Western Australia help define both individual and communal identity of the characters, through whom some fuller and better possibilities can be expected for renegotiating man/nature relationship and reworking the world-view and traditions held by white Australians. Furthermore, they even acquire an "ecological identity which aims to resolve the legacy of alienation from the earth" because theirs are stories that seek "a ground of continuity not *separation* from but in *connection*" with nature (Plumwood, *Feminism* 102).

2.4 An Environmental Campaign: Awakening People's Eco-responsibility

To some extent, creating nature's children characters serves as a prelude to the launching of the environmental movements to protect nature. Nature's children don't deny their dependency on nature and won't treat nature in an instrumental mode. The mutual relationship between the two involves "respect, benevolence, care, friendship and solidarity" (Plumwood, *Feminism* 155). When nature and wild species are endangered, they won't sit by but would take actions to save them. In many aspects, Winton's protagonists have many affinities with the

Aborigines on account of a sort of kinship gradually developed as they grow up in natural surroundings. Hence, their actions to protect nature are spontaneous, their objectives clear, and their resolution firm. Now the analysis will turn to Winton's eco-fiction *Shallows* again to explore the awakening of people's environment-protection consciousness in the 1970s at the fictional whale town Angelus.

In the first chapter, I have explored whale exploitation in the pioneering days of the 1830s and the focus of discussion has been on serious alienation and spiritual disequilibrium felt by the early whalers on account of the estranged labor of whaling. But there was no worry about problems such as depletion of resources and extinction of the species then. The analysis in this section will revolve around the situation of whaling industry by the end of 1970s.

The Australian whaling industry was well-established by the end of the Second World War, but the world's cetacean resources had shrunk dramatically as a result of relentless overfishing over the centuries. Hence, the "last land-based Australian whaling station, at Cheynes Beach near Albany in Western Australia, was forced to close in the late 1970's" (Turner 79 ~ 80). It is against this historical context that the story happens. The town of Angelus, taken Albany as its prototype, is where Nathaniel Coupar was forsaken and where the last land-based whaling Company, the Paris Bay, locates. It is "a montage of fictional pasts and multiple presents" (Tyas 219). And the campaigns against whaling are set in 1978 when the traditional industry of whaling is struggling for its survival.

According to John P. Turner, many details in *Shallows* correspond with the real occurrences that took place at Cheynes Beach in 1977 (80). For one thing, history records that the Norwegians came at the end of the nineteenth century armed with Svend Foyn's newly invented harpoon gun and pursued whales with "relentless havoc" (Turner 79). In *Shallows* we read that the Paris Bay Whaling Company was initiated by some Scandinavian companies in 1910 and came under Australian ownership in 1918 (35). For another, the numerous head-on confrontations between the eco-group and the whalers are based on historical facts:

> Winton bases the superplot of his novel on three of the most dramatic episodes in the confrontation, the failure of Greenpeace's small boat engines, causing the whalers to win the first day's confrontation, the near-miraculous appearance of dolphins in usually shark-infested waters, and the firing of a harpoon gun dangerously close to the anti-whalers. (Turner 80)

Since ecological protection is a topic closely related to social reality, the awareness that *Shallows* echoes real incidents will greatly enhance the significance of the novel and the researches into it.

Winton began to write *Shallows* in his college time and didn't finish it until the birth of his first child in 1984. Despite the young age, Winton was determined to load his book with a heavy sense of history. Therefore, in the novel, three obvious storylines are perceptible, namely, the brutal whaling time in the 1830s as recorded in Nathaniel's logbook, the bitter clashes of the Great Depression in the 1930s as revealed through the flashbacks of Daniel, Pell, Hassa and Des, and the crisis of whaling industry in the late 1970s. Historical elements intertwine with fictional ones to form the legendary family saga of the Coupars.

This link between whales and the Coupars initiates from the American whaler Nathaniel Coupar and persists till Queenie Coupar, the fifth generation. Nathaniel Coupar lost faith in God and bathed himself in despondency till death due to the estranged labor of whaling that he had done in his youth. Unlike her ancestor, Queenie was brought up in close contact with the sea and she could interpret the information annually brought by whales, "God's appointed messenger", although there is a lack of scriptural evidence about the belief that whales are the messengers sent by God (Winton, *Shallows* 16). By calling whales thus, Winton endows them a halo of mystery. Throughout the novel, whales remain stubbornly loyal to the cycle of life and out of man's comprehension. Since observing whales' seasonal migration has been a family tradition to the Coupars, their entanglement with the whales also assumes an air of mystery and tragedy.

Queenie has to put up with the fact that Angelus is a doom place to the adorable species. Paris Bay is a place of interest for "sightseeing" where people come to witness the butchering of whales with their own eyes. It is perverse and unthinkable that humans would seek fun and amusement from watching the killing of other species. Her job as a tourist guide exposes Queenie more frequently than others to the nightmare scenes of dissecting and flensing whales at the local whaling factory. Visits to the local whaling operation sites are a kind of torture on her conscience, which aggravates the agony and plunges her into an abyss of confusion so that sometimes her anger is vented on the tourists. That's why Queenie thinks the stink of boiling blubber serves as a convenient punishment to the visitors. In a way, Queenie's job of guiding others to visit the last land-based whaling venture and her revulsion against the modern whaling industry constitute the tension that can only be solved by some dramatic changes in status quo and prelude the eruption of the protest.

Hence, on that day when some greenies, who pretend to be tourists, launch the protest in the course of the visit, almost compulsively, Queenie joins and she feels that she has done something useful for the first time in her life (63). To Queenie, the demonstration makes her realize that something can be done to change the situation. So to speak, Queenie's consciousness of environment-protection is initiated and her passion for saving the species is ignited so that the energy buried deep down begins to burn fiercely. However, it's necessary to note that her opposition to whaling has been spontaneous and subconscious until the ecological campaign, though her involvement isn't without struggles as will be discussed later in this book. Maybe she does not know much about eco-activities, let alone scientific facts or theories concerning whales and stranding. Neither does she like high talks. "It was action that she wanted, not Brent's sleazy press conferences, not more talk" (125). In brief, she just wants to do something for the angelic sea life.

Tim Winton places much hope on Queenie, a protagonist who embodies the author's ecological ideal and would take actions to stop the crimes against nature. It is through her lens that the bloodiness and brutality of modern whaling are exposed. Queenie's voluntary aversion to "weapons in water" makes her an instinctive environmentalist (5). And Queenie is a character with firm conviction. Once a decision is made, she won't waver from it whatever happens, including being opposed by her husband and being held as a public foe by the town people. Most important of all, she is not only an observer but a doer.

"Angelus' confrontation with outsider eco-activists and the inevitable loss of its major industry is an apt vehicle to discuss some of the major questions of the late twentieth century — spiritual malaise, the failure of leadership, and the plundering of the earth's resources" (Turner 80). In the head-on strife with the whaling ships of the Paris Bay Company, the eco-warriors are in a serious disadvantageous position because of the poor equipment they can obtain. Unlike Ahab's chases of the white sperm whale in *Moby Dick*, predominantly fights against elements of nature, Queenie and her fellow eco-warriors' twentieth-century sea chases are battles against the Leviathan of technology and environmental degradation rather than the ocean or the whale itself (Tyas 225). In addition, some campaigns are not fully prepared while others are aborted for all kinds of reasons such as the boycotts from the workers' unions, the breakdown of the engines, or even accidental occurrences like the ironic rescue of the shark-hunter etc. That the campaigns are launched by outsiders and women renders it more "dubious" and "unreliable". However, despite the clumsiness and immaturity of the greenies, they are pushing things in the right direction. They render whales' voice audible for the first time in the town's history, which disturbs the serenity of the town life, engenders contemplation and initiates a chain of reactions at the whaling town. "Long-dormant passions are awakened by the arrival of the conservationists, who threaten the town's livelihood and disturb the fragile peace under which its inhabitants live"①. It's the very thing that holds the small whale town by its collar to make it aware of the crimes that have been committed by human race against their intelligent mammal brothers (as repeatedly stressed by the author in the text) that are on the brink of extinction. It's the first "match" that ignites humans' passion for the marine species that they have long depended on for subsistence (258). "An ocean without whales is like a wilderness without trees" (152). We cannot afford to be "the silent majority" that "use[s] soap and fertilizer and margarine and ice-cream and candles and lipstick ..." made out of whale blubber. Immediate actions are called for before it's too late (236).

Like Nathaniel Coupar's journal, embedded in the text are "excerpts from journals and newspapers, books and television scripts, government documents, copies, carbons, cuttings" (49). "Each scrapbook entry is a separate voice articulating a particular environmental perspective". "Using scrapbook cuttings, Winton contrasts the passionate subjectivity of Queenie's reverie with the studied objectivity of biological description and zoological concerns" (Tyas 222). We have to bear in mind that what was for Winton the long and arduous job of writing *Shallows* was done before environmentalism became a widespread phenomenon in the mid-eighties (McGirr, *Writer and Work* 31). So, people did not know

① From Back blurb of the UK Picador Edition of *Shallows*.

much about the marine species though whale fishery used to be the pillar industry. In a way, the book helps disseminate knowledge about the whales and makes people aware of the dangerous situation that the species is in.

When talking about why he works to save the whales, Fleurier attributes it to the influence from his father, who, as he sees it, wasted his life on "looking for Atlantis, the lost civilization". It's pitiful that the talent was not used on something more constructive and beneficial — promoting mutual communication and cultivating friendly relationship between human race and marine species. Fleurier puts it frankly that it's ill-advised to allow him to chase relics instead of guiding him towards the future, for "our future lies in communication between the species, co-existence with the environment" but not in "the follies of the past" (48), which is the core of Winton's ecological ideal. As a matter of fact, cross-species communication is a law stressed by Aborigines. Paddy Fordham Wainburranga, an Aboriginal Rembarrnga man of Arnhem Land, stresses that while travelling across the country one has to talk with the country rather than walking quietly (qtd. in Rose, *Nourishing Terrains* 14 ~ 15). In that case, one is as rude as passing by one's acquaintances without greeting them. Through talking or singing out, one is having active and effective interactions with all the plants and animals kinfolk who are the countrymen (ibid.). That is, Aboriginal cultures expect constant communications between human race and other species in the natural surroundings. They believe if one sings out, the birds hear and are happy. In western culture, human race is assumed to be the only species that is gifted with the talent for language which is taken as the major means of communication. Yet, not only can Aboriginal people talk to their bird relatives in human language but it's implied that other species may have their own languages as well. One clipping in *Shallows* has it that "whales make a variety of groans, ticks and high whistles which, it can be assumed, are used in communication as well as echolocation and that each whale has a unique voice, as do humans". These quotations show that each species holds its own specific ways of communication, breaking the hyperseparation between man and non-human animals. Therefore, there are only differences between them. What's more, Winton is optimistic about the possibility of cross-species communication as another documentary quote points out — "it is theoretically possible for this communication (of whales) to be understood and interpreted by humans [...] a kind of sensual telepathy [...]" (50). In Winton's *Blueback*, a modern fairy tale for young readers, interspecies communication between the protagonists and their fish pal is touching and impressive. In short, communication between species is something that Winton passionately advocates and may be a way out of the mastery mode of man-nature relationship and implies a rosy dream of harmonious coexistence between humanity and other species.

Despite the obvious ecological motif, "*Shallows* is far from rosy-eyed about the environmental movement" and the author himself was not a mature environmentalist with firm confidence then (McGirr, *Writer and Work* 31). Like protagonists Queenie and Cleve, the author was, in effect, experiencing the same process of building up conviction in environmentalism. And he admits that Queenie and Cleve are each a part of himself in spite of their incompatible attitudes to whaling (McGirr, *Writer and Work* 37). Winton's complicated state of mind is clearly embodied by Queenie in her attitude towards the international eco-warriors. She doesn't like the Frenchman's "accents" which makes "her dizzy". And her feelings towards the matter are a mixture of "an exhilaration and a compulsion and some shaft of doubt" (46). Her "curious and dangerous mixture of feelings" is more frankly described as "half of her wanted to defend the town against these invaders, the other half of her made her wish she was one of them" (48). Sometimes she even cannot tell whether she is an "activist" or an "accomplice" (45).

Despite all the perplexities, she is baptized by such experiences as washing in whales' blood, being cursed by an old friend, losing her job, and gradually shifts to an eco-heroine who "felt a renewed purpose, an enthusiasm" so long as she is doing something for saving whales (150). Loyalty to one's town is a value cherished by Queenie, which reflects the author's attachment to his homeland. However, the care about the whole ecosystem undoubtedly should outweigh the allegiance to one's folks for the time being. Like the land itself, "the sea country" is also included in this care and love, as the Aboriginals do. So to speak, Queenie's decision to stay on the greenies' side partly suggests Winton's potential to grow into an unwavering environmentalist and an eco-patron later.

Winton's vacillation is more apparent on Cleve who reflects another profile of the author. Like the publican Hassa Staats and the majority of town folks, they share common fascination for the traditional industry and they all admire the type of masculinities embodied by the whalers. Disturbingly, to the town people, it's the whalers who are assumed to best represent the hegemonic masculinities and are national heroes that enjoy high esteem. They believe that "it was the whalers that made this country" (41), alluding to the historical fact that whaling was once the leading industry in Australia. Winton confesses his contradictory emotions: "I used to live in Albany. The whole whaling thing affected me deeply. Seeing these sperm whales hacked up for oil. And yet I liked the whalers' spirit, their tradition" (McGirr, *Writer and Work* 37). Likewise, "Cleve had marvelled at the size of the whales and admired the men who hunted and dissected them" (36) when taken to witness the operations at the Paris Bay. Besides, Cleve is fond of reading books such as *Moby Dick*, which reveals his fascination with the whaling industry. Moreover, he is deeply captivated by Nathaniel Coupar's logbooks, which causes a fierce brush between the couple and leads to the split. It is again an either/or proposition and the choices before the locals are whales or jobs, the same story as in *Scumbuster*. Cleve attaches much significance to the whaling factory mainly on account of the job opportunities they offer for people to feed their families. Additionally, Cleve embraces naïve ideas about the government, which is assumed to be the very agency that tackles such matters. All these render him reluctant to help when the greenies need to rent ships from him. Like most other town people, Cleve takes them as intruders and he is full of antipathy to them.

The author's hesitation in the eco-campaigns can also be felt in his description of a hunger strike held against whaling in front of Parliament House. A big woman named Sally Miles has fasted for five days, living in a tent on the steps of Parliament House. She is supported by Cachalot & Company, the international eco-group that Queenie joins. She is probably a local eco-volunteer. Four parties are involved in the episode, each holding a dissimilar attitude to the matter. Firstly, the media generally adopt a bantering tone while the government ignores but believes that whaling is indispensable. The third force comes from the union of laborers, which represents the working class in the town. Their appeals stand diametrically opposite to those of Sally and the eco-team. Here, the local working class with families to support is set against foreign hippy greenies with rich parents, the fourth party involved. Judging by the diction and arguments, Winton's sympathy goes to the former, which is certified by Winton's own words that "I was on the side of the greenies but I sympathized with the locals who were faced with unemployment" (McGirr, *Writer and Work* 37). Opposition is also constructed between genders. His depiction of the woman hunger striker is prone to arouse suspicion of sexism again. It is ironic that as a hunger striker, Sally Miles is depicted as a bulky woman. No wonder the workers' union protesters hold the placards which read "HIPPIES GO HOME; YANKS GO HOME; WOMEN GO HOME" (146 emphases original). But one thing must be admitted. At Angelus, a handful of people have come to realize that it's time to stop killing whales and they are taking righteous actions to put things right. Sally cares about whales true-heartedly and she hopes to stop the whaling industry right now through her efforts.

As mentioned above, the author admits that the novel owes much to his sojourn in Albany for more than three years. The description of the blood-stained scenes of whale dissection is a replay of the author's personal experiences:

> As a schoolboy in Albany I saw this clearly for the first time. A true wonder was dragged up onto a flensing deck and dismantled like a machine in a wrecker's yard, all so it could be rendered into oil and fertilizer. I saw that day what the ocean could produce and was amazed; I realized what humankind was likely to make of such creations and was dumbfounded. (Winton, *Land's Edge* 22)

Young Winton was astounded not only by the colossal size of the whales but by the way they were treated by humans. The shocking memory has been hanging him until he is old enough to put it to pens and share it with others through the anti-whaling novel *Shallows*. If the depiction of whaling in the 1830s throws light on the spiritual alienation of man, then the narrative of whaling operation in the 1970s underscores the objectification of nature and hegemony of instrumental reason.

Unlike Moby Dick that could still pose enough threat to the whalers in the early time, whales in the late 1970s were in absolute disadvantaged position. Whalers in modern society are far better equipped than their counterparts under primitive circumstances so that whales become easy preys to satisfy humans' gluttony. That is, under the hegemony of instrumental reason, whales are in effect rendered completely voiceless, powerless and hence subjectless and are exposed to the whim of human race, the sole speaking subject.

Winton puts it himself, "it was then that I realized the sea and its many wonders were not invulnerable. The ocean I grew up in might not be for always after all" (qtd. in McGirr, *Writer and Work* 30). Michael McGirr comments that the years Winton spent in Albany were the ones in which he developed beliefs about the importance of protecting the physical environment (*Writer and Work* 30). With the aid of the modern mechanics and tools, flensing and dissecting the gigantic marine mammal is just like dismantling "a salvaged vessel" (36). To them, whales towed in for processing are no longer held in awe as Leviathan. Neither are they taken as fellow living creatures. Instead, they are simply the "raw materials" to be worked on, not much distinct from iron ore dug out of the ground only that disgusting smells stink heavily. Besides, since the whales are held as senseless objects, no morals or ethics need to be observed at all. This is the typical attitude adopted by people in industrial society where nature is instrumentalized as the provider of raw materials for sole exploitation by human beings. In this case, whales are not taken as lives with desires and needs of their own that should be respected and thus are objectified. Namely, " in anthropocentric culture, nature's agency and independency are denied, subsumed in, or remade to coincide with human interests, which are thought to be the source of all value in the world" (Plumwood, "Decolonizing" 59).

The inhumanity and atrocity of the work especially when it is done with the aid of modern equipment are what the author takes great pains to disclose to stir up discomposure. Disturbingly, unlike Nathaniel Coupar and his generation of whale hunters, modern whalers are increasingly numb to the slaughter and are no longer annoyed by moral struggles. Compare the scenes of physical immersion in a visceral environment, a hellish experience to which two generations of whalers respond differently. When Nathaniel was wading about in entrails, he was stricken with a sense of profanity. In contrast, while working, the modern whalers are almost physically soaked in blood but emotionally untouched. The shift in attitudes implies more severe alienation of modern man from nature. The indifference and numbness to the elimination of other life as embodied in the whalers at Paris Bay manifest the extreme man/animal split, which must be abolished if a harmonious relation is to be reestablished in the eco-system.

Holistic worldviews of the Aboriginal cultures take the trees and birds as their relations. It's reasonable to infer that they tend to assume a sort of kinship with marine life as well, though no solid evidence has been established for much intimate contact between the two①. It is humanity's duty to ensure the prosperity of all species in the country. In this sense, the Aborigines are caretakers and nurturers while the European settlers are ravagers and plunderers. By adopting a semi-Aboriginal attitude, Winton lets the hunger striker Sally Miles claim that the whale is her brother and the earth the mother. To young Queenie Coupar, whales are old childhood friends and mysterious messengers who come back seasonally. However, the biggest mystery about whales resides in their stranding on the shallows that happens from time to time, which is one of the multiple implications of the fiction's title *Shallows*.

Tim Winton consciously mentions several cases of whale beaching in the fiction. Martin, Nathaniel's son and Daniel's father, once organized an inexpert flensing of a whale that stranded on the beach below the farm. People then assumed that it's "mindless suicide" (274). But Daniel refutes the opinion, because in his eyes whales are sentient animals who know well what they are doing. Queenie saw the stranding of a pygmy whale through shallows at the age of sixteen and took it for granted that it's brutal suicide. In fact, the suicide hypothesis has remained the most popular guesswork amidst the common people till today.

Interestingly, the issue of whale beaching is one that attracts wide

---

① Evidences prove that they don't mind eating whales that stranded. See Martin Gibbs's essay listed in the works cited.

attention from both laymen and experts. If Daniel and Queenie's opinion are subjective and sentimental, then Fleurier and Mark's judgments are more objective and scientific. They are both members of "Cachalot & Company". Fleurier, the French eco-battler, denies the suicide hypothesis by pointing out the huge size of whale's brain, which implies the possibility of high intelligence. Therefore, in his view, it is ridiculous to draw the conclusion that whales commit suicide without knowing anything about "what goes on in that enormous cavity" (46). One of the scrapbooks Fleurier hands to Queenie reads that "... even the killer whale has not been found guilty of suicide ..." (50). More scientific speculations as to the causes of stranding are found in Fleurier's information bank, i.e. disease, sonar fault, loyalty, distress signals, stress, and other unknown reasons (211), which are to be elaborated on by the American stranding expert Marks in the fiction. In a word, documentary materials widely quoted in the novel seem to exclude the possibility of suicide hypothesis, a crime against the Creator's will according to Christian doctrines. Winton implies that the main reason why whale grounding is assumed to be suicide is that there is a severe lack of understanding of the marine species.

Both Aboriginal values and Albert Schweitzer's concept of "Reverence for Life" admit that every form of life naturally possesses the "will-to-live", which requires no justification. Winton holds similar view as to wildlife's natural right of existence expressed through Marks. Despite being an expert, Marks is never lack of passion and his arguments are not pedantic at all. He doesn't bother to argue or deduce in an academic way but considers that the whales are "inhabitants of the earth—they need protecting, that's all, because they are meant to be here. Needs no justification". That is, we do not have to prove that a species possesses intelligence to justify the legitimacy of its existence. In this sense, to live and to let live as a kind of ecological justice is self-evident and it is the common good that must be known to all. In Winton's fictitious world, scientists or experts are unconventional. They are practical movers rather than pedantic high talkers. Like Queenie, Marks believes that they should spend "more time and money protecting them and less time trying to make the poor bastards talk and do Rorshach tests!" (152). Actions speak louder than words.

Marks also emphasizes that human race should "know good, bad, big, small" and "know their place" (ibid.), which touches upon the root of the problem with modern people who virtually fail to distinguish right from wrong. If they turn a blind eye to the right place of man allocated by nature, do not care much about the common good, or can't tell the difference between big (the holistic exuberance) or small (man's sole prosperity), the consequence will be that they have to come to terms with possessing only half world and being half people (ibid.). The beautiful world will be spoilt and humanity suffers the loss with it. Therefore, as advocated by the Aborigines, human race has to shoulder the responsibility of looking after their "country" and everything inhabiting in it. "The preservation, promotion, and enhancement of life in general" are the anchor of both Aboriginal eco-wisdom and Schweitzer's ethics (qtd. in Nash, *Rights of Nature* 60). The extinction of any one species may be a heavy toll taken on the whole system of life, for every component has its own intrinsic worth. Hence, to ensure that our children "grow up to see whales" is a duty that cannot be neglected (152). In this indigenous cultural matrix, whales are not silent objects but speaking subjects whose needs and desires are discerned and met.

In addition, Winton also wants to highlight a number of virtues possessed by whales, which probably indicate that in many aspects whales are at least equal or even superior to human race as a species, which overthrow the artificial hierarchy that gives human race top place in the ecosystem. In the fourth section of chapter Ⅰ, I've cited an instance in which the cow whale attempts to save her baby by exposing herself, which vividly demonstrates great maternal love that is the instinct shared by both human race and wildlife. Fleurier insists that whales are "the most amazing creatures alive" and they have "intelligence, wit, compassion" (156). Daniel attributes such qualities as faith, loyalty, and innocence to whales. They have been faithful to the ancient pattern of "moving, feeding, mating" over the years (274). In the case of a mass stranding, the rescued whales will stubbornly return to the beach once they pick up the distress calls released by the leader (211), which attests to their loyalty to the herd leader. Marks offers more evidences for such features. He is amazed at the "complicated loyalty" possessed by whales, for "if one goes, all go". When picking up the distress signal transmitted by the stranding whale, "they'll all go to help and get caught like him". Therefore, "if a pod leader ... gets into trouble, there's almost a certain stranding of the pod" (151). Undeniably, the author intends to highlight the loyalty and devotion in whales. Therefore, how can we witness the demise of them without doing anything? As Marks suggests, human interferences are necessary and should be done in a constructive way. Humanity used to kill whales but now they need to protect them from extinction. Put it another way, it is "redressing previous interruptions with more interruptions" (152). To stop the slaughter is just the first step in rescuing the huge marine animal.

Another virtue that humanity dearly lacks but whales possess is innocence. As Daniel sees it, there is no innocence in human race that has "rotton to the core with pride" because they are always "s'posed to *know*". In contrast, other species "just *do* and it's enough" and thus retains innocence (ibid.). Here, knowledge and innocence are held as a pair of binary opposition. He asks: "Why do we have to know? Why can't we be innocent?" (274). These interrogations allude to the root of original sin and degeneration in Christianity: after stealthily eating the forbidden fruit from the tree of wisdom, man loses the innocence and begins to degenerate. According to Lynn White Jr., in Latin West, efforts had been made to "understand God's mind by discovering how his creation operates" since early thirteenth century (11). Almost all major scientists explained their motivations in religious terms and the trend was kept till the late eighteenth century when it became unnecessary (ibid.). But historical facts have proved that the more humans know about nature, the more they lose their innocence and the more nature is spoiled. In *Shallows*, we are informed that to acquire more knowledge about whales, "[...] the projectile had to penetrate deep into the muscles of the back [....]" (49). That is, whale researches are conducted by mutilation instead of by close touch and communication between species.

According to Aboriginal cultures, knowledge is necessarily local. Put it another way, the Aboriginal system of knowledge does not "invite people to assume that they can or they should know everything. Nor does it commend itself to people who believe that they can and should (or already do) know everything" (Rose, *Nourishing Terrain* 13). In a way, the author is more or less skeptical of modern spirit of science and knowledge and even education. Readers familiar with Winton's fiction know that his major protagonists are definitely non-elites. That is, they are either slow learners or dropouts from school. However, transplant them into the natural settings, they'll demonstrate superb capacity to survive there, which proves that they possess adequate knowledge about their natural home where they frequently go to stay, to seek fun or to contemplate. Winton's interpretation of knowledge is akin to Aboriginal idea in that it is obviously local and specific to places. Their territory is in wilderness — places away from human civilization but near to wild nature, the nurturer and instructor.

In sum, besides refuting suicide hypothesis, Winton endows the whale virtues, which actually denies the superiority supposedly possessed by human race as the highest form of life. Moreover, the similarity between the two species far outgoes the hyperdistinction between human beings and non-human animals. Like what the Aboriginals have been doing over the thousands of years, it is necessary for humans to learn to understand and communicate with whales to uncover the mystery of whale stranding and to promote common prosperity and coexistence.

Scriptural elements were prevalent in Winton's texts and they arouse constant research interests. According to the Bible, humans were created in the image of God himself and granted many privileges including domination over all forms of life which were "for man's benefit and rule: no item in the physical creation had any purpose save to serve man's purposes" (White 9). "Man shares, in great measure, God's transcendence of nature." Thus, Christianity "not only established a dualism of man and nature but also insisted that it is God's will that man exploit nature for his proper ends" (White 10). No wonder Judaism and Christianity are widely taken as the major theoretical sources for anthropocentrism, "the philosophical viewpoint arguing that human beings are the central or most significant entities in the world",① "in the sense that they are considered to have a moral status or value higher than that of other animals". Anthropocentrism implies "the assessment of reality through an exclusively human perspective".② Ethically, anthropocentrism holds that human life has intrinsic value while other entities (including animals, plants, mineral resources, and so on) have only instrumental value and are resources that may justifiably be exploited for the benefits of humankind.③

The famous Chinese critic of Australian literature, Yuanshen Huang notes that scriptural quotes and allusions frequently appear in Winton's early works and he proceeds to comment that they are predictive and

① http://www.britannica.com/EBchecked/topic/27493/anthropocentrism.

② http://en.wikipedia.org/wiki/Anthropocentrism.

③ http://www.britannica.com/EBchecked/topic/27493/anthropocentrism.

help upgrade the protagonists to the holy realm (黄 389)[①]. However, the Bible is widely quoted in *Shallows* to blame humanity for their absurdity and arrogance and to call for them to mend their ways. In Nathaniel's logbook, a text from the great prophet Isaiah was quoted and taken by the whalers as the motto: *In that day the Lord with his sore and great and strong sword shall punish Leviathan the piercing serpent; and he shall slay the dragon that is in the sea* (123 italics original). Superficially, "Old Testament references to the sperm whale as 'Leviathan the piercing serpent' present an archetypal image of evil" (Tyas 222). Admittedly, it's the most forceful justification for the slaughter of whales. Winton follows the above quotation with this condemnation: "The ignorant fellows believe the sperm whale to be the Serpent, agent of the Evil One" (123). Therefore, the quotation actually implies that sperm whales were wrongly demonized as "the Serpent" by western people due to their prejudice and ignorance.

Biblical allusions are also employed to explore such themes as sin and redemption, abandonment and hope in *Shallows*. In Daniel's pursuit of salvation, he realizes the crimes committed by human race against other species. A line from Jeremiah runs: "*How long will the land mourn, and the grass of every field wither? For the wickedness of those who dwell in it the beasts and birds are swept away*" (76 italics original). It directly lashes out at anthropocentrism, which always triumphs human interests over those of the nonhumans and the environment, and sees humans as the center of the universe or the ends of creation (Minteer 58). The ruthlessness and relentlessness of humanity in the exploitation of nature have yielded serious consequences. Plants and animals on the land, birds in the air and fish in the sea are all to be eliminated, which will eventually lead to the collapse of the whole ecosystem. "But pride

① Translation mine.

waits until all else has withered" (284). Human arrogance, the root of the evil, is now putting all species in an endangered circumstance and it's high time to wake up. Nature's backlash is impending and man cannot wait any longer.

Queenie's nightmare of being trapped in the whale's stomach is an obvious parody of the allusion of Jonah which is repeatedly referred to by Pell, Daniel and Queenie in the fiction. Jonah the prophet was also the whalemen's favorite (124). In the Bible story, God appoints the whale to swallow Jonah to prevent him from being drowned in the storm. Jonah's experiences resemble those of Jesus Christ in that he has spent the same amount of time — three days — inside the whale as Jesus Christ does in the tomb. Like Christ, Jonah also preaches salvation to the lost. In her dream, Queenie is in the whale's belly and sees the half-digested limbs of many acquaintances, such as Staats, Des Pustling and even Cleve, who are all obstinate supporters of whaling. Queenie's dream is a parody of Jonah's story and so Queenie is the modern Jonah who is expected to rid her fellow men of the sin of whale hunting and lead them to salvation — the harmonious coinhabitance, which is a possible aim to strive for since all signs hinted at the unnecessity and irrationality of modern whaling industry in the late 1970s.

Throughout the novel, the readers not only feel the author's compassion for the miserable marine species but his ambiguity towards the eco-participants, especially to the outsiders. However, the protests and demonstrations made by the eco-activists prompt one to contemplate the necessity of the continuous existence of the whaling industry in modern society. It's undeniable that whale hunting had laid the foundation of the colony and had been contributing to the development of the settler society all the time. People had got used to relying on it for subsistence. Whale oil was used as lighting oil and "for fishing and for lubricating old machinery" and it was once the raw materials for daily necessities such as soaps, candles, etc. (274). "The baleen from whales' mouths served as the flexible material in items ranging from corset stays to coach springs" (Gibbs 3).

The industry has always been economically lucrative and socially beneficial but turned out environmentally destructive. After a long history of exploitation, it's time for humanity to stop and think. Firstly, the products mentioned above are no longer made of whale oil, for better replacements have been found. Secondly, we do not kill for meat either. In the argument between the couple, Cleve says: "They're just animals [...] Some animals are killed so we survive" and Queenie refutes: "And some, [...] don't need to be killed. We don't eat them. Even the by-products are all obsolete" (64). Since whales are held as Leviathan in traditional western culture, the westerners feel sick of eating whales, which can be evidenced by Nathaniel's narration. So Cleve's argument is unjustifiable. Interestingly, Aboriginals don't mind eating whale meat. According to Martin Gibbs, "prior to the whaling era, Nyungar people, including the Mineng, had traditionally consumed whale meat on an opportunistic basis when animals stranded on the beach or carcasses washed ashore" (4). On the rare occasions when whale meat was available, neighboring tribes would get together to feast. They didn't waste food and they shared it. Therefore, another excuse for whale hunting turns out to be shaky. Thirdly, in the face of the rapid shrinkage of the number of whales plus uncanny beaching of whale herds, no one can stay aloof to the matter. All signs indicate that there is "no need of whaling industry" in modern social context (49).

What's more, it is human race's duty to take good care of their land or country. As Deborah B. Rose observes, in Aboriginal cultures action toward a place is intended to be nurturant, and to elicit more life from the site. Aboriginals are doing the work that keeps the place engaged with everyday life and time ("The Redemptive Frontier" 52). In contrast, wherever the westerners go, they destroy the natural environment there. And as they keep pushing further into the inner territory of nature, their actions result in not only the hyperseparation between human race and nature but the disequilibrium of the whole biosphere which is the cradle to all creatures on Earth. Unlike the early settlers, Winton makes endeavors to construct new identities for European Australians who care about the natural surroundings, who strive for a harmonious coexistence, who would learn to look after the place by hearing the voice of the indigenous people and who are willing to reestablish a kinship link to the adopted land as their native place. Put it another way, they are fully aware of the eco-responsibility on them and are learning to love the land in the right way, from which a sense of belonging is expected to derive.

2.5 An Ecotopia: Reestablished Harmonious Symbiosis

After cultivating the consciousness of environmental protection among his compatriots, Tim Winton succeeds to depict an ecotopia where humanity and marine species happily coexist side by side in *Blueback*, the winner of the 1998 Wilderness Society Environment Award. Although targeting young people as its primary readers, the short novel is ambitious enough to cover such major marine environmental issues as oil spills, changing weather, and over-exploitation of sea resources. The conflicts between conservationists and plunderers are no less severe than those in his other novels. It merits the honor as "a text with strong environmental consciousness" (Marca 9). Unlike his other stories that involve quite a few turns and twists downward in the lives of his characters who are mostly solitude souls, this narrative centers more on heart-felt love between human protagonists and their pals in nature. The human race and other members in that bio-community give you a strong sense of family. Scenes of friendly interactions between man and marine life are fantastic and impressive. In this contemporary fable, we are supposed to meet a group of characters who are passionately attached to the sea and claim a belonging to it. They become caretakers of it when its prosperity is impaired. The author portrays the Jacksons' stoic life in tune with the environment as a combination of pastoralism and utopianism, which is somewhat idealized but reveal the author's best wishes. In brief, *Blueback* depicts the harmony between human race and nature in a utopian world where the major protagonists make moderate use of and in the meantime take good care of the land and sea as the Aborigines do to their country.

The marine world has been what Tim Winton knows and loves most. He has impulsive propensity to choose it as the place for his stories. The same comment applies well to Rachel Carson, the avid lover of and excellent writer on the sea. Winton and Carson have a lot in common. Among the numerous similarities are the obvious facts that they share common interest in the mystic blue world and its inhabitants there; they both attempt to let others learn about it; and they are both keen observers with imagination.

And the distinctions are self-evident as aforementioned though. Here, another difference is discerned. Equipped with the competency in both marine biology and poetic writing, Rachel Carson demonstrates her devotion to the mysterious world impressively in her marine trilogy. But the only pity is that she lacks personal intimate touch with the sea that she is so obsessed with. The only experience of underwater dive, if any, came "in less-than-ideal conditions" (Lear XI) a decade later after her "Undersea" was published by *Atlantic Monthly* in 1937, "the top literary magazine of the day" (Lear X). Tim Winton is comparatively lucky to be an excellent diver and surfer as well as a good writer. In a way, Carson's observations are grounded on solid scientific knowledge and hence mostly second-hand whereas Winton's are personal and first-hand. Therefore, it seems Winton's comprehension of the marine world is intuitive and imaginary rather than scientific and rational. However, it is their response to the natural world of the sea and their sense of wonder and delight in it that link the two names.

Winton sees eye to eye with Carson that the sea is "the great mother of life" and we belong to it (Carson, *The Sea Around Us* 3). In *Blueback*, Winton desperately hopes to impress his readers with the fact that the Jacksons are a clan of swimmers and divers who enjoy their sojourn in the blue world. Dora Jackson describes her son Abel thus: he has been "swimming inside her all that time" and it's difficult to "get him out of the water" as a baby (144). Abel admits that he can "never remember a time when he could not dive" (6).

Abel's father was killed in his thirties by a tiger shark while working as a pearl diver. To Dora, there is deep grief towards his early death but no grievance against the sea. Neither does her son feel indignant about it. Virtually, they have taken a "peppermint tree" as "a kind of shrine to his father" so that they can express their love and yearning for him (51). But generally two points stand out about Abel's father. Firstly, he was able to swim like a fish. Secondly, his death is taken as a sort of re-entering the mysterious sea world. Rather than being tragic and melodramatic, it is assumed to be natural and reassuring. Moreover, his return is never lack of mystery and romance that evoke rich imagination and free association. Young Abel assumes his father knows all the secrets of the sea since he is now in one with it. Partly on account of this, Abel and his mother always feel akin to instead of alien from the sea.

In Abel's eyes, unlike "his schoolmates' mothers" who buy fashionable clothes and drive flash cars and chirp like birds, Dora is "quiet, tough and sun-streaked" with her hands "lined and calloused" (74). Most important of all, like Queenie Coupar in *Shallows*, "she was a beautiful swimmer, relaxed and strong" (6). So to speak, the author portrays Dora in the images of the land and sea that has made her (74). Abel's journey through the novel is an awakening to Dora's connection to the land and the sea (Marca 2), or to her country, the word in its aboriginal sense. As mentioned in the first section of chapter Ⅱ, country contains everything in an ecosystem or biotic community, as Aldo Leopold calls it, in which all things are interconnected like kindred. When this connection develops to its highest form, one loses the self gradually and becomes part of the whole. In Abel's dream, when Dora dies, she transforms into something like seaweed or a starfish, which indicates her reuniting with the marine world and her death is a sort of returning to the sea whence she came from, and she is accompanied by the gulls, terns and Blueback, the giant blue fish. Abel's dream of her death is just a re-affirmation of Dora's affinity with the natural world.

As a matter of fact, people get to know their country mainly through two major means: indirect experience and direct experience. The former is done through school education whereas the latter by living in and becoming part of it. Abel admires the way her mother gets to know the sea, namely, "by staying put, by watching and listening" and by "feeling things", which exactly resembles the way that knowledge is acquired about one's country in Aboriginal cultures. Abel gradually comes to realize that you don't need "a computer, two degrees and a frequent flyer program" to know your place, which is a claim indicating a clear endorsement of and identification with Aboriginal values (129). Interestingly, when Abel is away for school, Dora doesn't feel lonely in that she thinks "this place is a kind of friend" and she says that "maybe I'm a bit odd" (74). Then why and to whom is she "odd"? According to traditional western culture, a place is either a property, or something to be exploited, but is hardly a friend. Unlike other westerners, Dora talks to trees and communicates with fish, the sea and the land. Her viewpoint again suggests the appropriation of Aboriginal values.

Blueback is such a special story that persuades one into believing that human race belongs to the sea, which is the very thing that Dora repeatedly stresses before her death. When she dies, her spirit returns to the blue mystic world, reuniting herself with the timeless eternal. In a manner of speaking, both Dora and her husband become part of the endless cycle of life in the marine world, one physically while the other spiritually. All the descriptions are reminiscent of Rachel Carson's narration in the opening chapter "Mother Sea" of her second book *The Sea Around Us* (1951) in the trilogy. Rachel Carson traces the long process of life evolution from the formation of the earth itself to the appearance of the primitive life form in the sea then to the first pioneer of land life on the coastal shallows to human race and eventually man's return to the sea, which forms a loop in the mysterious cycle of life. Rachel Carson claims that "standing on its shores, he (man) must have looked out upon it (the sea) with wonder and curiosity, compounded with an unconscious recognition of his lineage" (*The Sea Around Us* 14~15). The sea is "a world long lost" to such a terricolous species as human race. But it's also "a world that, in the deepest part of his subconscious mind, he had never wholly forgotten" (*The Sea Around Us* 15). John F. Kennedy's words corroborate the intimate bond between humanity and sea: "All of us have in our veins the exact same percentage of salt in our blood that exists in the ocean, and therefore, we have salt in our blood, in our sweat, in our tears. We are tied to the ocean. And when we go back to the sea, — whether it is to sail to watch it — we are going back from whence we came" (qtd. in Marca 8). To the Jacksons in Winton's fiction, that "we come from water" and "we belong to it" is something the protagonists perceive and identify strongly for their existence (145). Transcending the demarcation as terraneous beings, they demonstrate strong affiliation with the marine world despite the fact that it does deprive life. To Dora and Abel, the sea is not only the stable source of livelihood, but the spiritual home with marine species as the endearing family members.

The fishermen establish close tie with the underwater world not only via building boats to venture out on the surface but via descending to the shallow parts of its floor, carrying with him the air that, as a land mammal long unaccustomed to aquatic life, he needed to breathe (*The Sea Around Us* 15). Ever since he was a ten-year-old boy, Abel has been adept at diving with the aid of the usual dive gear including wetsuit, fins, snorkel and mask, which immediately turn him to an agile fish so that he obtains a temporary sojourn in the marine world.

And the sea is like a magnetic field attracting our protagonists all the time. Dora has never uprooted herself from it despite the developers' the temptations and threats. She is a stubborn patroness of her country. Abel has to leave for education, but for the two decades from his early teenage to his early thirties, home has always been the place that his heart yearns for.

That the sea is both a real and spiritual source of life was essential to Dora's interpretation of the world. Their life is a perfect combination of pastoralism and harmonious symbiosis between humanity and nature. Winton depicts Dora Jackson as a stoical independent and an Aussie battler with strong physique. The author sets their almost reclusive way of living against town life which is the joint product of materialism and consumerism. They are living a serene and self-contained life on their own without disturbance from the hustle and bustle of modern life. Besides fishing, they grow fruits in the orchard and vegetables in the lean bush soil. Moreover, poultry are kept for meat and eggs and goats for milk. Three facts about the idyllic life they lead make it an eco-friendly model. One is the special organic fertilizer they use for enriching the soil. The self-made compost is made up of tree bark, vegetable scraps, seagrass as well as chopped fish (19). Besides, pilchards and salmon are also netted and dug into the sand for natural fertilizer (ibid.). Second, rather than using pesticides or chemicals, they hang bells on fruit trees to keep away the birds. Thirdly, "there was no mains electricity out at Longboat Bay, no water except rainwater and no TV" (20). Dora and Abel's home is a place that is not yet consumed by and digested into the body of modern industrial civilization. It clearly embodies the author's romantic and utopian ideal of anti-modernism. In his view, the most desirable way of living is one that minimizes its impact on nature. The benefits of it are evident. Abel enjoys roaming in the national park, swimming in the sea every day (20). Watching the kangaroos gather in the orchard should also be listed among the bonuses (21). What's more, Winton highlights Abel's distaste for the suffocating urban life that is noisy, "ugly and dreary" and lack of vigor and vitality that can be felt back home in nature (110).

On the top of the long list of boons stands his playmate Blueback. The eponymous protagonist is a giant blue groper that lives in the reef area off the Longboat bay. For his charming naivety and playful faculty, the Blueback endears itself to Abel and his mother that become its guardian angels. For years, playing with Blueback and feeding it with the abalones are what fascinate Abel who gives the fish the name. The groper becomes a bond with Abel and Dora at one end and the mysterious blue world at the other. Winton portrays an unforgettable image of the fish that is endowed with complicated changes of emotions and moods. "Some days the fish didn't show. Other days he was nervy and distant, but often he was simply bold, even mischievous" (37). He can even be indignant. Dora once punched him to rescue him from greedy hunters' gun. After that, Blueback kept clear of her for the rest of that summer (88). This is the "smart" (12) and "crafty" (23) old thing that accompanies Abel's whole childhood and makes him decide to major in marine biology to meet his curiosity about the mystery that lies in the fish as well as in the ocean.

Like genuine old friends, Abel understands the big fish and knows his preference. By and large, Blueback is sociable and fond of the communication with humanity if they mean him well. And he even allows physical intimacy. When Abel stretches out and touches him under the chin, Blueback's eyes roll, watching him and his fins vibrate (30). Abel is also deeply moved by the enormous weight of the fish's body as it brushes him (30~31). Such games are played for numerous times, with the boy and the fish fooling about safely in silence, back and forward, familiar as old mates (31), which forms the most touchy scenes of harmonious coexistence. Moreover, in the direct contact with the sea, Abel is constantly aware of humanity's littleness and transience in the face of nature's grandeur and eternity, namely, the insignificance of himself who is "like a speck, like a bubble on the sea left by a breaking wave, here for a moment and then gone", which adds to his reverence and awe to the immensity of the sea that is full of wonders (67). The intimate touch also instills in Abel the idea of modesty in man's relationship with the ocean, which is an attitude harbored by the author himself towards nature. And the smaller we come to feel ourselves compared to nature, the nearer we come to participating in its greatness (qtd. in Naess, *Ecology, Community and Lifestyle* 3).

Blueback has walked into Abel's soul and becomes an indispensable part of his life. While he is away, Blueback is the colour of all his dreams (151). Abel's pursuit of studies in town far away from home seemingly not only insulates him from the natural environment but splits the allegiances to his ecotopia. Dr Susan La Marca believes that Blueback has become "a symbol of the Bay for Abel, representative of everything he loves about his home and also a clear measure of the health of the Bay"①, to which I'd like to add that the relationship with the big fish is the touchstone of a harmonious relationship with nature.

Blueback is the major but not the only source of happiness. Not infrequently may they encounter dolphins on the sea and Abel touches them "with his rolled-up towel". Sometimes schools of tuna rise around him, "feeding like packs of wild dogs on terrified baitfish that leapt

① Susan La Marca. "Teacher's Notes — *Blueback* by Tim Winton." <http://www.puffin.com.au/extras/33/9780143304333/educational-text/Teaching%20Notes.pdf>.

across his boat" (68). Such are the happy times of harmonious coexistence enjoyed by the pair of mother and son as a routine but can be taken as a privilege by others.

The relationship between our human protagonists and the sea is obviously one of mutual support and care. Dora Jackson is a widow who willingly shoulders the responsibility of looking after her son Abel and her country that includes the Jackson land and the Longboat Bay. Having long been patronized by the sea, Dora and Abel assume it their duty to look after it in return. Looking after your country and you will be looked after by it. This is the system of reciprocity and mutual respect in Aboriginal cultures as aforementioned. Moreover, they feel great affinity with biocentric sentiments and seem to concur with the aboriginal value that goes though mankind is entitled to get food from nature yet one should be very careful but not greedy in the use of it. In their opinion, if nature is well cared, both will prosper.

Abalone picking is a major source of income for Dora and Abel. She is consciously moderate in the exploitation and always picks some, "leaving the rest to breed and grow" (7 ~ 8). In the good old days, other divers such as Mad Macka observe the same principle that runs taking some and "leaving plenty behind for next year" (41). Therefore, the undersea world where they work is in a state of equilibrium with the prosperity of both marine life and human race.

But life is not always rosy, as Dora puts it, "it's getting harder to hold on to good things" (71). Winton records his personal experience in an essay: "In the 90s I got used to diving longer and deeper to find abalone where, not long before, getting my quota had been easy work." Winton proceeds to comment that "you didn't need to be any sort of boffin to know something was wrong; every time you donned a mask and fins the evidence was right in front of your face: there it was — more and more of less". Winton comes to see that "the wider problems facing our marine environment were suddenly no longer over the horizon" and, therefore, "we needed to change our behavior, to reduce our consumption and set aside areas of sanctuary for regeneration" ("Sea Change" 7). Activism is possibly the only way out. In reality, Winton is the patron of the Australian Marine Conservation Society and a collaborative partner of Australian Conservation Foundation working together to create a network of marine sanctuaries in Australian waters. Moreover, the reclusive author found himself "in a sustained role as a public advocate" in the campaign to save Ningaloo Reef in Western Australia in the early 2000s, the experience itself looks back at many plots in the small book *Blueback* which was published in 1997 and is a reduced version of the strife and a utopian version of reestablished harmony between human race and the marine world.

Surfing "uncrowded waves" and fishing for food are privileges admitted by Winton who feel grateful for inheriting "a living ocean" ("Sea Change" 7). However, greedy plundering of the sea resources must be condemned. In his fiction *Blueback*, Dora's voluntary temperance that derives from an intuitive care about marine creatures forms a sharp contrast with the gluttony of a new abalone diver named Costello who has the notorious reputation as "a reef stripper" (59) that means taking "everything he sees" (69). Seeing Costello plundering "bag after bag of abalone", Abel is anxious and protests that "it's wrong" (76). Abel's viewpoint is remindful of Aldo Leopold's renowned theory of the land ethic.

Aldo Leopold (1887—1948), the father of wildlife conservation in the U.S., is Albert Schweitzer's American contemporary and he puts forward his theory of environmental concern — the land ethic, which echoes the former's core thoughts despite differences in details. Since the U.S. is listed among one the of nations that initiate the modern environmental movements, Leopold's influence is no less than that of Schweitzer and some even hold that the land ethic advocated by Leopold is the "most prominent American articulation of an environmental ethic"

(Freyfogle Vol 2, 21).

Leopold's "land ethic" affirms wild life the basic right to continued existence in a natural state and "changes the role of *Homo sapiens* from conqueror of the land-community to plain member and citizen of it", which "implies respect for his fellow-members" as well as the biotic community (240). As Leopold sees it, a land ethic "reflects the existence of an ecological conscience, and this in turn reflects a conviction of individual responsibility for the health of the land" (258). Dora and Abel are particularly conscious of the environmental ethics discussed above in their close touch with wild life. The care and compassion for marine species and the conscious temperance in utility of marine life are the excellent footnotes to the land ethic in that their way of living "tends to preserve the integrity, stability, and beauty of the biotic community" (Leopold 262). Hence, Costello is "wrong" on account that his deeds "tends otherwise" (76).

Abel, the voluntary caretaker of the bay, is determined to take actions to stop Costello in spite of his young age. Dora follows immediately though, as an adult, she is fully aware of the potential danger of the action. Winton is especially good at presenting ferocious scenes to create strong visual impact on readers, as he does in depicting the scenes of flensing whales in *Shallows*. This is the messy scene on the deck of Costello's fishing boat:

> The deck of Costello's boat *was awash with blood*. [...] Fish lay in *huge* slippery mounds and so many of them were *undersize*. Abel saw blue morwong, trevally, [...] and samsons *stiffening in the sun* or *quivering slowly to death*. Behind the steering console stood crates of writhing abalone and a box of *illegal* crayfish. (78 emphases added)

The bloody scene is nothing less than a massacre and the accusation is more vehement as seen through the lens of a thirteen-year-old boy.

Need is always easy to meet whereas avarice is insatiable. Carson mentions that the fishing boats pose deadly threat when they come, "towing their nets along the bottom" (*Under the Sea-Wind* 151). In that case, fish of all sizes are trapped, which accelerates the exhaustion of fishery resources. Likewise, what disturbs Dora and Abel is Costello's relentless pillage, which endangers the common welfare of both fish and human race in the long run. But what emboldens Abel to empty "crates of abalone over the side" of the boat must be something more sentimental than rational (79 ~ 80). He just cannot stand by when the greedy new divers are wreaking havoc in the Bay. Their concern about the destiny of the marine species bears much resemblance to the care about one's kinfolk, which is somehow reminiscent of Aboriginal concepts of kinship. One more reason for his anxiety is Blueback, whom he befriends.

However, this action of him only throws his mother and the giant groper in greater danger. Tempted by the abalone, Blueback suddenly emerges and soon becomes the new target of Costello and his pal. The action for saving abalones is soon turned to one of rescuing Blueback. Dora has no other choice but "put her body in the way" between the spearguns and the groper (82). She is virtually running the risk of hurting herself in the attempt to save the fish. To make the matter worse, the old fish knows nothing about the perilous situation he is in and like usual he wants to play the old game with Dora, which traps them both in deadly hazard. The whole rescue activity is about to end in disaster when Dora punches Blueback in the head in the split second and scares him off (83). As a patroness, Dora is not only courageous and passionate, but resourceful and prudent. All these merits help to pull her through one obstacle after another in the long process of defending and looking after her country.

However, Costello has other ecological crime to his name. One day, Abel sees a tiger shark towing "a big red buoy on a length of chain" (89). Every time it tries to dive to seek food, the buoy drives it back to the surface so that after desperate struggles it is now dying of exhaustion and starvation. The "pitiful sight" tortures Abel who can not take his eyes away from it the whole day and finds it dies the next morning. Replacing the buoy by "some lead weights", Abel gives it a decent funeral by sending it back home to the deep ocean, which shows deep reverence for life. He accidently discerns that the name stenciled on the buoy is COSTELLO (91). Costello's voracity and irresponsibility make Abel aware that "there was nothing in nature as cruel and savage as a greedy human being", which well expresses the author's own indignation (ibid.).

Another battle Dora fights single-handedly while Abel is at school is against the commercial developers. Since "the develop-at-all-costs mindset" (Winton, "How the Reef was Won" 22) still prevails, the Jackson land catches the developers' attention due to its good location adjacent both to the national park and to a lovely bay. The businessmen have long cast a covetous eye at the Jackson land, where "a hotel, golf course, swimming pool and a marina could all fit on". The Longboat Bay can be said to be "a goldmine". In addition to yacht trips and playing golf, tourists here can enjoy the privileges of watching "kangaroos grazing at the edge of the forest", whales spouting and dolphins hooting on the sea and even playing with the old groper Blueback (97). The fabrication in the fable is virtually a simplified version of what happened at the Ningaloo Reef area in the early 2000s. There are quite a few similarities between Ningaloo Reef and the reef at Robbers Head in the novel. They are both close to shore and hence vulnerable to human impacts. They are both seen as an ideal site for eco-tourism in that they have good potential of being converted to a luxury resort featured by a huge marina and golf course by the commercial developers. What can be foreseen is that the "massive imposition on the landscape" and the "long-term intrusion into the inshore habitats of whales, turtles, mantas and sharks" will spoil an area eligible for sanctuary since "the resort proposal was completely incompatible with its environment" (Winton, "Sea Change" 6~8).

"Yet the plan had great support in state parliament and many boosters in the WA media" (Winton, "Sea Change" 7), which again echoes the plot in the story. The businessmen and even government's fellows alternate between bribery and coercion, yet Dora just won't sell. To Dora, the place isn't just a property, but a life, a friend or a husband as well (99). Her stubbornness and patience eventually outlast them. Winton points out in a speech "How the Reef was Won" that to develop or not is actually "a battle of world views". That is to say, the traditional western views see a pristine place as "a resource to exploit, an opportunity to engineer and improve nature for quick profit" while "a new generation prefers nature unrenovated". Of course, Winton would see to it that "the health of the natural asset" be put "before commercial consideration" either in fiction or in reality (22).

But the modern society won't leave even a remote fishing bay alone. Tourists from all directions pour in to swim with the old blue fish. One day "an oil tanker cracked in two off the coast of Longboat Bay" (119). More erratic and ominous signs are found in the sea. After a "fierce and erratic" storm (123), history unearths itself suddenly (126) by exposing the whale bones and broken teeth on the shore to Dora who has walked over them for forty years without knowing (125). That the first generation of Jacksons came here as whalers obviously forms intextuality with the plot in *Shallows* and *Blueback* proceeds to tell us what happens more than a century later. As Rachel Carson sees it, the sea shores are places where "there are echoes of past and future: of the flow of time, obliterating yet containing all that has gone before" (*The Edge of the Sea* 215). The tides and the beat of surf are constantly shaping and changing the shore. Yet they can't eradicate historical traces and the whale bones stay to remind people of the past and warn them of the future. Dora knows the family story well, yet she is still astounded by the sight and realizes that "now it was time to help the sea live" and "she must protect the bay for all time" (126).

With Abel working away from the Longboat Bay, Dora is determined to give the issue a thorough solution. She begins writing letters to politicians, bosses, scientists and even newspaper editors, anyone who cares or may be of help. In reality, the environmentalists for protecting the Ningaloo Reef also wrote letters to the government. They also rallied and marched, which makes Winton aware "how much they love their country, what real patriotism is" ("Sea Change" 8).

Her stubbornness and patience again win her the victory — Longboat Bay was declared a sanctuary, a marine park where everything that grew and swam there was protected by law (128). Likewise, the campaign the author actively involved for saving the Ningaloo Reef ends in surprisingly good result:

> In 2003, WA Premier Geoff Gallop knocked back the resort proposal and rewrote the laws for coastal planning in WA so that inappropriate development was discouraged, not wooed as it had been previously. The marine park was enhanced so that a decent percentage of reef was off-limits to drilling and fishing. Last year (2011) the Ningaloo was finally added to the World Heritage Register. (Winton, "Sea Change" 8)

From the above analysis, we find that strives in fiction parallel those in reality and together they constitute the author's all-round activism against irresponsible behaviors towards the precious natural heritages passed on to their hands, only that *Blueback* was published before this environmental campaign, showing the author's foresight. And it's not difficult to perceive Winton's strong sense of duty to keep as much as possible of that treasure to pass it on to the coming generations.

As her son puts it, Dora is a great woman who saves a place with her love. When she is too old to look after her beloved home, Abel feels the calling of the place (136) and resigns his job to succeed her role as the caretaker. Like the catcher in the rye, Dora and Abel become the lifelong guardians of the Bay. There, "people and country take care of each other" and therefore constitute "a system of reciprocity and respect" (Rose, *Nourishing Terrains* 49, 44). In this ecotopia, the campaigns for protecting the big fish "Blueback" and the stretch of water against the commercial developer win success. Then it seems that man and nature will live in harmony with each other in the small fishing town.

Big Issue comments that "though containing suspense, indignation and sadness, the overwhelming tone of the book is an affirming vitality"①. In *Blueback*, the eco-issues receive satisfactory solutions and eco-protection activities always end in victories. Costello was caught on the spot by Fisheries patrol boat (88) and put out of practice before causing more serious consequence. Dora wins two battles single-handedly, one against developers, the other for setting a sanctuary in the bay. As a matter of fact, the greenies in his other novels are never so lucky as can be seen in the previous analysis. The differences in plots show the author's wishes that the young readers should be more cheerful and optimistic about the possible harmony between us and our endearing mother nature.

Winton says *Blueback* is only a fable in which "an old woman and her son fight off a development juggernaut". But "there were times during the Ningaloo campaign when I felt I was inhabiting a grisly, and far less wishful version of the same story, that it was a tale I might never escape". It's true that the shift of mind is gradual and slow. However, "people do change — individuals, families, nations — and the pace of transformation need not to be geological". A single book or a campaign can be hardly said to be fundamentally revolutionary. Yet, as the author

① From the blurb of the back cover.

puts it himself, it can engender hope ("Sea Change" 8).

To sum up, this chapter has explored the great endeavors made by the author to reconstruct an "umbilical" bond between the white Australians and the inherited land, which has become an indispensable and iconic motif in his oeuvre. The author draws inspiration not only from western eco-critical theories such as Albert Schweitzer's "reference for life", Aldo Leopold's land ethic, but also from Aboriginal eco-wisdom like the notion of looking after your country, which jointly become the internalized codes of behavior for his protagonists. In handling the animals, waste of life is despised and due respect and awe for life are advocated by Winton's characters and it is hinted that basic environmental ethic should be observed in developing agriculture. Winton consciously depicts characters as children of nature, who feel allegiance to the land and would fight to protect it. These characters are most likely to agree with Aboriginal values and ideas about relationship with nature and would defend ecological justice even at personal expense. *Shallows* and *Blueback* are both eco-fiction with the former highlighting the immense challenges and difficulties met by the pioneer eco-heroine Queenie and the latter unfolding a romantic ecotopia in which every eco-endeavor ends in victory. They express Tim Winton's eco-ambition that his Australian compatriots would shoulder the eco-responsibility of looking after the land and the sea so that as much as possible of them can be possibly preserved.

Chapter Ⅲ Retreat to the Wilderness

3.1 Wilderness

Etymologically, the word "wilderness" derives from the Anglo-Saxon "wilddeoren", denoting "deoren" or beasts existing beyond the boundaries of cultivation (Garrard, *Ecocriticism* 60). Another etymological explanation goes that in medieval and Renaissance English, the word "wilderness", earlier *wyldernesse*, Old English *wildeornes*, means "place of wild deer," or possibly "wild-deer-ness" (*deor*, deer and other forest animals) but more likely "wildern-ness" (Snyder 11, Giblett 85).

As a cultural, natural, and social construct, wilderness has a multiplicity of connotations which defy easy definition and it is never "a fixed concept, but one that remains constantly subject to changes in cultural construction and perception" (Bremmer 44). In Archaic Greece, the mountains functioned as a kind of "liminal space" between the civilized world and the world outside Greek Civilization and hence were seen as wilderness (Bremmer 43, 25). "The very earliest documents of Western Eurasian civilisation, such as *The Epic of Gilgamesh*, depict wilderness as a threat" (Garrard, *Ecocriticism* 61). William Robertson Smith (1846—1894), a celebrated Scottish biblical critic, theorist of religion, and theorist of myth, discerns that "the wilderness is the domain of demons, of evil, of wild beasts, and of physical danger" whereas civilization is "the domain of gods, of good, of domesticated animals, and of safety" (Segal 229). Smith's opinion is quite representative and highlights the complicated religious significance of wilderness in Christianity. Roderick Nash and many other scholars have noted that "in the Hebrew Bible wilderness was seen as a place to escape" (B. Taylor 294). Greg Garrard admits that the "Judaeo-Christian conception of wilderness is ambivalent in that it combines connotations of trial and danger with freedom, redemption and purity". Jehovah guides Moses to lead the Israelites out of Egypt into the wilderness of Sinai where God confers The Ten Commandments. Hence, wilderness is "a more hospitable place than the civilised but enslaving Egypt". Garrard also observes that after being driven out of Eden, man has to struggle for subsistence in the wilderness which is both a place of exile and hospice (*Ecocriticism* 61). Wilderness becomes a desolate place set in contrast to "the Garden of Eden". However, the "ambivalence of the Judaeo-Christian tradition towards wilderness had to be resolved in early modern philosophy and literature into something approaching outright hostility" (Garrard, *Ecocriticism* 63). Furthermore, for "the early Western explorers of the New World, the idea of wilderness implied opposition to civilization and to an agricultural ideal understood as the divinely sanctioned order. The wilderness was seen as a place to be defeated and not a place of dwelling for humans" (Hornborg 223).

The derivations and definitional developments of the concept of wilderness in Occidental culture is succinctly summarized by Gary Snyder: firstly, a "large area of wild land" "with original vegetation and wildlife"; secondly, a "wasteland" "unused or useless for agriculture or pasture", thirdly, a "space of sea or air"; fourthly, a "place of danger and difficulty" "as contrasted with heaven"; fifthly, a "place of abundance, as in John Milton, 'a wilderness of sweets'". While commenting that the last meaning "catches the very real condition of energy and richness of wild systems", Snyder also admits that "wilderness has implied chaos, eros, the unknown, realms of taboo, the habitat of both the ecstatic and the demonic". In a word, wilderness is "a place of archetypal power, teaching and challenge" (Snyder 11).

However, Anne-Christine Hornborg discovers that one people's wilderness may be another people's "cultured environment" and home (222). The opinion "seems definitive of the colonial exercise of invasion, expropriation and settlement, especially when based on the Doctrine of Christian Discovery and assertions about *terra nullius*" (Harvey 265). Paul David holds that in European societies and their settler diasporas the mute and inarticulate wilderness is the antithesis of home and is the unhomely (Giblett 90 ~ 91). Nevertheless, Australian "Aboriginal people use 'wilderness' to refer to spoilt country, country damaged by agriculture, mining, pastoralism and cities as distinct from country that is cared for. Wilderness for them is not country remote from agricultural, mining, pastoral and other industries, but that country itself used by those industries" (Giblett 92).

It is interesting to note that the above discussion just mirrors two types of wildernesses explored by Graham Harvey respectively from the European and Indigenous perspectives. Wilderness in the first sense refers to "spaces that are unmarked by humanity, nature untouched by and remote from human culture. [...] Human absence and distance is definitive of this view of wilderness" (Harvey 270). Self-admittedly, the first interpretation is the most common among the westerners and implies that wilderness is not our domain, not the right place for modern people.

The second type of wilderness is in direct opposition to the first: Wilderness refers to "places fatally damaged by too much activity of inappropriate kinds, usually by humans who decline to dwell harmoniously and work cooperatively alongside other species. Put it another way, wilderness is the result of human disruption. Human activities create rather than destroy this wilderness" (Harvey 271). This interpretation of wilderness precisely reflects Indigenous Australians' cosmology. The deserted mining towns depicted by Winton in *Dirt Music* can be the most eloquent examples of this kind of wilderness, which just conjures up images of wasteland that seems to be the unavoidable consequence of the invasion of western industrial civilization into the territory of nature.

The nineteenth-century witnessed a process of rediscovering the sacredness of wild nature in European world which is regarded as "a reaction against formalistic rationalism and enlightened despotism that invoked feeling, instinct, new nationalisms, and a sentimentalized folk culture" (Snyder, *Practice of the Wild* 80). In recent decades, people's attitude to wilderness has undergone dramatic changes on account of environment deterioration. As Harvey notes, the wilderness that was once the domain opposed to the civilized, "is now more commonly celebrated" and "more often viewed as a domain that has been fortunate to survive" (Harvey 270). Moreover, according to Max Oelschlaeger and Daniel J. Philippon, this wilderness is "to be protected and honoured, either for its potential to save over-civilised, overly urban humanity, or for its preservation of biological, scenic or other forms of positively valued diversity" (qtd. in Harvey 270). Wilderness, either as "natural places out there beyond invasive human intervention" or as "the places damaged by humans" (Harvey 271), is a theme that has aroused increasing attention from environmentalists, ecologists, authors as well as ecocritics.

Wilderness is an important motif in western literature, which can be dated earliest back to the ancient Greek epics: *Iliad* and *Odyssey* in which the hero Odyssey achieves the spiritual maturity through ordeals and tortures on the sea. In Renaissance literature, wilderness plays a vital role in characterizing the tragic flaws of the protagonists' personality. In *King Lear*, it is in the heath that King Lear and the Earl of Gloucester realize the blunders they have committed and achieve spiritual epiphany. Going bush is also a major theme in Australian literature. Patrick White's *Voss* (1957) is a modernist narration of an exploration into the continent in the mid-19th century, during which the protagonist Voss and his team experience much adversity in outback Australia. With the perishing of almost all members, the exploration ends in failure but the image of Voss is almost deified and his soul sublimated. The protagonist Heriot, a white missionary, in Randolph Stow's masterpiece *To the Islands* (1958), becomes disillusioned after years of working in an Aboriginal mission but experiences spiritual salvation on the road out of civilization to the islands of death, the resting place for Aboriginals' ancestors.

Given Tim Winton's Irish cultural heritage, it's appropriate to analyze wilderness in his fiction mainly from the western perspective, supplemented with Aboriginal cosmology. Definitions quoted above will effectively facilitate the interpretation of the wilderness in his fiction and the analysis of its ecological significance.

From the discussion, it is clear that wilderness is conventionally judged with utilitarian yardsticks in western cultural context. Despite the changes in recent ages, wilderness is seldom the sphere for daily life and interactions, especially for European Australians. Researchers agree that ever since the mid-nineteenth century, Australia has become "one of the most urbanised countries in the world", with the majority of its population living in a handful of metropolises along the coast (Carter 251). Moreover, their cultures and customs are predominantly European and urban. Hence, most white Australians are definitely city fellows who stay away from the nature and spend most time in air-conditioned houses. Then here is the problem: how can they develop an allegiance to the land and affiliation to nature by staying away and aloof? Returning to wilderness makes "people feel a deep sense of belonging and connection to nature and a sense of its sacredness, which is accompanied by feelings of kinship with other organisms and a corresponding belief in their intrinsic value" (B. Taylor 315 ~ 316). So to speak, Winton's fiction attempts to unfold post-settler Australians' growing ability to interpret and understand the landscape and to survive in wilderness, primarily for establishing new national identity, in the meantime also for strengthening the bond between mankind and the land and cultivating the ecological care towards nature. Therefore wilderness possesses special significance in Tim Winton's oeuvre.

In Chapter Ⅲ, I will attempt to analyze the intimate link between the white Australians and wilderness as constructed and depicted by Tim Winton in his short story as well as novels. Wilderness, in a way synonymous with pristine nature, is the most desirable place for the author to render his protagonists in direct contact with their natural surroundings. Retreat to wilderness is the means through which the white Australians indigenize themselves, or root themselves physically as well as spiritually in a land where they feel alien (Toorn 43). If one can survive in the country, one knows it well enough to claim it one's mother land and one belongs to it as identity is shaped by place. Besides, to a contemporary author who demonstrates obvious identification with romanticism, going "back to nature" also seems to be an antidote to and a reaction against the myth of development and consumerism prevalent in modern society. As is depicted in *Capricornia* by Xavier Herbert, who is "concerned with the failure of Europeans to understand or come to terms with the land", the half haste boy Norman regains his vitality and spiritual maturity by returning back to the tribal bush land, because in white city society, he was oppressed and suppressed (Goldsworthy 123). Through the analysis, we'll see how Winton's protagonists, who have been corrupted by society, resume their good nature in wilderness.

3.2 Coping with Growing Crises in the Wilderness

In this part I am going to interpret Winton's virgin work *An Open Swimmer* (1982) to shed some light on the role played by wilderness in helping a young adult cope with his growth pains from boyhood to adulthood and overcome his childhood trauma. Among the three parts of the novel *Swimmer*, two are set in the bush, highlighting the importance of the natural setting in the story. Part One narrates the crisis in mateship experienced by the hero whereas Part Three deals with his incestuous love with his friend's mother.

The friendship between Jerra and Sean is forged partly owing to the unstable childhood of Sean who even doubts whether Jim is his physical father, for his mother Jewel seems to be a promiscuous woman. Worse still, his own parents even can not give him a home when he was young. That's why both he and his mother spend a lot of time with Jerra's family, the Nilsams, during which Jerra develops brotherly friendship with Sean and deep affiliation to Aunt Jewel.

What's noteworthy is that Jerra and Sean used to spend lots of time fishing and camping together in the wilderness. While camping on the beach, they feel "the air cooling towards twilight", smell the "peculiar smell" from "wet granite", and hear the "mutterings of the gums" (*Swimmer* 9). In a manner of speaking, they grow up in natural surroundings. Hence, they accumulate rich experience and cultivate in themselves strong ability to survive in the wilderness along the beach. They collect wood from the nearby bush to cook and they know what wood burns well; they know what stone is fit for a fireplace; they fish when food is running out. In brief, they are also children of nature and the frequent sojourns in wild nature make it possible to resume the most natural pattern of living — to rise at sunrise and to retire at sunset. Their camping life fully embodies a harmonious state of man's inhabitation in nature without much influence of human civilization.

However, the ideal mode of life has to come to a halt as they grow up on account of different choices of future life. The discrepancies between the two young fellows are increasingly obvious. Jerra drops out of university while Sean stays long enough to get a degree which entitles him a decent job and stable place in the society. From Jerra's point of view, Sean has "sold out to the very economic and social structures which destroyed Sean's own mother" (Watzke, "On the Verge" 17). But Jerra is laid off from the fishing job which he enjoys very much and later is dismissed from his new job at the local deli. That's to say, Sean has settled down in city with a stable income whereas Jerra, a university dropout, is on the crossroad in his life and the problem before him is whether to "finish at Uni" (13) or to follow his heart by doing something that enables him to stay as near as possible to nature.

Another interesting difference between them lies in their pool of knowledge. Sean majors in history in university, which implies that he knows much about the past of human civilization and he is ready for social life. In contrast, Jerra's childhood life and his work at the fishing boat furnish him with adequate information about fish. One type of knowledge is from institutional education while the other is from nature, which obviously doesn't assume equal importance to the survival of individuals in human society. That explains why a college degree is held up high by all. With it a decent life and a smooth way to success are ensured; without it one cannot see any prospect of future. In fact, it is school education or civilization that effectively drives men away from nature. With the accelerating speed of urbanization, the bond with nature as felt by modern people further slackens off. This state of affair leads to wanton plunder of natural resources with no regard to the welfare and wholesomeness of other cohabitants in nature and even the earth itself. Winton's young characters are not top students at school. Neither are they good at human communication in society. But like Jerra, they are in most cases great outdoorsman who can survive in rough natural environment. This is the anti-elitism as some critics call it.

Like most other young people, Sean moves to city, leaving behind a pattern of living that involves intimate contact with the bush and beach. But unlike Sean, Jerra's devotion to nature and a natural way of living seems more stubborn and unshakeable. In a way, Jerra's hesitation to join the society also owes to his reluctance to be converted to a "cultured" man from a natural being, which reveals the author's skepticism about modern civilization. Jerra is virtually a prototype of a number of natural individuals that Winton persistently portrays in his later fiction. These protagonists with natural bent are fish in water in wilderness but are misfits in human community; they are ingenious and resourceful in nature but somewhat maladroit and incapable at school. Therefore, they feel deeply affiliated to nature, enjoy themselves in nature but abominate all types of cultural traps. Their psychic need can only be met by doing jobs that won't sever the link with nature. The depiction of such characters attests to the Romantic attributes on Tim Winton, namely, "a deepened appreciation of the beauties of nature" and "a general exaltation of emotion over reason, or a valuing of senses over intellect" (叶 162). No wonder Jerra loves the job on the fishing boats very much, which retains the innocence in him. To such a child of nature as Jerra, to finish university and then to work for a company is giving in to "corruption" (13), though a conventional routine for many young people in community.

Interestingly, a subtle affinity exists between Winton's conception of knowledge and that of Henry David Thoreau, who has always been regretting that he was not as wise as the day he was born in *Walden* (qtd. in Oelschlaeger 155). After long-term direct touch with wilderness, Thoreau came to realize that knowledge, in the form of Indian wisdom that represents the primal intelligence, does not derive from "mensuration, quantification, differentiation". It is in the wilderness that one is to learn "the essential laws of existence" and get "some sense of the cosmic whole" (Oelschlaeger 155). School learning just numbs our senses, dulls our responses to nature and thus makes us less wise than the day we were born. Therefore, the innocent time when one can't count and doesn't know any letter of the alphabet should be cherished as the golden and responsive time in an individual's life. The communication between a human being and nature then is direct and smooth. Virtually, Thoreau's idiosyncratic theory of knowledge and wisdom has been inspired and stimulated by Jean-Jacques Rousseau, the renowned philosopher, writer, educator as well as composer, who is also called the father of

Romantic Movement. "Rousseau thought that human beings were naturally good and they were corrupted by bad institutions such as governments, schools, cities and armies"①. Like Rousseau and Thoreau, Winton doesn't trust school education very much. In an ABC (Australian Broadcasting Company) radio broadcast he says that the spontaneous feelings are "slowly beaten out of children through our education until we become hard and skeptical buggars who can't get on with anything" (qtd. in Miels 41). Again like Rousseau and Thoreau, Winton also emphasizes the belief that true knowledge comes from living in close consort with nature while modern civilization cuts and blocks up the link between the two.

Last but not least, Jerra's attitude to the unnamed hermit that they run into at the beach is at odds with Sean's. Being men of the coastal bush, Jerra and the old man both show strong interest in fish and demonstrate similar reverence for life as shown in my discussion in chapter Ⅱ. Obviously, their similarities are more than those between Jerra and Sean. No wonder it's easy for Jerra to understand and, to some extent, identify with him. But Sean's attitude to the old fellow is discernibly cynical and ungracious.

Part One of the novel narrates Jerra and Sean's final camp trip to the wilderness. This trip is of special significance on account that it happens when Sean has accomplished the transition to adulthood while Jerra is still lingering at the threshold. To Jerra who "hopes desperately to locate some sense of meaning and direction now missing from his life", the trip offers an opportunity for him "to renew and reaffirm a relationship which has up to now confirmed Jerra's sense of mateship and identity" (Watzke, "On the Verge" 16 ~ 17). The loss of their friendship will further knock out the support from under him and add to his bewilderment and self-denial. But unfortunately it turns out that the

---

① http://novaonline.nvcc.edu/eli/eng252/romanticstudy.htm.

trip only foregrounds the discrepancies between them and affirms the irrevocability of the trend of split between friends.

Even the old hermit discerns the discordance between them and points it out to Jerra, which renders him uneasy and uncomfortable about all this. Despite any endeavor, Jerra has to admit that they are "growing apart" (39) and "it was all over between them; it was a matter of time" (40). The author handles the delicate changes in the relationship in a subtle way in which landscapes and seascapes play an indispensable role for the development of the story. Beth Watzke comments that "Winton uses the physical details of Australian bush and beach to both illuminate and reveal characters and conflicts compelling their actions, driving on the action of the story itself" ("On the Verge" 17). Beth also notes that "the physical details of specific locales in Western Australian and Jerra's interaction with these places permeate the text, shaping Jerra and the way he sees everything" ("On the Verge" 20). The surfing scenes attest to the author's feat in putting the stimulating and fleeting sport in vivid language, which in the long run becomes a hallmark attached to Tim Winton fiction. Deep diving unfolds the mysterious world under the sea, which symbolizes the protagonist's chaotic inner world and his relentless quest for answers. The descriptions reveal the role played by the seascapes in healing the trauma inflicted by the corrupted human society.

Undoubtedly, the numerous fishing trips of Jerra and Sean, sometimes with the company of Jerra's father, in the old days established the brother-like affection between them. But in this trip Sean declares that fish is "not the only bloody thing there is". Sean has outgrown the childhood interest in diving, which is just "swimming in circles" to him now (45). His interest in wilderness camping also fades, which explains why in the final trip Jerra has to collect the wood for fire, clean the fish and do other chores despite slight complaints. It's ironic that Sean would rather spend the daytime reading books than fishing, or diving, or surfing with Jerra in the ocean. What's more, even in the great Aussie bush, he bothers to be in a suit and tie. All these details prove that Sean has lost the innocent heart to feel nature. Eventually, he decides to leave one week ahead of the schedule and thus declares the end of the mateship between them. As a social individual, Sean is virtually alienating himself from the natural landscape as well as his childhood mate, which can be said to be a sort of betrayal. No wonder when Jerra calls the seagulls "Bloody scabs" (15), Sean is watching him. The final trip to the coast witnesses the end of the childhood mateship between Jerra and Sean, which frustrates Jerra very much. As one grows up, everything is not the same anymore. The bush, which should have been a place of refuge, escape and self-confirmation, becomes oppressive and foreboding as the deterioration of Jerra's and Sean's friendship becomes clear (Watzke, "On the Verge" 17).

Crisis in friendship is accompanied by Jerra's worry about the exposure of the secret love with Sean's mother, Aunt Jewel, another major impediment to his growing up. Undeniably, his hesitancy on the cusp of adulthood should mainly attributes to the unsolved boyhood trauma left by his seductive neighbor — Auntie Jewel.

"Freud asserts that during the late infantile stage (somewhere between 3 and 6), all infant males possess an erotic attachment to their mother" (Charles E. Bressler, 124). To grow up, Jerra has to outgrow his incestuous desire for the woman of his mother's age. Although Winton doesn't mention the exact age of Jerra when the affair occurs, we can deduce that the relation forms over long period of intimacy dating back to Jerra's infancy. Jerra has an aptitude for poems from young age. His grandfather once taught him C. J. Dennis①, poems and he was able to

① C. J. Dennis (1876-1938) was an Australian poet known for his humorous poems. He is often considered among Australia's three most famous poets together with Banjo Paterson and Henry Lawson. < http://en. wikipedia. org/wiki/C. _J. _Dennis >.

write some clumsy poems as a child. As a little boy, Jerra felt close to his neighbor Auntie Jewel mainly out of their common love for poems. Thus they spent a lot of time together reading or even composing small poems, which became the beautiful memory of his childhood. But, as he grew up, their intimate relationship was shadowed with a hazy feeling of incestuous love, which involved the young Jerra in a nightmare memory of Auntie Jewel after she went lunatic and was eventually drowned or murdered in an accident on the sea. Jewel is a whore figure in the novel and she is a lunatic. She is obviously promiscuous so much so that she lures a boy. It is implied that Sean is probably of "illegitimate origin" and may have "a beautiful foreign bastard brother soon" (83). Jewel was expecting a baby when she was drowned. Is she murdered by Jim because the new baby disgraces him much? The plot forms obvious intertextuality with *Rebecca* (1938), the masterpiece of famous British female author Daphne Du Maurier (1907—1989). It also incurs the criticism that Winton is misogynistic or heavily prejudiced against women. Jewel and Eva in his later book *Breath* are both women loose enough to lure young boys to dispel their loneliness or to satisfy their lust. Boys or men are always the victims while women are victimizers. "Male trauma is transformed into stories of confession and redemption voiced through the recollection of the female body as displaced Other — stigmatised, threatening and demonized" (Schürholz, "The Poetics of Domesticity" 75). It seems that to grow up means to degenerate. Adult world is already corrupt. Having been lured to experience sexual relation with adult women, young boys are unable to love others, or to live a normal life. The hurt is perpetual.

Tim Winton says in an interview: "Kids become obsessed with sex and my feeling is that they should be encouraged to take things slowly, not in a rush to grow up, but I don't want to go the other way and be down about it. I know trying to arrive at these two aspects I walked a tight rope, but kids are both puritanical and randy at the same time"

(Alf 19). Lockie Leonard, the protagonist in his trilogy, is the ideal teenager in this term. However, "Jerra Nilsam's childhood had been invaded by the corruption of adult world in a way that he neither understood nor could control" (Matthews, "Childhood" 64). His entanglement with Sean's mother throws him into the nightmare of extreme agony. On the one hand, wanting to forget, but he seems to be enlaced even tightly in the painful memory of the time spent with her. On the other, Jewel revisits his dream and thus attests to Schürholz's censure that "the female in Winton's fiction is abstracted as a ghost" ("The Poetics of Domesticity" 75).

Jerra is stricken with the shock of incest. Worse still, the abnormal relationship between them is neither perceived nor suspected by anyone. Hence, Jerra is unable to share his agony or seek any help. With Jewel's accidental death, only their correspondences consolidate its existence. Without sharing, without condemnation, the affair is eventually converted to heavy psychological shackles on Jerra. Since there is no punishment, there is no remission.

Winton says "for many of my characters, the sight of the ocean is either reassuring or it's kind of confirmation of all your worst suspicions" (qtd. in Watzke, "On the Verge" 15). Hence, Jerra's idiosyncratic love of camping in the bush near the coast offers a possible way out of his personal trauma. To dispel the psychological burden, Jerra chooses to separate himself from the secular world and turns to his natural territory for consolation and disengagement. Jean-Jacques Rousseau advocates going "back to nature" to regain "the natural state of human goodness"①. This is what we read in Part Three of the novella: escape to the bush. This part of the narration "details the alternation of Jerra's physical journey to the bush and ocean and his inner journey through memories of Jewel and her death, thus setting up a correspondence

① http://novaonline.nvcc.edu/eli/eng252/romanticstudy.htm.

between inner and outer reality" (Watzke, "On the Verge" 18).

"Going bush" is the classic route of escape for Australians (Watzke, "On the Verge" 16). To Jerra, fishing, diving into the ocean and camping on the beach are something really reassuring, for the ocean is "a space of freedom and solace at this time" (Watzke, "On the Verge" 17). He dives repeatedly deep in search for the pearl supposed to be found in the big fish's head. But in essence he is seeking guidance and clues to his personal predicament rather than the pearl itself. This plot has a lot to do with the author's personal experiences. Winton admitted that diving deep in the ocean meant much to him as a teenager:

> When you're a teenager you feel overcome by all these problems. Everything seems enormous. Everything seems big. You seem tiny and bewildered. So, in a way, jumping into the ocean and diving deep was a way of getting over myself, [...] a way of leaving myself, not worrying that I wasn't tall enough, that I wasn't skinny enough, that I wasn't smart enough, [...]. You jump in the water and [...] It was like a hallucinatory experience, you know? (qtd. in Chen 64)

Since the sea is taken as "a source of dramatic wonder and soothing calm" (Steger, "The Sea Side" 26) in both physical and spiritual sense, diving plays multiple roles in a boy's growing up: to alleviate growing pains, dispel worries, and efface the scope of self. And in this process one befriends such sea animals as fish, seals, and even sharks and becomes a member of the mysterious marine world. Time and again, Jerra puts himself in danger by diving deeper and deeper into the ocean, which yields nothing but ironically proves that the pearl supposed to be in turrum's head is just a legend among fishermen or an illusion from his young age. But why must he find the pearl? What's the significance of the pearl? Beth Watzke's analysis sheds some light on this:

> Jerra can't articulate to anyone, much less himself, what he's after. The nearest he can get to it is the pearl, which he believes contained in the

> kingfish, the "open swimmer" of the title. [...] The pearl (and the story of the pearl) crystallises all Jerra yearns for into an object forged out of nature, solid yet also retaining mystery. ("On the Verge" 17~18)

First of all, it is obvious that Jerra's seeking for the pearl insinuates his relentless love for Jewel as "a pearl is a type of jewel" (Watzke, "On the Verge" 18). Secondly, considering Jerra's age, we are well-grounded to speculate that the pearl also symbolizes the purity and innocence that he cherishes much but lost too early. To seek for the pearl implies Jerra's psychological desire to resume the pure and innocent relationship with Aunt Jewel or to regain the innocence of childhood, which is full of pure happiness. Thirdly, Jerra is tortured by the secret and desire, which is unspeakable. If the pearl is to be found, then Jerra will be able to dispel the agonizing burden of memories about Jewel and return to a normal state of life and set sail on his new life. Thus, looking for the pearl symbolizes seeking for a way out of his growing crisis. Fourthly, in a broader sense, the pearl refers to any aim in one's life which is out of reach. Or it is a dream that will never come true.

Rather than mere physical journeys, Jerra's retreat to the bush is more an explorative and contemplative odyssey through which he gradually comes to face his past boldly, sort out his problems and fumbles a way out. The final epiphany is inseparable from the protagonist's firsthand contact with nature, namely, his sojourn in the wilderness of coastal bush. The hero as a cultural being is reduced to its minimum form while his self as a natural entity is maximized. In my view, it is the magical power possessed by nature to tranquilize one and appease one's trauma that eventually causes Jerra's epiphany.

When he discovers that the pearl in the fish's head is a mirage, Jerra is overtaken by extreme despair and collapse in the inner world, which is echoed by the atrocious thunderstorms in natural world. "Winton's texts do not seek closure in the traditional sense of fictional narratives; they have inconclusive endings which fail to offer up incontestable 'meanings'" (F. Murphy 74). However, Yvonne Miels believes that although "*An Open Swimmer* is also dark with Jerra's guilt and uncertainty" (33 ~ 34), it "ends with a positive cleansing by fire and water and Jerra's desire for increased self-knowledge" (34). So, a favorable turn for the better can be expected after the utmost misery. Jerra's disillusion evaporates; a bundle of envelopes are burned; the hermit dies. It's not until then that the psychological cross on the young lad begins to be removed, and the trauma begins to heal. As Wachtel puts it, the idea of water (in the sea or in the river) is compelling to Winton. "The water is dangerous but it can offer a kind of empowerment" for Winton's characters. "Some of them, (like Fish in *Cloudstreet*), are very badly affected: there are accidents that maim them. Others derive a kind of epiphany or purging; something positive happens to them" (72). Fire and water jointly purify a young soul corrupted by the adult world and wilderness offers the ideal locale for Winton's traumatic protagonist to cope with his growing crises.

3.3 The Dilemma of Modern People in the Wilderness

Scission (1985) is Tim Winton's first collection of short stories that deal with protagonists whose lives are jeopardized and whose hearts are broken. The volume includes stories that have appeared in various publications and achieved good acclamation. Among the thirteen stories, "Neighbours" has been translated into Chinese. "Secrets" has also become a classic one to be read by literary students in class. Victoria Sen comments that in this anthology many characters have to struggle with "change and disintegration"①.

Included in the collection is a short story entitled "Wilderness", first published in *Westerly* in 1983. Three protagonists are found in the

① From the back cover of the Penguin version.

story, namely, a couple who are fond of bushwalking and a crank who attempts to build a shack in the wilderness. All are unnamed. The encounter between the two parties is fortuitous, yielding a series of mystic and funny results. Despite the brevity of the narration, "Wilderness" demonstrates the author's excellent modernist writing skills, for the text is full of fragmentary flashbacks, stream of consciousness, and interior monologues. Interesting comparisons are deliberately made by the author to unfold complicated and profound human nature in cultural and natural settings respectively. In addition, many conflicts are explored, such as those between wilderness and civilization, nature and culture, as well as between instinct and reason. Religion and mysticism also flavor the story. All these render it a lovely short story worthy of critical scrutiny.

"For FIVE days and five nights the man and the woman had been in the wilderness" thus begins the story. The couple is different from others due to their devotion to outdoor life (61). "In their five years of marriage, they had become connoisseurs of national parks and wilderness trails" (64). With the passage of time, they develop a taste for it and their walks become more adventurous.

Oddly, their love of wilderness trekking does not derive from deep love for nature. Neither does it come from a tradition in Australia, though the nation, especially the state of Western Australia is never lack of such a tradition. The Bibbulmun walk is a convincing proof①. Winton

---

① Tim Winton mentions the Bibbulmun walk in this story, but spells it as "the Bibulman walk" (62). The Bibbulmun Track is one of the world's great long distance walk trails, stretching 1000km from Kalamunda in the Perth Hills, to Albany on the south coast, winding through the heart of the scenic South West of Western Australia. <https://www.bibbulmuntrack.org.au/> The name comes from the Bibbulmun, or Noongar people, Indigenous Australians from the Perth area. <http://en.wikipedia.org/wiki/Bibbulmun_Track>.

points out in his text that their passion for bushwalking does not visit accidentally. Instead, it is the conclusion drawn after many negotiations between the husband and wife. "Being afraid of religion and expense, they choose bushwalking" (64). Put it other way, it results from scrupulous weighing the pros and cons, i.e. rational contemplation. The importance of rationalism is purposefully and sarcastically highlighted by the author in the story. It seems that the couple does everything in a rational way inflexibly. Moreover, they are both teachers by calling, of which the husband is quite proud, for a teacher is "a man of reason, disseminator of rational learning" (71).

That the hobby is decided by rational deduction is just the tip of the iceberg. Other details fortify the speculation that the couple is enslaved to rigid rationality. The trekking can't be done without essential outdoor facilities such as map, compass, torch and duck-down sleeping bags. And they upgrade it when they can afford. Then, it is obvious that every walking is well-planned beforehand: "They mapped out their journey; they walked from A to B to C without unnecessary deviation or lingering at any point" (67). It is stressed that the walking in the wilderness is carried out mechanically. One can't help wondering how they can manage to enjoy the freedom and absorb the tonics from wilderness as Henry D. Thoreau did if "deviation or lingering at any point" were believed "unnecessary". To them, bushwalking sounds more like task-accomplishing than soul-relaxing.

Not only do they have accurate plans but they usually follow them rigorously. When they deviate from their "planned route" or breaking the "timetable" (62), they will feel uncomfortable. The adjectives such as "strange" (62), "amazed" (63), "annoyed" (65) and finally "uneasy" (70) imply the deterioration of their moods when they fail to follow the route. With the development of the story, they become increasingly upset as the whole matter just goes from bad to worse. Eventually they attribute it to the ominous digression from normal itinerary as if a spell were cast on them. In fact, the root of the whole thing turns out to be "a metallic glint" that flashes, which is unexpected and inexplicable since "this is wilderness" (62, 63), where traffic tools have no access according to the widely admitted definition of wilderness. Curiosity kills the cat. To trace down the matter, they go astray and eventually pay a high price. Not only is the walking spoilt, but they end up making tremendous efforts to carry the sick crank that becomes invalid while transporting building materials across uneven hilly road in a barrow under the moon.

Attention now turns back to the preparations for walking. As mentioned above, the couple would firstly get the necessary outdoor facilities and then draw up a plan. It's interesting to compare these preparations with those required by the great wilderness walker Henry D. Thoreau. Like the protagonists in "Wilderness", Thoreau stresses adequate preparation for walking. He underscores that firstly "the walking of which I spoke has nothing in it akin to taking exercises [...] but is itself the enterprise and adventure of the day" ("Walking" 600~601). Neither is it the hobby, or topics for gossip, an opinion held by modern people like the couple in Winton's tale. Secondly, sauntering through the wilderness demands that one be "free from all worldly engagements" ("Walking" 599). Instead of being ready in material terms, Thoreau highlights that "walkers must prepare themselves for the adventure, essentially by clearing the mind, forgetting the conventional wisdom, the din of parlors, thoughts of work", as insightfully interpreted by Max Oelschlaeger (164). Namely, they must remove the disturbances from the secular world and be ready in psychology and mentality for the immediate and potentially liberating encounters with wild nature. Thirdly, Thoreau believes that "there is a subtle magnetism in Nature, which, if we unconsciously yield to it, will direct us aright" ("Walking" 607). Rather than the metaphor of compass, what the modern bush travelers need is the compass itself as an indispensable tool for bushwalking. It's unimaginable for modern people to follow nature's guide as if they were "the needle of a compass" that can feel the magnetism in nature and get the guidance from it, because they have been hyperseparated from nature for too long (Oelschlaeger 164). The radical exclusion, borrowing Val Plumwood's term, makes it impossible for modern people to perceive and respond to direction from nature. Through the comparison, we see Thoreau foregrounds the preparation in mental and emotional aspects, which is something dearly lack in our protagonists who stress preparation in rational terms, including material equipment and rational knowledge.

Modern wilderness trekkers choose to depend on information from books rather than on intuition and first-hand experience. Book knowledge is another necessary preparation for walking to the couple. Before setting off, they usually do some reading and the wife even brings along the bird identification book with her. She reads it while walking because in her view to be able to "name all the birds" "makes seeing them worthwhile" (61). Naming (places or wildlife) is a major means to colonize nature through which flora and fauna become others that are categorized into objective systems of knowledge, which "overshadows the subtle interactions that create and sustain an ecosystem" (qtd. in Corderoy and Baker 5). Tom Griffiths (1996) has pointed out that

> even those settlers who were most enamoured of the flora and fauna in their adopted homelands saw themselves as either hunters or collectors, and wanted to assert their mastery over the wildness that they simultaneously admired and feared, or to collect specimens that could be named and safely deposited in museums (Adams and Mulligan 5).

Additionally, the female character's behavior exactly attests to Henry D. Thoreau's mockery that "most of our boasted so-called knowledge is but a conceit that we know something" ("Walking" 625). As a matter of fact, John Muir, the wilderness sage, takes nature itself as a book, "the Book of Nature" (Oelschlaeger 176). Muir reads "it largely as an early nineteenth-century scientist might, with the assurance that it was a sacred book" (qtd. in Oelschlaeger 176). Albert Schweitzer once said "it is not through knowledge, but through experience of the world that we are brought into relation with it" (*Anthology* 263), which seems to be an opinion agreed upon by Tim Winton. The intellectual tradition of western world holds that reason is the way to know and understand the world, but the author, like other ecophilosophers, embraces intimate contact with nature as the truer way of understanding the world.

Hence, both the idea and the act of the female protagonist in "Wilderness" seem stupid and ridiculous. Funnily, "she stumbled on a stump and fell to one knee". The crux of the matter lies in the ironic fact that "while you've got your beak in that book you're not even seeing the birds" (61), as pointed out by her husband. Here, she takes wilderness as the object of observation and exploration, which is an attitude typical of many westerners who bother to come into close touch with nature. Self-evidently, they withdraw from human community to wilderness in order to sojourn and see rather than to return and feel. Rigid modes of rational thinking make them unable to place themselves in nature heart and soul and have active and constructive interactions with nature. While walking in wilderness, they can't feel "the absolute freedom and wildness" as felt by the American naturalist and hiker Henry D. Thoreau, for they can't perceive themselves as "inhabitant, or a part and parcel of nature" ("Walking" 597). They are not aware that the problem with them is that "they did not believe in things that were ends in themselves". They just settle for the fact that "they had *done* this walk and *done* that wilderness trail" (emphases original). But when they try to share experiences about their walking, their friends and colleagues obviously feel apathetic. To the couple, bushwalking is "a means to an end" other than the ends themselves (67). Namely, they just move a small step forward than their fellow urbanites who would rather read *Walden*, or watch TV programs produced by *National Geographic* than go to the natural world to have direct contact with the other-than human world, which will offer them the immediacy they need to reestablish an umbilical bond with nature. In the binary opposition between nature and culture, they are always members of cultural community. However, in wilderness, one is always expected to open the arms to embrace nature with abandon. Winton wants to dispel the estrangement and reestablish normal rather than alien relationship between modern people and wilderness. To that end, he appeals to man's animal instincts, the irrational aspects. That is to say, he arranges rational characters to perform irrationally or passionately in the natural surroundings, which weakens their cultural attributes and boosts their natural features and thus reestablishes humanity's status as a member of the natural community.

Firstly, Winton begins to dismantle the rigid rationality via discussing why people are "always walking to water" in wild nature, which is a petty question in life (62). Habitual rational mindset prompts the couple to seek a rational explanation for every phenomenon. Behind the couple are the shadows of such rational philosophers and scientists as Francis Bacon (1561—1626), René Descartes (1596—1650) and Isaac Newton (1642—1727) who saw nature as a huge machine "reducible to an assemblage of parts functioning according to regular laws that men could, in principle, know in their entirety" (Garrard, *Ecocriticism* 61~62). Furthermore, it was also assumed that "knowing the force and action of fire, water, air, the stars, the heavens, and all the other bodies that surround us", human race might become "masters and possessors of nature" (qtd. in Garrard, *Ecocriticism* 62). However, that water, the source of life, is needed by all species does not need explanation and it is by instinct that all species choose to live near water. That the couple would resort to "commonsense" for a reasonable explanation sounds like bringing owls to Athens (Winton, "Wilderness" 62). Common sense is a catchy phrase for practical sense or knowledge. According to the Scottish philosopher Thomas Reid (1710—1796), common sense is "natural judgment from a set of innate principles of conception and belief implanted in the human mind by God" and can be taken as "the antecedent of the concept of inspiration" (Crammer 64). The author here is playing on the animal instincts of human race to mock at the rigidity and stupidity of modern urbanites and intellectuals.

Secondly, Winton forces his protagonists to encounter the wildness in their physical body face to face, a tentative attempt at subverting the western culture that "alienates itself from the very ground of its own being — from the wilderness outside (that is to say, wild nature, the wild, self-contained, self-informing ecosystems) and from that other wilderness, the wilderness within" (qtd. in Oelschlaeger 275).

When standing on the peak of Mount Ktaadn, Thoreau discerned the sublime of miles of mountainous landscape, but more surprisingly he also felt "the permanently threatening proximity of that other wilderness, the human body" (Garrard, *Ecocriticism* 67), which rendered him speechless:

> This matter to which I am bound has become so strange to me. I fear not spirits, ghosts, of which I am one, -that my body might, -but I fear bodies, I tremble to meet them. What is this Titan that has possession of me? Talk of mysteries! Think of our life in nature, -daily to be shown matter, to come into contact with it, -rocks, trees, wind on our cheeks! the *solid* earth! the *actual* world! the *common sense*! *Contact*! *Contact*! *Who* are we? *where* are we? (*Maine Woods* 64)

As observed by Oelschlaeger, the problem is to embrace the existence of wildness within himself without threatening his identity as a distinctive human being (161). When an individual is placed in such a setting, surrounded by the genuine natural elements, one can hardly deny the existence of one's corporeal body which is not only a thinking entity but first and foremost a natural being.

Long-term hyperseparation between man and nature renders it difficult for westerners to recognize the wildness in our physical body so that when they are aware of it they are scared. And in this quote Thoreau, despite his enthusiastic passion for wild nature, just took it as Titan that entrapped him. Wildness is an intrinsic component of human psychology. But, human beings in most cases have lost it over the process of education and civilization. However, "as a quality intrinsic to who we are", the wildness in human won't die but is temporarily repressed in our unconscious (Snyder, "Cultured or Crabbed" 49). In western culture it is assumed that the possession of such mental attributes as rationality and intellectuality is what distincts humans from other animals. According to Val Plumwood, "the ideals which are held up as truly worthy of a human life exclude those aspects associated with the body, sexuality, reproduction, affectivity, emotionality, the senses and dependence on the natural world" (*Feminism* 71). If walking to water makes a slight dent in indicating man's dependence on nature, more dramatic effects may be produced when elements of sexuality, corporality, and passion are felt by human beings.

When her husband is feeding her chocolate, the female bushwalker has planned to say something to kill time. But as if out of nowhere, she feels "another sensation, a springing of nerves in her pelvis, in her chest, her feet". Released the selves from the limitation of rationality, the trekking couple embark upon the most spontaneous foreplay of lovemaking. Everything occurs in the most natural way. "It was passion. It made no sense" (68).

Val Plumwood notes:

> ... accounts of the mind/body and reason/nature relation (are) associated with the Platonic, Aristotelian, Christian rationalist and

> Cartesian rationalist traditions that exhibit radical exclusion as well as other dualistic features. Thus the body and the passions belong in Plato's account to a sharply distinct lower realm, homogenized and defined by exclusion, to be dominated and controlled by superior reason, and to be used in its service. (*Feminism* 70)

But the development of plots in Tim Winton's "Wilderness" indicates that you can't control the sexual impulse as you can't explain it. Put it another way, sexuality, as a human instinct, is uncontrollable and inexplicable especially in the context of wilderness. Mankind, in some respects, has been overcultured so that no room is left for the wild nature in them. Being wild doesn't mean being savage. It is the wildness in us that forms the genetic link with nature because passion and sexuality are something that humans share with other animals in the natural world. Reason, the very thing that separates humans from the sphere of nature, just cannot manage to root up the wildness in human race no matter how hard it tries or how eagerly rational philosophers hope so. As feared by Henry D. Thoreau in the above quote, the wild instinct in the form of sexuality in human beings erupts all of sudden in the wilderness, which defies any attempt on rational explanation. Thus, the couple's images as rational beings collapse immediately and the dichotomy of reason and instinct dissolves.

We may dwell a little longer on the life led by the pair. "Winton's narratives often present the themes of alienation and isolation as the consequences of modernization" (Ben-Messahe, *Mind the Country* 62). The husband and wife in the story are lucky exceptions in Wintonian clan, most of whom are solitary souls. However, their life in town, like most other urban dwellers, is far from satisfactory as is indicated by the description of their home. As the locus of privacy, home should have been the most appropriate place for intimacy between couple. But "their home was a place of business", implying that there is no demarcation between work and life at all. Furthermore, efficiency is the currency in modern society so that "no time, no gestures, no thoughts (are) wasted" even while they are at home. Winton presents daily life and work of the couple in such an exaggerated way that it impresses his readers that it goes on like a machine operating on a fixed and precise procedures. Namely, it is a reductionist and mechanic rather than an organic life with time for both work and play. Sarcastically, this state of life is assumed to be quite normal and even desirable in people's eyes as "it was not a frivolous life" (67). "Urban society fragments the individual into compartmentalized roles" so that the space for interpersonal communication is greatly misappropriated (qtd. in Ben-Messahe, *Mind the Country* 62).

Compare this with their interactions in the wilderness. On the same page, we read: "He fed her tiny bits of chocolate [...] She took it on her tongue silently as a communicant, tasting the salt on his fingers, holding one fingertip captive between her lips until his thumb buttoned her nose back and he smiled". This flirting scene is so romantic with the most natural and spontaneous affection between lovers. Pitifully, "there was none of this at home" (67). Their attitudes towards life best represent the so-called modernistic mode of living that "understands both the natural and cultural worlds on the basis of a machine metaphor" (Oelschlaeger 202). In urban life the most natural factors are missing so that humankinds can hardly be aware of the mere fact that they are beings with flesh and blood. Retreating to wilderness awakens the passion for each other buried deep down in the collective unconsciousness of human race. Hence, wilderness is where modern people shake off the hypocritical mask and shackle of civilization to enjoy freedom and relaxation and feel the residue of wildness per se. And hopefully they may eventually become "part and parcel of nature".

All three protagonists are living in twofold realms: the constructed urban area, the realm of culture; and the pristine wilderness, the realm of nature. Wilderness is the raw material out of which man has hammered a diversity of cultures (Leopold 264). Wilderness is "where humans have not yet imposed recognisably human-originated and human-benefiting order" (Harvey 273). And the realms in the story are incompatible. So here arises the question: why bother to go to the wilderness since urban environment obviously ensures a better and easier life for them all? The hippie couple possibly does it in order to strengthen the bond between husband and wife. It is also implied that they do this in order to find the topics for staffroom gossip. Sarcastically, their friends and colleagues grow more aloof from them because they show no interest in either their peculiar hobby or their stories.

To the eccentric man, wilderness offers a spiritual sanctuary where he is determined to retreat under the guidance of a mysterious voice. He had an epiphany while sitting in the staff room a year ago. The "ragged noticeboard" suddenly transformed to a window, through which he envisioned a landscape with bush and sky. He emphasized that in the visionary scene there was only "lonely, untouched, risky-looking bush" (76), namely, the bush in wilderness. After that, more uncanny things occurred. The students in his history class, which implies that he is also a teacher, sometimes lose their heads sometimes have their heads. All these drive him to the edge of nervous break-down. To dispel the fearful feelings, he goes to the bush where "he heard the voice coming out of the ground" — "Go into the wilderness and wait" (77). He assumes it the voice of God and thus concludes that his salvation resides in wilderness.

A big plan comes into being soon and is carried out by him stealthily, stubbornly, and single-handedly for the whole year which results in the "frame of a dwelling" in wilderness (63). As the definitions of wilderness indicate, that there is no permanent dwelling of human race is a basic feature of wilderness①. No wonder both the

① See the definition in the American Wilderness Act issued in 1964 by the U.S. Congress.

husband and wife are amazed when they come across it accidentally. Although even Henry D. Thoreau admits that a man would construct his shelter as naturally as a bird builds its own nest in nature (*Walden* 41), he also highlights that "the wisest have ever lived a more simple and meagre life than the poor". Hence, in Thoreau's opinion the comforts of urban life are "not only not indispensable, but positive hindrances to the elevation of mankind" (qtd. in Oelschlaeger 153). However, the house-builder in our story takes it for granted that "not even God would make a man wait out here without a roof over his head" (78). His story is not one of return to the wilderness but one of escape to nature, laden with heavy burden of civilization. So it's not hard to imagine that even if the house were built, the eccentric could hardly acquire serenity and redemption.

The house-builder demonstrates the spirit of Sisyphus when attempting to build the shack on his own because it keeps falling to the ground. And he holds the conviction that "nothing was impossible" (78). As a history teacher he knows well about the major feats in human civilization, such as the pyramids, accomplished by the ancient Egyptians under primitive working conditions with strong willpower. All these make him believe that strong will is the only thing needed for any ambition. In brief, the history teacher best represents blind conceit and arrogance of humanity who think that they can defeat nature. And his intention to build a house in wilderness epitomizes this ambition, which involves scarring the wilderness by hacking the bush, flattening the vegetation and so on. The crank's anecdote is one employed by the author to suggest that before the westerners harmonize their relationship with nature, the further they contact with nature, the more serious nature will be spoilt.

Why does the odd man need to seek redemption via withdrawing himself from the human community and from his mother? Salhia Ben-Messahe notes that Winton's stories are frequently concerned with "split communities and individuals" (*Mind the Country* 60). The unnamed eccentric is a split individual who lives in a ruptured society, which can be proved by the alienated relationship between him and his mother, who is portrayed as a hollow person. It is in the evening of the day when epiphany occurred that "he saw his mother's skeleton inside her" (77) as if "he saw her in X-ray vision" (75). In his eyes, his mother is "an empty vessel" (75), which obviously is reminiscent of the images of hollow man portrayed in Joseph Conrad's *Heart of Darkness* (1902) and further developed in T. S. Eliot's poem The Hollow Men (1925). In the former, we find that the protagonist Mr. Kurtz went to Africa as a brilliant, eloquent and ambitious young fellow but degenerated into a hollow man who was overwhelmed by greed and power in the darkness of ivory trade that involved plunder and embezzlement. Hence, Mr. Kurtz was the agent as well as victim of western civilization and colonialism and his decadence in both spirit and morality epitomized the dilemma of modern westerners who were faced with the predicament of the fall of their civilization. This type of spiritual desperation and hollowness was even more explicit in the latter. They are "stuffed men" whose heads are "filled with straw" and whose voices are "dried", and "quiet and meaningless"①. In Winton's image of hollow men, we find a careless mother who does not understand her son that is on the brink of nervous breakdown: "She, even this past year, had never suspected, never known where he had been coming every weekend, never even understood or detected his sudden and vast dissatisfaction with his life, with her, with his useless job" (75). What she does is to give him the shelter over his head, a room to sleep in and some chops to fill the belly. There is neither care nor affection between the two. The odd character even foresees the future when he is to be absent from home, her mother would find a boarder as the replacement for him as the company at dinner table, which is assumed to be the role he plays in his mother's life.

① http://baike.baidu.com/subview/1287866/11989961.htm#4.

Therefore, the highly alienated and indifferent mother-son relationship can only be explained by her being a hollow character. Under the spell of some uncanny force, the son has to turn to wild nature for a vital source of solace.

When the room-maker falls to the ground and can no longer get up, the couple decides to save him right away. For want of any transportation, they have to utilize the very barrow that the odd man has used to transport the construction materials. Funnily, though in desperate physical agony and exhaustion, the old crank immediately "recognizes" them as the angels who come to rescue him and take him to heaven. He is then in a state of half stupor and half illusion and it seems that he resumes the long-lost sense of satisfaction and serenity at that moment. He assumes that he is parting with his careless mother and the meaningless life in this world and is led to another world by compassionate angels. Winton concludes his salvation in a surreal way — he is saved by two angels: one male, another female, who turned out to be the couple who are wilderness travelers. The old crank's religious cosmos and the couple's secular cosmos overlap in the coincident encounter between them. The consequence is that one party gets on the way to heaven while the other to hell, which reveals the story's nature as a modern tragicomedy.

In brief, Winton's short story "Wilderness" sheds light on the fact that modern people's return to wilderness may degrade to a ridiculous farce without adequate psychological preparation and right attitudes. It just exposes the dilemma of modern people who desire for nature but cannot return due to the fact that they are cultural beings who are deprived of the ability to survive in wilderness.

3.4 The Reconciliation in the Wilderness

Dirt Music (2001) is another major fiction that won Tim Winton his third Mile Franklin Literary Award and was shortlisted for the Man Booker Prize in 2002. The motif of the novel is generally agreed to be the love story between Luther Fox, a local poacher and Georgie Jutland, the partner of the head fisherman Jim Buckridge, or a triangle love story involving the three protagonists. Bárbara Aritzi takes it a typical trauma story on account that the "story of love-at-first-sight" between Fox and Georgie "is short-circuited but also fuelled by their own and other characters' unsolved traumas" ("Personal Trauma" 176). Admittedly, all three characters in the fiction are stricken with traumatic personal experiences of one sort or another. Georgie, the former nurse, is beset by broken relations with her family and a nightmare of being chased by Mrs Jubail, a former patient whose face is misshaped by tumor. Jim is haunted by both notorious family tradition and a sense of guilt in that he has committed adultery with Sal, who happens to be Lu's sister-in-law, and thus is trapped in contemplation of sin and redemption. Luther Fox is the only survivor of a series of family tragedy.

Sunday Telegraph's endorsement reads that it is "an extraordinary depiction of a man coming to terms with his soul in the tropical wilderness of northern Australia"①. Lu's seeking for redemption scratches from leaving his hometown at the White Point, a fishing town, reaches its climax at the wild island on Coronation Gulf. *Dirt Music* also possesses some features of a road novel. But my research interest guides my attention to the wilderness of the remote island where his trauma heals and reconciliation is achieved. Therefore, I see eye to eye with Kylie Crane in her idea that *Dirt Music* also belongs to the category of "into the wilderness narrative" (*Myths of Wilderness* 61). Retreating to wilderness, or "back to nature" as Rousseau calls it, is believed by many eco-critics and eco-philosophers to be the fundamental channel

① From "Praise for Dirt Music" listed before the title page of the novel.

through which to resume the good nature in an individual, or to reconstruct the severed bond between humankind and nature. Hence, the research into Lu's rehabilitation in the wilderness is also of ecological significance. Bárbara Aritzi's essay offers me the very inspiration to further the study into trauma and its recovery. Based on her research, I would like to shed new light on the role played by wilderness in a variety of reconciliations depicted in the novel, such as the reconciliation between man and shark (wild life), culture and nature, man and himself (past), the white and the aboriginal (though quite dubious), and eventually humankind and nature.

Undeniably, Tim Winton is fortunate as an author who achieves early success and has a happy family. But Bárbara Arizti points out that "the lives of his fictional creatures are often scarred by trauma in various shapes" ("Personal Trauma" 176). In Winton's oeuvre, trauma may come from all manner of sources such as neglect, abuse, accidents, violence, and alcoholism etc. Luther Fox stands out among the traumatic characters and his family tragedy is somewhat unparalleled among others. His mother died of a bough that went through her chest in a gale when he was hardly ten whereas his father died of mesothelioma due to his work on the asbestos mine as explored in chapter I. Later he became the only survivor of a car accident in which he lost his elder brother's family. The ways that Winton's protagonists get out of traumatic situations also vary from one to another. Some depend on a mythic inner voice while others turn to God. Still others retreat to an isolated world of one's own.

In her essay "Personal Trauma/Historical Trauma in Tim Winton's *Dirt Music*", a chapter in *The Splintered Glass*, Bárbara Arizti contends that "Lu's working through his personal trauma relies on elements that both expose and play down the foundational trauma of the Australian nation: namely, the appropriation of the Aboriginal land" (176). She considers that it corroborates the "white settler envy or trauma envy" put forward by Marc Delrez, which refers to "the ambivalence of trauma studies in Australia, where the idea of trauma is often displaced from the native Australians to the settlers". That is to say, the Aborigines' trauma is often overshadowed by highlighting all sorts of trauma felt by the white settlers. My dissertation has claimed that Tim Winton always endeavors to construct new national identity through establishing "umbilical" bond between the settlers and their adopted land in chapter Ⅱ. Hence, rather than purposefully overshadowing the historical trauma experienced by the Indigenous, "what white Australians seem to be envious of is the Aborigines' emotional link with the land and the legitimacy of their relationship with it", as pointed out by Arizti ("Personal Trauma" 186). It's true that due attention ought to be paid to Winton's constant efforts to locate characters back in natural landscapes, which is a matter of more environmental than political significance for him as an eco-author. Through my analysis, I hope to dig out the ecological implications buried in the obvious facts that Winton consciously has his protagonist act in an aboriginal way and resolve personal trauma in the wilderness.

In the first section of this chapter, I've briefly combed the historical changes in attitudes towards wilderness in western culture and pointed out that wilderness assumes more ecological significance in contemporary context owing to the deterioration of natural environment and the awakening of people's consciousness of ecological protection. It seems that the situation is going from one pole to another. Instead of treating wilderness as dangerous other, "wilderness is shown to be a key word for tourism". A good case in point is the enthusiastic lovers of bush walking in Winton's short story "Wilderness". But the short story was published in 1983 when wilderness tourism was just taking shape and winning popularity in Australia (trips to wilderness enjoy a much longer tradition and history in the US). *Dirt Music* comes out in 2001. The temporal gap reveals the author's persistent interest in wilderness trekking and witnesses gradual changes in his attitudes to wilderness tourism. So to speak, when in his early 20s, he was ambivalent about the matter. What concerned him then was the dilemma of urban people — how to cope with temporary sojourn in bush. His budding contemplation mainly centered on such basic questions as reasons for, means of and purposes for going to wilderness. Paradoxically, the crank's walking only "'devalue[s]' wilderness as the pristine, human-free natural world" (Crane, *Myths of Wilderness* 60). What they lack is a heart-felt love for and need of nature and genuine skills of living in wilderness, which can all be found in Luther Fox, another character Winton portrays as a wilderness hero after an 18-year interval.

As indicated in his "Wilderness", Winton is dubious about wilderness tours. In fact, Winton does not show much interest in modern tourism, which can be corroborated by more details in his other fiction. In his short story "Laps" (1987), his protest against the construction of tourist infrastructure like the hotels on the beachfront is vividly demonstrated through images such as cranes, steel skeletons, bulldozers, diggers which are taken as representative tools of instrumental rationality. In fact, Winton ironically calls Western Australia "a state of small people with big bulldozers" (*Land's Edge* 22). Bulldozers on the beach imply that human race's encroachment of natural territory has been expanding to the edge of the land — the coastlines, "one of the fastest-shrinking categories of wilderness" (Leopold 266). Aldo Leopold warns in 1949 that "no single kind of wilderness is more intimately interwoven with history, and none is nearer to the point of complete disappearance" than the shorelines (267).

The descriptions of the tourist town of Broome in *Dirt Music* convey similar information. The old-timey lovely landscapes in nice dream towns are being replaced by large-scale shopping malls and car parks catering to the demand of a booming modern tourism industry. Wilderness trip has become a vogue among successful elites. They pay handsomely for "a week's mad-dog sportfishin[g]". But it ends up in their being scared and lying awake all night. As Red, the tour guide in *Dirt Music*, puts it, they are not scared by any particular species of wildlife but are "terrified of the wide, brown land" (414), namely the wild nature. Highly educated professionals like lawyers, surgeons, and CEOs are the very people who are highly alienated from nature. Therefore, when displaced from human civilization to pristine wilderness, they are unavoidably trapped in a sort of "cultural shock" resulting from the state of hyperseparation. This plot insinuates the ironic fact that the better educated one is, the more alienated one becomes, which again hints at the author's anti-elitist propensity.

Despite all this, "they're back every year for more". Georgie calls it "ritual humiliation" (415). Maybe they are prompted by the call from the wilderness, the spiritual home of mankind. Therefore, it's hard to tell whether the tourists genuinely entertain the "freedom and safety" they claim to obtain in the wilderness (414). Then how to look at Luther Fox's retreat to the wilderness? What does the wilderness mean to this "Robinsonade" character? Will he be scared by the wildness of wilderness? These are all the puzzles to be solved in my discussion.

In her monograph *Myths of Wilderness in Contemporary Narratives*, Kylie Crane takes the island of wilderness that the three protagonists converge as the key object for research. She considers the novel a "Robinsonade story of being shipwrecked on an isolated island", an opinion I can hardly see eye to eye with (59).

Firstly, Robinson Crusoe is the one "being shipwrecked" but Luther Fox chooses to retreat willingly. Namely, one is passive while the other is active and voluntary. The following quote from the text best shows Luther Fox's desire for going to wilderness:

> What he wants is to slope off into the bush somewhere, [...] instead of slinking around the edge of White Point like a feral dog. If you want to be left alone then clear out. Go somewhere clean. Some place with water and food so you're not skulking at the margins to keep yourself alive. A place where you can stand alone, completely alone. No roads, towns, farms — no bloody civilians. Just walk off into the trees. [...] The idea of a place to be truly alone in — wilderness. (294)

"While almost all men feel an attraction drawing them to society, few are attracted strongly to Nature" (Thoreau, "Walking" 627). Luther Fox is one of the few. Thoreau deems the most significant role of wilderness is spiritual: "When I would recreate myself, I seek the darkest wood, the thickest and most interminable and, to the citizen, most dismal swamp" (Thoreau, "Walking" 616). This explains why Lu decides to go deeper into wilderness to an unmanned small island away from the mainland coast. "Wilderness narratives share the motif of escape and return with the typical pastoral narrative" (Garrard, *Ecocriticism* 59). Obviously, Lu's is a voluntary escape from society and also a willing retreat to nature because he wants to be left alone, to have a place where he is free of secular worries. That's to say, he hopes to insulate himself from the civilized world. He retreats to stay in the wilderness rather than to visit.

Secondly, Robinson's conquest of the island metonymically represents the British Empire's colonization of the world. He established agriculture and husbandry on the island and enslaved the indigenous people and demonized them as man-eaters. Friday was portrayed as an obedient slave who was filled with admiration and worship for the civilization possessed by Robinson whereas Robinson assumed that Friday's only diet was human flesh. The novel even describes a scene of the "savages" eating the flesh of their enemies to strengthen their stereotype as the cannibal other. Portraying the indigenous people as cannibal savages in fact meets the need of constructing the pair of binary opposition: Christian European culture verse indigenous cannibalism to justify "the suppression of the threatening 'other'" (Huggan and Tiffin 168). Ironically, "while there was little evidence of native anthropophagous practices (among the indigenous), there *was* some evidence of European cannibalism, albeit in extreme situations of shipwreck and starvation" (emphasis original), which can be certified by a plot from *Shallows*. In addition, "because many non-European cultures identified their selfhood in relation to animals — e.g. as totems or ancestral continuities rather than as their absolute antithesis — the force of cannibalism as *discourse* had considerably less significance for them than it did for their European counterparts" (Huggan and Tiffin 170).

In contrast, Lu withdraws to escape the corruption of civilized human society and to recover from pains but not to conquer. Lu's life on the remotest small island can be described as a fish back to water and like Henry D. Thoreau, Lu takes the island "as a sacred place, — a *sanctum sanctorum*" ("Walking" 616). In addition, the trajectory into the wilderness taken by Luther Fox evokes a "post-settler dynamics of belonging in the wilderness" (Crane, "Wilderness as Liminal Space" 60). Luther Fox resumes his identity as a member of nature and he enjoys living "like the wild animals, gleaning nourishment here and there from seeds, berries, etc., sauntering and climbing in joyful independence of money or baggage" (qtd. in Oelschlaeger 188). Playing with his shark mates is the unexpected boon to him in spite of tough living conditions in the wilderness and his weakening physical constitution. Put it succinctly, "an edgy blend of sharp realism (about the true nature of these places) and colourful romanticism (about their restorative possibilities) emerges in conversations and activities during 'retreats'" (Harvey 282).

"He chooses his camp primarily for its proximity to drinking water but he recognizes its defensive virtues" (Winton, *Dirt Music* 351). This is interpreted as a sort of colonist mentality by Kylie Crane who believes that "although Lu does not engage in settler activities, [...] he cannot let go of the need to be settled, to 'have' a place" (*Myths of Wilderness* 60). But I can hardly agree. The advantage of this camp is that he will not be found easily but he can detect it if other people come, which is quite possible as Fox happens to find the tourist service station on the island. So, what he wants is to be left alone but not the control of the land the way Robinson does. This can be proved by his quick withdrawal from his favorable camp when he notices the arrival of a helicopter, which is done at the risk of a worse place to live in.

Finally, the differences between the two works should be attributed to the historical contexts in which they are written. "As is well known, *Robinson Crusoe* was written at a time of European territorial and capitalist expansion, and it has become almost commonplace to read it as paradigmatic of colonial encounter". Almost all major subjects for colonial exploration are covered, such as "*Terra Nullius*, the cannibal 'other', land use, race relations, attitudes to animals, personal labour as the route to salvation, the conversion of others to western/Christian values, the efficacy of capitalist accumulation over mere exchange" (Huggan and Tiffin 169). By comparison, *Dirt Music* was composed at the post-colonial era of modern Australia where descendents of the white settlers are beginning to "redress the past wrongs, and contribute to healing and reconciliation in the present" and thirsting for a bond with the land and a harmonious relationship with nature (Toorn 38). Social contexts decisively determine the value inclinations of the texts.

Retreat to the wilderness from the corrupted human community has always been a major motif in European and American literature. Many classics narrate stories of spiritual redemption through physical ordeal in primal wilderness. The trip that occurs in the physical world is de facto a metaphor of the psychological journey through spiritual predicament to epiphany or sublimation. It symbolizes a painful rediscovery of lost self after disillusion (黄 284~285)①.

It's easy to discern that going into the wilderness is not anything that hits upon Luther Fox all of a sudden. Virtually, his life story is one gradual process of being driven increasingly away from human community toward its antipode — primitive nature. Even before his escape to the north, Lu has been living on the margin of the small coastal fishing town White Point which is implied to be on the margin of the nation geographically, culturally and politically. Marginality is a key concept to the interpretation of *Dirt Music* and many other works in Winton's oeuvre. The narrative has enough traces insinuating that Lu's brother Darkie and sister-in-law Sal were drug addicts, which gives the family a notorious name. And Lu's reclusive way of living by poaching only adds to the family's bad fame. To make matters worse, he was taken as an ominous person by the town on the ground of the family tragedies, which further segregates him from others. Having destroyed the documents certifying his membership in human society, Lu converts his life into "a project of forgetting" (103). So to speak, to Luther Fox, wild nature is more hospitable than the alien fishing town.

Dirt Music glimpses at how a white Australian copes with the antagonistic environment of wilderness, and comes to terms with the land and its concomitant postcolonial issues (Crane, "Wilderness as Liminal Space" 60). Before cocooning himself in absolute isolation from others, Lu encounters two quasi-Aborigines. The much-discussed plot has it that Axle, the younger Aborigine, burns all his maps and tells Lu to walk "on the country" rather than "on the map", which shows the author's sympathy for the historical trauma suffered by the Indigenous (312). In contrast to his depiction of the Aborigine in *Cloudstreet* (1991), Winton's

① Translation mine.

sense of responsibility for historical issues has obviously increased. Rather than mystifying Aboriginal characters, here he approaches historical trauma squarely and figures out some strategies for racial reconciliation though his ideas may be too naïve and thus impractical in reality. Map-burning is a symbolic counterattack against the colonists for their dispossession and displacement of the Aborigines in history. Walking "on the country" reflects an obvious reference of the walkabout tradition in Aboriginal culture. After the ceremony of initiation the young lad will embark upon a sole travel across his country, which is virtually a test of his capability of independent survival in that territory. His passage to adulthood cannot be accomplished until he proves himself competent through the walkabout tour. What's more, it is also through this bush walk that Aborigines' kinship bond with his country is continued. In a manner of speaking, walking "on the country" hints at the possible way for settler Australians to establish "umbilical" link with the land. Wilderness is the environment where "the feelings of belonging and connection to nature, and perceptions of its sacredness, that characterize earth and nature-based religions in diverse cultures and periods around the world" can be cultivated (B. Taylor 302).

Winton attempts to handle historical issues in an artistic way. Axle, the younger Aboriginal, possesses a guitar but cannot play it, which clearly shows the influence of white culture. Surprisingly, Lu offers to play him a tune. This plot is of twofold significance. To the individual, it's the first time that Lu willingly allows himself to approach music — a torture to him ever since the car accident. You may still remember that on his way to the north, it's repeatedly stressed that he is painful to hear music of any sort because music unavoidably reminds him of his deceased family. Out here in a space of purity — Axle's country and Lu's wilderness — an unbelievable thing occurs. Lu plays the guitar and "the melody gets hold of him" (306) so that it turns to a mode of "shuttle going despite himself" (307). In the end, music is not aching. Lu strides the first step towards rehabilitation from personal trauma. To the nation, the guitar playing episode symbolizes Winton's best wishes for racial reconciliation. In a way, music in this specific context functions as a means of cross cultural exchanges and a solution to racial issues. The contact between Lu and the two Aborigines is short but fruitful and double-win. Axle enjoys the mesmerizing melodies played by the gifted dirt musician whereas Lu gets a kayak as a present from Axle in return for his wonderful guitar improvisation. Strikingly, Axle is able to read Lu's mind (an Aboriginal skill that strains the comprehension of the white Australians but may be possibly interpreted as something mystic or superstitious) and knows what he needs. The kayak proves of great help for his stay on the island. Winton's story indicates that communication between the white and black Australians are reciprocal and sometimes this communication does not need to be based on mutual understanding to say nothing of converting one to the other. Good will is cross-cultural and mutual respect is indispensable.

The sounds that Lu hears when sleeping in the open air on his way to the north also conjure up Aboriginals and their culture (232). As my discussion in chapter I indicates, the mixture of sounds resembles those produced by Aboriginal shaman in all sorts of ceremonies or corroborees, acquiescing in the existence of Aboriginal spirits who are looking after their country all the time. On another occasion, while wandering on the island, Lu bumps into a cave where he sees Aboriginal paintings on the cave wall, which makes him "keenly aware that the wilderness to which he 'retreats' is not at all pristine natural environments" (Harvey 281). Filled with awe, he says hello and gets out. This plot forms obvious intextuality not only with Patrick White's *Voss*, but with Stow's *To the Islands*. It shares quite a few affinities with the latter, confirming Stow's impact on Winton. Firstly, both Heriot and Fox willingly choose to retreat to the wilderness from civilization that they have been fed up with. Secondly, the places that both protagonists aim for are remote littoral areas, or islands. The difference is that Heriot finds that the islands do not exist at all but Lu arrives at an ideal unmanned island. Thirdly, they both enter a cave with Aboriginal rock paintings. Winton does not give much information about the cave. Stow's narration sheds more light on the significance of this encounter. This cave should be the burying ground for the Aboriginal ancestors and it is the sanctum sanctorum for Aboriginal spirits and gods. It is thus the forbidden place for the living. Different from Lu, Heriot sees the cave as the final home. Besides, Heriot passionately expresses his identification with Aboriginal culture to his Indigenous brother Justin and in the meantime denies his belief in God and Heaven. Heriot's exclamation that "after so long — but we're always foreign" exactly expresses the white Australians' agony of being refused by the indigenous culture and yearn for belonging (Stow 200). In this sense, Stow's desire for racial reconciliation is far stronger and more explicitly expressed than that of Winton.

Even so, the scattered information in the text at least indicates Winton's acknowledgement that the white man's wilderness is virtually the Aboriginals' home country or their sanctuary blessed by their ancestors. Self-admittedly, this is far from enough, though the position itself indicates a sort of respect for history. Lyn McCredden concerns herself with the postcolonial reading of Fox's redemption and her question is: "Are we able to read the beginnings of Fox's redemption as, in part, his learning to live in and through the land as both other and as nurturer?" (52). McCredden is insightful in pointing out the contradictory sentiments towards the land held by people like Luther Fox. In *Dirt Music*, the land's role as the nurturer is vehemently stressed, overshadowing its historical status as the other. What concerns Tim Winton is mainly how to get the white Australians enrooted in the land and how to eliminate the alienation from nature rather than how to deal with the tough issues of the Aborigines. Hence, Winton just flirts with the Aboriginal issue but won't push further into it. Most undesirably,

Aboriginal cultures here only serve as convenient means and inspiration for solving white protagonist's personal problem. McCredden's challenge lashes the author for his romantic handling of such thorny issues as Aboriginal ones, which obviously demand more wisdom and courage. It's really a pity that Winton fails to give due concern to the matter concerning the racial discordance.

Luther Fox's sojourn on the unmanned island is in essence a process of self-rehabilitation and self-salvation and wilderness witnesses the protagonist's alchemical changes there. When being told to walk "on the country", Lu is uneasy and at a loss. With the burning of the maps, the dependence on civilization is all but erased. Lu now embarks upon the passage to self-salvation in genuine wilderness, leaving everything behind. And his stay on the island is a perfect interpretation of the Aboriginal catchword "walking on the country", which proves to be the truer path into the wilderness. The author hopes to highlight the fact that white Australians can manage to survive in the wilderness as well as, if not better than, the Aboriginals, which means so much to the construction of the new national identity to them. However, Lu's going to bush was interpreted by Bárbara Aritzi as "cultural appropriation of the Aborigines' special bond with the land" ("Personal Trauma" 186). In my view, Winton shouldn't be blamed for borrowing eco-wisdom from the Indigenous cultures. What the author wants to underscore is that we (the white Australians) are connected to the land and we belong here, which is something near to Aboriginality. It's understandable that as a white writer Winton hopes to construct the legitimacy for his compatriots and thus reduce the awkwardness of their national identity. However, striking new bond between the white Australians and the land doesn't necessarily deny or remove the traditional kinship link between the Indigenous and their country. Any author with historical conscience should not purposefully dwarf the significance of the Indigenous issues in contemporary Australia. But one needs to be more tolerant, more open-minded and more creative and imaginative to solve these problems.

"In a new context, (here in the wilderness of the island) the primary educator as well as the lawgiver and the primary healer would be the natural world itself" (T. Berry 15). There is something in the wilderness that "feeds the spirit and inspires" (Thoreau, "Walking" 611). It's interesting to note a description of going to wilderness given by Gary Snyder,

> One departs the home to embark on a quest into an archetypal wilderness that is dangerous, threatening, and full of beasts and hostile aliens. This sort of encounter with the other — both the inner and the outer — requires giving up comfort and safety, accepting cold and hunger, and being willing to eat anything. You may never see home again. Loneliness is your bread. Your bones may turn up someday in some riverbank mud. ("Cultured or Crabbed" 48)

The description is frightful to hear, but it's partly true especially to those who take wilderness as alien other, those who cannot discern its beauty and sublimity. But to our protagonist, the outdoor man who revels in the life of the senses, who loves to hunt and fish, life in natural surroundings is not so formidable. Instead, it "grants freedom, expansion and release. Untied. Unstuck. Crazy for a while. It breaks taboo, it verges on transgression, it teaches humility" (Snyder, "Cultured or Crabbed" 48). The toughness and reticence in Luther Fox are vividly demonstrated.

Readers are deeply moved by the great variety of wild species in the ecosystem of the island presented in the text. It seems every species enjoys a carefree life on the island — a haven unspoiled by human civilization. Largely left untouched, the small island is the wildest place that Lu can find. The only pity is that Lu soon discovers a service station in which adequate necessities for wilderness survival are stored. The discovery really upsets him, though times again he returns to renew food supplies when he reaches impasse.

Having made a fine camp on the small island, Lu begins to live by seeking food from nature "according to the tide". Leaving human society behind, Lu immediately turns to a primitive forager. Fishing is the rudimentary skill and he even learns to "eat fish raw" (352). Thanks to good season, foods are quite abundant and he takes great pleasure in tasting new food, such as green ants, mangrove snails and wild fruits like figs, berries and nuts. As Henry D. Thoreau puts it, "from the forest and wilderness come the tonics and barks which brace mankind" ("Walking" 613). Lu is so content with the gifts bestowed by nature that he can hardly believe it's true. His feelings corroborate Paul Shepard's claim that "humans are genetically programmed for wild environment and that there is a normal genetically based human ontogeny that involves bonding with wild nature" (Session 325). Sigurd Olson, who spent a lifetime guiding in the boundary waters of Minnesota, observes that "once city folk are a day or two into the backcountry with everyday demands left behind, ancient rhythms again resonate with human spirits, and they are lifted up, renewed in body and soul" (qtd. in Oelschlaeger 2).

Having "nothing personal to protect himself from", Lu begins to resume the ability to feel "comfort" and "safe in a way he hasn't felt since early childhood", which can be taken as major indexes for rehabilitation (353). His lack of security derives both from losing his parents young and his means of living by poaching in the fishing town. That an individual feels safe and comfortable in the wilderness must sound unconventional and anti-mainstream to white Australians, which demonstrates "Winton's lament of the lack of a sense of community" in human society and in the meantime serves as a foil to the author's wish for human race's poetic reinhabitation in wilderness (Quin 7).

"Unexpected pleasures" also come from the boab trees. The cute shapes of young ones "delight" him whereas the "asymmetrical splendour" demonstrated by the huge ancient tree "makes him smile" (353). As a matter of fact, when nearing the town of Derby from where he may take a chart or helicopter for his ultimate destination, Luther has noticed the adorable boab trees that "stand fat and close" and "to Fox they're preposterous and lovely, like a crowd lining the highway, hip to hip, all arse and head-dress in the sun" (297). Lu also expresses his fancy for boabs on the island on account of the feeling of warmth of their skin after the sun sets (387). Kylie Crane gives a detailed analysis of the covers of different versions of *Dirt Music* published domestically and internationally and notes that the image of an adorable boab tree stands before each section in the eight chapters of the novel as well as the front cover of the novel (the Picador version published in 2004). Boab trees appear repeatedly in the text and the paratext so that its special significance should be put under scrutiny. Boab trees, also known as baobab, upside down, bottle and monkey bread trees, are indigenous to Madagascar, Africa and Australia. They are also a typical plant in the tropical area in Kimberley.

> Various species of birds and insects nest on the branches and in the body of the tree. Animals chew on the moisture-laden bark to stay hydrated, especially during drought. Farmers will feed their cattle and other livestock pieces of the wood as well as the seeds for the same reasons. Pulp from the fruit can be made into a sweet drink believed to relieve certain illnesses such as diarrhea. Young boab leaves contain vitamins and can be eaten.①

So image of boab trees brings people blaze of hope for the various benefits animals as well as human race can get. What's more, love for

① http://www.gardenguides.com/97969-boab-tree.html#ixzz38rtdHrFz.

boabs also reflects an affiliation to the indigenous plant of his country.

"The animate vitality of nature pervades the cosmos" (Oelschlaeger 184). Winton puts it thus: "If you sit still long enough the bush or the sea will produce an event" (*Dirt Music* 354). Winton's descriptions of the wild landscapes with indigenous flora and fauna stimulate "an aesthetic and spiritual appreciation for wilderness" that can frequently be found in poetry of Romanticism (Nash, *Wilderness & American Mind* 44), which "gives primary concern to the emotions experienced in confronting the sublimity of untamed nature and its picturesque qualities"①.

It is implied that Luther Fox is a reader, or an enthusiast of Romantic poetry, to be specific. For one thing, Lu's love for books is expressed by the repeated depictions of his uneasiness at failing to bring along some books while travelling north. "He wants to be alone, God knows, but not without something to read" (222). During his sojourn in the wilderness, this desire for something to read sometimes grows to an unbearable degree so that "Fox would content himself with a phone book, a shopping list" (355). For another, Georgie notices that there is "a bricklike poetry anthology" in his study and British Romantic poets such as "Wordsworth, Blake and Keats were bruised with underscorings" (333). What's more, when the English teacher Bess, one of those who give him a lift on the journey to the north, says "Beware Greeks with freebies", Lu responds "Troy just spoiled it for the rest of us", which consolidates that he has read widely and is well-cultivated (243). As a result, Lu impresses Bess favorably so that more discussions are evoked about literature, which includes great men of letters such as Thomas Hardy, Earnest Hemingway, Lord Byron, William Blake, and William Wordsworth, who are either influenced by Romanticism or Romantic poets themselves except Hemingway. When he is immersed in the drone

① http://en.wikipedia.org/wiki/Romanticism.

music, Lu's consciousness returns to his family library, where there is a rich storage of romantic poetry as noticed by Georgie. William Wordsworth's *The Prelude* and *Tintern Abbey* in particular occur to him in his spiritual trip back home. The former, as one of Wordsworth's masterpieces second only to *Lyrical Ballads*, "traces the growth of the poet's mind by stressing the mutual consciousness and spiritual communion between the world of nature and man"①. The latter is actually the abbreviated form of Wordsworth's poem "Lines Composed a Few Miles above Tintern Abbey", which is a description of the landscapes of the banks of River Wye. But like other romantic poems, the focus is more on revealing the elevated joy felt by the poet from his close contact with nature and his intellectual and philosophical contemplation on the sublimity of nature. Thus Romanticism is also believed to be "protoecological" (Garrard, "Radical Pastoral?" 185).

"Winton's fiction has long been testing out the idea that characters who are enlightened, or who seek understanding, use forms of art, especially poetry, to help them" (Mapstone 26). In *Dirt Music*, Lu's emotional reactions to wilderness are akin to those of Romantic poets. With romantic sensitivity, Lu Fox also demonstrates an obvious propensity to notice the delicate beauty of nature and perceive the simple pleasures from sublime nature. Like Wordsworth, Lu feels the grandeur and wonderment of nature. What's more, to Luther Fox, wilderness is animistic or pantheistic, which echoes the Aboriginal culture: "he knows he would have tried to explain this sense of the world alive, the way they articulate your own instinctive feeling that there is indeed some kind of spirit that rolls through all things, some fearsome memory in stones, in wind, in the lives of birds" (Winton, *Dirt Music* 370).

Traditional western opinions of wild nature as the object to be either

① http://en.wikipedia.org/wiki/The_Prelude.

loathed or conquered are not to be found on Lu. His journey of self-recovery becomes an odyssey of rediscovering and re-enchanting nature in the intimate touch with wilderness. Direct contact with myriad plant and animal life-forms offers him a new way of experiencing and perceiving the wilderness and contemplating his life. To Lu, wild plants and animals are "sources of solace, of wonder and adventure", which can be felt in his interactions with the sharks (Oelschlaeger 184).

Anything can happen in the remote world of wilderness on the wild island and Lu's life is imaginably full of risks and wonders. One day when Lu is cleaning fish and throwing the heads and backbones into the water, a bunch of sharks appear on the shallows. Thus begins an unusual friendship between man and sharks. Lu is half scared but soon he is sure that the sharks mean him no harm. As he becomes bolder, he "feeds them, applauds and taunts them until dark when he heads up to his camp facing a hungry night" (356). More incredibly, the sharks return every day ever since then to seek fun with Lu. The sharks become his play mates and their arrival becomes the only thing he expects every day, which greatly cheers him up. Their relationship grows more intimate with time going by so that the sharks snatch meat directly from his hands and in return they allow Lu to stroke them when they lunge forward (ibid.). Besides the feeding routine, Lu and his shark mates also play tug-of-war. With these close interactions, mutual trust grows so that "the games escalate until Fox is manhandling them and they're bumping and passing him in the shallows" (ibid.). Winton's depictions of the harmonious coexistence between Lu and sharks are impressive and full of fun:

> He loves the sport of it, the mad reckless play, but it's the bodily presence of them that he treasures most, the weight of them in his arms, against his legs, the holiness of their power, and the carnal sociability of the buggars. Everyday they come like a bouncing, bickering pack of dogs,

> and after they're sated with food they tug on an empty vine until Fox laughs so hard he gets hiccups. (Winton, *Dirt Music* 365~366)

Like John Muir, in the course of walking on the wild island, Lu takes on an "aboriginal tone [...] in which the distinctions prevalent in Western civilization between men, plants, and animals begin to be broken down and are replaced with a kind of mystical reverence for all forms of life" (qtd. in Oelschlaeger 183). More importantly, pure happiness derives from the intimate touch with sharks. In this process, Lu resumes the ability to laugh, to love and to trust, which clearly boosts a positive mood and attitude towards life. Besides, a new and reciprocal relationship between mankind and wildlife derives out of this close contact.

However, to the ordinary readers it's just unimaginable to play with sharks as if they were dogs. The question was cast at the author during an interview by Amy Brown and Catherine Bisley, to which Winton responded that they are authentic personal experiences:

> I've done that, yeah — a number of times. It's incredible. In fact, a documentary was being made about me while I was writing *Dirt Music* and they got footage of it, to prove it. A friend of mine has a camp up in the Kimberley and he'd do it everyday. And, the strange thing is that I know a lot more about cetaceans than I do about sharks and I understand that dolphins, and whales to some extent, have a kind of play factor in their culture, but it's interesting to me to see that sharks have the capacity to play too. Initially we would just, over and over again, with a big barramundi head on a rope, just throw it out and play a tug-of-war with these things and sometimes they'd be dragged up the beach, they'd roll back down, do a lap then come back up for some more. And when the fish head was all gone they'd keep coming back, like dogs, like a Kelpie, like "can we do it? Can we do it again?" And they responded to physical contact. All the things you wouldn't normally associate with sharks. So they are quite sociable.

> Crocodiles are quite sociable as well, but probably not the same capacity for safety. ("The Quiet Australian")

Winton makes every endeavor to show that sharks as well as other colossal marine creature like cetaceans, dolphins are "sociable" animals but not direful cannibals as depicted or imagined by human beings. Each species may have its own "culture" usually beyond our comprehension, but we do have something in common with other life forms. The "play factor" is a case in point. So, the harmonious symbiosis with them is not an illusion. Therefore, the stereotyped opinions of sharks and other marine animals should be altered and inter-species communication may be possible.

It will be a pity if I leave the talk about the story between Winton and sharks here, for the author not only writes about sharks in his work but makes relentless efforts to protect them in reality. The status quo of sharks is far from optimistic in Australia. As the Western Australian vice-president of the Australian Marine Conservation Society, Tim Winton has campaigned for sea-life like turtles, dugongs, dolphins and whales as is mentioned in the introduction. In 2010, he appealed to the Australians to "leave the sharks alone" (Skatssoon 42). He points out that the abomination of sharks is deep-seated: In the landmass of Australia, there are few large carnivores. So the shark becomes the devil, or the Satan, the bogeyman (ibid.). "Australians have an almost supernatural fear and hatred of sharks" (ibid.). Likewise, another author Robert Drewe also points out that the shark and the dingo are conventionally held as "archetypal threats inherent" in the Australian natural environment (27). Winton accuses Australians of the crimes against sharks: "Consciously or unconsciously we've made the shark the infidel. It's the creature to which we license ourselves to do everything unspeakable". To raise awareness of the plight of sharks, Winton says sharks are at the forefront of the imminent collapse of global fisheries, with some species, such as the hammerhead, already 89 per cent gone. He underscores that "Australia is complicit in their threatened demise". For example, fish and chips are the most favorite food in Australia but today one is eating shark and chips without knowing it. Another major reason is the consumption of shark finning, "a barbarity on par with practices like harvesting bile from bears" (Skatssoon 42).

Like other Australians, Winton also grew up with the traditional fear and abomination of sharks, but he was fortunate enough to have opportunities to swim with sharks so that he dispelled the fear and learnt to appreciate its unique beauty. In Tim Winton's semi-autobiography *Land's Edge*, his personal experiences of swimming with dolphin, eight-metre shark, bronze whaler, whale shark are lavishly narrated. He takes great pride in these "rare and precious encounters" and considers them a blessing as well as a privilege (22). Winton stresses places such as Shark Bay, Exmouth, Ningaloo along the West Australian coast are the only places in the world where you can touch or swim with them. Therefore, persistent endeavors are needed to protect them from over-development of tourism in modern society. The good news is that with the unremitting efforts of a bunch of dedicated marine environmentalists Shark Bay has been listed in the World Heritage followed by Ningaloo in 2011. "Western Australia, most traditionally seen as the nation's quarry, suddenly looks as though it could yet become a world leader in the management of fragile places and a trailblazer for sustainable eco-tourism" (Winton, "How the Reef was Won" 20). Tim Winton expounds his views on its ecological significance:

> The frenzy at Cape Cuvier, the presence of the whale sharks at Exmouth and (to a lesser extent, thanks to long term studies) the dolphins at Monkey Mia, are barely understood phenomena, but ones which must be regarded as privileges to behold. I find them stirring, inspiring, strangely unifying and even religious in their nature. I don't believe there's anything

> cosmic or divine or morally superior about whales and dolphins or sharks or trees, but I do think that everything that lives is holy and somehow integrated; and on cloudy days I suspect that these extraordinary phenomena and the hundreds of tiny, modest versions no one hears about, are an ocean, an earth, a Creator, something shaking us by the collar, demanding our attention, our fear, our vigilance, our respect, our help. (*Land's Edge* 27~28)

Winton's intuitive ideas are better expressed by Aldo Leopold in his famous essay "The Land Ethic". Like *Homo sapiens*, "these creatures are members of the biotic community and if its stability depends on its integrity, they are entitled to continuance" (Leopard 246 ~ 247). Winton's close contact with big marine wildlife becomes raw materials for literary composition. So we read Abel's swimming with the big old groper in *Blueback* and Lu's having fun with the sharks in *Dirt Music*. That elements of nature are always highlighted by him echoes a line by Satish Kumar — "Nature seen as inanimate machine becomes an object of exploitation whereas nature seen as sacred becomes a source of inspiration for the arts, culture, architecture and of course religion" (134). "When we experience nature we develop a deep sense of empathy and love for nature and when we love something we care for it, we conserve it and we protect it" (Kumar 135). Deep sense of awe and respect grows naturally out of such interaction and communication. Thus, the intrinsic value of life, small or large, should be valued and protected, as is advocated by Arne Naess, the Norwegian philosopher and deep ecologist. Winton interprets these "extraordinary phenomena" as messages from God or Creator and hopes his readers hear it and act accordingly. From reverence for life to harmonious symbiosis, the author's attitude towards wild life undergoes essential evolution.

Finally, the analysis will turn to the reconciliation with self achieved by Luther Fox in wilderness, the predominant motif of *Dirt*

Music.

As time goes by, the excitement of dwelling in the wilderness begins to recede and daily tasks of food-seeking can no longer compose him. Boredom grows out of absolute solitude. Insulating himself completely from the human society, having nothing to fill his mind or to occupy his thoughts with, Lu is on the brink of emotional breakdown. The absence of human culture and civilization becomes increasingly apparent. Everything indicates that as a cultural and social being, a person can't function properly in absolute isolation unless one fumbles a way to achieve the psychological equilibrium. As mentioned above, Luther has refused to play or listen to music ever since the family tragedy. But instead of letting the past go as he expects, the longer he maintains the discipline, the heavier the burden grows. Playing guitar for Axle is the ice-breaking step towards reconciliation with music. On the deserted island, dirt music, "a sound just outside nature but not dissimilar to it", again becomes the boredom-killer and best medicine (368).

In the text, Lu explains to Georgie that dirt music is a sort of "rootsy" and "old timey" stuff that somewhat resembles blues, country, or folk music (95). You can play it with such instruments as guitar, mandolin, fiddle on a verandah and the music is nostalgic. So dirt music is closely related to place and to one's affiliation to the land. Like romantic poems, it is also a direct expression of one's emotions and a convincing mark of one's identity, as Kylie Crane insightfully points out in the essay "The Beat of the Land: Place and Music in Tim Winton's *Dirt Music*". So, in a way avoiding music is denying one's identity in the community and restraining one's emotions. But when Lu Fox happens to create a sort of music by tying a length of fishing line between two limbs of the fig tree, things are different. Not only is there no hurt, but he is so excited that he can't help "humming and stamping and chanting" with the drone. Then "he growls out a chant, his throat burning with pleasure [...]" (368). So how shall we define this peculiar music happened to be discovered, created, and played by Lu in the wilderness? Isn't it also dirt music? I think yes. Dirt indicates place. Dirt is also land, soil, or nature. Music created out of nature is dirt music, which may be another interpretation of the title of the novel.

As a matter of fact, many Chinese folk artists make musical instruments such as bamboo flutes out of materials from nature. Some can even play music with something directly out of nature. The willow leave "flute" is a good example. It's not a genuine flute but gives the sound of flute when blown between the lips skillfully by the folk artists. That's to say, in Chinese culture music has been traditionally closely related to nature; some music resembles the sounds from nature; and musical instruments are made of materials from nature. In brief, nature is the major source of inspiration for music composition and music is the combination of nature and culture. The discussion about Chinese folk music sheds some light on the interpretation of Lu's dirt music in the wilderness. "If music is thus clearly a part of culture, the question whether it alienates nature [...] or is in sweet concord [...] clearly depends on the nexus of man as a 'music-making animal', and his or her own relationship to place, society and nature in the process of identity formation" (Crane, "The Beat of the Land" 22). Lu's musical instrument is an accidental combination of a nylon line, obviously a product of industry or culture, and the fig tree, element of nature. Namely, what is obviously a cultural thing is created out of nature, spanning the demarcation between culture and nature.

Later, as reprising the nylon string becomes disheartening (387), Lu notices the sounds from nature: "Crows do their monkish improv all day beyond the ridge and the creek tinkles a layered monotone and the fist baler shell you find after the spring tide kicks you into action with its endless whorrrrr against your ear" (sic) (ibid.). In brief, nature is never lack of "music".

Ever since its invention, most of his free afternoons are consumed in the newly-discovered dirt music and "within that long, narcotic note there are places to go" (369). Music creates the framework in which the character's stream of consciousness flows back and forth freely. Bárbara Arizti remarks that *Dirt Music*, like many other novels of his, is written as "a discontinuous narrative in which fragments of various lengths [...] alternate, presenting flashbacks, digressions, and events in parallel, and bringing about a certain degree of confusion in readers" (Arizti, "Personal Trauma" 179). On the one hand, apparent modern and postmodern features in Winton's writing constitute the major impediment to complete and thorough comprehension. On the other, they challenge the reader's capability to reconstitute a traumatic story in the process of reading. Fragmentary writing caters well to delving deep into the character's inner world and tracing the process of psychological rehabilitation.

Since "music's wordlessness allies it with the unspoken, the felt", in an uncanny way, the dirt music helps to restore the spiritual equilibrium of our protagonist Luther Fox who acquires great fun from it (Mapstone 26). By synaesthesia, an important artistic form in modern poetry which means involuntarily associating one sensory or cognitive feeling to another, Winton puts it that "within the drone, sound is temperature and taste and smell and memory" (368 ~ 369). Within the music, Lu is able to mediate upon his past life. His memories jump and flutter intermittently. At first, scenes of his former life sparkle before his eyes. Flashbacks unfold scenes of young Darkie (his elder brother) playing music, Lu's restraining from touching the guitar during the years of his self-imposed isolation, and his going back to his family library. Subconsciously, he chants lines by William Wordsworth with his music in "a kind of monofilament manifold monotone that feels inexhaustible" (369). Art is the spontaneous overflow of powerful emotions. Gradually, he comes to realize that he needs to share these emotions with others. To be more specific, how he wishes to share his ecstasy with Georgie

Jutland who sees him as the genuine dirt musician.

In music, Lu's consciousness also returns to the pinnacles where he puts a tea can. But instead of fishing it out of the stone fissure like usual, "a gout of blood and water" runs out of it, which frightens him because it's not memory, but something mythic, ominous, or portentous (372). Soon the bodeful feeling is confirmed by the message of Bess's death that Lu receives through the familiar music that is hanging him while he is working the next day. When it disappears, Lu suddenly realizes it is "Bess's music" and she is gone (373). Music is endowed with mystic significance by the author. It's not until then that Lu becomes conscious of the fact that his life has been pestered by dead people or death. And a strong desire for something alive grows.

Having reconciliated with wildlife and music, it's time for Lu to sort out his agonizing past that keeps eating at him and to come to terms with himself. "Wild places are where spiritual re-creation — recreation we now call it — takes place" (Scheese 310). The restorative power of nature is fully demonstrated here.

His trauma is a complex with multifold layers. As mentioned above, superficially, the tragedy is the loss of family in a car accident. Pushed further, the trauma seems to be Lu's self-doubt and self-negation due to his blind adoration for his brother Darkie and his sister-in-law Sal on account of their talent for music. But virtually it goes far deeper than that. Traumatic memories are the very things that must be faced with to dispel the psychological hurt. As passions for the drone hums fade away, memories cannot stop. "And yet memories flash at him, persistent and chaotic" (375). Remote from the noise of humanity, the larger-than-human wilderness is "a good place to contemplate, meditate, and seek alternate visions of the reality" (Harvey 281).

Stream of consciousness reveals the crux of his trauma, which is tightly related to Darkie and Sal. Winton juxtaposes the emotional torture at tracing down the root of the psychological trauma with the extreme physical agony of digging "skerrick of black shell" out of his feet with the tweezers, which serves as a foil for the battered inner landscape of the protagonist and together pushes the development of the plot to its climax (378). "Great insights have come to some people only after they reached the point where they had nothing left" (Snyder, *Practice of the Wild* 22). So to speak, suffering is a kind of redemption (McCredden 44~45).

First, Darkie and Sal were irresponsible parents. "Their need for one another was ravenous but it didn't extend to anybody else. They were fond of you and they loved the kids in their distracted way but there was no passion, no sacrifice in it" (379). As a result, they left their duties completely with Lu who virtually had to undertake almost all the house chores like cooking, washing, cleaning and baby caring. Rather than a younger brother who needs care, Lu was the free housekeeper for them and his efforts to please were capitalized on and taken for granted.

Second, they not only abused Lu's admiration and affiliation to them but hurt him in an immoral and unethical way. From school days, Lu was exposed to the ugly scenes of their flirts and this state persisted till their adulthood "as though he's no more present than a dog under the table" (370). Lu couldn't tell whether they did it out of "carelessness" or "they enjoyed the cruelty", but they did that "for years" (380). In brief, the deep-seated trauma derives from psychological impairment inflicted by his brother and sister-in-law and the self-denial arising from that abnormal relationship rather than the tragic deaths of his family.

Gradually and painfully, he comes to realize that his love and sacrifice for his brother's family was only abused. When he is aware that "music wasn't *in* them" and "Darkie was an inspired mimic" (379 emphasis original), the causes for that blind admiration and worship are also rooted out. Hence, it is only his illusion that they earned him "that last grudging shred of respect in the district" (378). Eventually, he comes to realize that he should let go rather than revenge. "Winton's fiction is informed by Christian concepts of an immanent and suffering God, seen in characters who are simple, stripped down, punished and vulnerable, and finally purified" (McCredden 45). Luther Fox is a typical character that goes through this process exactly. After this catharsis, the desire grows in him for "some wit, some memory, some kindness, someone who saw him, saw through him, saw the music of him", which virtually indicates that he has outgrown his traumatic past and is ready for a new life (380).

In sum, wilderness possesses a magic power that is missing in western civilization. Some changes take place on Lu and the wild island becomes the loving and nurturing home in spite of its potential dangers. The male character Luther undergoes an alchemical rebirth into someone better and more unified than he was before landing the island though he is seriously impaired in physique. This transformation begins with the gradual alteration in his actions of returning to wilderness, which could be interpreted as a shift from seeking death to seeking life. It is accompanied by the change in Lu's attitude towards shark and music, to be specific. To establish a new identity as an integrated man, the psychic rebirth is accomplished (P.D.Murphy, *Farther Afield* 32).

This chapter has delved into the significance of wilderness in Winton's relevant fiction, which confirms that retreating to the wilderness becomes a major channel to discard his personae's psychological trauma and regain spiritual equilibrium. In *Swimmer*, Jerra outgrows his childhood trauma in the coastal bush. Winton caricatures the predicament of modern bush trekkers in their trip back to the wilderness that only exposes the estrangement felt by modern urbanites. Luther Fox is the one who achieves reconciliation with himself via going back to nature. He gleans simple pleasure from boab trees, wild fruits and nuts and seeks fun with sharks, which symbolizes the much anticipated reconciliation between humanity and nature. Music plays an indispensable role in all kinds of reconciliations. That Lu plays music for the Aboriginal boy Axle obviously hints at the best wish for racial reconciliation; the music Lu invents in the wilderness not only serves as the key to the solution of personal trauma but insinuates the reconciliation between nature and culture. The psychological self-recovery is accomplished in the course of treating the physical wound, both of which are extremely agonizing. Wilderness is the very place for Lu to boldly face the harsh facts and go out of the shadow.

Conclusion

"Civilised man has marched across the face of the earth and left a desert in his footprints" (qtd. in Schumacher 73). The statement, though exaggerated, depicts vividly the European settlers' domination over the land of Australia, which leads to a variety of environmental issues. History has witnessed the rise and fall of a number of civilizations that have spoilt their favorable environment and thus are forced to seek new land. However, the awkward fact today is that the planet has almost been fully packed by a huge population of human race, leaving almost no new land to move to (qtd. in Schumacher 74). Therefore, we have to cherish what we have. As an author with strong affiliation to his mother land and deep solidarity with nature, Tim Winton is a poet with intuitive and spontaneous eco-awareness and he consciously shoulders the responsibility of educating and awakening people of their eco-obligation and transmitting eco-centric ideas to reconstruct harmonious coinhabitancy between human race and the nurturing ecosystem. Eco-persuasion has become an organic factor of his writing, which in time grows into an idiosyncratic ecosophy.

From my analysis above, I draw the conclusion that Winton's ecosophy has three components. Firstly, anatomizing the pathology, namely, presenting serious consequences elicited by the estrangement between humanity and nature. Tim Winton virtually concerns himself with almost all major environmental issues in his oeuvre, such as salinization of topsoil on the farmland, depletion of natural resources, deforestation of the usable timber, denuding the grassland with overgrazing by livestock or by imported pests, destruction of natural habitats for endemic species, pollution of the harbor by industrial sludge, extinction of colossal marine species such as sharks and whales. This study views the mentality of domination and conquest over nature in traditional western culture as the philosophical root which decisively determinates the split and alienation between human race and nature.

Winton ruthlessly exposes "how European Australians are 'always doing things to the land'", a euphemism for plundering and despoiling nature. Then he turns to Aboriginal culture for spiritual tonics in nurturing an intimate connection with the land of Australia, though accused of effacement of Indigenous issues in his fiction. Thus, Winton's attitude to the land is obviously "more akin to the Aborigines' than to the Europeans'" (Arizti, "Personal Trauma" 185). In other words, Winton is equally passionate for establishing a harmonious bond with nature and consolidating the legitimacy for white Australians' inhabitancy in the land, the second major element in Winton's ecosophy. Winton demonstrates his spontaneous ecological ethics towards animals, which goes from "reverence for life" (*Swimmer*) to protection of wildlife (*Shallows*) and then to a harmonious coexistence with animals (*Blueback*). He not only shapes a pioneering white, female eco-warrior but depicts an ecotopia where man and nature enjoy a harmonious symbiosis.

Thirdly, the outcast characters in Winton's novels are often returned to the wilderness to experience catharsis and epiphany and then to restore equilibrium or gain salvation, displaying his reverential love of nature and implying that wilderness is nourishing, revitalizing and regenerating as is lauded by great wilderness-trekkers like Henry D. Thoreau, John Muir, etc. Rather than escape, this retreat to wilderness is re-placing humanity in its right slot in the holistic and balanced ecosystem. Only by making people recognize their dependence on nature as the only supporter and nurturer of life can an umbilical bond be built between them. Additionally, returning to nature offers the possibility to resume a harmonious, symbiotic bond with other members in the bio-community, to feel the spirituality of other-than-human species and nature and to enjoy simple joy from the interactions with them.

The Chinese eco-philosopher Suyuan Lu believes that the unification of nature and man more often than not lies in genuine poets and poetry (7)①. Winton has been labeled a "late romantic writer" who often plays on the healing power of wilderness (qtd. in Walker 41). Admittedly, he shares with romantic poets common love for and sensitivity to the sublimity of nature. Yet, the distinctions are equally apparent, one of which is that he does not take nature as the vehicle to transmit personal emotions. Like the landscape poet Gary Snyder, he "distances himself from the egotism and appropriation plaguing most Romantic landscape poetry" (qtd. in P. D. Murphy, *A Place for Wayfaring* 46). He would like to see his personae derive vitality from nature and feel that one's identity is tied to immediate nature.

As early as in 1967, Roderick Nash claimed that Muir "valued wilderness as an environment in which the totality of creation existed in undisturbed harmony ... [in wilderness humans] could feel themselves 'part of wild Nature, kin to everything.' From such knowledge came respect for 'the rights of all the rest of creation'" (Sessions 324). Through the discussion, we find that in Winton's fictional world, it is in wilderness that reconciliation is expected to be achieved either between man and nature, man and himself, or between white culture and aboriginal culture. And the dichotomy between culture and nature is also dismantled. Winton once said in an interview "I rarely deal with this (environmentalism) explicitly in my fiction, but my characters are quite obviously immersed in nature and the forces of nature impinge upon their lives in quite direct ways. I'm interested in this elemental connection" (刘,《当代外语研究》61). While reading his stories, the readers feel

① Translation mine.

close to nature and this is a way to relocate human beings in nature through fiction. As Gary Snyder puts it, our body is a vertebrate mammal being — And our souls are out in the wilderness ("Cultured or Crabbed" 49). We might safely claim that Winton is consciously creating an awareness of environmental protection among his readers through his stories and reconstructing an "umbilical" bond between humanity and nature. An ecocentric world order may derive from efforts like this.

Having explored the ecosophy in Tim Winton's oeuvre, still I am not bold enough to claim that I have exhausted the ecological significance of his fiction. But I hope this research can be acknowledged in terms of its originality that lies in:

Firstly, it is the first attempt at surveying the author's somewhat intuitive ecological consciousness prevalent in his works, establishing the logical link between his being an environmentalist and an author with obvious propensity to transmit this care and concern about nature through fiction.

Secondly, as a comprehensive study, it breaks the demarcation of separate works to draw up a trajectory of the development of the author's ecological thoughts. The book argues that Winton's ecosophy scratches from his depictions of the alienation of man-nature relationship elicited by man's wanton conquest of nature. Then the focus is laid on shaking off the estrangement and reestablishing a nurturing umbilical bond between the two. Given the not so cheerful state of affairs, the author just returns his protagonists back to nature, or wilderness. Retreat is virtually taken as the feasible means for reconstructing a harmonious relationship with nature for the time being.

Thirdly, the research attaches due attention to Winton's ecological care towards wildlife. Through scrupulous studies into relevant texts, the researcher concludes that thanks to the joint influence of western culture and Australian Aboriginal culture, Winton's ecological ethics goes from reverence for life to the protection of wild species and then to cross-species communication and symbiosis as its eventual goal.

Fourthly, integrating the research results so far, the study attempts to interpret the author's regionalism, affiliation to place, sense of belonging, as well as consciousness of constructing new national identity, which "is still being discovered and defined" (Carter 264), through the lens of ecocriticism to shed light on the intrinsic link among them.

Works Cited

Adams, William M, and Martin Mulligan. Introduction. *Decolonizing Nature*: *Strategies for Conservation in a Post-colonial Era.* By Adams and Mulligan. Eds. London: Earthscan, 2003. 1 – 15.

Alarcos, Ma Pilar Baines. "She Lures, She Guides, She Quits: Female Characters in Tim Winton's *The Riders.*" *Journal of English Studies* 8 (2010): 7 – 22.

Alf, Mappin. "Tim Winton." *Magpies* 2 May (1990): 18 – 19.

Andrew, Darby Hobart. "Author Winton Joins Artists in Logging Boycott." *Age* 6 Nov. (2002): 9.

Appleton, Jay. The *Experience of Landscape.* London and New York: John Wiley and Sons, 1975.

Arizti, Bárbara. "Personal Trauma/Historical Trauma in Tim Winton's *Dirt Music.*" *The Splintered Glass*: *Facets of Trauma in the Post-Colony and Beyond.* Eds. Dolores Herrero and Sonia Baelo — Allué. Amsterdam and New York: Rodopi, 2011. 175 – 189.

Assya, Pascalev. "Agricultural Ethics." *Encyclopedia of Environmental Ethics and Philosophy.* Eds. J. Baird Callicott and Robert Frodeman. 2 vols. Detroit: Macmillan Reference USA, 2009.

Barsam, Ara Paul. *Reverence for Life*: *Albert Schweitzer's Great Contribution to Ethical Thought.* New York: Oxford UP, 2008.

Beal, Chris. "Sea, Spirit and Salvation: A Theological Reflection on the Writings of Tim Winton." *St Mark's Review* 221.3 (2012): 47 – 54.

Bell, Sarah. "The Wheatbelt in Contemporary Rural Mythology." *Rural Society* 15.2 (2005): 176 – 190.

Ben-Messahe, Salhia. *Mind the Country — Winton's Fiction.* Crawley: U of WA Press, 2006.

---. "'More Blokes, More Bloody Water!': Tim Winton's *Breath*." *Antipodes* 26.1 (2012): 13 - 17.

Bennett, Bruce. *An Ocean of Stories*. St Lucia: U of Queensland P, 2002.

Berry, Thomas. "The Viable Human." *Deep Ecology for the Twenty-First Century*. Ed. George Sessions. Boston & London: Shambhala Publications, 1995. 8 - 18.

Bordian, Stephan. "Simple in Means, Rich in Ends: An Interview with Arne Naess." *Deep Ecology for the Twenty-First Century*. Ed. George Sessions. Boston & London: Shambhala Publications, 1995. 26 - 40.

Bradford, Clare, et al. *New World Orders in Contemporary Children's Literature: Utopian Transformations*. New York: Palgrave Macmillan, 2008.

Bradshaw, Don. "Conservation and Land Mis-management in the South-west of WA: a Cautionary Tale!" *Australian Biologist* 15.1 (2002): 13 - 25.

Bremmer, Jan N. "Greek Demons of the Wilderness: The Case of the Centaurs." *Wilderness in Mythology and Religion: Approaching Religious Spatialities, Cosmologies, and Ideas of Wild Nature*. Ed. Laura Feldt. Boston: De Gruyter, 2012. 25 - 54.

Bressler, Charles E. *Literary Criticism: An Introduction to Theory and Practice*. 2004. Beijing: Higher Education Press and Pearson Eduation, 2007.

Brown, Amy, and Catherine Bisley. "The Quiet Australian: An Interview with Tim Winton." *The Lumière Reader* 7 June 2012 <http://www.lumiere.net.nz/reader/item/1077>.

Brunton, Nicholas. "Holidays by the Sewer: Coastal Water Pollution and Ecological Sustainability." *Australian Environmental Law News* No.2 June/July (1996): 37 - 47.

Buell, Lawrence. *The Environmental Imagination: Thoreau, Nature Writing, and the Formation of American Culture*. Cambridge: Belknap Press of Harvard UP, 1995.

---. *Writing for an Endangered World: Literature, Culture, and Environment in the U. S. and Beyond*. Cambridge: Belknap Press of Harvard UP, 2001.

Callicott, John Baird. *Earth's Insights: A Multicultural Survey of Ecological Ethics from the Mediterranean Basin to the Australian Outback*. Berkeley, Los Angeles and London: U of California P, 1994.

Carson, Rachel.*Under the Sea-Wind*. 1941. London: Penguin Books, 2007.

---. *The Edge of the Sea*. Boston: Houghton Mifflin, 1955.

---. *Silent Spring*. 1962. Beijing: Science P, 2007.

Carter, David. "The Influence of Immigration on Australian Literature." 大洋洲文学研究. Ed. 詹春娟. 合肥：安徽大学出版社，2014. 250 - 266.

Chen, Emily. "Surf's up: Lockie Leonard in the Classroom a Study Guide." *Screen Education* 55 (2009): 60 - 66.

Corderoy, Erin, and Michaela Baker. "Toward a Negative Aesthetic of Sustainability in Tim Winton's *Dirt Music*." <http://www.academia.edu/4677457/Corderoy_E. and_Baker_M._2013_._ _Toward_a_Negative_Aesthetic_of_Sustainability_in_Tim_Wintons_Dirt_Music_>.

Cosgrove, Denis E. "Introduction to Social Formation and Symbolic Landscape." *Landscape Theory*. Eds. Rachael DeLue and James Elkins. New York: Routledge, 2008. 17 - 42.

Cramer, Jeffrey S, ed. *The Maine Woods: A Fully Annotated Edition*. New Haven and London: Yale UP, 2009.

Crane, Kylie. "The Beat of the Land: Place and Music in TimWinton's Dirt Music." *Zeitschrift für Anglistik und Amerikanistic* 54. 1 (2006): 21 - 32.

---. "A Place in the Wilderness? Tim Winton's *Dirt Music* and Margaret Atwood's *Surfacing*." *Territorial Terrors: Contested Spaces in Colonial and Postcolonial Writing*. Ed. Gerhard Stilz. Wurzburg: Konigshausen and Neumann, 2007. 71 - 87.

---. *Myths of Wilderness in Contemporary Narratives: Environmental Postcolonialism in Australia and Canada*. New York: Palgrave

Macmillan, 2012. 59 – 82.

DeLue, Rachael, and James Elkins, eds. *Landscape Theory*. New York: Routledge, 2008.

DeLue, Rachael. "Elusive Landscapes and Shifting Grounds." *Landscape Theory*. Eds. Rachael DeLue and James Elkins. New York: Routledge, 2008. 3 – 14.

Dinham, Judith, and Glen Phillips. *Landscape and You*. Ed. George Karpathakis. CD-ROM. Perth: Edith Cowan University, 1995.

Dixon, Robert. "Tim Winton, *Cloudstreet* and the Field of Australian Literature." *Westerly* 50 Nov. (2005): 245 – 260.

Drewe, Robert. "Where the Yellow Sand Stops." *Westerly* 47 Nov. (2002): 25 – 74.

Edelson, Phyllis Fahrie. "The Role of History in Three Contemporary Australian Novels." *The Journal of Popular Culture* 23.2 (1989): 63 – 72.

Edemariam, Aida. "Waiting for the New Wave." *The Guardian* 28 June 2008 3 Sep. 2014 <www.guardian.co.uk/books/2008/jun/28/saturdayreviewsfeatres.guardianreview9>.

Flannery, Tim. "Foreigners in a Strange Land." *Issues* 58 Apr. (2002): 37 – 39.

Freyfogle, Eric T. "Land Ethic." *Encyclopedia of Environmental Ethics and Philosophy*. Eds. J. Baird Callicott and Robert Frodeman. 2 vols. Detroit: Macmillan Reference USA, 2009.

Garrard, Greg. "Radical Pastoral?" *The Green Studies Reader: from Romanticism to Ecocriticism*. Ed. Laurence Coupe. London and New York: Routledge, 2000. 182 – 186.

---. *Ecocriticism*. London: Routledge, 2004.

Gelder, Ken, and Paul Salzman. *After the Celebration: Australian Fiction 1989—2007*. Melbourne: Melbourne UP, 2009.

Gibbs, Martin. "Conflict and Commerce: American Whalers and the

Western Australian Colonies 1826—1888." *The Great Circle* 22. 2 (2000): 3 – 23.

---. " Nebinyan's Songs: An Aboriginal Whaler of South-west Australia." *Aboriginal History* 27 (2003): 1 – 15.

Giblett, Rod. *Living with the Earth: Mastery to Mutuality*. Cambridge: SALT, 2004.

Glotfelty, Cheryll. Introduction. *The Ecocriticism Reader*. Eds. By Cheryll Glotfelty and Harold Fromm. Athens and London: Georgia UP, 1996. XV-XXXVII.

Goldsworthy, Kerryn. "Fiction from 1900 to 1970." *The Cambridge Companion to Australian Literature*. Ed. Elizabeth Webby. 2000. Shanghai: Shanghai Foreign Language Education P, 2003. 105 – 133.

Griffiths, Tom. *Hunters and Collectors: The Antiquarian Imagination in Australia*. Cambridge: Cambridge UP, 1996.

Grogan, Bridget. "The Cycle of Love and Loss: Melancholic Masculinity in *The Turning*." *Tim Winton: Critical Essays*. Eds. Lyn McCredden and Nathanael O'Reilly. Crawley: UWA Publishing, 2014. 199 – 220.

Guy, Elizabeth. "Tim Winton Writing the Feminine." *Women-church* 19 spring (1996): 31 – 37.

Hartsock, Nancy C. M. "Foucault on Power: A history for Women." *Feminism/Postmodernism*. Ed. Linda J. Nicholson. New York: Routledge, 1990. 157 – 175.

Harvey, Graham. "Ritual Is Etiquette in the Larger than Human World: The Two Wilderness of Contemporary Eco-Paganism." *Wilderness in Mythology and Religion: Approaching Religious Spatialities, Cosmologies and Ideas of Wild Nature*. Ed. Laura Feldt. Boston & Berlin: De Gruyter, 2012. 265 – 291.

Head, Lesley. *Cultural Landscapes and Environmental Change*. Key Issues in Environmental Change. London: Arnold, 2000.

Hefner, R. "Winton on Cloud Nine after Reviews." *Canberra Times* 21 April 1991: 23.

Hensher, Philip. "Ruling the Waves." *The Spectator* 3 May 2008: 36+. <http://ezproxy.ecu.edu.au/login? url=http://search.proquest.com/docview/201247381? accountid=10675>.

Hemingway, Ernest. *The Old Man and the Sea*. 1952. Nanjing: Yilin Press, 1999.

Hill, Ben. "Every Breath You Take; Insight." *Sydney Morning Herald* 27 Feb. 2001: 11.

Hochman, Jhan. "Green Cultural Studies." *The Green Studies Reader: From Romanticisim to Ecocriticism*. Ed. Laurence Coupe. London: Routledge, 2000. 187 - 192.

Holding, Clyde. Forward. *Kakadu Man Bill Neidjie*. By Big Bill Neidjie, Stephen Davis, and Allan Fox. N. S. W.: Mybrood P/L inc., 1985. 8 - 9.

Hornborg, Anne-Christine. "Making a Garden out of the Wilderness: Landscape, Dwelling and Personhood in the Encounter between European Settlers and the Mi'kmag in 'New France'". *Wilderness in Mythology and Religion: Approaching Religious Spatialities, Cosmologies and Ideas of Wild Nature*. Ed. Laura Feldt. Boston & Berlin: De Gruyter, 2012. 205 - 228.

Huggan, Graham, and Helen Tiffin. *Postcolonial Ecocriticism: Literature, Animals, Environment*. London: Routledge, 2009.

Hughes-d'Aeth, Tony. "The Shadow on the Field: Literature and Ecology in the Western Australian Wheatbelt." *The Littoral Zone: Australian Contexts and Their Writers*. Eds. CA Cranston and Robert Zeller. Nature, Culture and Literature 04. Amsterdam and New York: Rodopi, 2007. 45 - 70.

Jackson, Sue, Deborah Bird Rose, and Steve Johnson. "A Burgeoning Role for Aboriginal Knowledge: [Interviews Conducted by Kendall, Gillian]." *Ecos* 125 June - July (2005): 10 - 13.

Kinsella, John. "Wild Radishes." *Peripheral Light*, New York: W. W. Norton, 2004, 63.

Knox, Malcolm. "What the Boom won't Leave Behind." *The Monthly* 85 Dec/Jan (2012/2013): 69 – 72. <http://search. informit. com. au/documentSummary; dn = 009579903241591; res = IELLCC>.

Kuhlenbeck, Britta. *Rewriting Spatiality — the Production of Space in the Pilbara Region in Western Australia*. New Brunswick: Transaction Publishers, 2010.

Kumar, Satish. "Three Dimensions of Ecology: Soil, Soul & Society." *Spiritual Ecology: The Cry of the Earth*. Ed. Llewellyn Vaughan-Lee. Point Reyes, California: The Golden Sufi Center, 2013. 129 – 141.

Langton, Marcia. "The Resource Curse: New Outback Principalities and the Paradox of Plenty." *Griffith Review* 28 (2010): 47 – 63.

Lear, Linda. "Introduction." *Under the Sea-Wind*. 1941. By Rachel L. Carson. New York: Penguin, 2007. IX – XX.

Leopold, Aldo. *A Sand County Almanac: with Essays on Conservation from Round River*. 1949. New York: Oxford U P, 1966.

Lowie, Robert H. *Primitive Religion*. New York: Boni and Liveright, 1924.

Lynn, White, Jr. "The Historical Roots of Our Ecologic Crisis." *The Ecocriticism Reader: Landmarks in Literary Ecology*. Eds. Cheryll Glotfelty and Harold Fromm. Athens and London: The U of Georgia P, 1996. 3 – 14.

Macintyre, Stuart. *A Concise History of Australia*. Cambridge Concise Histories. Shanghai: Shanghai Foreign Language Education Press, 2006.

Manes, Christopher. "Nature and Silence." *The Ecocriticism Reader*. Eds. Cheryll Glotfelty and Harold Fromm. Athens and London: The U of Georgia P, 1996. 15 – 29.

Mapstone, Sally. "From Go to Whoa." *London Review of Books* 24.17 (Sept. 2002): 26.

Martin, Barbara Arizti. "The Crisis of Masculinity in Tim Winton's *The Riders*." *Commonwealth: Essays and Studies* 24.2 Spring (2002): 29 – 45.

Martin, Mike W. *Albert Schweitzer's Reference for Life: Ethical Idealism and Self-Realization*. Chippenham: Antony Rowe Ltd, 2007.

Marx, Karl. *Economic and Philosophic Manuscripts of* 1844. Trans. Martin Milligan. Moscow: Foreign Languages Publishing House, 1927.

Matthews, Brian. "Childhood in Tim Winton's Fiction." *Reading Tim Winton*. Eds. Richard Rositter and Lyn Jacobs. Sydney: Angus & Robertson, 1993. 59 – 71.

Melville, Herman.*Moby-Dick*. 1851. New York: Bantam, 2003.

McCredden, Lyn. "Tim Winton: Dirt Music and Dreams of Renewal." *Luminous Moments: The Contemporary Sacred*. ATF Press, 2010. 41 – 53. <www.slwa.elib.com.au/patron/FullRecord.aspx? p=63114>.

McGloin, Colleen. "Reviving Eva in Tim Winton's *Breath*." *The Journal of Commonwealth Literature* 47(1) (2012):109 – 120.

McGirr, Michael. *Tim Winton: The Writer and His Work*. South Yarra: Macmillan Education Australia PTY, 1999.

McPhee, Hilary. "On Publishing Tim Winton." *Tim Winton: A Celebration*. Comp. and ed. Hilary McPhee. Canberra: Pan Macmillan Australia, 1999. 19 – 25.

Minteer, Ben A. "Anthropocentrism." *Encyclopedia of Environmental Ethics and Philosophy*. Eds. J. Baird Callicott and Robert Frodeman. 2 vols. Detroit: Macmillan Reference USA, 2009.

Miels, Yvonne. "Singing the Great Creator: The Spiritual in Tim Winton's Novels." *Reading Tim Winton*. Eds. Richard Rositter and Lyn Jacobs. Sydney: Angus & Robertson, 1993. 29 – 44.

Moore, Clive. "Colonial Manhood and Masculinities." *Journal of Australian Studies* 56 (1998): 35 – 50.

Murphy, Ffion. "History and Tim Winton's Fiction." *Reading Tim Winton*. Eds. Richard Rossiter and Lyn Jacobs. Sydney and Auckland: Angus & Robertson, 1993. 73 – 86.

Murphy, Patrick D. *Farther Afield: In the Study of Nature-Oriented Literature*. Charlottesville: UP of Virginia, 2000.

---. *A Place for Wayfaring: The Poetry and Prose of Gary Snyder*. Corvallis: Oregon State UP, 2000.

Murray, Stuart. "Tim Winton's 'New Tribalism': *Cloudstreet* and community." *Kunapipi* 25.1 (2003): 83 – 91.

Musk, Arthur W., et al. "Asbestos-related Disease from Recycled Hessian Superphosphate Bags in Rural Western Australia." *Australian and New Zealand Journal of Public Health* 30.4 (2006): 312 – 313.

Murrie, Linzi. "Changing Masculinities: Disruption and Anxiety in Contemporary Australian Writing." *Journal of Australian Studies* 22.56 (1998):169 – 179.

Naess, Arne. "The Deep Ecological Movement — Some Philosophical Aspects." *Deep Ecology for the Twenty-First Century*. Ed. George Sessions. Boston & London: Shambhala Publications, 1995.64 – 84.

---. *Ecology, Community and Lifestyle: Outline of an Ecosophy*. Trans. David Rothernberg. Cambridge: Cambridge UP, 1989.

Nash, Roderick Frazier. *Wilderness and the American Mind*. 1967. 4th ed. New Haven: Yale UP, 2001.

---. *The Rights of Nature: A History of Environmental Ethics*. Madison: The U of Wisconsin P, 1989.

Neidjie, Big Bill. Stephen Davis, and Allan Fox. *Kakadu Man Bill Neidjie*. N. S. W.: Mybrood P/L inc., 1985.

Nicol, Tim. "WA's Mining Boom: Where does it Leave the Environment?" *ECOS Magazine* Oct.-Nov. 133 (2006): 12 – 13. <http://www.ecosmagazine.com/? act = view_file&file_id = EC133p12.pdf>.

Oelschlaeger, Max. *The Idea of Wilderness: from Prehistory to the Age of Ecology*. London: Yale U P, 1991.

O'Reilly, Nathanael. "Mind the Country: Tim Winton's Fiction." *Australian Literary Studies* 23.3 (2008): 359 – 361.

---. "Testing the Limits of Endurance." *Antipodes* 22.2 (2008): 169 – 170.

---. "From Father to Son: Fatherhood and Father-Son Relationship in Scission." *Tim Winton: Critical Essays.* Eds. Lyn McCredden and Nathanael O'Reilly. Crawley: UWA Publishing, 2014. 161 - 182.

Quin, Rod, and Robyn Quin. "The Edge of the World: Study Notes". *Metro Education*, 16, (1998). 20 Mar 2014 <http://search.informit.com.au/documentSummary; dn=720020368297003; res=IELHSS>.

Palmer, Helen, and Jessie MacLeod. 1954. *The First Hundred Years.* London: Longmans, 1962.

---. *After the First Hundred Years.* London: Longmans, 1961.

Pickering, Michael. "The Physical Landscape as a Social Landscape: a Garawa Example." *Archaeol Oceania* 29 (1994) 149 - 161.

Plumwood, Val. *Feminism and the Mastery of Nature.* London and New York: Routledge, 1993.

---. *Environmental Culture: the Ecological Crisis of Reason.* London and New York: Routledge, 2002.

---. "Decolonizing Relationships with Nature." *Decolonizing Nature: Strategies for Conservation in a Post-colonial Era.* Eds. William M Adams and Martin Mulligan. London: Earthscan, 2003. 51 - 78.

Rolley, Chip. "Natural Born Writer: Interview." *Australian Author* 34.2 Aug (2002): 27 - 29.

Rose, Deborah Bird. *Nourishing Terrains: Australian Aboriginal Views of Landscape and Wilderness.* Canberra: Australian Heritage Commission, 1996.

---. "The Redemptive Frontier: a Long Road to Nowhere." *Dislocating the Frontier: Essaying the Mystique of the Outback.* Eds. Deborah Bird Rose and Richard Davis. Canberra: ANU E Press, 2005. 49 - 65.

Rossiter, Richard, and Lyn Jacobs, eds. *Reading Tim Winton.* Sydney: Angus & Robertson, 1993.

Rudiyanto, Arifin. "Managing Marine and Coastal Resources: Some Comparative Issues between Australia and Indonesia." *Maritime Studies* 118 (2001): 6 - 28. <http://search.informit.com.au/documentSummary;

dn=141194377217670;res=IELAPA>.

Scheese, Don. "Desert Solitaire — Counter-Friction to the Machine in the Garden." *The Ecocriticism Reader: Landmarks in Literary Ecology*. Eds. Cheryll Glotfelty and Harold Fromm. Athens: U of Georgia P, 1996. 303 – 322.

Schumacher, Ernst Friedrich. *Small is Beautiful: Economics as if People Mattered*. London: Blond & Briggs, 1973.

Schürholz, Hannah. "Shadow of the Dead: Stories of Transience in Tim Winton's Fiction." *Westerly* 57.1 (2012): 164 – 181.

---. "Gendered Spaces: The Poetics of Domesticity in Tim Winton's Fiction." *The Journal of the European Association of Studies on Australia* 3.2 (2012): 59 – 79.

---. "'Over the Cliff and into the Water': Love, Death and Confession in Tim Winton's Fiction." *Tim Winton: Critical Essays*. Eds. Lyn McCredden and Nathanael O'Reilly. Crawley: UWA Publishing, 2014. 96 – 121.

Schweitzer, Albert. *Albert Schweitzer: An Anthology*. Ed. Charles R. Joy. Boston: Beacon P, 1947.

See, Carolyn. "Young Men and the Sea." *The Washington Post* 27 June 2008: C05. <http://www.washingtonpost.com/wp-dyn/content/article/2008/06/26/AR2008062604164.html>.

Segal, Robert A. "William Roberson Smith on the Wilderness." *Wilderness in Mythology and Religion: Approaching Religious Spatialities, Cosmologies and Ideas of Wild Nature*. Ed. Laura Feldt. Boston & Berlin: De Gruyter, 2012. 229 – 240.

Sessions, George, ed. *Deep Ecology for the Twenty-First Century*. Boston & London: Shambhala Publications, 1995.

Skatssoon, Judy. "Shark Attack Author and Marine Conservationist Tim Winton is Calling on Australians to Leave Sharks Alone." *Townsville Bulletin* 24 July (2010): 42.

Snyder, Gary. *The Practice of the Wild: Essays by Gary Snyder*. San

Francisco: North Point Press, 1990.
---. "Cultured or Crabbed." *Deep Ecology for the Twenty-First Century*. Ed. George Sessions. Boston & London: Shambhala Publications, 1995. 47 - 49.
Spirn, Anne Whiston. "'One with Nature': Landscape, Language, Empathy and Imagination." *Landscape Theory*. Eds. Rachael Ziady DeLue and James Elkins. New York and London: Routledge, 2008. 43 - 68.
Stackpole, Edouard A. *Whales and Destiny: The Rivalry between America, France, and Britain for Control of the Southern Whale Fishery*, 1785—1825. Amherst: U of Mass. P, 1972.
Steger, Jason. "A Big Night in for Miles Franklin Winner." *Age* 14 June 2002: 1.
---. "The Sea Side of Tim Winton." *The Age* 26 Apr. 2008: 26.
Stow, Randolph. *To the Islands*. 1958. Middlesex: Penguin Books, 1975.
Taylor, Byron. "Wilderness, Spirituality and Biodiversity in North America — Tracing an Environmental History from Occidental roots to Earth Day." *Wilderness in Mythology and Religion: Approaching Religious Spatialities, Cosmologies and Ideas of Wild Nature*. Ed. Laura Feldt. Boston & Berlin: De Gruyter, 2012. 293 - 327.
Thomas, Roie. "Inspire, Expire: Masculinity, Mortality and Meaning in Tim Winton's *Breath*." *Journal of Men, Masculinities and Spirituality* 4.2 (2010): 54. *Literature Resources from Gale*. Web. 10 June 2011.
Thompson, Paul B. *The Spirit of the Soil: Agriculture and Environmental Ethics*. London and New York: Routledge, 1995.
Thoreau, Henry David. "Walking." *Walden and Other Writings of Henry David Thoreau*. Ed. Brooks Atkinson. New York: Random House, 1937. 597 - 632.
---. *The Maine Woods: A Fully Annotated Edition*. 1864. Ed. Jeffrey S. Cramer. New Haven and London: Yale UP, 2009.
Tiffin, Chris. "Five Emus to the King of Siam: Acclimatization and

Colonialism." *Five Emus to the King of Siam*: *Environment and Empire*. Ed. Helen Tiffin. Amsterdam: Rodopi, 2007. 165 – 176.

Toorn, Penny Van. "Indigenous Texts and Narratives." *The Cambridge Companion to Australian Literature*. Ed. Elizabeth Webby. 2000. Shanghai: Shanghai Foreign Language Education P, 2003. 19 – 49.

Turner, John P. "Tim Winton's *Shallows* and the End of Whaling in Australia." *Westerly* No.1 Autumn (1993):79 – 85.

Tyas, Gillian Mary. "Transformations: Landscape in Recent Australian Fiction." Diss. Deakin U, 1995.

Wachtel, Eleanor. "Eleanor Wachtel with Tim Winton." *Malahat Review* 121 Issue Jan. 1 (1997): 63 – 81.

Walker, Shirley. "Coming and Going: a Literature of Place." *Australian Fiction* 2001—2002. *Westerly* 47 Nov. (2002): 38 – 51.

Watzke, Beth. "Where Pigs Speak in Tongues and Angels Come and Go: A Conversation with Tim Winton." *Antipodes* Dec. (1991): 96 –98.

---. "On the Verge: Place in the Early Fiction of Tim Winton." *Reading Tim Winton*. Eds. Richard Rossiter and Lyn Jacobs. Sydney: Angus & Robertson, 1993. 15 – 28.

Whitehead, Albert North. *Science and the Modern World*. New York: the Macmillan Company, 1948.

Wilde, W. H., Joy Hooton, and Barry Andrews, eds. *The Oxford Companion to Australian Literature*. 1985. 2nd ed. Melbourne: Oxford UP, 1994.

Willbanks, Ray. "Tim Winton." *Australian Voices*: *Writers and Their Work*. Austin: Texas UP, 1991. 187 – 200. Rpt. in *Short Story Criticism*. Ed. Jelena O. Krstovic. Vol. 119. Detroit: Gale, 2009. *Literature Resources from Gale*. Web. 10 June 2011.

---. "Shallows." *World Literature Today* 69.1 (1995): 221.

Winton, Tim. *An Open Swimmer*. Ringwood: Penguin Books, 1982.

---. "Wilderness." *Scission*. Ringwood: Penguin Books, 1985. 61 – 80.

---. *That Eye*, *the Sky*. 1986. Camberwell: Penguin Books, 1998.

---. "Laps." *Minimum of Two*. 1987. Camberwell: Penguin Books, 1998. 75 - 87.

---. *Cloudstreet*. 1991. Ringwood: Penguin Books, 1998.

---. *Land's Edge*. Sydney: Pan Macmillan Australia, 1993.

---. *Blueback*. 1997. Sydney: Pan Macmillan Australia, 1999.

---. "How the Reef was Won." *Habitat Australia* 31.5 (2003): 20 - 25.

---. *Dirt Music*. 2001. Sydney: Pan Macmillan Australia, 2004.

---. *Breath*. 2008. Camberwell: Penguin Books, 2009.

---. "Silent Country: Travels through a Recovering Landscape." *The Monthly* Oct. (2008): 30 - 38, 40, 42.

---. "Sea Change." *Habitat Australia* 40.3 July (2012): 6 - 8.

Wright, Alex. *Carpentaria*. Sydney: Giramondo. 2006.

Zhang Fangjie. *Oxford Advanced Learner's Dictionary of Current English with Chinese Translation*. 1st ed. 1988.

黄源深.澳大利亚文学史[M].修订版.上海:上海外语教育出版社,2014 年.

刘云秋.蒂姆·温顿访谈录[J].当代外语研究,2013 (2):61 - 65.

刘云秋.蒂姆·温顿访谈录[J].外国文学,2013 (5):149 - 155.

鲁枢元.生态批评的空间[M].上海:华东师范大学出版社,2006.

徐在中.追求超常生活的代价:论《呼吸》对反文化运动的反思[J].当代外国文学, 2013 (4):89 - 97.

叶胜年.西方文化导论[M].2 版,上海:上海外语教育出版社,2013.

詹春娟.颠覆背后的含混——论温顿作品中的女性意识[J].当代外国文学, 2012 (3):117 - 124.

Appendix

1. The Works of Tim Winton (From Wikipedia)

Novels

- *An Open Swimmer* (1982)
- *Shallows* (1984)
- *That Eye, The Sky* (1986)
- *In the Winter Dark* (1988)
- *Cloudstreet* (1991)
- *The Riders* (1994)
- *Blueback* (1997)
- *Dirt Music* (2001)
- *Breath* (2008)
- *Lockie Leonard* (1990—1997)
- *Eyrie* (2013)

Short Story Collections

- *Scission* (1985)
- *Minimum of Two* (1987)
- *A Blow, A Kiss* (1985)
- *The Turning* (2005)

Children's Books

- *Jesse* (1988)
- *Lockie Leonard, Human Torpedo* (1990)
- *The Bugalugs Bum Thief* (1991)

- *Lockie Leonard, Scumbuster* (1993)
- *Lockie Leonard, Legend* (1997)
- *The Deep* (1998) — picture book illustrated by Karen Louise

Non-fiction

- *Land's Edge* (1993) — with Trish Ainslie and Roger Garwood
- *Local Colour: Travels in the Other Australia* (1994), republished in the U.S. as *Australian Colors: Images of the Outback* (1998) — photography and text by Bill Bachman, additional text by Tim Winton
- *Down to Earth* (1999) — text by Tim Winton and photographs by Richard Woldendorp
- *Smalltown* (*book*) Penguin Group, 2009 – text by Tim Winton and photographs by Martin Mischkulnig

2. Awards and Nominations

- Four time Miles Franklin Award winner, 1984, 1992, 2002, 2009
- Two time Booker Prize nominee
- Winton was included in the Bulletin's "100 Most Influential Australians" list in 2006
- Australian Society of Authors Medal in 2003

Full List of Awards and Nominations

- *An Open Swimmer*

  1981 Australian Vogel National Literary Award
- *Shallows*

  1984 Miles Franklin Award
- *Scission*

  1985 Western Australian Council Literary Award
- *Lockie Leonard, Human Torpedo*

  1990 Western Australian Premier's Book Award for

Children's Fiction

1993 American Library Association Best Book for Young Adults Award

- *Cloudstreet*

  1991 Miles Franklin Award

  1991 NBC Banjo Award for Fiction

  1991 West Australian Fiction Award

  1992 Deo Gloria Award

- *Lockie Leonard, Scumbuster*

  1993 Wilderness Society Environment Award

- *The Riders*

  1995 Booker Prize for Fiction (shortlist)

  1995 Commonwealth Writers Prize (South East Asia and South Pacific Region, Best Book)

- *Blueback*

  1998 Bolinda Audio Book Awards

  1998 Wilderness Society Environment Award

  1999 WAYRBA Hoffman Award for Young Readers

- *Lockie Leonard, Legend*

  1998 Family Award for Children's Literature

- *Dirt Music*

  2001 Western Australian Premier's Book Award Premier's Prize

  2001 Good Reading Award, 2001

  2002 Australian Booksellers Association Book of the Year Award

  2002 Man Booker Prize for Fiction (shortlist)

  2002 Miles Franklin Award

  2002 New South Wales Premier's Literary Award, Christina Stead Prize for Fiction

  2002 Kiriyama Pacific Rim Book Prize, Fiction, 2002 — shortlist

- *The Turning*

2004 Colin Roderick Award, 2004 — joint winner

2005 Queensland Premier's Literary Awards, Best Fiction Book

2005 New South Wales Premier's Literary Awards, Christina Stead Prize for Fiction

2005 Inaugural Frank O'Connor International Short Story Award — shortlisted

2005 Commonwealth Writers Prize, South East Asia and South Pacific Region, Best Book — commended

- *Breath*

2008 Age Book of the Year, Fiction — winner

2009 Miles Franklin Award

Acknowledgements

This project initiates from a grant from the Australia-China Council that gives me the opportunity to visit Edith Cowan University in Australia to embark upon the researches into Tim Winton. In the long process of project design, argumentation and drafting, many people give me the most unselfish help and support.

My first and most enduring gratitude is extended to my supervisor Zhang Dingquan. His lectures on contemporary western literary criticism provide me with a panorama of theories in literary research. He gives me invaluable assistance with his wide-ranging knowledge and provides the intellectual stimulus to this book. He was tolerant during the long period of its gestation and it's so nice of him to read the drafts and gives me constant guidance and encouragement.

I feel deeply indebted to Professor Li Weiping who taught me so much about modernist and post-modernist literature, Professor Qiao Guoqiang who introduced narratology to me, Professor Shi Zhikang whose splendid lectures on *King Lear* let me appreciate the unique charm of Shakespeare's play and many other professors in Shanghai International Studies University whose lectures on various occasions arouse my curiosity and stimulate my interest in literary and cultural studies.

I would mention in particularmy my Australian mentor Honorary Professor Glen Phillips of Edith Cowan University who looked after me during my visit there and gave me inspiring advice and immediate feedbacks to any puzzles I had. I feel greatly grateful for Professor Ye Shengnian who encourages and supports me all the time and Associate Professor Liu Yunqiu for her unselfish sharing of the script of her interview in English.

Finally, I am grateful to my parents who always support my work and study in so many years. And I must also mention my husband Yang Yongchun who collects a lot of research materials during his stay abroad as a visiting scholar and my son Tony who suffers so much but is generally supportive.